STRAY CAT STRUT

STRAY CAT STRUT

BOOK 5

RAVENSDAGGER

Podium

Cover design by Edink

ISBN: 978-1-0394-2799-0

Published in 2023 by Podium Publishing, ULC
www.podiumaudio.com

STRAY CAT STRUT

CHAPTER ONE

GOOD INVESTMENTS

Was spending some precious points on a kiddie pool a good investment?

No.

Did I do it anyway?

Yes.

Was I currently sitting in my brand-new pre-inflated kiddie pool, shirtless and with only some panties on while watching the news with some five-hundred-percent-daily-recommended-sugar-intake drink in hand?

Also yes.

When I gave Lucy a bunch of resources and told her to furnish the house, that had apparently included getting a TV wide enough that even sitting across the room from it, I had to turn my head to see the entirety of it. It was very extra and I loved it. Exactly the kind of stuff I expected some super-rich celebrity to have in their house and that I'd dreamed of having one day.

Now all I was missing was a useless private jet and a butler. Or maybe some maids? I could get a maid uniform for Lucy, she'd love that.

The door to the room opened, and I prepared to chuck my can in case it was a kitten walking in. Instead, it was Lucy with a tablet held up to her chest. She paused halfway in to read the little door-hanger sign I'd left hooked on the door. "Don't Tits Open Inside?" she read.

"What? No, you're supposed to read it from the top down, then left to right," I said with a demonstrative wiggle of my can. "Don't open, tits inside."

"And that's supposed to keep people away?" Lucy asked.

I shrugged, then grinned as I noticed Lucy's attention straying downward. Hell yeah. "What's up?" I asked.

She closed the door with a click and moved over. "Why are you in a kiddie pool naked—"

"I'm not naked," I interrupted.

"—without me?" she continued.

"But I could be with very little persuasion," I said. "I was just relaxing, watching the news. The whole world got messed up pretty bad, you know. It's my job to keep up with all of that."

"While mostly naked in a kiddie pool?"

"The job description never included any details about how I should keep informed. Or that I should bother at all. Actually, my job comes with very little by means of instructions, which is great because I'm iffy with those."

Lucy pulled a chair over from next to a little makeup table tucked in what had become 'her' side of the room. She set it next to the pool, took off her shoes and socks, and dipped her feet into the water. "Oh, that's cold!"

I scooted over and placed her feet on my stomach, then started stretching the muscle in the arch of her foot. "It's meant to be a chill-out pool," I said.

"We're not actually leaving this here, are we?" she asked. Her eyes went half-lidded, as they usually did when I put some effort into a massage. "Because it doesn't fit the decor at all. Also, while I'm totally down for trashy-chic, a pool in the bedroom's a bit weird."

"If it's inflatable, it's deflatable too," I said. "Rac can toss it into the matter reconfiguration machine later, get some exotic plastics out of it or whatever. What's with the tablet?"

"I was doing some homework," Lucy said with a knowing smile. "Have you done yours?"

I sank a bit deeper into the pool until the water was up to my nose and I had an excuse not to open my mouth.

"Cat," Lucy whined. "Come on, it's not that hard, is it?"

I pushed myself up a bit. "But it's *homework*. Come on, we're too old for that."

"No we're not. We're basically college-aged. Plenty of people our age have homework to do. I've done mine." She wiggled her tablet for emphasis.

"But it's so boring," I said.

Lucy sniffed. "I'll tell Grasshopper," she said. "Can you imagine how disappointed she'd be? Not even angry or pissed off. Just, like, sad. She'll look you in the eye and be like, 'I understand, it's okay.' But deep down you'll know she's sad because you didn't even make the effort to try." I glared up at Lucy until she broke down into a cruel cackling fit. "Okay, okay, I'll stop. But you really should do your homework."

I pushed myself up until I was sitting on the edge of the pool, legs pulling back until my feet splashed. Grasshopper had spent the evening with the kittens, going over lessons that we were probably all supposed to get if we had ever had a proper education. She was . . . actually a pretty good teacher.

Her weirdness helped. So did her ability to liberally spend points to summon up teaching aids. It was one part lesson, one part live comedy show, and the kittens had eaten it up. So had Lucy and I, admittedly.

Then the lessons had ended. Grasshopper gave us all homework and left without a hint as to when she'd return, but only the ominous promise that she would.

My homework was in two parts. One was a set of questions meant for someone in early high school, covering things like chemistry and math. Grasshopper left a note saying I could cheat as long as I understood how the cheating worked . . . I didn't know what that meant, exactly. The second part was a link to a matrix-location where there was an online shooting arena.

I think my bad aim had offended her, somehow.

I had been planning on working on that for a while anyway, so no harm in actually trying. "I'll get to it," I said. I let my hands drop with a pair of dismissive splashes. Was I being a petulant little shit? Yes, yes I was. It was nearly noon, on my only day off in a long while, and I had planned on doing nothing of import all day.

I'd even set some rules for myself, such as the 'you can only wear less clothes, not more' one, which had so far served to make the day passively entertaining and relaxing.

"I'll make sure you do," Lucy said. "If I wasn't so sore I'd make a game of it or something."

I nodded. Grasshopper had kind of blueballed us yesterday. The making up of that afterward was great, but I wasn't ready for more just yet. Maybe in an hour or three. "I need to go over my purchases too. Can't just spend everything on cool furniture."

Lucy nodded. "You should. Your armor looked a bit . . . cooked last night. You'll need something better."

"Yeah, that's on the list. I'm thinking of getting something big too. For moving around." I gestured to the TV. "Looks like things around New Montreal are cooling down. Literally and otherwise."

That massive heat bomb Gomorrah and I had dropped next to the city had made the news. Some environmentalists were whining about it, others were complaining that it had been a massive and unnecessary destruction of property and infrastructure. But most commentators were happy that they hadn't been eaten by plant monsters overnight, so the mood was pretty grateful overall.

Other cities weren't able to complain as much, with the media people being on the same menu as everyone else as far as the Antithesis were concerned. Some places had come out of it better than we had. Other places had gotten utterly screwed. The full tally wasn't out yet, but it seemed that even just a couple of days into it, this global incursion was probably one of the biggest losses of human life in a short span since the first world war.

Then the news cut out to an ad for burgers with free at-home delivery.

"Okay, I'm gonna get this training shit out of the way. We can do the rest of this homework stuff later, alright?"

Lucy pulled her feet out of the water and wiggled them dry. "Sure," she said. "Want help with that? Either part?"

"Uh, yeah, I can't remember where I put that matrix stuff. I probably shouldn't shell out for another when I still have one that's perfectly usable."

"Oh, I know where it is, give me a minute!" Lucy darted out of the room, slipped on wet feet, then caught herself with a giggle by the door. "Running's complicated, you know."

I nodded, then waited for the door to click shut before I started to stand up. Now, where could I find a towel?

I think I was supposed to feel a bit guilty about relaxing at home while the world burned, but it felt so distant. The people dying were far from home, and I had a whole heap of little distractions to deal with between now and then.

I'd feel guilty about it later, when it became my problem to fix all of the world's many, many issues. For now, I was busy debating whether or not to wear a shirt.

CHAPTER TWO

FINALLY GETTING GOOD

Mesh Sex is the best, no worries about birth control, there's always someone willing, and no matter the kink, you will find a group of enthusiastic
weirdos to talk to about it!

—An enthusiastic Meshizen, 2039

I wasn't about to go gallivanting in the matrix while in the kiddie pool. Nah,
I was going to do that on the bed. I laid down, fiddled with my augs until I
found my Full-Dive System, and I flicked it on. There was that weird sensation of sneezing backward as I dove in.

*One of these days I'll convince you to buy better neural augmentations.
Then you won't need to set up all of these extraneous things.*

"I told you, I'm not super fond of having my brain messed with. Also,
where am I loading into?" I asked. For the moment, I was a shapeless nothing in a void, which . . . while not exactly unpleasant, wasn't nice either.

Then the world turned on, as it were, and I found myself in a room with
cement walls all around. There were a few tables to one side, then a couple
of booths overlooking a long, long room with some holographic targets
floating at the end. They looked like glowing orange model threes, though
these were entirely stationary, and a bit cartoonish.

"Is this the place Grasshopper wanted me to see?" I asked.

*This is a training facility. The tablet to your right allows you to pick and
choose a weapon, as well as attachments and equipment. The range is to your
left. You shoot things from there. Time is slightly dilated here, so that three
hours training in Mesh will count for one outside of it.*

"Uh-huh," I said as I walked over to the little panel and picked it up.
Then I stared at my hand. It was . . . a hand. My hand. Mostly. I squinted and
noticed that the texture of the skin wasn't quite right. "Right, VR bullshit-
tery," I said. Outside of the Mesh, that arm was cybernetic. I glanced down
at myself, just to be sure. I looked . . . like me, but in a dull gray jumpsuit.
The only hint of personalization was the nametag "CAT" over my left breast.

You can hardly train with a weapon if you're not in your own skin.

"Yeah, I suppose," I said before tapping the panel. It lit up and I found myself with a dozen options. "Assault rifles, DMRs, Bolt-Action Rifles, Handguns, Shotguns, Exotics . . . I'm guessing these are the bigger categories for guns? How many guns are on here?"

All of them.

"When you say that," I said.

A large number of gun enthusiasts have re-created nearly every weapon ever made by humanity as faithfully as they could, including many prototypes and otherwise lost weapons. The latter were designed from existing photographs and records. All of these are available for you to play with.

"Wow, what a bunch of nerds," I said.

I also took the liberty of adding digital versions of the weapons available to you through your current catalogs. All seven hundred thousand of them.

"Oh," I said. "Well, that's a bit much, isn't it?"

I don't think anyone expects you to memorize all of them. This space should let you try things out on your own, though.

I tapped on the shotguns list, because I happened to be fond of those, then frowned as it subdivided itself some more. Automatic, Semi, Pump, Heavy. I didn't know what Heavy was, so I pressed on that, and was greeted by a long, long list of guns. Each had a little thumbnail next to its name and some information that went over my head. I guessed that ROF was Rate of Fire, and the weight and ammo count were self-explanatory, but a lot of it was clearly meant for nerdier nerds than me.

Heavy, as it turned out, meant the kind of guns that required two normal humans to operate, or that were loaded onto a vehicle. I could probably manage them with my power armor on. I scrolled down, then stopped on one in particular that looked cool enough to try.

"Okay, how do I get this one?" I asked while pointing to a HMSG-m49. The name wasn't as sexy as the gun itself. The rifle was an all-black thing, with a curvy trigger guard and handle that swept up to the stock at the back.

Tap the selection, then configure the weapon as you please. Afterward, press the Ready button on the bottom right and the weapon will appear on the range bench.

I tapped on the thumbnail, which brought up a 3D version of the gun with little lines pointing to all the things I could modify. There were drop-down menus. The drop-downs had their own drop-downs. "Oh shit, this is getting complicated," I said as I got lost in barrel-length options.

Perhaps keep the weapon stock for now and modify it as you find things you dislike?

"Right, right," I agreed. This was giving me a whole new appreciation for the crap Myalis did. I asked for a gun, and she just gave me one with the bells and whistles all set up the way I liked.

The heavy shotgun appeared at one of the waist-high tables in the range and I walked over to it. It was bigger than I'd imagined from the picture, a meter-long gun with a barrel as big around as my forearm and sleek heat-sinks covered by polished steel.

The box below the bench will contain ammunition for whichever gun you summon. They will not—with some exceptions—appear pre-loaded.

"Makes sense," I said. If this was meant to be training of some sort, it made sense to have reloading be part of the simulation. I fiddled with the box magazine that went into the gun for a bit before it fit into place, then I pulled back on the bolt and leaned into the stock. This gun had a cheap ironsight mounted on it instead of all the fancy holographic stuff I was used to. Still, I held my breath and placed the crosshair over the distant form of the model three target.

The kick was . . . wrong.

My body moved back, but the sensation of it didn't make any sense. I supposed that I'd run into one of the limitations of the Mesh. Sensations in here were a little muted already, so it tracked that recoil wouldn't work the same.

A smaller copy of the target appeared on the table next to me, with pinpoints showing me where I'd hit it.

"Hey, that's . . . nearly a bullseye," I said.

You have been improving. Though your accuracy against moving targets is still lacking.

"Look, I spent most of my life with just one eye. I'm not tripping over myself now that I've got working depth perception, but it's still hard to tell where something is moving to."

Understandable. With time, the discomfort will pass and you'll grow more accustomed to tracking and firing upon moving targets. Practice will, of course, help.

"That's what we're here for," I said. "Uh, I'm not feeling this gun. It's too . . . big? Chunky? Maybe it'll feel better with power armor on, but right now, eh."

I understand. The gun is limited by being a model entirely designed by humans with limited crafting capabilities. There are some very potent weapons available to you from your various catalogs.

"I'll definitely be needing something more potent," I said. The last little while had me running into a lot of bigger, meaner aliens. My current level of firepower wasn't keeping up with the amount of resistance the bastards I met could put up.

Fighting the Antithesis was something of an arms race, one that I definitely wanted to be on the winning side of.

"So, what do the Sun Watchers have that's decent?"

This one might interest you. It's actually a relatively common medium-to-short-range gun. It is technically a shotgun because it fires shells and it's a smoothbore gun, but I think most modern classifications would consider it a PDW or submachine gun based on weight and ergonomics alone.

The big gun on the table disappeared, replaced by a much smaller, much sleeker weapon. Not to say that this was any less lethal. I picked up the gun and checked it out. Bullpup, meaning it had the opening for the magazine just under the stock, and with a set of holographic sights at the front and middle. The barrel was a bit bigger than the joint on my thumb, which I imagined let it pack a punch.

"What's this called?" I asked. "And what does it fire?"

Its actual name is a single word whose meaning has no equal in English. It roughly translates to "the captivating way a beam of light travels across the ground." As for its ammunition, this can use a number of fifteen millimeter shells. Mostly fin-stabilized discarding sabot seeking rounds with miniaturized warheads.

"Oh, neat." The gun had fire-modes too and seemed compatible with my eye's software. "Yeah, I'll try this out. Got all day to figure out how to shoot straight, right?"

CHAPTER THREE

A NOT-SO-QUIET HOME LIFE

Samurai don't tend to show marked improvements in their abilities. At least, no more than you would expect from a normal person.

They don't learn at rates that are superhuman, not unless they are specifically purchasing items to help them do so.

It's this researcher's opinion that this might be a good thing. It's comforting to see that anyone, if they apply themselves and are sufficiently motivated, can become just as talented as a samurai.

—"On the Learning Rates of Samurai," academic paper, 2026

I spent a good couple of hours practicing with the Laser Pointer. The gun took a bit of getting used to. It didn't have the same kind of kick as my Bullcat had, but it still needed careful handling. The punch it delivered was nice, though.

Myalis started me small, with mid-range targets that stood still. Then she summoned an image of myself shooting and pointed out how I could change my stance to improve. That . . . made some sense, a little. Really, the important thing was pointing the end of the barrel at what you wanted dead. How you held the gun didn't matter.

Not unless you wanted to be *consistent*.

We worked out a few kinks, Myalis proving surprisingly patient. Eventually the targets started to move around slowly, mostly from side to side, and I started to see the value in basically posing while aiming.

Eventually, Myalis moved me into a digital building with concrete walls and lots of little rooms. The targets were still stationary, though they were replaced with holograms that lit up in passing. I had to turn and shoot them as quickly as I could.

Myalis said that the next step would be moving targets in changing environments, with "kills" only awarded on immediately fatal hits, but she rattled out some statistics about my accuracy and target-finding speed, which had noticeably improved in just a couple of hours.

A few more sessions like this and I'd be halfway competent, according to her. Personally, I was pretty happy. The time spent in the range had been fun too, and it didn't even leave me feeling sweaty or anything.

Once we were done playing with guns, Myalis brought up one of my next big purchases.

You have used two suits of armor recently. Both have been damaged. One by falling debris, the other by high heat exposure. While you still have both of them, and they are repairable, it's possible that future engagements will also lead to situations where your current armor is just not capable enough to keep you safe.

"Yeah," I said. "I need something bigger and tougher, then?"

Not necessarily. Larger armored suits do provide more space for armoring. Thicker plates of conventional materials and reactive sections as well as more room for internals generally means that the larger a suit is, the more protection it will give.

"You're about to tell me that that's not always true?" I asked.

You have met other Vanguard who have been fighting for considerably longer than you have. Do you recall their equipment?

Deus Ex came to mind. The first time I saw her, other than these two massive pilon things, she was wearing some pretty thin armor. Just a few panels over what looked like a padded skinsuit.

I didn't take her for someone who would put looking cute over being well protected. "I think I see where you're going with this. I imagine the magical third factor here is cost?"

Essentially, yes. I would suggest two purchases. While the suits I would suggest to you now are mostly part of the Sun Watcher technology tree, there are several advances in material sciences that are above what they can provide at the tiers you've unlocked for that catalog. Therefore, I would suggest buying a tier two Power Armor catalog, then investing in a single powerful suit that can cover all of your needs.

That sounded like it would cost a lot. But then, I had a *lot* of points to spend. Nearly six figures worth.

"That sounds fair enough," I said. "I liked the big armor, but it was a bit . . . big, you know? I can't imagine using it to get around."

Perhaps something more like a medium suit of power armor? Fully enclosed, but not as bulky. I'm certain we can fit all the devices you desire into something like that.

Myalis started to summon models of the various armors she had in store for me. Mostly they fit a single, very obvious theme. Sleek, a bit taller than I was, with a long cat's tail and protrusions above the head for my ears.

I didn't mind the look, and from the looks of things, I could pick out the colors as I saw fit, which only made sense since most of the examples she laid out had the kind of stealth system I was growing really fond of having.

I didn't need to make a choice yet. In fact, I was supposed to have a day off, and this was starting to look a lot like work. Was I even supposed to train on my one day off after so long without? "Myalis, I think I've had enough of the Mesh for a day," I said.

I logged out of the Mesh, the matrix fading away even as I regained sensation across my body. There was a weight pressing down on my stomach. I glanced that way to find Lucy, with a pillow set onto my bare stomach, sleeping soundly while curled up in a ball. She'd covered a bit of me in a blanket, but had clearly not gone through too much effort.

I reached down and ran my fingers through her hair, as if attempting a futile effort to straighten her curls out.

That woke her up, and she blinked dumbly for a bit before smiling. "Have fun?" she asked.

"So-so," I said. I'd have to get her an aug like my own so that we could spend time together in the Mesh. There was so much weird stuff to see there that I kind of wanted to dive in and just explore for a day or two, but that would be infinitely more fun with Lucy around. "I'll bring you next time. Myalis had me going through weapons drills and that kind of stuff, you might find it fun."

"Hmm, commando Lucy," she said. "Battlefield expert. I like the idea."

I laughed. "Alright, now get off me."

"You don't want to snuggle?" she asked.

"Your weight's pressing into my bladder," I said.

Lucy laughed and rolled off of me. "Fine, fine. Are you hungry?"

"Did you cook something?" I asked as I swung my legs off the side. "Because if so, no." That earned me a smack to the back of the head with her pillow.

Lucy scooted off the other side of our frankly too-large bed then bounced to her feet. "I'm starving!" she declared. "Let's order more trashy food than we could eat in a week."

"Sounds wasteful," I said as I walked over to the en suite (with only one sink, because two was stupid).

"We can shove the leftovers in the fridge. Besides, have you seen how much the kittens eat? You'd think they'd never seen food before, the way they can empty a fridge out. Maybe if they continue to eat that way, they won't all grow up to be little runts like us."

"Hey!" I called back. "I'm not a runt."

"You're too thin," Lucy complained. "I want something to grab at, and you're all bones."

"Then grab my bones," I snarked back as I left the washroom. I realized that one of the downsides of not having pants on was nothing to wipe my wet hands on after rinsing them off. I could have used one of the towels next to the sink, but they looked clean and almost decorative. Lucy had spent a lot of time picking them out.

We ended up sitting on the bed while ordering from three different places, just picking out the items that looked tasty, which was most of them since we were both hungry.

After that, I scrounged around for some clothes to wear, realized that I basically had none, and then I suffered through Lucy and Myalis buying some shirts and pants from a basic catalog, which I was obliged to model for Lucy.

There was something incongruously wrong about modeling an outfit that had rips and tears in it as part of its design.

We had to cut it short when one of the kittens screamed through the door that there was a nervous delivery guy waiting outside.

As it turned out, deliveries were supposed to be drop-and-go, but the poor driver didn't want to just leave a stack of food at some samurai's door in case something happened to it—delivery theft being an entire career as it was—so he stood there with the food and waited until I grabbed it from him and sent him on his way.

And then, for the rest of that day, we ate, talked shit, and made merry.

All in all, it was a pretty nice day off.

CHAPTER FOUR

WHERE THE FUCK IS BURLINGTON?

It's unfortunate that, in times of crisis, the common man cannot trust his government and his co-citizen. Now we need to trust in these samurai. Some of them are true, red-blooded Americans, sure. But just as many of them are foreigners, strangers here to lord over God's chosen people!

I say it's about time we do something about it.

—Pastor Loud, during his last televised broadcast, 2026

Very, very early in the morning, two days into my semimandatory break, Lucy and I were sitting in our dining room (which was still weird to think about) contemplating life, love, and fast-food fries.

"Why," I asked as I dabbed a sad, pitiful fry into some ketchup, "Do these things always taste like shit once they're cold?"

Lucy pressed three fries of her own into a plastic container of some sort of mustard-ish stuff. It was yellow and tasted strange, but she liked it. "I don't know," she complained before chewing down.

These were the leftovers from two days ago. The choice stuff was all gone already. Picked over by the kittens and Rac as if they were a flock of starving scavenger birds. The burgers were the first to go, then the pastas and the chicken and rice, and all the other food slowly disappeared over the course of the day.

Now all that was left were six family-size boxes of fries and a mixed assortment of dipping sauces and packets of ketchup.

"We need to buy better food," Lucy said as she grabbed a few more fries.

"Mm," I agreed. I could have ordered something, but the effort was just too much. Honestly, it was a wonder that I was out of bed at all. Last night, Gomorrah had sent me a message, asking me if I wanted to head out today, and I'd said yes.

We were supposed to meet at her church in the morning, so I had diligently set an alarm and woken up early.

I regretted it. Not that I didn't love spending time with Gomorrah, it was just the obligation that weighed on me.

Then I got a ping from Gomorrah between one fry and the next. "Huh," I said.

"What's up?" Lucy asked.

"Gomorrah's here." I sent her a quick reply, telling her to come in. If the door was locked then . . . well, she could figure that out, I was sure. "We're here!" I shouted back.

The clonk-clonk of my favorite pyromancer's boots echoed through the halls until she stepped into the dinning room. She was in her full regalia, all shiny black not-leather and full face expressionless mask. "I thought we were going to meet this morning," she said.

"Hi, Delilah," I said before gesturing to the fries on the table. "Have you had breakfast yet?"

Gomorrah stared me down, hands on hips. I could just imagine the frown she was wearing at that moment. "Cat, it's eleven."

"A.m.?" I asked, just to be sure.

"Yes, a.m.," she said.

"So . . . I'm not late?"

Gomorrah stared some more, then she reached up and undid her mask to reveal her unamused face. She was still as pretty as ever . . . though there was something weird about her that I couldn't quite place. Maybe when it wasn't so early I'd figure it out. "Hello, Lucy," she said, much more sweetly than she'd addressed me.

"Hi, Delilah," Lucy said. "How are you doing? Oh, how's Franny?"

Delilah's cheeks flushed, not brightly, but enough that I noticed. And if I noticed, then it might as well have been a siren for Lucy. "She's well. We're well. I think."

"Oh?" Lucy asked. There was a weight of *implication* on that single syllable that had Delilah standing a bit taller. "Well is good. I can't wait to meet Franny again. I'm sure we have a whole bunch of things to talk about."

"I'm sure the opportunity will come up," Delilah replied.

"So, what are we doing today anyway?" I asked.

"Well, you might start by putting some pants on," she said.

Lucy giggled, then poked me in the shoulder. "Your undersuit thing's in the bedroom. It's a bit melted though."

"Yeah, I'm just going to buy a new one, I think. Hey, do I have time to shower?" I asked Gomorrah.

The look she gave me was priceless, especially when I started laughing. "What's so funny?"

"No, I'm kidding, I showered already," I said.

"But you're not wearing any clothes," Delilah said. "Did you just . . . shower, then change back into sleepwear?"

I pinched the front of my shirt. It was one of those Lucy had made. It said, *If you can read this you are in range.* "Okay, first, this isn't sleepwear, it's an oversized T-shirt for sleeping. It's different. Second, I didn't change into fresh clothes, I just put this back on."

"Cat, that's disgusting," Delilah said.

I sniffed. "Look me in the eyes and tell me you never did it," I said.

She didn't. "You can literally just buy something. It's like, a single point."

"Uh-huh," I said. It didn't matter what she said, I'd won the argument and we both knew it.

Gomorrah sighed and shook her head. "Go get dressed. We have things to do."

I laughed as I got up. "Yeah, alright. You still haven't told me what you're planning though." I ran off to our bedroom and got changed. Most of my gear really had melted, so I had to get new stuff. Fortunately, what I had last time was pretty decent. "Hey, Gomorrah!" I shouted, head sticking out of the bedroom.

"What?" she called back.

"What are the chances we'll be shot at or something will try to eat us in the not-fun way?"

"Low?"

"Thanks!"

I shut the door. So I didn't need to buy that new power armor yet. I settled on asking Myalis for a new set of formfitting suit. Something worth a fair bit more than what I'd been wearing so far.

What I got from that was an outfit that wouldn't fit me if I gained any weight at all. It was all black, with pads covering every surface. "Does this have temperature control stuff?"

Of course. As well as being hypoallergenic and airtight from the neck and wrists down, it has a heating and cooling function, can instantly harden to resist blunt blows, and is obviously tear- and puncture-proof. It has its limits, but it should provide a level of comfort that will leave you safe and comfortable against most low-risk threats.

That seemed decent enough. I took off my shirt and underthings then slid into the suit, which was pleasantly cool to the touch.

Then I ordered a long coat that could turn invisible on command.

I didn't bother bringing a gun other than my trusty Trench Maker. It had been with me through a lot, and I kind of trusted it to carry me through some more shit. The sword was coming, of course.

"Alright," I said as I bounced down the stairs. "I'm ready for . . . well, not whatever, but maybe some light fighting and such."

Gomorrah nodded. "I think we'll mostly be meeting people at first," she said.

"Is this the part where you tell me what's up?" I asked.

"Maybe on the way over. I said I would arrive by one, and at this rate we'll be cutting it close." Gomorrah refit her mask, then nodded to Lucy. "It was nice seeing you again, Lucy. I . . . I'll let Franny know that you asked about her. I'm sure she'd love a call though."

"Ah, we're both in a similar situation," she said. "Oh, we should start a club exclusively for the girlfriends of samurai."

Gomorrah stumbled, but caught herself quickly enough. "That . . . that might be nice. See you later."

I ran over to Lucy, pulled my new helmet off, then gave her a quick smooch. "See you later," I said.

"Be safe," she said.

I nodded, then ran off to catch up with Gomorrah. "Alright, so what's up?

"Things have been developing while we were sitting back and relaxing," she said. "Not all of it good."

"The news seems pretty positive, which is usually a pretty bad sign, yeah," I agreed.

Gomorrah nodded. "We had a few more experienced samurai going around and clearing out bigger hives around most cities. And I think something like seventy percent of all cities are now in orange–green zones. It'll take a while to properly clear the surroundings, but it'll get done. The big issues are the coastal cities and a few holdouts."

"Are we heading all the way to the coast?" I asked.

"No. There's a problem in Burlington. Laserjack asked if we could go over and see what we could do to help."

I paused. "Where the fuck is Burlington?" I asked.

"It's a small city to the south. What used to be Vermont, now it's a corpo-state for like, retirees and such. The city barely had any walls, and it got overrun pretty hard. They lost a few samurai already, and now the population is holed up in half the city while they wait for help to arrive or for the Antithesis to give up."

"So we're their only hope?" I asked.

"No, the Family's asking other samurai to pitch in too. It's just that we might be the first volunteers to arrive. Everyone's busy, and most places didn't get out of things as easily as we did here."

"Well, that's encouraging. And why, exactly, did you tell me I didn't need to come loaded for bear?"

"Because we're just going to meet the locals, not fight," she said. "Not unless something goes terribly wrong."

CHAPTER FIVE

LEADERSHIPPING

It takes the average samurai three incursions before they reach a level of comfort and stability with their own abilities and tools to be completely effective. Some take longer, and others are naturally inclined toward the lifestyle of a samurai. A few rare examples flake out and decide not to take part in combat and alien-hunting directly."

—*The Family's Guide to Working with Noobs*, 2051

"So, what do you know about the locals?" I asked as I followed Gomorrah outside. I immediately put my question on hold as I took in the car sitting on my landing pad.

The Fury had been Gomorrah's baby. I think the only things she loved more than that car were fire, and maybe Franny, in that order.

The car sitting ahead of me wasn't the Fury, not unless Gomorrah had gone really nuts with the modifications. It looked a bit like her old ride though, but bigger and meaner. The car was stationary, but it *looked* like it wanted to be breaking every speed limit in the province.

Four meters of pitch-black, obviously armored skin on a chassis that reminded me of an old-timey muscle car, with sharply angled paneling. It sat low on the pad, fat wheels tucked deep within. "Damn," I said.

"Pretty, isn't she?" Gomorrah asked, clearly proud. "I'm calling her the Fury Resurrected. It felt like an appropriate name. Bigger engines, a better environmental control system, actual space-capable thrust, and a lot more armor than the first Fury."

"Wait, it can go to space?" I asked.

"Yes, but not for long. And not very well, honestly. If I wanted something space-capable I'd just buy something specifically designed for it. I'm just saying, it's a lot faster and can take more of a pounding. Oh, and it's better armed too. Two Gatling guns at the rear, a forward-firing railgun, a missile-launching system, and flamethrowers for up-close work. It won't be knocked out of the sky by an unlikely strike from a passing model eleven. Oh, and the interior's big enough to accommodate power armor."

"Oh, that's a nice change," I said. The doors to the new Fury opened up, gull-wing style, and I slid into the passenger seat while Gomorrah went around. "Hey, is this real leather?"

"Real fake leather," she said with a nod as she sat behind the wheel. The interior really was more spacious, though I still pitied anyone that had to squeeze into the back.

"Nice," I approved. "So, are we heading straight south? What's the plan here?"

Gomorrah reached to the console in the middle of the dashboard and touched a few buttons. A hovering map appeared between us, projected from a tiny pinprick hole in the ceiling. New Montreal was impossible to miss, at least until she zoomed out and moved south across a bunch of nothing toward a city that looked a good deal smaller than ours.

"This is Burlington," she said. "It's a fairly small city. Population: just over half a million. There's a big university there, and not too much else. It's mostly a retiree city."

"So chock-full of old people?" I asked.

"Just about," Gomorrah agreed. She set the new Fury into motion and we smoothly rose up and away from my place, then turned and started flying just under the skylanes that had the most traffic. "The place is guarded by three samurai. They're all new. Like, very new."

"We're not exactly old," I muttered.

"Compared to these three, we might as well be," she said. "All three of them became samurai near the start of the global incursion. Like Jimothy. But they've had it a bit worse. They were the only ones around to defend the city, except for the local cops, and maybe a small militia."

That sounded like a hot mess. I could see why Laserjack or whoever wanted us to fly over and check on the place. "What are things like?"

"One in five dead, nearly half the city lost, it's just not looking very good, and while the big-name samurai have been actively breaking most hives, I don't think they're destroying those inside of cities."

"Why not?" I asked.

"Too much collateral. There are shelters and people hiding that would die just because there's a tiny hive nearby. Look, Atyacus will send you the package."

I got a ping, and when I checked it (it had taken surprisingly little time for me to get used to not having pop-ups and ads shoved through my augs at all times of the day) it was a set of compressed files from Gomorrah.

I leaned back, trusting the nun to drive while I looked over what she'd sent. There was a lot there. Maps, connections to live satellite feeds, historical documentation about the city, the location of shelters and projected numbers of survivors. Just heaps of stuff. But it was also organized so that I wasn't instantly swamped without a clue of where to start.

The thing that caught my attention first was a time-lapse of the Antithesis movement in and around the city.

They started on the edges, but most of them seemed to come from this big lake right next to the city. The aliens poured out right onto beaches and behind waterfront homes that had no defenses. The defenses the city did have were all outward-facing from the outer edge of the city. Nothing faced the waterfront.

That was a mess and a half. The city was effectively split in half, with the Antithesis quickly taking over a big chunk of it and only stopping once they were nearer to the less clustered sections to the north of the city.

There seemed to be a lot more homes with big yards where the Antithesis had taken over, with the occasional bigger complex or stretch of suburbia. The parts still holding out were the more urban areas with apartments and stores all jammed together.

Downtown Burlington wasn't all that impressive, not compared to the megacity I'd spent most of my life in. It looked like everyone was being forced to get real close to each other while the few defenders the city had built barricades pointing outward and tried to keep the aliens at bay.

"Only three samurai, right?" I asked.

"Yeah," Gomorrah said. "You're going to be in charge of the four of us."

I blinked. "Um. Can you go back for a second there. Be in charge?"

"Yes," Gomorrah said. She glanced my way, and even if I couldn't see her face, I had the impression she was smiling. "And before you ask, yes, I really did mean *you*."

"What? Why?"

"Because someone has to be," Gomorrah said. "And I'm not exactly the leadership type. You, on the other hand, are actually somewhat experienced."

"I'm used to bullying children."

"So you'll have no trouble with samurai," Gomorrah replied. "Look, it was partly my idea, but Laserjack approved of it. Someone needs to take charge in Burlington. The samurai there now are too green, the political situation is a mess, and you're good at blowing right past those kinds of issues."

"Yeah, but I'm . . . fuck, I don't know," I said.

Gomorrah shook her head. "You won't be alone. And I don't think anyone's expecting you to be perfect at this. Just see what you can do, I'll help where I can. The Family will be redirecting reinforcements to the city before the week's over."

"That's five days from now," I said.

"So we just need to hold out for that long," Gomorrah said. "We've done worse, I think. Besides, we're not far from home. We can drive back every day so that you can sleep in your own bed if you really want."

I worked my jaw. I didn't like it. But . . . yeah, maybe this wouldn't be too bad. I did like giving people orders a lot more than I liked taking them. I flitted through the files until I found dossiers on all three samurai.

Two men, one woman, all fresh as newborn babes. They didn't have good photos of them. By the looks of it, every picture was taken by a civilian aug and uploaded somewhere. The samurai themselves had only had very light communication with the Family so far.

The first on the list was a guy in his late twenties. Whip-thin and rather scrawny. Going by the name Sprout. He seemed to be leaning toward a specialization in biological weaponry, mostly plant-based things.

That sounded outright stupid when dealing with the Antithesis.

Next guy didn't have a samurai name yet. He was Sprout's opposite. A big guy with heavy body mods. Couldn't see anything about his fighting style or what kind of stuff he was getting.

The last, the woman, was in her thirties. The only photos they had of her were taken from afar. She had some sort of coat on, with lots of spikes on it, and seemed to be in the thick of it. They were calling her Manic.

"Holy crap, these are like, the dregs," I said.

Gomorrah scoffed. "We weren't much better at the start," she said.

"I mean, sure, but still." Maybe I was too used to working with professional . . . ish samurai. Those that, if they weren't professional, were at least experienced enough to make their weirdness work.

This was going to be a spectacular mess, I could just tell.

CHAPTER SIX

OUTRANK

A samurai in motion outranks everyone.

The complexity in this situation lies in deciding if you should run with them, or in the other direction.

—*US Core of Special Ordnance Disposal: Technicians' Manual*, 2050

I almost fell asleep as Gomorrah drove us across the afternoon sky. We received a few warning calls as we left New Montreal's flight space, mostly automated messages telling us that we were shit out of luck if some flying aliens decided to munch on us, but a few calls came in with actual people on the other end, again to tell us that we were on our own the moment we left the area immediately around the city.

It wasn't illegal to move (after all, some folk were going to leave no matter what, and if they left, that was fewer mouths to feed), but it was pretty damned stupid to try and cross any distance while no one was around to protect you.

Telling the nice concerned people that we were samurai was usually enough to reassure them that we knew what we were doing. Although one guy from an insurance place insisted that he could sell us great travel insurance, and I ended up hanging up on him.

I had a lot of reading to do about the situation over in Burlington, but I got bored of reading reports on my augs. It wasn't exactly a strain to use the fake floating screens projected onto my eyesight via my augmentations, but it also wasn't as easy to focus on those. I could be looking at pictures of kittens or girls with nice butts.

Burlington was about forty-five minutes away, if you flew in a straight line with no traffic. With Gomorrah behind the wheel testing her new Fury's engine, it took ten minutes, and half of that was spent decelerating.

"We need to travel somewhere farther," Gomorrah said. "Maybe across the ocean?"

"So that you can push the acceleration to the max?" I asked.

"We barely hit three-fifty an hour before I had to start slowing down," she complained. "This beauty can go a whole lot faster. I'm talking fast enough that the planet's curvature becomes an issue."

I shook my head, but I was pretty happy for her. If Gomorrah's fun came from burning things and going fast, then I could get behind that.

"There's the city," she said, gesturing ahead of us.

I sat up straighter, pulling out of my slight slump so that I could see the place we'd be dealing with, with my own flesh-and-blood eyes.

Burlington matched up to what I'd seen pretty well. It was a smallish city, with a large downtown area in its southern end and a sprawl of homes and estates around that. Even from the air it was pretty obvious that this was a place for the semi-well-to-do.

Gomorrah flew in a wide circle around the city, and I took note of a few things that hadn't shown up in the first pages of the report I skimmed.

From what I read, most of the resistance was located in the downtown portion of the city, which made sense. That area basically sprouted from nothing. It went from a few streets with apartment buildings and little stores to suddenly a wall of larger complexes and buildings that stuck out of the landscape like sore, stainless-steel thumbs.

They weren't anywhere near as big as what I was used to. My own building was on par with most of the skyscrapers here, even, and it was obvious that they lacked the sort of elevated platform setup that a proper megacity had.

Still, there was a kilometer-wide square of larger commercial and high-density housing which was, in turn, surrounded by barricades and defenses. I saw lines of barbed wire next to flipped-over hovercars and debris being used to create a wall. Lots of greenery in that wall too, but I'd inspect that once I was on the ground.

The problem was that the downtown area wasn't the only defended one. A section of the city near the lake had a few dozen armed cars around it, some actively moving around, and someone had set up guard towers and cement blockades with gun nests behind them.

They looked a lot more professional than the downtown defenses.

"That's going to be trouble," I said.

"That's going to be *your* trouble to sort," Gomorrah pointed out.

"Are you happy about that?" I asked. "Because I'm pretty sure I'm not. I don't like politics."

Gomorrah shrugged. "You've handled them well before."

"I threatened to shoot the mayor."

"Yes, and?" She asked. "That's exactly how a samurai does politics well. With collateral damage. Personally, I don't have the constitution for it."

"What's that mean?" I asked.

She hummed. "I think I'm too used to listening to people in authority? I grew up with nuns telling me how and when to do every thing. Franny was always the rebellious one. I can follow along with a bit of anti-authoritarianism, but it's not something that comes naturally to me."

"You're really painting me as a rebel here," I said.

"You're not?"

I chose not to argue that point, sensing that I'd probably lose. But really, I wasn't that rebellious, was I? "Land downtown, there's more people there. Bet they have more problems that need solving. Did the report say they have a headquarters?"

"They do. There's a mall. It's central to the area, so I suppose it makes sense to use it as a staging area," Gomorrah said.

We flew down and through the downtown area. There was some traffic out, but it was exceptionally sparse. No callouts or warnings came as we slid to a halt over a busy road. People in hoodies and jeans were moving around, carrying boxes onto vans or shuffling around in little teams with shovels and picks.

There was some organization. People were wearing bands in different colors on their arms, or tied around their heads, and usually people with the same markings were together.

Our arrival caused something of a shift, mostly because Gomorrah parked half-on and half-off the sidewalk right in front of the building. "Nice place to park," I muttered.

"I don't want anyone scratching the paint," she said. "That might set off the Fury's self-defense mechanism, and I don't want flambéed civilian on my conscience."

"Hey, I'm not a parking cop," I said. "You can argue with them about it." I adjusted my coat, made sure my helmet was on straight, then loosened my shoulders. "You ready for the spotlight?"

"Always," she replied.

With that, we pushed the car's doors open and stepped out. This Fury was a little taller off the ground, which was nice. It made my exit a lot easier, and at a glance, it looked like I'd need to make a good entrance.

One thing became immediately clear now that I was on the ground. These people weren't doing so good.

It wasn't just the cheap, work-dirtied clothes. Those were normal in a situation like this. It was the look on their faces. They looked one part hungry, one part desperate, and all tired. I don't think "hopeless" has an expression, exactly, but what I was seeing now was pretty damned close to that.

We *were* the hope these people were waiting for. It put a bit of weight on my shoulders to discover that so suddenly. This was a city of hundreds of thousands, and they were relying on five of us.

There was a group of police officers milling around the entrance in full riot gear and army surplus junk. They straightened up as we approached. "Hey," I said. "Where're the local samurai at?" I asked.

"Uh," the one I addressed said. I saw the gears clicking in his head, waffling between two choices. Be a normal police officer and use his own authority to try and bully me, or act like a proper human being when faced with something bigger and scarier and just give me what I wanted. "They're inside, ma'am," he decided. "By the McDonald's."

"Thanks," I said.

I stepped past him and entered the mall. It was surprisingly busy inside. Someone was brushing broken glass aside into a large heap to one side while others were stacking clothes into boxes that were being carried out by others. It looked like properly organized looting, mostly carried out by young adults and older teens with yellow bands.

Gomorrah and I walked across as if we owned the place, and we were followed by a wake of whispers and pointing.

Honestly, I felt pretty damned cool at the moment. I just hoped that we could earn all that coolness in the next few hours, because as I entered the food court and found three people arguing next to a tipped-over table, I was getting the impression that it wouldn't be all that easy.

CHAPTER SEVEN

BIG GUN POLITICS

If given the option between being poor and rich, choose to be rich. That's what my father used to tell me. He was a good man, worked hard for what he earned.

As I grew up, I learned that there was more to it than that, especially here in America. This land has the greatest legal system in the world. It's one of the easiest to buy your way into.

Remember though, it's a legal system, not a justice system.

—Mister P. J. Vermille of River Heights, 2034

I came to a stop and crossed my arms as I took in the scene.

Of the three people arguing, one was clearly a samurai. An inexperienced, new one, but he was undoubtedly like me and Gomorrah. It wasn't even just the strange gear he had on that gave him away. There was just . . . something about the way he stood that said he was a weirdo and had no business being anywhere near anyone in charge.

The other two were entirely different. A woman in the kind of business-chic that screamed "high-end secretary" and a man in a square-cut corpo-military outfit, with a plastic pistol strapped to one hip and the obligatory complement of low-ranked mooks standing at attention in the background. A few people had noticed us, but no one was telling the three of them.

The way everyone was milling around felt like kids watching their caretakers having a nasty argument. It would probably have been best for morale if this circus happened behind closed doors.

"I'm going in," I told Gomorrah as I turned on my stealth systems and faded away. "Stay around here?"

"Sure," Gomorrah said. "I'm going to go check on the civilians, try to get an idea of how things are organized on the ground. Call me when you need help."

"Thanks," I said before walking over to the morons fighting in public.

"We can't allow the defenses around River Heights to fall," the secretary-lady was saying. "Just in the last twelve hours we've lost seven guardsmen, and the Villmont estate had to be abandoned, which required that we move our defenses back. Restoring the estates later will be a significant expense."

The samurai guy shook his head. "We can't, we barely have enough here. General Wilkinson can barely spare ten soldiers per entrance, and our green-tags aren't able to keep the Antithesis at bay on their own."

The big army guy, who I guessed was this General Wilkinson because I wasn't a moron about reading context clues, nodded along. "We are severely undermanned at the moment," he said. "We might be receiving reinforcements, but not for another two to three days. My men can hold out for that long, but they will need some R&R soon or the constant stress will reduce their effectiveness. Also, we are losing too many around the River Heights area."

"Look, we're doing what we can," the samurai said. He was a skinny, rather tall guy. Lanky, I think, was the right term for it. He had to be Sprout, the plant-specialist samurai. His gear was very . . . civilian. Jeans with a plain T-shirt under a vest covered in pockets. He had a sort of gardening belt hanging low to his side with some handles sticking out of it and what was obviously a handgun shoved into it.

He looked entirely out of his depth.

The secretary woman sensed that weakness and pounced. "If Downtown wants River Heights's continued protection, then we expect Downtown to provide compensation. We're already sharing supplies and allowing the people here to profit from *our* hard work. The least that can be done is diverting more help to us. Maybe we can renegotiate the samurai rotation?"

"Rotation?" I asked as I shut down my stealth gear.

The three jumped and spun around. I was sitting on one of those half walls that malls loved to use to divide up their food courts.

"Yo," I said with a hand raised to wave. "So, Sprout, who're your friends here?"

The young man (who was a few years my senior, but it didn't feel like it at the moment, not when it looked like he had a spine made of canned spaghetti) straightened up and nodded to me. "You're Miss Stray Cat?"

"Yeah," I said.

"Oh, uh, hello," he replied. "This is Miss Baker, she's representing River Heights."

"The preeminent community in Burlington," she replied with a winning smile. "We're a small, private group who are working to assist the rest of the city in its time of need."

I nodded. "Okay. And you're General Wilkinson?"

"Yes ma'am," he said. I had the impression he was holding back from saluting. "I command the Vermont Militia's local branch."

"Nice, nice," I said. "Right, I've just arrived. I read the reports thoroughly, but I like seeing things for myself. What's the situation here?"

"We're . . . surviving," Sprout said. "But it's getting harder. There's only three of us, and the Antithesis are getting stronger while we're losing people."

They were caught on the wrong end of exponential growth then. Maybe Gomorrah and I could make a difference there. We were both pretty good at making a mess. "I think that'll be our first priority then, making sure that defenses hold up. Then we'll see about heading out and culling any local hives."

"Oh," Sprout said. He looked a bit wide-eyed at the idea. He was real green.

"If you're here, that means we now have four samurai?" Miss Baker said. She sounded pretty excited by the idea. "We can have two at River Heights now."

I raised a hand. "What the fuck's a River Height?"

"As I said, it's the premier living space in Burlington."

I turned to Sprout, who squirmed. "It's the nice part of the city? A few mansions all placed close together. It's a gated community."

"How many people live there?" I asked.

"Twenty-six families," Miss Baker answered. "With additional staff, of course."

"Give me a solid number," I said. "How many people are there now?"

"Nearly six hundred in all, ma'am, including a fifth of my men and logistical support crews," the general replied.

I blinked. "So one in five of our best-trained troops are protecting a couple dozen homes?" I asked, just to be sure.

"Yeah," Sprout said. He sounded ashamed of it all.

"Okay, and how many people are in the downtown area?"

"Downtown had sixty thousand people. Right now, we're not entirely certain. A number of people evacuated from around the city to here, where it's safer," the general said. "We are working on a census to better distribute supplies and work."

"Right," I said. "Any reason we shouldn't abandon the River Heights area and relocate the troops here? Sounds like they'll be more help defending the greater number of people."

"River Heights is very defensible," Miss Baker said. "A number of the homes have tall fences and automated defense mechanisms that can't just be moved. Not to mention the historical value of the location."

I blinked, then I raised a finger and texted Myalis. "This is bullshit. Right?"

It does seem that a few people are living quite comfortably in a location not too distant from the center of the city. Cross-referencing family names and local business owners suggests that a number of them own a lot of property within the city.

So, rich fucks who'd built a small defensible kingdom for themselves, and now that shit hit the fan they were staying in their castles.

Honestly, I didn't mind that too much, but they were interfering with the protection going to the rest of the city. I hummed, then spoke up. "We have a samurai over at River Heights?" I asked.

"We do," Sprout said. "Johnny. He's there now. It's his turn."

"Right, I'm going to replace him for a bit. General, I'll be texting you some information. Sprout, follow me."

I fell off the wall I was perched on and started walking deeper into the mall. The newer samurai jumped to keep up.

As soon as we were in another section of the multistory mall, I spoke up. "How are things?" I asked. "Don't hold back, I can handle bad news."

"Not great, probably not terrible," he said. "I . . . need time to set up and be useful, but we've been running around putting out fires all day for the past few days. Johnny got us some pills that make it so that we don't need sleep. Without those I'd have crashed."

"And the other samurai?"

"Manic?" he asked. "She does her own thing. I'd complain, but I really can't, she's killing more aliens than Johnny and I together. She doesn't really do orders or anything."

"And the local politics?" I asked.

He winced. "Complicated."

"I'll be taking over those then," I said with an evil smile. "I'm good at politics, or so I've been told."

"That would be a relief," he said. "Look, River Heights is . . . a pain to deal with, but we kind of need them right now. They control payroll for the militia and run nearly half the businesses in this city. *I* worked for them until two days ago, I guess."

"Hey, don't you worry. I'll handle this with grace and decorum."

Once I was done, the rich morons would be gracing us with all of their goods and decorums.

CHAPTER EIGHT

RIVER HEIGHTS

Charity has proven to be nothing but a mistake. You give and give, and while it might help some, most of those you pull out of the pits of poverty merely drop back in as soon as you stop helping them.

No, if a person in need of charity doesn't want to need it, then all they need to do is work harder.

—Hope Rutherford, professional philanthropist, 2026

"Hey, you," I said while gesturing to Miss Baker. She jumped, probably not expecting me to call her out. She was with a small group of well-dressed folk—mostly they looked like more corporate stooges, the type of failed human whose entire identity is tied to a single company.

"Miss Stray Cat," she said with a nod. "Can I help you? We were about to return to River Heights with the good news."

"Really? That's perfect. I'm bumming a ride," I said.

She blinked, then turned to her groupies and pointed one out. "Jacob, stay here, please. Check on our offices and maybe press Mr. Daniels to get the accounting done fast. If he complains, refer him to me."

The man nodded, then picked up a briefcase and walked off.

"There, now there's plenty of space for you," she said with a saccharine smile. "Are you going to stay at River Heights for long?"

"Not planning on it," I said. "Just want to check the defenses there, get an idea of what needs to be shored up and where. How do you travel to and from River Heights to here?"

"We fly over," she explained. "The roads between Downtown and the better part of the city are patrolled lightly, especially as we have convoys that travel back and forth, but the area is still relatively dangerous."

I nodded along. "How's the state of the wider city?"

"The wider city?" she asked. "You mean the sections we've had to abandon?"

"Yeah. Sounds to me like this divide between Downtown and River Heights would be a lot easier to handle if the defenses circled the entire city, not just two sections of it. We're going to need to take the rest of it back anyway."

Miss Baker nodded, enthused by the idea. "Quite a few members of the River Heights council believe the same thing. Though I'll admit it's a somewhat divisive issue. Some would rather wait for assistance to arrive to clear out the city, but others do wish we could scour the Antithesis away. When the global incursion began, there was a vote on whether or not River Heights's defenses would be used to protect the wider city, but in the end we chose to protect what's most important first."

My flesh eye twitched a bit. "Yeah, I totally understand," I said.

I don't think she caught onto the sarcasm, which was probably for the best.

She led me, and, consequently, her gaggle of aides, out of the mall and into the parking lot just above it. The area was nearly empty, which was a bit off-putting. I hadn't seen many empty parking lots in my time.

Baker and friends had a trio of cars waiting for them. Two larger, armored trucks with some of those militia-PMCs hanging around them, and a car that looked like it cost more than most people made in a lifetime. It was one of those fat, sleek Bentley-like cars, with all of the bells and whistles a rich dipshit needed on their car, like bulletproof glass and anti-riot measures. The kind of stuff they needed to stop angry folk from just blowing them up.

"Did you want to ride with me?" she asked.

I shrugged. "Sure," I said. Then I ignored her spiel about the car's seats being made of real leather sewn together by Peruvian orphans or whatever.

It wasn't nearly as comfortable as Gomorrah's ride. Then again, this car wasn't made for someone wearing even basic body armor. If I was wearing my bigger power armor I'd have to horrify Miss Baker by riding on the roof.

We took off, the bigger hovercars flanking the nicer one. They had proper gun emplacements on the bottoms and tops, probably to dissuade chasers and such, but I imagined they worked well enough on Antithesis.

"Slow down on the edge of Downtown," I said.

"Pardon?" she asked. I'd just interrupted her talking about the historical value of the architecture near central Burlington.

"The edge, slow down once you get there. I want to see what the defenses are like with my own eyes."

"Oh, yes, we can accommodate that," she said before relaying instructions to the driver. When we reached the edge of Downtown's skyscrapers (which really didn't take long) we lost some altitude and slowed way down until we were barely moving at a crawl.

I pressed my head close to the window and looked down. The roads out of the downtown area were blocked by stacked cars and furniture. Whatever people could drag out. There were also a number of trees and bushes, of all things.

"Are the plants Sprout's doing?" I asked.

"Yes! He has been providing us with different plants that we can use as defensive measures. Mostly these tough bushes that are covered in nasty barbs. They're difficult to handle, but from what I understand the Antithesis tend to get caught in them quite well. They're an acceptable replacement for barbed wire fencing."

I nodded along. That might actually have some potential, as long as the Antithesis didn't discover a way to subvert them. And if they did, that would just mean that we were dealing with barbwire aliens too, which was actually kind of messed up.

We shot past the barricade, and I noticed a number of civilians looking up. Most had green bands around their arms. A lot of them gave us the finger.

My impression that the normal people were getting fucked over grew just a little.

Then we were flying over the no-man's-land between Downtown and River Heights. That entire area was filled with hollowed-out apartment buildings, burnt-down shops, and abandoned buildings of unknown purposes. The city, though it was a rather small place, had a number of parks and larger buildings with some land around them. Those had probably served to slow down the spread of any fires.

"The entire area's been evacuated?" I asked as I noticed something weird.

There were people on the roof of a larger building. A hospital, I think. The roof had a fence all around it, and they'd put up boards and sheets of crap in the way to roof it up completely, but it was clear that there were at least a dozen people on there. Scavengers, maybe? But then, why build defenses if they were just grabbing things?

"More or less, yes. There are several shelters across the city that are networked together. A number of those are reading as having people within them, but we can't yet spare the people to go and retrieve them. I believe Miss Manic has been instrumental in escorting people from the shelters nearest Downtown."

"So, some people have been locked together in a single large room for . . . what, four, five days?" I asked.

"Standard shelters should have supplies for up to a week," she said.

I didn't like that, not one bit. "What are we doing about that?" I asked.

She blinked. "Well, that seems more like a concern for the residents of Downtown. The River Heights shelters are all empty. We did run a few rescue missions for persons of interest who were in locations nearby. The sons and daughters of River Heights residents."

"Of course," I said.

We flew over the edge of River Heights. This chunk of the city was a quarter the size of Downtown but couldn't fit a hundredth as many people. It was all McMansions with little lots around them. I spotted the clear blue water of pools hidden under glass domes and manicured gardens and lawns.

The entire area was walled off. Two-meter-tall cement barriers were set around the compound, with prebuilt towers sprouting up every twenty or so meters apart that were equipped with automated guns.

I noticed a patrol making their way around on the safe side of the wall, five guys in body armor with submachine guns. The place was guarded better than a pharmacy that sold opiates.

We came in for a landing on the main street cutting through the center of the area, where a few large vans and PMC trucks were parked on the sidewalks and where tents were set up. The area was dominated by an AA emplacement that was unfolded out of the back of a trailer.

I pushed the car's door open and stretched up to my full height. "Right, I'm going to find the samurai that's supposed to be stationed here. Don't go too far, I might need you."

"Um, okay? Are you certain you don't need an escort? I would be glad to show you aro—" She froze as I activated my stealth equipment and faded from view.

Now all I had to do was find that still-unnamed samurai and see what he thought about all of this, because at the moment I wasn't feeling all that charitable.

At least I had that much in common with the locals, it seemed.

CHAPTER NINE

EYY

There is rich, there is wealthy, there is classy. They are not mutually exclusive. To be a good wife, you must embody all three in due moderation.
—*A Future Wife's Guide to Presentation and Poise*, 2045

River Heights was a nice place. The road had a thing in the middle with little trees in it. The sidewalks were wide. Every house I walked past was either an older home made of glass and stainless steel or a newer mansion made of reinforced concrete and sharp angles. They almost all had a gate, but the fences were a few steps back, leaving enough room for some grass to grow.

I bet they had some sort of homeowners' association kind of thing.

I bet they actually owned their homes too.

"Myalis, do you have any idea where what's-his-name is?"

The nearest Vanguard? He is three hundred meters to your northeast.

I pointed.

A bit more to the right, around the intersection.

I headed that way, only pausing to take in a yard where all the hedges had recently been trimmed to look like animals. This place was rich. It was a different sort of wealth than I'd occasionally seen from far below in New Montreal. This wasn't supercars and designer brands rich. It felt more understated than that.

I guess it was a class thing, but I wasn't in any position to make much commentary about that.

In the end, I was here for a purpose. Save the city. That meant saving the city's people. It included the people in these little mansions as much as the folk living Downtown.

Fuck me if I wasn't conflicted. These rich fucks here had done the right thing. They'd prepared to face an invasion. I walked by a checkpoint in the middle of the road. It was a small fixed base, with enough room under it for a car to drive while militiamen sat above manning stationary guns.

The checkpoint was fixed to the ground by cement bases that were clearly already sunk into the earth long ago.

They'd prepared for this, or for something like it. It was almost unfair to ask that they relocate to Downtown.

At the same time, Downtown was more important. There were more people there. The sheer human value made it a clear choice.

"Hey, Myalis, have the people living here been doing anything skeevy? Like, I don't know, keeping kids in their basements, eating people, that kind of stuff?"

A cursory scan suggests nothing of the sort, no. Though there are plenty of suggestions of white-collar crime and possibly business fraud.

"Darn. it would make it a lot easier to burn this entire place down if the locals were dickbags."

You're in a difficult position, then. Did you want to talk it out? I'm a surprisingly good listener. I am also smarter than you.

I laughed. "No doubt. Yeah. Look, I'm responsible for this shithole. That means I need to keep as many people safe as possible using what I have on hand. So, that means making sure the aliens don't hit us too hard and then arranging things so that we can hit back."

I understand.

"Now, these fucks have got it all figured out. They basically don't need me here, which is fine. Downtown's messy though. The defenses there look like crap, the people don't look prepared, and I imagine they're not in the best of moods."

There is certainly a growing morale issue.

"Right. Now . . . if River Heights is calling the shots for Downtown and prioritizing their own safety, then that'll make my work harder, yeah?"

Yes.

I stopped walking. "So I'll tell them to fuck off." I nodded to myself. "They've done well for themselves, so they can keep handling themselves. We'll stop supplying them with any more than they need while focusing on keeping Downtown safe. Once we start hunting down the local hives, that'll help everyone everywhere."

That seems like a perfectly workable solution.

"Thanks," I said as I started walking again.

You're welcome.

"You . . . didn't actually say anything helpful there, you know. Don't need to sound so smug."

Ah, but I correctly predicted that you would eventually draw a reasonable and workable plan if you only spent some time thinking about it without needing additional input on my part.

I scowled. "And that makes you feel all smug inside?"

My genius is as unparalleled as your predictability, Catherine.

What a bitch. I chuckled as I continued on. There was a small group of militia guys up ahead, taking a coffee break next to what looked like a very normal and misplaced food truck. Had it flown all the way here across restricted airspace just to deliver lukewarm coffee and sandwiches?

The Vanguard you're looking for is within that group ahead.

So, the new guy was slumming it with the locals? Cool. I flicked off my invisibility and walked over while trying to figure out which one of them was the samurai. It wasn't all that hard. The militiamen were all in army-surplus style uniforms. Jumpsuits with bulletproof vests on top, all covered in pouches and with plenty of gear hanging off their belts.

The only guy without any of that was standing to one side. He was a massive guy, easily half a head taller than I was, and I wasn't the shortest of girls. He wasn't just tall though, his chest was huge, and he was quite proud to show it off, judging by his shirtlessness.

A couple of the soldiers noticed me and one smacked him on the arms and gestured in my direction.

"Oh, hey!" he said. "You're the Cat woman!" He moved around the group and headed my way, an arm extending to shake.

Not a normal meat arm either. At some point this guy had replaced his arms with a pair of massive prosthetics. The hands were all metal, but the arms were covered in artificial musculature under a thin transparent film. Every joint gleamed and the corded material beneath looked like it was straining even with just a simple gesture. They were probably protector-made. That, or Johnny here had spent all of his money on the arms and didn't leave any over to buy a shirt.

"Hey," I said. "Stray Cat, apparently in charge. You're Johnny?"

"Ey, that's me, babe."

"Uh," I said. "Babe?"

"Yeah?" he asked.

We stared at each other for a moment, then I snorted. "Okay, whatever. Call me babe if you want, but I've got a girlfriend already, and you're not my type."

"Not even with these guns?" he asked. Then he raised his mechanical arms and flexed, the artificial musculature within straining while servos whined audibly.

"It's not that equipment that disqualifies you," I said. "I came over to check on you. Or that's what I told that Baker woman. I'm really here to see how things are going here. You alright so far?"

"I'm fine, and so's that Baker lady. I love a well-organized woman, you know?"

"I guess. Hot secretary was never really my thing."

Johnny shook his head. "You're missing out, Cat, babe. A nice woman in a nice suit, telling you what to do, all stern and forceful. And did you see her thighs? Damn."

This was not the conversation I thought I'd be having.

"You know what, I didn't actually look."

He gave me a weird look, backing up a half step to side-eye me. "Babe, you sure you're gay?"

"I'm pretty sure, yeah," I confirmed. "Right, I came here to talk, but not about that."

"Can't think of anything more important," he said.

"What about saving lives?" I asked.

"Ah, yeah, making all the babes thankful that me and my guns were there to make them safe." He flexed. Again.

I had no doubts about this guy being a samurai, even setting aside Myalis's confirmation. No one else could afford to be so strange at a time like this. "You've been patrolling River Heights with the militia?" I asked. "How's the place holding up?"

"With me and Sprout keeping things nice and safe, we haven't had any trouble at all. A few plants tried to sneak in, but most get taken out by the auto-defenses long before we get to them, and Sprout's stuff takes care of the rest. Lot less work than keeping Downtown safe."

"That's tougher?" I asked.

"Oh yeah, constant fighting. There's always something that's blowing up and the aliens have a million ways to sneak in. Get to put my guns to good use."

"If this place is so safe, then why are you here? Just need a break?"

"Nah, the nice lady asked, and Sprout agreed that one of us should be here. One of us isn't worth more than the dozens of guards they send to Downtown in exchange for us staying here."

"Right," I said. That might even be true. I certainly couldn't beat a dozen competently trained soldiers after only a day or two of being a samurai, at least not when it came to playing a long-term defensive game.

Still, I didn't like it.

"I think I'm going to have to renegotiate that one," I said.

CHAPTER TEN

HOPE

Hope is a currency that's hard to define.

But that doesn't mean you can't buy some anyway!

Hopebucks! A non-fungible semi-monetary unit that you can buy, keep, store, and place your hope in!

—Typical NFT advert, 2023

Myalis had General Wilkinson's contact information ready for me, of course. It included the locations of all of his troops and their current dispositions.

I was able to confirm that nearly half of the militia was located in River Heights.

"Miss Stray Cat, ma'am," the general said.

"Hey," I said. I glanced around myself, taking note of the militia guys leaving the food truck and the owner of said truck packing things up. The guy pointed at me, then the stall, and I shook my head and waved him off. Nice fella. "So, I'm at River Heights. Be honest with me, how overkill are their defenses?"

"They are far above standard. As it stands, and assuming normal Antithesis progression, the area should be entirely safe for another seventy-two to ninety hours before we would need to increase its defensive potential."

"Uh-huh," I said. "And Downtown, the defenses there?"

"Abysmal, ma'am. Samurai Sprout's plant-based defenses are helping, and Samurai Manic's frequent excursions are culling some of the alien threat, but the defenses are manned by civilians with little to no training. Those who did have training were conscripted into the militia."

"Right. We're moving things around then," I decided. "Find out what the minimum number of militia you need in River Heights is, leave that number behind. I want you to set up a few rapid response teams. I think my fellow samurai and I will be heading out to cull some of the nearest hives. So we won't be manning the walls."

"I understand. I can have them transferred over within the hour."

"We're not in that big of a hurry. Do it naturally. I'm heading downtown in a little bit. Also, your report has a section on missing supplies. That's like things you wished you had but don't?"

I scrolled through that section. For the most part it was ammunition counts, some additional guns, more armor. Whoever the general had serving as quartermaster was pretty good at keeping track of what they needed.

"We've opened our storage caches, where our ammunition and additional weapons were stored, and discovered that a number of them were either mismanaged, robbed, or simply had unmaintained equipment. As it is, with our current rate of consumption, we'll be running out of certain kinds of ammunition within the next two days. We'll have to switch off certain weapons platforms for others, which means using that ammo faster."

"Right," I said. I . . . might be able to help with that. "We'll see about that problem later. If you guys are actually getting close to running out, make it a priority to annoy me about it."

"Yes ma'am. Will you be handling the fallout with the River Heights leadership?"

I frowned. "What fallout? I'm telling them what to do. If they're not happy, they can go live in a city that's someone else's responsibility."

I cut off the comms with the general after a few more pleasantries, then I sighed, stretched my back out until it popped, and started walking back the way I'd come. Johnny was waiting for me nearby, the absent twitching of his fingers suggesting he was scrolling through something.

"Doomscrolling?" I asked.

"Hm? Oh no, I'm looking at my matches. I never had trouble with the ladies before, but since getting these arm rockets"—he paused to strike a pose—"my DMs have been on fire!"

"Uh-huh," I said. Guy must have been attracting every gold digger within a ten hour's flight. "Well, you can flirt with folk once I'm done with you."

"Oh my," he said.

"Not that way," I sighed. "I mean I want to start clearing the area of Antithesis around Downtown and River Heights. That'll mean taking out hives and blowing up plenty of aliens."

Johnny grinned. "Hey, think we can get someone to film us at work? I need some new pics for my dating sites."

"I'm sure we can find someone with nothing better to do," I said. "But first, let's find a way back to Downtown."

As it turned out, Miss Baker wasn't too far from where I'd left her. She rushed over to us, or at least, walked over as quickly as she could in her little high heels and pencil skirt. "Ah, you found our local guardian," she said with a plastic grin.

"Yup," I said. "I'm taking Johnny here out."

"And you'll be staying to replace him?"

"No," I said. "We're going to start a counteroffensive. The sooner we begin, the easier it will be. We don't want to let the hives grow too big. Also, do you happen to have a list of the shelters across the city?"

"I . . . yes, we have one."

"Good, I'll need that. We'll cross-reference it with the public shelters. I think we can start by saving those we can."

She reached out and grabbed my bicep. "Miss Leblanc," she said, all serious now.

"Yes?" I asked. It was a little unnerving to be called by my proper name while acting the part of the samurai.

"Are you planning to abandon River Heights?" she asked.

"Do you think I'd do that?" I asked.

She nodded. "We aren't clueless, Miss Leblanc. Not all of us working here were raised with silver spoons. Some of us understand there's . . . enmity toward the kinds of people who live in places like these. But abandoning them now would be a mistake."

I touched her hand. "I might be a bit of a bitch, but my job's to keep people alive. All the people, alright? Now, if your precious River Heights people give me trouble, that'd be another story, but if they mind their own and help where they can, then this will all be so much easier. We'll do our part, get some weeding done, then be out of their hair. You can go back to playing house or whatever."

"Thank you," she said. "I'll hold you to that. And I'll explain things to the community leaders as well. I think seeing you in action protecting the city will reassure them that we can allow a certain amount of . . . leeway in our defenses."

I nodded along, then gently pulled her hand off my arm. "On that note. Mind if we borrow your ride back to Downtown? We need to get planning."

"Certainly," she said.

The ride back was . . . cramped. Johnny took up a lot of space. I wasn't one to complain about manspreading, but this guy took it to a whole other level. The only thing that saved me was the distraction of trying to arrange everyone to meet up at one central place. Sprout agreed right away, as did Gomorrah, but the other samurai, Manic, was quiet.

"She doesn't talk much, does she?" I asked.

"Manic? Nah, she's the quiet and deadly sort of babe. When I gave her the ol' one-two kapow she almost ripped my head off."

"The what?" I asked.

He then mimed pointing to someone, then pointing back to himself and thrusting his hips out.

This man was samurai material?

The Protectors were probably laughing their alien guts out from which-ever hole they lived in. "Yeah, uh, I can't actually see that working on a woman. Ever."

"Ah, it works on the right kind of babe," he said with a wink.

"Has it ever worked for you?" I asked. It was morbid curiosity, really.

He looked away. "One day, it will."

"I mean, there's a billion eligible girls out there. You keep trying, my dude," I said.

The driver brought the car around and landed us in front of the mall. It seemed like the shopping center really was the headquarters for the entire Downtown area.

It was disheartening to step out of the car and see Downtown. The place was a mess compared to the otherwise impeccable River Heights. It wasn't just the architecture and the cramped, too-populous nature of it all, or even all the trash left on the roadside and in overflowing bins. It was the people. They walked as if expecting the shadows to jump out at them at any time.

Then I saw the way they looked at us. Johnny did his whole flirting and flexing thing, looking like a fool the entire time, but that still worked. There was a light in their eyes on seeing us. Augs flashed on and I knew we were being filmed from a dozen different angles. People were less worried with us around.

That was kind of a nice feeling. I just hoped I could live up to it. Giving people hope and taking it away wasn't something I wanted practice with.

CHAPTER ELEVEN

IRON SPINES

This is going to be a fabulous merger, I'm telling you.

Are you sure? We make prosthetics. They literally make bombs.

I know! It's a match made in heaven.

—Discussion between MetalArms CEO and CFO
before their merger with Noeing in 2031

The mall hadn't changed much in the last hour or so. It still felt like a terrible place to be holding any sort of meeting, especially out in the middle of the food court where anyone could spy on us.

Then again, we weren't planning to do anything too skeevy, were we? And a bit of public accountability couldn't hurt. I imagined it was the same reason why most companies didn't hold important meetings where anyone could overhear them.

Sprout was waiting at one of the central tables already, back bent over a trio of tablets that he was poking at and studying carefully. Next to him, a man in a militia uniform was standing at attention. He had a few pips on his chest which suggested that he had some sort of rank in the organization.

Surprisingly, they both had Frappuccinos next to them.

"Hey, boys," I said as I came over.

Sprout looked up, then smiled weakly. "Oh, hello," he said.

"Ey! Sprout! Haven't grown too much since I left?" Johnny asked as he flopped down onto the bench next to Sprout, wrapped an arm around the much smaller man's back, and pulled him into a bro hug.

"No, not really," Sprout said. "Like, really not much. The amount of points I make from my plants is kind of pathetic."

"How's that?" I asked.

"Huh? Oh. Well, you know how it is. They're not directly used by me, so I don't get as many points from them. But hey, passive point income is nice, they're mostly paying for themselves now."

"Oh, yeah, of course," I said. I cleared my throat. "Anyone seen Gomorrah around?"

"She's coming," Sprout said. "She went to the northern entrance. There was a small wave pushing at the barricade over there and she cleared it out. I, ah, heard some concerns about fire?"

"That sounds like a reasonable concern to have around her, yeah," I said. That didn't seem to reassure him much. "What about Manic?"

"Whether or not she comes is up to her. She doesn't strike me as someone who does meetings," he said.

I nodded. "And you?" I asked the militia man standing next to our little table.

"I'm here as a representative, ma'am," he said. "If you need anything relayed to the general, I can assist you. I'm linked into the militia's net as well, I can pull up information for you."

That made sense. The general probably wanted to keep tabs on us as well. "Alright. Well, while we're waiting on the others . . . Myalis, can I get some sort of mini-projector?"

Certainly. There are a few inexpensive options available. I imagine you don't want something permanent?

"Just something cheap would do," I said.

Ten points later, a box appeared on the food court table and unfolded itself. A projection sprang to life above it, a stylized cat head with a grenade pin in its mouth and a cybernetic right eye. It was even in my colors, pink and dark blue.

I chuckled. "Nice."

I've been working on it for entire milliseconds. It's a more refined version of some of the logos I've seen attributed to you online.

People were drawing shit about me online? That was kinda weird.

"You talk to your AI out loud?" Sprout asked.

I blinked. "It's, um, for your benefit. I want to show you what a good AI–Vanguard relationship looks like."

You are, to put it into terms you'd understand, so full of shit.

"Anyway, Myalis, my dear, my pal, my buddy, can we have a wireframe of the city?"

The projection changed to a loading screen, which was a depiction of a kitten running after a ball of yarn, then it snapped back to a map of the city, each building sticking out as a set of thin wirelike lines.

Sprout leaned forward. "Okay. Nice. We've blocked off these streets here, here, and all of these out entirely. We have patrols that check and see if the barricades are still working, but that's about it." He pointed to some roads, which highlighted them in green.

"Nice," Johnny said. "I know there's good fighting to be had down the main avenue out. Lots of babes to check you out too."

"Um, yeah, the main roads were too large to block at first, so we're keeping them mostly open. The idea is to have areas where the Antithesis can enter with little initial resistance. These are spots that are guarded day and night. They act as killing fields for us," Sprout said. That added four orange areas around the edge of Downtown.

"Clever," I said, then I half turned as I noticed someone approaching. It was Gomorrah, who placed her flamethrower atop a nearby table before joining us. "Hey."

"Hello," she said. She nodded to the other two. "Sprout and . . . you don't have a samurai name yet, do you?"

"Oh, babe, you can call me whatever you want," Johnny said. "Are you a nun? Because I'm a sinner, and I need your help tonight." He winked and fired some finger guns in her general direction.

Gomorrah turned to me. "Can I burn him?"

"No, please don't," I said. "Johnny, she's got someone already."

He tsked. "The hot babes always do."

"That's right," I agreed. "Now stop flirting with her for a minute, we've got work to do."

"How did things go at River Heights?" Sprout asked.

I shrugged. "Well enough. We're pulling more militia back to Downtown. No more sending samurai over either. It's a bit of a waste of our time, unless they really need us. In the meantime . . . Gomorrah, how were the aliens?"

"Crispy when I was done with them," Gomorrah said. "Honestly though, there weren't as many as I expected to see. Certainly not as many as we saw in New Montreal. The defenses are getting hit frequently enough, but the numbers are always small."

"How small?" I asked.

"Forty to fifty models, usually on the lower end with a sprinkling of the bigger single digits. By this late into the incursions we should be seeing double digits, maybe low twenties. This is far below what I'd expect to see."

"Huh, that does sound a little weak. Any ideas why? I don't know if the area was culled by a higher-tier samurai earlier."

"The area around the city was," Sprout said. "Once near the start, then again two days ago. There were lots of explosions and the weather shifted around. People were worried about it. We lost power for a while, but it was re-established. The internet went down as well."

"Alright," I said. Something wasn't adding up then. "Seeing as how Manic's not here . . . should we proceed?"

"Proceed to what, exactly?" Gomorrah asked.

"I'm thinking the wisest course of action right now would be to wipe out some of the nearest hives," I said. "We can pair up—a noob and someone with more experience hitting hives together. Once we've cleared out the easy ones, we'll be able to range out farther, and it'll mean that the new guys here will have more points to spend on themselves."

"That sounds fair. There's only two of us and three new samurai though," Gomorrah pointed out.

"I don't mind staying behind or switching out later," Sprout said.

"Well, there you have it," I said. "I'll go and see Manic. I should say hello at least once if she's technically my responsibility, right?"

Gomorrah nodded, and I had the impression she was proud of herself under that mask.

"Anyway. You, can you tell the general to increase the alert level while we're out? There won't be as many samurai around to keep things safe. But if we succeed, that'll mean fewer aliens too, so I think the general will be happy enough with the trade."

"Not that you need his permission," Gomorrah said.

"It's just polite," I said. "Will you be okay with Johnny here?" I pointed to the big guy with a thumb.

"As long as he doesn't touch me, he won't get burned."

"Oh, that's a hot mama," Johnny said.

"Significantly hotter than you could ever manage," she said. It was a threat.

Johnny grinned, but he didn't push his luck, which was probably for the best.

Was sending him with Gomorrah a good idea? Probably not. But if she cooked him, then that was just Darwinism at work.

"Right, I'm going to check on Manic, then head out to find some trouble. Sprout, keep me apprized. If Manic doesn't want to play, we might switch out."

"I can do that," he said.

I patted him on the back. The dude could use some of Johnny's spine. And Johnny could use a bit less. Maybe sticking them together would end with a nice middle ground? I'd have to see.

CHAPTER TWELVE

ALMOST COOL

Omg! When Deus tripped over a pipe and bashed her face against that wall?

That bit after, where she stomps her feet, it's already a meme.

How can someone so dangerous be so cute?

—Chat from SamuraiBloopers.net, 2048

"Myalis, got a bead on Manic?"

Her location is known. She's past the west-side barricade, about three hundred meters out, close to the waterfront. I can guide you there, if you wish.

"That'd be nice," I said as I stood up. Sprout had run off to check on things already, and Gomorrah and Johnny—who really needed a proper samurai name already—were walking out. She'd pointed to a hive just to the south, which was close enough to Downtown and River Heights that taking it out would help both.

By the looks of it, Manic was faffing about some ways away from the place everyone else was working to protect.

I couldn't blame her though, she was killing aliens, and that's all that mattered. There was a suspected hive a few blocks over from where she was, so we would hit that after saying our hellos.

"I feel a little underdressed for alien hunting," I said with a tap against my chestplate. The gear I had was probably more than enough to tango with some single-digit plants, but if we were going to hit a hive, then I'd want something a little tougher.

Besides, I wasn't properly armed.

I nipped into a washroom, because while I didn't mind eyes on me, the bodysuit I was wearing under my coat was so tight in some places it looked painted on, and I didn't need Lucy seeing images of my ass across her media feeds. Scoring higher on the popularity boards wasn't worth it.

"You remember that armor you showed me in the Mesh?" I asked Myalis.

I don't forget much. Is that what you want now?

"Yeah," I said. "But make sure it's heatproof. Good cooling and stuff. We're working with Gomorrah often enough that not having something fireproof is just asking for trouble."

That's understandable. Do you want the usual otherwise? Thagomizer tail, finger-mounted blades, shoulder-mounted guns?

I nodded along. "Sounds perfect, yeah. Oh, and those jump-jets from last time."

Those will be difficult to fit in . . . I can add smaller ones, but their range will be somewhat limited unless you want to purchase a whole new catalog specifically for that kind of technology.

"How limited?"

You won't be jumping any higher than five meters vertically.

"That's more than enough, I think. Make sure it's got the usual stealth stuff." I said. There were a few gizmos I didn't use much. The claws were something I'd never messed with, and the tail was almost more for show than anything else. Still, it kind of fit the image. The stealth stuff was a must-have though, I was getting used to going invisible. "I think . . . the usual color scheme? Oh, and I'll need a scarf too."

I'm on it.

A box appeared next to me with a dull thump. The top unfolded and a metallic figure unfurled itself until it was standing as tall as I was. The sides of the box slid to the ground, and I was able to shuck my coat and just walk into the armor, hands fitting into the glove-like spaces for them and chest pressing up against the front of the suit.

It closed around me, and for a split second I felt claustrophobic before it passed, like a wave of vertigo.

Shifting my shoulders then my hips, I made sure I had full control of the suit even as the space before my eyes flicked on and ran through a diagnostic so fast it was more of an afterimage.

I was left looking at the inside of the unisex bathroom through a screen with better resolution and frames than my own flesh and blood eye. The HUD was small and out of the way, easy to forget. The way I liked it.

"Sometimes I think you're too good at this," I said to Myalis.

I am.

I walked over to the mirror after picking up my coat and slipping into it. The person looking back at me in the mirror was armored from head to toe in sleek black power armor with a few dark sections over the more armored parts and some glowing pink highlights along the edges. I had a scarf around my neck, bunched up nice and neat under my coat. The trailing edge had that cat-head logo, with the grenade pin in its mouth.

"That'll do," I said.

I could pick up a weapon later, when I needed it. And I had my Trench Maker in case things got a little out of control, but mostly it was good for intimidation.

I left the box behind—it wasn't littering if the stuff you left behind was worth a lot—and headed out of the washroom and through the mall's cafeteria.

It was interesting to note how much more attention I was getting now compared to before. I guess my more casual outfit didn't scream "samurai" as much, and even Gomorrah's gear looked very nunlike. This was different.

Once I was outside, I checked a map, found Manic's location, my own, and the simple route I'd need to take to get there. It wasn't all that far.

I could have gotten a car, or hitched a ride with someone, or even just splurged some points on a scooter or something, but I didn't mind a short jog. It was only a couple of kilometers.

I regretted my decision about six hundred meters later. The power armor was great, it took out a lot of the effort I had to put into moving. Without that, I wasn't sure I'd be able to move at all with its added weight. Still, moving was moving, and I wasn't in the most perfect shape.

You might want to consider either more cybernetic enhancements or, seeing as how you're wary of those, perhaps supplements to help your body grow more comfortable with this degree of exercise.

"Like steroids?" I asked.

Yes.

"Well, I don't have a dick to shrink, I guess," I said.

I'd hardly give you something with negative side effects.

"I mean, fair, but isn't that cheating?"

You could argue that everything a Vanguard does is cheating.

I laughed until I had to stop to focus on my breathing. Soon enough, I was by the barricade and I stopped my run to a slow jog and finally a normal walk.

The barricade wasn't much to look at, but it was still impressive in its own . . . mishy-mashy way. A group with brown bands around their arms were off to one side, grinders screaming as they cut through some metal plates. Others were behind a small partition, the actinic spark of welders going off brightening up the entire street.

The wall itself was made of cars turned on their sides, with metal braces bolted in place to keep them there. There were enough of them stacked up that they rose a good five or six meters up. They'd built catwalks behind the cars just high enough that someone could stand up and see over the edge of the wall. A few guns were mounted up there too.

"Hey," I called out to a militia guy who jumped to attention. "How do you get to the other side?" I asked.

He looked at the wall, then back at me. "There's a tunnel, under the street," he said. "We use it to get to the other side when we need to burn the corpses. Um, you can get around through that building too, but it's locked up to hell, ma'am." He gestured to one of the buildings next to the barricade.

"Ah, that's alright then," I said.

I walked up to the wall, bunched my legs up under me, then jumped.

And then I landed about a foot ahead.

"Myalis," I growled.

Yes, Catherine?

"Was it not obvious what I was trying to do?" I asked.

It was. But now I have a video of you doing a bunny hop while thinking you'd look very cool.

"Don't you dare," I said.

Sent to Lucy already. I apologize, Catherine. She asked nicely.

I grumbled. Well, Lucy would enjoy it, and I was pretty much immune to embarrassment at this point. "Just turn on the jump-jets this time? People are watching."

Certainly.

I jumped again, and this time the jets near my ankles fired with a nearly quiet hiss that propelled me up and to the side of the catwalk. I latched on and used the momentum to swing myself over, then I planted a foot on a small ledge and basically stepped over the top of the barricade and leapt off the other side, coat flapping with a snap behind me.

I landed with a grunt, knees bending so much that I almost hit myself in the chest before I stood and continued to walk. I was vaguely aware of people over the wall staring.

"That's more like it," I muttered. "Now, where's Manic?"

CHAPTER THIRTEEN

ACTUALLY COOL

A ground-based city is a city whose infrastructure isn't—yet—designed to accommodate sky-based traffic. These cities require that hover vehicles use ground-level commercial and public traffic lanes and are generally accessible for people on foot, or on self-powered vehicles (e.g., bicycles, Rollerblades, scooters).

As megacities continue to become more popular, living in a ground-based city is seen as something less desirable and more mundane. People living in these places are often called Dirt, or Ground Pounders.
—*Modern Dictionary of Modern Slang*, fourth edition, 2045

The city past Downtown wasn't all too different from the city within the barricades. It wasn't like they'd stopped right on the edge of the high-rises. Though the farther out I walked, the shorter the buildings became. Most of them were older constructions, the kinds of building styles that were popular in like, the early bit of the century.

These were pre-Antithesis buildings. Cheaper, designed to be prettier. They'd been retrofitted, of course. All that flat space on their sides was wasted if it wasn't plastered full of ads.

The place was a mess now. More windows were broken than not, and I suspected that had more to do with looters than any alien presence. A couple of places had gone up in flames, and I stepped over the hood of a car that had merged into a few others in what was obviously a spectacular pile-up.

Burlington, it seemed, was very much a ground-based city.

She's to your right, around the intersection and one floor above ground level.

"Thanks," I said. I looked around for any signs of the Antithesis and found a whole lot of nothing. Strange. I would have expected them to be swarming almost nonstop. Wasn't that what happened in New Montreal?

Why was it so different here?

It couldn't have been Manic. She was alone and still relatively new. The area around the city had been culled, probably, but . . . no, I had a worrying feeling in my gut that said that something was off here, and I couldn't place exactly what it was yet.

The missing aliens were part of it, though.

I poked my head around the next intersection and scanned the space. A shopping area? There was a music store, an aug clinic, and a few chain restaurants with flashy ads competing for attention. Or they would have been if they weren't off. Neon wasn't nearly as impressive when it was powered down.

The second floor on the music store was blown out, the entire facade missing. Music was coming from there, which . . . was a little strange. The street seemed entirely unpowered, so what was making the noise?

After checking for stuff that might shoot at me and finding none, I stepped around the corner and started toward the store.

The music continued. It was just a guitar being strummed, something acoustic, if I had to guess (and I did have to guess, I didn't know jack shit about musical instruments). The sound carried well across the empty street. Without half a hundred air-conditioning units and neon tubes humming along and no cars passing by or catchy ad jingles competing for ear-space, the street was a nice, echoey place for a haunting, slow song to linger.

I didn't know music, but I knew emotions, and that song was as melancholic as any.

I stopped in the middle of the street in front of the music store, head tilted back to watch the player.

She was older than I'd imagined, somehow. A thirty-something woman with pale blue hair tossed up in a pompadour and shaved on the sides with a clean fade. She was aug'd to the tits (which were, admittedly, fantastic), with shockingly blue eyes and a few wires just under the skin of her face.

Her jacket, a thick black thing that was definitely Protector-made, with little spikes on the elbows and shoulders and a teal interior that matched her hair, was rolled up to let her hands free.

She was half-bent over an old guitar, one of those wooden ones with a starburst pattern inlaid into the grain. Manic continued to pluck at the strings, and the song turned a little less sad, and a little more . . . inquisitive?

"So, who the fuck are you?" she asked.

"Stray Cat," I said. "You play well."

"You don't know shit about music, Stray Cat."

She stopped. It was the wrong place to stop the music, though I couldn't explain why. With a sigh, she stood up from the pile of rubble she was using as a bench and carefully placed the guitar back on a rack next to a few others that didn't look like they'd weathered whatever destroyed the wall as well.

Then she walked out of the store's second floor, coat billowing out and legs straight until she crashed into the ground with a grunt and a hard bend of her knees. "Fuck. Knees aren't as smooth as they used to be," she complained.

"Buy new ones," I said. "You're Manic?"

"Yeah," she said. "Glad introductions are done. What do you want?"

Well, I was either going to get along with her or we'd end this in a cat-fight, and there was no middle ground. I figured we'd both be finding out which it was sometime in the next five minutes.

Manic was sizing me up. Her hands were in the pockets of her pants, real close to a pair of large handguns hanging off her belt. I couldn't tell if she was being casual or if that was some sort of threat.

I took a deep breath and considered what I was going to say next. I didn't have a lot of time to do that considering in, though. "I heard you were a gigantic bitch," I said.

That was a nice opener.

She scoffed. "Wanna see it for yourself?"

"I'd love to," I said. "There's a hive nearby. Whole fuckload of aliens that need killing. Actually, there's a bunch of them. You can pick."

"What is this, some sort of test shit?" she asked.

"Do I look educated?" I asked.

She shrugged and pulled a hand out of her pocket to gesture vaguely at me. I supposed I was wearing some pretty fancy shit instead of my usual less-than-fancy thrift-store-chic.

"Alright, fair enough," I said. "Want to come or not?"

"I don't like working with people. They're cunts."

"Can't have a band with just one player," I said.

"Bitch, you don't go making music analogies at me."

I laughed. "Sorry. Couldn't resist. But really. If you want, hit up the hive yourself. I can stand back and blow shit up when you can't handle it anymore."

"Girl, I'm too old for that kind of double-think trickery," she warned.

I shook my head. "One way or another, we've got hives to explode. You can work with me, you can go at it alone. Either way, we have work to do."

"Says who?"

"Says me," I said.

"And you're the boss of this place?"

"Literally, yeah. Some fuckwit who's never seen the outside of his little beige heaven assigned me to protect this backwater shithole of a city. Trust me, I'd rather be back home wearing a lot less and frying my brain out on my media feeds while fondling my girlfriend. But no, instead I'm out here giving orders that I hope won't get anyone killed and trying to lead around a bunch of noobs who don't know any better. So yeah, either work with me, or work for me."

"Those are my two options?" she asked. She stood taller, and I realized that she had a good half head over me. Still, something about her posture, the way she crossed her arms and scowled . . . yeah, we were on the same page, more or less. At the very least, we were in the same book.

"Well, you can go back to practicing your guitar."

She tilted her head to one side, the cybernetics in her neck poking out of her skin in a disconcerting way until her spine cracked, then she did the same on the other side. "Yeah, alright, show me what you can do, Stray Cat. You some sort of top-tier samurai?"

"Not even close," I said. "Just been at this for a little longer than you have. Long enough to figure out which end of the gun goes bang."

"Hm."

"Myalis, nearest hive from here?"

Difficult to confirm. With local surveillance networks mostly down, I can only point you in the general direction. There are a few potential locations to visit. One is a botanical shop on the other side of the city, the other a sewage treatment plant, another—and this is the nearest—is beneath the Burlington Museum of Natural History.

"Cool," I said. "I love museums."

"Museums?" Manic asked. "Are we talking about the tallest cabinet thing?"

"What?" I asked.

"Yeah, never mind."

I frowned, but didn't ask. "Come on, it can't be too far from here. You can tell me your sob story as we walk."

"Fuck you."

"Only if you're real okay about threesomes," I replied.

CHAPTER FOURTEEN

OPPOSITES DISTRACT

It's an accepted fact that the average American diet was worsening year by year, but I think it really took a hit the day the FDA merged with Nars-Mestle.

—Chef Boy Kardi, last aired episode of his cooking show
Proper Dishes, 2034

We walked down the center of the road, mostly because it allowed us to keep an eye on everything and if something ambushed us, it would give us more time to see it coming and to react. Also, it was strange and novel to walk down the middle of the street.

"You ever been to the museum?" I asked.

"Do I look like the museum-going sort?" Manic asked right back.

I shrugged. "Hey, don't knock museums. I became a samurai in one."

"Wow," she said. "Talk about nerdy."

I blinked. Did she think I was that kind of girl? I . . . didn't care *that* much about the impression she had of me, but it still stung a little that she didn't think I was a punk. "Yeah. I was with the other kids from my orphanage. It was this big PR stunt thing. Then aliens came pouring out of the sky, crashed through the ceiling and things kinda went to shit from there. I ended up with a pipe through my chest." I tapped the spot. "Anyway, it turned out alright in the end."

"Huh," she said. "Don't have as much of a story as that."

"Really? Far as I know, most people that get picked to be samurai get a shitty start. It's fine if you're not ready to talk about it, though."

She scoffed. "I didn't get run through or anything. Me and a couple of . . . acquaintances all discovered that our go-to aug-doc was fucking with us." She touched her exposed stomach. "He sold us these colon-integrated stim injectors. CISIs, you know? They can give you a long-lasting hit of something fun if you activate them. You can load yourself full of Ziggy, or Propi, or your opioid of choice before a fight. Gets your heart kicking to the beat and with the right cocktail you can't bleed and you'll keep going for a minute after you've died."

"Something wrong with the installation?" I asked. I'd never been able to dream of affording that kind of self-modding. Not to mention, the orphanage was liable to rip anything too good right out of me to sell it off.

"Worse. He did good work, but someone from a band I know started running the numbers and it turned out three or four of us had the same serials on our CISIs. Which, yeah, that's not possible. Turns out he hawked out these cheap-ass Chinese knock-off models. 3D-printed, backroom shit. So we went off to kick his ass."

I nodded along. I was already iffy about modding myself any more than I had. It was . . . I don't know, just kind of squicky. I didn't mind the eye, or the arm, but that was because I needed them. The internals were pushing it. I might give in one day, but I'd put it off as long as I could. Her story was like a lesson on why it could be a bad move.

"Where do the aliens come in?" I asked.

"Oh, when we drove out to his place, it's near the river, we found it getting hit up by aliens. The others fucked off, but he had clients in there, you know? Mostly local whores and shit, but . . . yeah, they weren't going to last. Bummed a shotty from a friend of a friend and ran in."

"Big fucking hero, huh?"

She snorted. "Yeah, sure."

I checked a map of the city while we chatted. The Museum of Natural History was only a block down from where we were. "Just around the corner," I said. "You know the place at all?"

She made a vague so-so gesture. "A little? Driven past it enough times. Been living in this shithole city for five or so years now."

"Where were you before?" I asked.

"Mega-city York," she said.

I whistled. And she was calling this place a shithole? Then again, I couldn't complain too much, since this was about as far from the place I was born as I'd ever gotten. "Well, Myalis thinks there's a hive in there. I think we ought to check it out because something's not right about this incursion."

"What's not right about it? Aliens show up every few hours, we kill them, then more show up."

"That's the thing, we should be seeing a lot more. Maybe only a dozen show up on day one, but by that night there should be three dozen, and by the next morning it should be a hundred or two. Just a few little bands of low-tier models? Over days? Just got this feeling that something weird's going on."

She linked her arms together behind her back, then stretched until her spine popped. I tried not to stare at her chest. I didn't need to. I had a perfectly stareable chest back home.

"I'll go in first," I said. "Stealth's kind of my gimmick."

"And you're going to leave me behind?" Manic asked. She sounded a bit peeved about it.

"Hey, if you want to come, feel free," I said. "But I'm not big on babysitting."

"I can pull my own weight," she growled.

I grinned behind my mask. Gomorrah was going to be horrified when she met Manic. The woman was like an older, meaner version of me. I was impressed that we hadn't turned to blows yet, actually.

The museum wasn't anything as fancy as the museum I'd turned into my home. It was a three-story building with a large glass front. A screen covered one surface, from the ground floor all the way up. One of those perspective-based 3D advertising things that were real popular about ten years back.

It looked like the museum was actually pretty nice, otherwise. Not too many ads, and it seemed pretty clean. "What gives?" I asked.

"That place? Dunno. It's a museum some of the time, and the rest of the time it's used for like, fancy parties and shit."

"Ah," I said. Probably a place for philanthropists to hobnob then. "Well, whatever, through the front door, yeah? Myalis, can I get a Laser Pointer?"

One Laser Pointer, coming right up.

Manic gave me a strange look, but a box appeared next to me and I pulled the top off to reveal my new toy. One of those Sun Watcher bullpup SMGs I'd been practicing with in Mesh-space. There was a slight difference to the feel of it in real-space. It had more weight than a virtual world could properly simulate, but otherwise, it was pretty much the same.

"You armed, or you going to take them out with a winning smile?"

She laughed then reached to the small of her back. What she came back with was a relatively small handgun. "Got this thing. It fires a resonant frequency. Melts the aliens right up."

"Oh, hey, I used something like that before. A lot, even. It's a grenade though. Good AOE, keeps an area safe."

She nodded, then looked at my gun, then her own. Hers was a lot smaller. I could almost see the math being worked out behind her eyes. "Give me a sec," she said before frowning.

"We've got all night," I said, even though it was midday at most.

It took a minute, but eventually, Manic nodded. Then a box thumped down by her feet. She grinned, kicked the top off, then pulled out a much larger gun. It looked like the high-tech great-grandchild of a double-barrel. "Bass Cannon," she explained.

"Cool," I said with a nod.

"You wearing ear protection in that suit? Because this thing's loud as fuck."

I laughed. "I should be alright," I said. "Right, Myalis?"

One moment, I need to ask Vanguard Manic's AI the specifications of that weapon . . . yes, your equipment should be able to handle indirect fire. Please don't take a blast to the face unprotected though. It'll make your cybernetic eye malfunction, and also melt your brain.

"Should be good," I said with a thumbs-up.

Manic grinned, then the sides of her head shifted and the "skin" over her jaw moved up and over her ears while plates on the side of her skull lowered to meet them so that her ears were entirely covered and I could see the linkages and wiring of the augs planted into the bone of her skull and jaws.

"Let me try this thing," she said.

I stepped back.

Manic stepped up.

She cocked her gun, which whined like a microphone getting bad feedback. I stepped back a bit more as she started to laugh and pressed the gun in against her shoulder. The barrels flipped and extended, forming a pair of large, glowing disks. The noise grew and grew until the pitch hit a point where I couldn't hear it at all.

With a single heavy *whump* that displaced the air ahead of her, Manic fired.

The front of the museum exploded.

I was pretty sure they heard that all the way across the city.

"Ah, fuck," I muttered. "She's not like me. She's the opposite."

CHAPTER FIFTEEN

THE BAD KIND OF INTERESTING

The last game was stupid-hard, but the water level on this one? It's just not playable. It's streamer-hard, not casual hard.

—Most *Eldest Ring* forums, 2037

With the front of the Museum of Natural History being itself part of history, it wasn't exactly hard to find a way in. Though there was a lot of glass lying around and I wasn't sure if the building's structural integrity had taken a hit or not.

"You know, you could have tested that on another building," I said.

"This is the one the hive's in," Manic shot back.

"Yeah, but we could have snuck over to the hive. Now, unless they're all deaf in there, they'll know we're coming."

Manic shrugged. "So they'll come out to where I can shoot them better. That's not sounding like much of a problem to me."

I resisted the urge to roll my eye. She wouldn't be able to see it anyway. "Let's head in. They'll probably be on the lower floors if anything."

My boots crunched on loose glass and I stepped over a chunk of masonry before ducking into the museum. Manic followed, her gun refolding itself into a smaller configuration. I hoped that it had multiple settings and didn't just have a "blow everything up" mode, especially if we were going to be fighting indoors.

I paused once past the threshold and craned my neck back to take in the museum's layout. It seemed as if the main lobby area was a big open space, reaching all the way to the top of the building with balconies that let people entering peek into the second and third floors.

A huge whale skeleton hung from the ceiling by a set of metal wires. Some of the bones had been blasted off, but it was still obvious that it was a whale. A plaque hung next to it. *Martha, the Last Whale on Earth! Now on Loan from the Ocean and Seas Museum of America!*

"You broke the whale skeleton," I said to Manic as she stepped up after me while making noticeably more noise.

"Huh. Well, my bad."

"At least you own up to your mistakes," I said with a nod. She flashed me a glare, but I turned around and headed deeper in before she could get a word in edgewise. The second floor looked like more of a reception place than a museum, and the first floor had a playspace for kids, with tactile displays and cartoonish animals explaining things in simpler terms.

I imagined that the areas above were more adult-oriented.

A holographic sandwich board, probably battery-powered since it was one of the only things in the museum that was lit up, sat by a staircase leading up. "Fourteenth annual gathering for the benefit of the Burlington Music Society," I read aloud. "That something you're part of?"

She scoffed. "Please. This kind of stuck-up shit? They're all about the old-old stuff. We're talking fifties rock and classical bands."

"You're not a fan of the classics?" I asked.

"Oh, I love the real classics," Manic said. "Pre-diaspora Justin Bieber, Imagine Dragons before they went all cyborg. The real music from back in the day, before AIs took all the soul out of it."

"Yeah, I'm not super into music. Never really developed a taste for it. I like some songs, don't like others. It's all just beeps and boops, you know?" I raised my Laser Pointer to my shoulder and started to scan the area. Fortunately, there was a handy map on one wall that I scanned for a moment. The maintenance access was a little deeper in. I figured that would be the best way to go down.

"How old are you, anyway?" Manic asked.

"Eighteen-ish," I said.

"Ish?"

"Orphaned as a kid, didn't exactly keep good track of things," I said. "Never really did birthdays much either."

"Huh," she said. "Well, I guess you still have time to acquire *some* taste before it's too late."

"Don't need to be such a bit—" I paused, then raised my off-hand in a fist above my head. Manic went quiet too. I focused some more on my hearing. There was something scratching at something nearby. "You hear that?"

Manic shook her head. The augs over her ears peeled back, and she frowned. "No, nothing."

I knelt down and listened more intently, letting my cybernetic ears do their thing. "Yeah, there's something below us. It's scratching something. Maybe digging?"

"You've got good ears," she said.

I pointed to the armored stubs above my helmet, both shaped like the cat ears they were protecting. "They're still newish. Anyway, let's find a way down. There's no way the Antithesis don't know we're coming, so we might walk into an ambush."

"Want to go first then, since you're all armored up?"

I nodded, then faded into invisibility. "I'll take care of it, no worries."

Manic blinked at where I stood, then I started to move and she didn't follow me with her gaze. "You can do that?" she asked.

"It's my specialty," I said from about two meters to the right of where she thought I was. "Myalis, want to give her AI an idea of where we are? I don't want to get Bass-Cannoned."

I continued on deeper into the museum, gun sweeping left and right as I started to look for trouble. A few of the displays looked like they'd been broken into, but I couldn't tell if that was looters or aliens. There wasn't any blood around, or many signs of trouble.

We crossed a section dealing with the local geography that looked entirely unbothered. It looked like most looters were more keen on throwing rocks than picking up new and interesting ones. Finally, we reached a maintenance door that was locked shut, the "Employees Only" sign printed on it a pretty clear indication that we weren't supposed to be pushing through. So, of course, I shot the door's hinges off.

"Huh, that's a quiet-ass gun," Manic said as I raised a hand and caught the falling door. I lowered it down until it was close to the ground, then let it fall with a *whump* of displaced air.

"Yeah. Not much of a point in being stealthy if you give yourself away with the first shot," I said. "Myalis, do we have blueprints of this place?"

We do. The reason I suspected that the Antithesis were around this building is because of an unusual heat buildup in the area. The interior of the museum is several degrees warmer than it should be.

"So, strange and mysterious warmth. That's not a perfect indicator of aliens," I said. "Maybe someone's growing something in the basement . . . is weed legal here?"

Manic shrugged. "It's easy to get, legal or not." She shouldered her Bass Cannon and looked into the maintenance area. It didn't have the benefit of a floor-to-ceiling wall of glass to allow sunlight in, so the interior was dark except for a flickering emergency exit sign.

I stepped in, the visor on my helmet compensating for the lower light levels a bit, though I supposed that better gear existed for that same purpose.

Manic sighed. "Give me a bit, I need more light."

"Might want to order like, a headset, or glasses that let you see in the dark. Or a helmet. You have no idea how dangerous it is to be fighting aliens without good head protection," I said. I was quite fortunate that I was resistant to my own hypocrisy.

I waited as Manic ordered something up. It turned out to be a sort of half-helmet visor thing that covered the top half of her face and wrapped around to the back of her skull. It let her hair out free. "That's better. I'm going to be low on points soon."

"We'll find something for you to murderize yourself back to a good number of points," I said. "Or I can donate my old stuff to you."

"I'd rather not," she said. "My gear looks good."

"Ouch."

The maintenance area wasn't all that grand. We crossed a tiny break-room with a wall of lockers, then a few other essentials: a couple of tiny offices, a closet with all of the breakers and servers for the museum, another closet with mops, buckets, and a few shut-down cleaning mechs.

There was a small warehouse space with shelves all over, but judging by how dusty it was, it hadn't been crossed by any aliens in a while.

Then we found a door leading to a second warehouse space. On opening the door I was blasted by a gush of warm air that I felt thanks to my suit's haptics. More shelves, more dust, but this room was unique because the last one didn't have a fuck-huge water-filled hole in the middle of its floor.

"Well, that's interesting," I said. I walked to the edge of the hole and looked down, only to find one of those monkey-like model tens staring up in our general direction atop a thick plant-like artery.

CHAPTER SIXTEEN

MAKING LOTS OF LITTLE PROBLEMS

It's true that the Antithesis are essentially plants, without a centralized hive-mind, or even a coherent structure of command. They are true aliens, unlike nearly anything that we've ever seen on Earth.

But don't discount their cunning.

—Professor Christie, lecture on the mysteries of the Antithesis, 2029

I lowered my Laser Pointer, placed the red dot in the sight over the model ten, then tapped the trigger to release a trio of rounds with a hush-like whisper and a faint kick to my shoulder.

The water around the alien splashed up and I stepped back a bit not to get hit by it. The rounds I fired pierced through the water and rammed into the little alien, two of the three finding their mark and ripping it up.

"Okay," I said. "This is fucky."

"Is this normal?" Manic asked. She flicked a rock into the hole with the tip of her boot. It splashed next to the corpse, which gently floated up and away from the root.

"I've never seen anything like it," I admitted. This was very strange. The root seemed to go on for a while. In fact . . . I knelt down and lowered myself over the hole, following the path bored into the ground. I couldn't see far, not with the lighting being as poor as it was and with my vision obscured by the murky water, but it was pretty obvious that the tunnel went on for quite a ways. Onward, and deeper too. "Myalis, what am I looking at?"

It looks like an artery root from an Antithesis hive. They are frequently grown along tunnels dug out by model eights and, of course, guarded by model tens. These will frequently link two sections of a hive together.

"There's an entire heap of bad implications there," I muttered as I stood back up. "We're going to need to call Gomorrah about this."

"I want to know where the root's leading to," Manic said.

"Trouble," I answered.

She scoffed, but didn't press. I think we both knew I was right. Now, that begged the question, why was there a root like this underground? Or . . . no, that was a stupid question. Higher-tier samurai than me had been smashing hives all over. This one was probably a lot harder to discover, hidden as it was underground and under a layer of water. It was beneath the city, too. I bet a cursory glance would just suggest that it was some piping or something normal instead of a giant alien problem.

I rang up Gomorrah, and she picked up within a few seconds. She was breathing hard on the other end of the line. "Hey," I said.

"Hello," she replied. "What is it?"

"Nothing super urgent, are you alright on your end?" I asked. She was breathing pretty hard. Was she in a running fight?

"Just burning some xenos," she said.

Ah. Well. That explained the heavy breathing then. I wasn't sure if Franny was a lucky girl or not. "Okay then. You find the hive?"

"No, actually. Atyacus pointed us to a place but there was nothing there. It was strange. My IR systems said the place was hot too, but nothing."

"Did you check underground?" I asked.

"No? There was a parking garage, but nothing in it."

I looked down the hole again. "Yeah, well, we found something neat over here. I'm with Manic, and while sniffing around we found this fuck-huge hole with a large root in it and a model ten. No signs of a proper hive, just a recently bored hole and the root. Myalis says it might be, like, a connection between two hive parts."

"Huh," Gomorrah said. "And we were right on top of it? That might explain why these model threes ran to our position, actually. I thought it was strange."

"A lot of them?"

"No, just a few," she said.

I looked at the root. It was about as big around as my torso, with gnarled skin and what looked like veins across its surface. "Yeah, no, something's fucky. This root here looks chunky enough. However much resources the hive put into growing this could have made a hundred model threes, I bet."

Gomorrah was quiet for a moment. "That's the last of the easy ones here. And it doesn't look like there's anything else. I think you might be right. Did you want to hit the hive from your end and we'll find out what we can here?"

I considered what to do for a moment. "Actually, I think I want more information first. Might just scout the root network out and then go from there. Can you hold off on burninating things for a little bit?"

"I've had my fill for the moment, though it wasn't quite as satisfying as I would have wished."

"That's nice. Manic and I will check things out. You cool down for a bit," I said before cutting out. I stretched my back until my spine popped, then gestured to the hole. "Okay. So we either buy scuba gear and go down there, hope we don't run out of air or get ambushed underwater, or worse, get stuck, or, and bear with me here, we toss in something AI-controlled and let that figure out where the root leads."

Manic chuckled darkly. "You're really living up to the cat stereotype if you're worried about getting wet."

"I prefer getting wet under the right circumstances, and this ain't it," I shot back.

"You're a real freak, huh?"

I nodded. I was proud of it too. "Alright, Myalis, I need something small that can swim through that crap and figure out what's what."

I can offer a pair of small semi-autonomous drones for twenty points each. Or, if you want something a little more versatile, stealth drones for a hundred points apiece. They're armed with a self-destruct mechanism and a number of stealth capabilities.

Stealth would be preferable. We didn't know what we'd be running into down there, and I'd rather it not know that we were around until we chose to let it know.

I ordered up two drones, and they appeared in a set of boxes next to me. I pulled the top off one of them, revealing that I should have asked Myalis to be a little more specific.

When she'd said stealth drones, I had a mental image of a small thing that hovered invisibly, maybe covered in cameras or something. What I found was a small robotic cat wearing a tiny set of scuba gear. I reached in, plucking the cat out by the nape of its neck. It weighed no more than a real cat, but looked to be cold to the touch.

"What?" Manic asked.

"No," I replied, even if it didn't make much sense. Then I flicked the cat into the hole where it landed with a splash and sank right down. The second drone joined it a moment later, and I kicked the boxes out of the way.

Myalis opened a pair of screens over my augmented eye's vision, one from each of the cat drones. So far, there wasn't much to look at but light-corrected footage of two dark tunnels.

"Are you getting that?" I asked Manic.

"Yeah, I've got it," she said. "Not much to see so far."

"Let them swim out for a bit," I suggested. I imagined that whatever these hives were hiding, it wouldn't be sitting just a few meters away.

One of the cats reached a fork in the tunnel and I cursed. The root split two ways, though one was clearly larger than the other. That was bad news in any case. The Antithesis had to have a whole network of these things.

Myalis directed the cat to follow the thicker root, and I watched with growing anxiety as it continued to swim along next to more and more offshoots and side tunnels. At one point the drone stopped as a pair of model tens scampered by, seemingly unbothered by the water around them.

The roots eventually turned downward, and I tightened my fists as I watched them lead into a much larger space. An underground cavern of sorts, with large sections dug out from the walls and the ground. Model eights, the big wormlike ones, were hard at work enlarging the space.

They weren't the only aliens around. The roots covered nearly every surface, and there were hundreds of pods lumped together like grapes on a massive stem, each with an unborn alien within.

Those didn't concern me as much as the really large, really disturbing pods taking up the center of the room, each one as large as a semitrailer.

"That's going to be a problem," I said.

Then the other cat reached a second chamber, and I closed my eyes. There was more than one of them.

We were sitting on top of a massive hive, one filled with every sort of Antithesis in the books, and I was willing to bet they were just looking for an excuse to pop up and make my life complicated.

CHAPTER SEVENTEEN

GROWTH

There's famous samurai, and then there's Famous ones. I'm not talking about your average Joe with an alien chip in their head and a bit of an attitude problem who likes saving orphans. I'm talking about the samurai who leave behind a legacy.

—Three Swipes, "Late Night With AI-567" interview, 2032

"Now what?" Manic asked.

I reached up to rub at the bridge of my nose, then let my hand fall. "Well, we're kinda fucked, aren't we?"

Manic shrugged. "Honestly, that's nothing new for me."

"Yeah, that's fair. Want to go out with a bang?" I asked.

She grinned. "Always imagined that the best way to go was while blowing something big up. A last, final show, you know?"

I nodded along. That was the big dream, wasn't it? Unfortunately, I had responsibilities now, and Lucy would be upset if I died, even if it was in a blaze of glory. So, basically I couldn't strap a nuke to my chest and charge at the aliens.

Besides, I didn't feel like swimming.

"Myalis, I need a few more of those cat drones. Can you start mapping out the underground for us? We need to know more or less where they'll be breaking through," I said.

Certainly. I've already begun, though I don't yet know the extent of the underground hive's reach.

That was fine. I let Manic open the boxes that showed up around me. I had to think in the meantime. Downtown was woefully underdefended for the number of aliens we were seeing. "Myalis, you're the expert here. When will they attack?"

An undisturbed hive will, generally, continue to expand, grow, and harden itself until such a time as it encounters resistance or a threat, at which time it will work to eliminate that threat.

So if I planted bombs down there and set them off, then we'd be swarmed within the hour. I started pacing the little room. It seemed as if I had three problems. I opened a text box and typed them up.

1. Fuckloads of aliens were going to mess us up soon
2. Downtown wasn't ready to deal with even a moderate swarm
3. All I had to work with were three noobs and Gomorrah

I hesitated, then added a fourth line.

4. Lucy was going to be annoyed if I wasn't back home for dinner

"Myalis, what could we do to mess the aliens up?" I asked. "I don't think we can just nuke them to hell."

"Nukes are an option?" Manic asked.

"Always," I said. "But they might be a bit rough here. How much of these hives are under the city where the people we're supposed to protect are living? Nah, we can't afford to nuke anything, I don't think. We'll have to be more creative."

Myalis brought up a map and superimposed it over a 3D representation of Burlington. It was pretty clear that the hive was stretching around Downtown, with a few little tunnels leading inward. Of course, we hadn't uncovered the entire thing yet. The two cat drones we'd sent ahead were still moving along, and the new ones were playing catch-up. It would take . . . well, I didn't know how long it would take to figure out the size of the hive. The bigger it was, the longer it would take.

I started cycling through options.

Resonators would melt the hive up nicely, especially if they couldn't turn them off in time. Just disconnecting the various root networks would fuck up the Antithesis's logistics for a minute. But that would be super obvious.

If we did that now, they'd react, and then Downtown—and River Heights—would burn.

Lighting everything on fire was an option too, but I figured we'd run into the same problem. Plus, fire would pour out into the city above, and then everything would *literally* burn. And the hives were underwater. I was sure Gomorrah had fire that burned underwater, but I imagined that would just make it more dangerous.

So, something more subtle than that.

Fuck, I wasn't too good at subtle.

"Myalis, you remember those nano-bombs? The ones that eat Antithesis meat?"

Of course.

"If we set off a number of them in the hive network, would that kill it all without alerting them too quickly?"

The nanomachines can be programmed to only eat the Antithesis after a certain set time has passed, ensuring a wider distribution.

"Oh, that could work," I said. We'd need to insert them all over, then find a good time to set the bots off . . . But yeah. Eating the entire hive all at once would be fantastic. "They're kind of slow-acting, aren't they?" I asked.

Depending on the mass of the subject being consumed and the number of available nanomachines, the amount of time spent "eating" will vary greatly. But, generally, they are a little slower.

I could still work with that. "Okay. Send everything we've found so far to Gomorrah and Atyacus. Prioritize finding routes in the hive that lead into Downtown. We'll use those to pour our nanomachine friends in." I tapped Manic on the shoulder. "In the meantime, we're getting back to Downtown. Once the swarm starts being eaten, I bet they won't just sit back and enjoy it. We need to defend the city, which means arming up the locals and setting up defenses that aren't as budget as what's there already."

"I'm not sure that's my kind of deal," Manic said.

I looked at her. No, I imagined her deal was charging in and making a mess of things, which was usually just fine, but not if she did that now. "Can you hold back for like, a couple of hours? Soon we'll have more aliens breathing down our necks than we'll know what to do with."

"I guess," she said.

Patting her on the shoulder, I gave the hole in the floor one last look before slipping out of the room. At the same time, I called Gomorrah. "We have a problem," I said.

"That's a fun way to say hello," she replied. "What is it?"

"The hive here's bigger than I thought. I think it's got double-digit models, maybe up to the low twenties, and they're all snoozing belowground right now. But hey, I've got a plan."

"Does it involve copious amounts of explosives?"

"No, actually," I said. I was pretty proud of myself in the moment. "We're going to poison the well, or however that expression goes. Basically, I need you back in Downtown ASAP. We need to up the defenses until they'll be able to survive the aliens getting all uppity."

There was a long pause before she replied. "I don't think the Antithesis get 'uppity,' so much as they get murderously angry."

"Potato p*otato*," I said. "We'll be killing them either way. Do you think you'd have time to make a quick run from here to New Montreal and back?"

"What for?"

"We've been making turrets at my place. We must have half a hundred of them by now. They're pretty cheap shit, but they'll work well against the weaker models," I said.

"I'd much rather stay here, but I can ask Franny to take the church van and grab them," she said.

I nodded along. "Much better idea. I'll send Lucy a text about it. We really need to get things moving. I think that every hour we waste adds a whole shitload of extra aliens we're going to have to kill."

"I know. We'll go over whatever half-baked plan you came up with . . . want to meet at the mall again?" she asked.

"Sounds good. We'll have to distribute better weapons and coordinate with the general, what's-his-name from the militia. We need everyone on their A-game. Talk to you in person in a bit."

Hanging up the call, I continued walking through the museum, Manic a step behind me. "So, where to?"

"The mall," I said.

"Fuck me," she replied.

"Don't like the place?"

"It's fine. It's the people I don't like. There's only one sort of person that hangs out in a place like that, and they're the worst sort of human around. Hyper-consumerist fuckwits who'd sell their own mothers for the latest micro-version of whatever's the status symbol of choice this week. Can't fucking stand the place. And you know it only exists for people to flash their wealth. Otherwise they'd just buy their shit online like the rest of us."

"I like malls," I said. "Used to go there with my girlfriend and stare at all the shit we couldn't afford, filch half-eaten meals out of the trash too. Great smoothies."

Manic snorted. "I guess we have different memories of that sort of place."

"Guess so," I said. "Anyway, it's where everyone decided to gather in Downtown, so that's where we'll be heading to."

"You can blame that Sprout guy, he chose it. I think he used to work there."

"Really?" I asked as I stepped out into the sunlight. I got my bearings, then started walking toward the bigger skyscrapers.

"Yeah. Worked in this little flower shop."

"Huh," I said. Then I put that out of my mind because I had bigger concerns to deal with.

CHAPTER EIGHTEEN

MEETING OF THE GREATS

They're idiots.

All their little minds can imagine as the pinnacle of this technology is a machine that looks and feels human. But why would you ever want that? Humans are stupid, humans can double-think themselves into believing that the god they were raised to think is real while their neighbor who worships another is a lie and a cheat and a fool, while also being aware that neither of them has any more proof than the other.

Humans are the bottom, the bare minimum when it comes to intellect and reasoning. Why in the world would you want your AI to be as smart as a human?

If we create AI and they're not entirely alien to us, then we will know that we've failed.

—Robert Vernes, head of the Open Institute for AI Research, 2029

Once I got back to the mall, Manic in tow, I sat around and started to look over our options.

I also started to nurse a migraine.

It wasn't a period migraine or the kind of thing that happened when you drank a high-addiction soft drink once and then didn't keep drinking it, but it was instead the far less fun, stress-induced kind of pain that throbbed across my head.

Do you want something for that?

Myalis didn't even need to ask for what. "Yeah, medicate me," I muttered low enough that only she'd hear. A tiny box appeared on the table before me, and I reached up and pulled my helmet off.

Manic glanced my way, and I found myself being observed a lot more closely than I'd usually be comfortable with. "You're younger than I thought," she said.

"I'm legal," I shot back as I opened the box Myalis gave me, took out a colorful pill, then tossed it back. It had a nice citrusy aftertaste. Nothing happened for a few long seconds, then it felt as if someone were carefully and slowly pouring cool water down atop my head and the pain washed away. "Oh, that's nice."

It's not chemically addictive, but try not to overuse that kind of medication. The last thing either of us need are permanent changes to your brain chemistry.

That was sobering. I sat up in the cheap plastic seat—bolted to the floor, of course—and glanced around. "Where's Gomorrah and the others?" I asked.

"Sprout's right there," Manic said with a nod to her left.

I glanced that way and saw Sprout jogging over. He was wearing a lab coat over a more skintight armored suit, the hems and front of the coat stained green and brown by what looked like dirt and plant stuff. "Sorry," he said. "I wasn't too close when the call came in. What's going on?"

"Give Gomorrah and Johnny a minute," I said. "She's the punctual sort, so she won't be too long in showing up. But . . . yeah, we're kinda fucked, so I wanted to hand out new orders and see what we could do to unfuck ourselves before we all die heroically."

Sprout stared, then nodded. "Okay then," he said before taking a seat as far from Manic as he could manage. Maybe that was because Manic was sitting on one of those dividers, knees folded up to her chest and fake plants arrayed behind her.

The next to show up were General Wilkinson and Miss Baker, whom I hadn't realized had returned to Downtown. Gomorrah and Johnny arrived a minute after, so we were spared having to do any sort of small talk.

"Alright." I said as I stood up. This didn't feel like the sort of conversation that should be had sitting down. I flicked a setting on with my augs and a map of the city sprung to life on the tabletop, a topographic map that outlined the extent of the hive beneath Burlington. "This is what we're dealing with," I said.

"Those don't look like sewer tunnels," Sprout said.

"No. It looks like the hive's been avoiding those, as well as any mainte-nance tunnels. Their passage pokes in, sometimes, but then they tend to divert away," I said. I probably sounded a lot more professional than I was. "My guess is that the hive's trying to be stealthy, which . . . well, it's worked so far."

"So, we go down and kick their asses?" Johnny asked. He grinned and shifted in such a way that his chest was puffed out even more and the mus-cles of his arms bulged. "I got to live up to my new name."

"New name?" I asked. This was a distraction, but I couldn't help but be curious.

His grin turned smug. "Babe Gomorrah gave it to me. I'm now known as Arm-a-Geddon. Oh yeah! Check out my nukes!"

I looked to Gomorrah, who seemed entirely to blame for all of this, but all she did was shake her head minutely as if to deny any involvement.

"Congratulations, Johnny . . . or, Arm-a-Geddon. I'm sure you'll live up to the name. We're going to have to cut the celebrations short for a minute, though, because we're all going to die unless we do something about this." I pointed to the hologram.

"Number of enemies?" General Wilkinson asked.

"Too damned many," I said. The hologram blinked as it refreshed, and the tunnels were all a couple of meters longer. My cat drones were still pushing through. From the looks of it, the majority of the hive was concentrated on the water-side of the city, sandwiched between Downtown and the coast.

Was it a coast if the coast was along a lake and not the ocean? I had no idea, and I didn't care enough to look it up.

"We still haven't discovered the size of the hive, but what we do know is that there are enough aliens waiting down there to overwhelm our shitty defenses ten times over. So, we need two things. First, to kill off the hive. I have a plan for that. Second, to defend the city better, which I also have a plan for, but my plan's kinda shit."

"Let's go over the defenses first," Gomorrah said. "It's more pressing, right?"

I nodded. "Probably, yeah. Right now we basically have a very thin barrier of volunteers and under-equipped militia between most of Downtown and a whole lot of very mean aliens that'll be coming out from . . . well, everywhere." I pointed to a few spots where the hive basically ran under Downtown.

"Our defenses are already penetrated, then," the General said.

"Basically. We need to clog up these holes, then make sure that the main defenses can actually hold up. My main plan is simple enough. Pump the hive full of these little drone-delivered nanomachines. They'll all start eating at the same time."

"Killing the entire hive all at once?" Gomorrah asked.

"Bingo. But I asked Myalis, and even the fastest-acting ones take a few minutes. And they're disproportionately expensive. We'll be mixing fast-acting payloads with much cheaper, slower-to-eat ones that we can spread around some more. Hopefully, we hit *all* of the hives. When they come out for revenge, they'll be half dead already, even if they don't know it."

"That's the whole plan?" Gomorrah asked.

"I'd love to hear better ideas. And I'm not being sarcastic or anything. Better ideas would be fantastic," I said. No one volunteered anything for a bit.

"So . . . I can't just walk in and punch everything dead?" Arm-a-Geddon asked. He sounded a bit disappointed.

I snorted. "I wish you could, but that'd wake the whole thing up. There are some double-digit models down there. Tens and up. We're going to be dealing with some big nasties soon. General, how quickly can you mobilize the entire militia?"

"You mean pull people off their relaxation time?" he asked. "I can have everyone in tip-top within the hour. It'll mean waking a lot of the night-shift people up though."

"Give them some coffee," I suggested. "Gomorrah, I bet you have a few points left over, think you can help me arm everyone up?"

"Sure. You're going to do the same?"

"I'm going to buy a heap of cat drones as a mobile force, then spend the rest on turrets and better guns. Hummingbirds cost very little and the civvies can use those no problem."

"Hummingbirds?" Manic asked.

I nodded. "Little smart-pistols. No aiming required, and they'll take out a weaker alien without too much fuss. We can set up mines and more creative explosives along the smaller routes leading into Downtown. We might want to pull people out of the towers on the outer edges though, they'll be hit by any area-of-effect stuff."

"What about River Heights?" Baker asked. I'd kinda forgotten she was there.

I considered what to say for a moment. "Well, if River Heights wants to use the protection afforded by Downtown, they have just under an hour to move. Things are going to get very messy, very soon."

We all had a lot of work ahead of us, and not much time to do it in.

Maybe I should have just called in the orders instead of pulling everyone into another meeting . . . a lesson for next time, I supposed.

CHAPTER NINETEEN

VITAL DEFENSIVE PREPARATION

I like the ship.

On the one hand, sure, it's classical trope stuff. The hardboiled, mean-spirited punk falling for the angelic nice-girl nun, but I mean, tropes exist for a reason you know!

Plus, I bet that in private, Gomorrah's totally the dom. I mean, have you seen the amount of faux-leather in her outfit?

—ShipBattles forum post by user Youralis, 2057

My plan had three basic steps, and of course I ran into trouble before the first one was out.

"Fuck," I said succinctly.

Myalis had continued to direct my drones through the hive tunnels, and that meant that with each passing minute we had a better picture of where the hive was. The good news was that few of the branching tunnels were under Downtown. Not none, but few, which was the second best option there.

Then Myalis, being the helpful little AI she was, kindly pointed out a big glaring issue that I hadn't considered.

If we wanted to spread the alien-eating nanogoop to as many aliens as possible, then we'd need to insert it in a few spots, and the best of those were all hard to reach. She overlaid a few locations in the tunnel network where we could do the insertion, but they weren't all close at hand.

"Okay," I said. My first thought was finding suicidal volunteers to head out and drop the packages off, but there were other, better options. "We send out drones. Same cat drones that we're using already, but with the bombs attached to them. Is that doable?" I asked.

Of course. The cats will also be able to reach the locations that I've designated as ideal spreading points with relative ease. Though this will take time, in any case, and there are few locations to insert them from. The hole in the basement of the museum is one of three locations I've found so far, and it's the most convenient.

I nodded along. It wasn't central or anything, but . . . yeah. Time to delegate. "Get me the general," I asked while I paced along the length of the food court. I didn't care if anyone saw me, really. Manic was still around, cleaning her nails out with a guitar pick. Sprout and Gomorrah had run off to prepare the defenses and Johnny—Arm-a-Geddon, that was—had run off to . . . I didn't know, try to get laid maybe?

A line opened up on my augs with a boring image of the general's face as the only indicator of who I was talking to. "Stray Cat?" he asked.

"You got any militia people with honking big testicles, General?" I asked.

He chuckled. "I might have a few. What needs doing?"

"I need a very precious cargo driven to a specific location and delivered to a specific hole. And no, this isn't any sort of innuendo. I need people to deliver a load of drones to the museum, specifically the basement where there's access to the Antithesis's tunnel network."

"Is this going to be the sort of mission where we only ask for volunteers?" he asked.

I swallowed. "I hope it's not that bad but . . . maybe ask anyway. We don't want cowards on this one. Give them your best gear too, and maybe I can throw in a few bonuses. Uh, while I have you on the line, where would be the best place to dump off a heap of Samurai-grade weapons?"

"Mall, second floor, we've taken over a row of shops there," he said. "I'll have someone meet you."

"Alright. Will you be able to distribute things quickly?"

"We'll try. No promises when it comes to the civilians though, they might decide to run and hide." There was no contempt there, just a matter-of-factness to everything that made it sound terribly truthful. Some civilians would run, and there wasn't anything we could do about it.

"Thanks, General. We'll deal with that when the time comes, I guess. Getting as many people as we can ready to receive the horde is more important for now."

With that done, I started to make my way across the mall. Of course, my pacing meant that I'd ended up as far from the nearest escalator bank as I could be without stepping outside. That was fine, it gave me time to get my next call out of the way.

Lucy answered on the third ring, and the first thing I heard was her breathing. Her breathing, which was hard and labored. "Uh," I said. "Hey . . . what're you up to?" I asked.

She laughed between pants. "Wouldn't you like to know."

"Desperately," I said. "You know, you can set your augs to record whatever it is you're doing in first person . . ."

"Oh?" she asked, the teasing note in her voice was impossible to miss. "Would you, ah, like that?"

I swallowed then glanced around as I slowed my walk. This was very much not the time to be looking at something like that, but yes, I totally wanted to see.

"Here, linking you in now. Enjoy the view," she said with a raspy chuckle.

I opened the link as soon as it came through and . . . watched through a floating screen in my vision as Lucy—in first person—knelt down and picked up one of those turrets we'd been fabricating at home and loaded it up into the back of a van. She stopped after it was in, hands on her knees to catch her breath.

"These things are way too heavy," she complained.

I snorted. "Yeah, I'll bet. How come you're loading them?"

"Isn't that what you called for?" she asked. She smacked her hands together and turned. I saw the front of our home. She was between the forelegs of the cat, just on the landing deck out front. The door was held open with a block of something and the kittens were carrying out turrets, working in pairs to lift them.

"Yeah, but how did you know before I called?"

"Because Gomorrah is better at communicating with her girlfriend than you are," she said. She turned and I saw that Franny was around.

The redhead looked up and blinked. "Girlfriend?" she asked. "Wait, who are you talking to?"

"I'm talking to Cat. Give me a bit?" Lucy asked. At Franny's nod she walked off to the side where she had a little bit more privacy. "So, what's up?"

"Uh, literally just called to ask about the turrets. How many do we have?"

"Forty-seven," she said. "And I think we won't be able to fit all of them in the van. Rac's working on making more as we speak, but they take like, twenty minutes each, so even if we did a round trip and then returned we wouldn't deliver that many more."

"That'll help," I said. "Also, what do you mean by 'we?'"

"We as in me and Franny!" Lucy said. "I'm going to be the door gunner!"

"Lucy, no," I said.

"Lucy, yes!" she cheered. "Come on, it won't be that dangerous."

"It's a van, not a gunship. There's no door to gun from," I said.

"I have a handgun," she replied. Then she looked down, unzipped the front of her blazer, and pulled a handgun out from where she'd tucked it into the waist of her pants. "See," she said.

"Disregarding how hot that was," I said. "Still no."

Lucy laughed and shoved the gun away after checking to see if the safety was still on. "You can't stop me, Cat. Besides, it's just a quick trip over, right? I'll kiss you in like, an hour, tops. Alright? Now, I need to get back to work. Love you!"

And then she had the gall to disconnect me.

Lucy was coming here. Oh, I could probably stop her, for now, but then it would become a challenge, and I really didn't want to stand in Lucy's way when she felt challenged about something. That wouldn't be healthy for our relationship. Besides, I did kind of miss her.

So, if I fucked up here, I wasn't just going to get a few thousand civilians dead, I was going to end up without Lucy too.

"Well, fuck," I muttered. "Myalis, how many points do I have left?" I asked as I ran up the escalator. The clock was ticking.

You currently have ninety-six thousand, four hundred and twelve points remaining. You have been spending without paying them much heed recently, but that amounted to less than three percent of your point total, so I didn't see the need to be overly concerned.

"Uh-huh," I said. "We're going to be spending a lot more. I need drones with those nanomachines, I need turret emplacements, I need entire crates of easy-to-use weapons, and I need cases of grenades. If we can't make the walls around Downtown impervious, then we'll just turn everything at street level into one big killing field."

Oh, wonderful! In that case, might I suggest a few catalogs?

CHAPTER TWENTY

NANOMACHINES, SON

Fuck logistics.

—Corporal Dimitry, Russian Eastern Incursion Front, 2029

First, nanomachines. Specifically nanobots that can be used in an offensive capability.

"I need a catalog for that?" I asked.

The only nanomachines you've used previously were specifically designed to dispose of Antithesis corpses. This is an entirely different use-case.

"Yeah, but those were also nano stuff," I pointed out.

Cat. The ones you want to buy for this hive are as different as a door handle is to a spacecraft. While both could technically be called machines, the degrees of complexity between them makes keeping both in the same general categorization idiotic and misleading.

I raised my hands in surrender. "Okay, yeah, fair enough." I imagined the nanobots we were preparing to deploy were going to be somewhat more complicated than those I'd used before. They needed to travel to specific places and wait for a specific signal before they started anything. "Any other catalog I should look into?" I asked.

Two come to mind. Basic Defensive Infrastructure for quick-to-install defenses. Then, Civilian-Grade General Combat Equipment. That last one is for the civilians, obviously.

"What does civilian-grade mean, exactly?" I asked.

The catalog mostly has helmets and armor that are relatively cheap, capable of keeping a civilian informed and connected while also keeping them safe from the weakest Antithesis. These are not rated for the level of combat a Vanguard would expect to face and aren't designed to last very long. The catalog includes weapons that are meant to be so easy to use that a child could operate them with barely any instruction without harming themselves or others.

I reached the top of the escalator, then nodded along. "Alright, fine. Grab the catalogs."

New Purchase: Class I Nanomechanized Warfare
Current Point Total: 94,564
New Purchase: Class 0 Civilian-Grade General Combat Equipment
Current Point Total: 94,464
New Purchase: Basic Defensive Infrastructure
Current Point Total: 94,264

"Nice," I said. "Hold off on buying stuff for a minute, though," I said. There were a predictable number of militia men loitering around a set of shops that had been taken over. Someone had installed steel plates before the windows and blocked the rest off with planks, leaving only one way into the area, with hip-high sandbags stacked up around it. Anyone coming in would have to get past the guys with rifles by the entrance.

Fortunately, I had someone running out to meet me already. A fresh-faced woman, maybe three or four years older than me, who came to a stop next to me and snapped a salute. "Second Lieutenant Smart, ma'am," she said. "The General said you would need some assistance."

"Hey, Smart," I said. "I think we all need a bit of help right now." She laughed and I stared at her for a long couple of seconds. That hadn't been funny. Was I dealing with my own yes-man? Yes-woman? Yes-cute-girl-in-tight-uniform?

I wasn't sure if I liked it or not. I preferred it when corporate stooges were angry at me, that meant I was doing the right thing.

"Did the General give you an outline of what's going on?"

She nodded. "Yes ma'am. We're looking for volunteers for your high-risk mission now. It might take a few minutes to gather everyone. The vehicle for their transportation is being readied as well. We just need the equipment they'll be using."

"Good," I said. Then I looked at the shops they'd taken over. A clothing place and a sporting goods store. The shelves had been pushed around and it was pretty clear that they'd done some last-minute renovations to make the place more suitable to their needs. It also looked like they'd set up a clinic of sorts and some spaces for their people to sit down and relax in.

That was all fine, but I needed more room than they could afford.

"Smart," I snapped. She straightened up as if I'd pinched her. "I need tables. All across here. Get me every nice flat surface you can find. It's not time for sitting around and looking clever, so get those guys over there working too."

"Uh, yes ma'am," she said as she followed my gesturing hand. I was just making a vague wave across the floor we were on. Half of the area was taken up by one of those open spaces that looked onto the floors below and above that malls liked so much because it made them look so much bigger.

The Second Lieutenant ran off to do as I'd asked, which *was* something I could get used to. In the meantime, I turned my attention toward Myalis. "Nano-bombs first," I said. "Enough to mess up the hive. I think price is a secondary concern here. Besides, they should pay for themselves."

They should, though don't expect them to be too profitable. Vanguard receive fewer points the more degrees of separation there are between themselves and a kill they score.

"Huh," I said. "Okay, I guess." Was it a way to keep samurai from making a literal killing without having to do any killing? I supposed that I'd been losing points here and there while using drones.

Don't worry. Most of the drones you've used have been deployed in close proximity to yourself. And any trap, explosive, or mine that you lay yourself doesn't suffer from any point-based penalties.

"Is it all there to slow progress down, or to discourage us from sitting at home buck naked while making a fortune?" I asked.

Why not both? Besides, you're not as interesting when you're cooped up at home.

I snorted. Chalk one up to the "Protectors using us as entertainment" theory. Which honestly never sounded plausible. If humanity could have storytelling AI that rivalled the combined minds of every poet and author ever put together, then the Protectors could generate their own drama without having to involve the likes of me.

"Just get us the nano-whatever we need," I said.

Certainly.

A case appeared at my feet, about a meter long and half as wide and tall, made of dark gray plastic with . . . was that my logo? The cat's head with the grenade pin in its mouth was present, embossed onto the case. "Really digging that logo, huh?" I asked.

I am, yes. It is . . . I think Lucy would call it cute.

I snorted. Well, whatever. It wasn't hurting me, and some Samurai, like Emoscythe, had a hard-on for branding and image stuff, so that might get them off my back.

"Is that one of the nano-whatevers?" I asked.

No. That's all of them.

"Really?" I asked. The box was large, but not that big. I could fit into it if I felt like contorting myself a little.

Catherine, what do you think nano means?

I rolled my eyes. "Right, I see what you mean."

Lieutenant Smart ran back over, with two guys behind her dragging along one of those plastic-topped tables with unfolding legs. "Ma'am, we're bringing every table we have," she said. "It'll take a moment though."

"That's fine," I said. "So, Myalis and I were thinking. First thing's first, the box here is full of nano-shit that'll melt the aliens for us. The general should have the outline of the plan already. Give this to whomever's heading out to the museum." I tapped the case on the ground next to me with the end of my boot.

"Thank you. We'll bring it over now."

"Good. Now, we'll be equipping the civilians, right?"

She nodded.

"So . . . yeah, Myalis, ideas?"

You can either buy a few hundred samples of each piece of equipment separately, or you could buy kits of them. There's no real point-saving either way, but the kits might make it easier to distribute to the civilians.

"I like that," I muttered. "So, a Hummingbird, something that packs a bit more punch? Then armor and a helmet with coms?"

That's most of what I would suggest. I'd also like to add a small first-aid kit and include a rig with the armor for additional ammunition and supplies.

That seemed perfectly logical to me. "Doesn't have to be pretty, just needs to work and be idiot-proof."

It should be. For a main weapon I'd suggest the Alley Purr, it's a suppressed smart-rifle with an IFF targeting lock to prevent accidental friendly fire. Perhaps we can add some explosives as well, since you have the catalogs for those?

I grinned. "Spread the love? Sure. But . . . maybe Resonators? They're a staple of mine and they're hard to mess up. The worst collateral they'll deliver is deafness."

Certainly. Each kit will cost . . . ninety four points.

I nodded slowly, then took into account how many points that was. "Hey, Smart, how many civilians will we be equipping here?"

"There are eighty thousand in Downtown, or close to that, we don't have exact numbers. Only about two percent are volunteering for guard and combat duty though."

That's a thousand six hundred.

And a thousand six-hundred times ninety four was . . . a lot. I opened a calculator app and punched into the numbers, then winced. That was way, way beyond my budget. "How many people volunteered to do guard duty already?" I asked.

"You mean the green bands?" she asked. "We have two hundred of those per rotation. Three rotations a day."

I punched in that number and liked it a lot more.

"Okay, so let's get half of them equipped then," I said. "We might be in this for the long haul, so let's not go too far. Oh, and Smart, this is expensive. Let's not have anyone running off with our gear, yeah?"

"Yes ma'am," she said.

CHAPTER TWENTY-ONE

SHOULDERING

It's sad, but a lot of us just kind of stop trusting people. You can only save people only to see them destroy themselves so many times before you start to lose hope.

But even when we've run out of hope, we don't stop trying, do we? I think that might be part of what makes us Samurai to begin with.

Uwu.

—Beatrice "Hyper Cutie Zoom Ranger Sparkle Girl Bubble-chan!" Smith, during her Twitch livestream of the 2042 Canberra Incident

Myalis came through with the equipment. Each set came in a large case with my logo on the front and a number stamped beneath from one to three hundred. Each case opened up to reveal a suit within, as well as a helmet, a gun, and a small bandoleer of grenades.

The suits weren't the prettiest of things. More like jumpsuits crossed with skaterpunk outfits equipped with some padding around the torso and elbows and knees. The entire thing was set up so that someone wearing the suit could just pull on a few straps and parts of it would fold up and could be tied down with a Velcro strap.

Basically, they were about as one-size-fits-all as a piece of clothing could be.

The helmets were a bit large, but they were also clearly samurai-tech, even if it was on the cheaper end of things.

Of course, the helmets had little stubs on the top that kind of hinted at cat ears.

At this point I was too tired to argue.

Second Lieutenant Smart got a volunteer, one of the green-band civilians, and the man suited up while we watched. It was clear she didn't pick the shiniest mind in the world, but the guy figured it out in the space of a couple of minutes. In the end, he stood at what he probably thought was attention, his Alley Purr rifle held up before him and his back straight.

"That'll do," I said with a nod.

The equipment was supposed to be resistant to lower-tier Antithesis threats, and I believed Myalis when she said so. The communications suite they had was rudimentary, but it wasn't awful. Enemies would be outlined in red, locations where they were needed would be at the end of a string of AR-pointers that only they could see, and allies were painted in green. It even came with built-in reticles.

If the first three hundred proved halfway competent, then we'd buy more sets and get more boots on the ground. I wasn't going to hold my breath though.

I couldn't recall any situation when a samurai had armed a large group of civilians so that they could defend themselves, and looking at how excited and frankly kind of dumb the locals were being as the militia directed them to get suited up, I could see why.

I wasn't going to be the one to order these folk around. For one thing, I didn't want to, and for another, I was far more likely to lead them into trouble. I'd let the militia do all of the heavy lifting there.

The militia who seemed one part envious, and one part amused. They looked like they wanted to get their hands on the civilians' guns, but the gear looked so generic and rather goofy that they were probably better off with their own military-surplus stuff.

I left the area when I got a call from Gomorrah. "Hey," I said as I answered.

"Is everything ready on your end?" she asked.

I looked back to the civvies still struggling to get into their jumpsuits. "Uh, more or less coming along. Why, what's up?"

"Time's up," she said. "Franny is about ten minutes out, and I've been following the progress of the militiamen bringing the nanomachines out, they've reached the museum already."

"So, we only have a few minutes left then," I said. I don't know why it was so strange to have my plan coming together. "How are the defenses coming?"

"Honestly?" she asked. "They're laughable. Sprout's planting more of his . . . plants, but it's not going to do much against a concentrated attack by a proper force of Antithesis. This city is not ready for a proper incursion. I've been buying automated defenses and setting them up where I can, but it's only going to dampen the front of the attack, not stop it outright."

I chewed on my lip. She was probably right. Even the gear Lucy and Franny were bringing wouldn't do much. A couple of dozen laser turrets? They took a second or two to kill a single model three. If we were dealing with a proper swarm then they wouldn't even kill a fraction of them.

I had a lot of points left, I could splurge on something to help, but I couldn't think of what. Mines? More cat drones? More equipment for the locals?

The Antithesis we'd be facing would, presumably, not be in the greatest of shapes, but that didn't mean they were harmless. I couldn't see an easy way to just wipe them all out and keep everyone safe that didn't involve nukes.

"Cat?" Gomorrah asked.

"Hmm? Sorry, my . . . brain isn't good at all of this," I admitted. "Just trying to keep up with everything. Uh, speaking of being a responsible human being, Myalis, can you AI-up a report with everything that's gone on so far and send it to the Family?"

Certainly. Though I'm curious as to why.

"I'm sure you can think of a thousand reasons why it's a good idea," I said.

And I could list them in alphabetical order and include little crayon drawings with all one thousand, but that wouldn't satisfy my curiosity as to why you, specifically, want me to send this report.

I huffed. "Because . . . look, I've heard too many stories about dipshits in middle management positions deciding to cover their asses by not telling people when they're swamped. Those stories are usually the ones that end with "and then the unmaintained equipment failed and sixty thousand infants were born with extra limbs" and I don't want to be that sort of dipshit."

That's understandable. Well done.

I glared at nothing in particular. "Don't patronize me, Myalis."

I was being both literal and sincere. When and if I chose to be patronizing with you, I'll be sure to point it out. And, to avoid hypocrisy, let me point out that the last statement I made was, in fact, meant to be patronizing.

I chuckled and shook my head. The bitch, living in my head and still thinking circles around me. "Anyway, Gom, I'm hoping we'll be able to hold out, but hope's not worth as much as bullets nowadays, so if you've got ideas, I'm all ears."

"We have chokepoints already, provided by the way the buildings in downtown are laid out. If we can abandon the buildings on the outer edge, relocate everyone inward, then we can turn the exterior parts of Downtown into a free killing zone. And . . . this is a little controversial, but I passed an idea over to Atyacus and he said it was plausible. You might like this one."

She sent over a file, and I opened it.

It was a 3D rendering of downtown. Some of the buildings were red, all along the outer edge. I was about to ask what it meant when large red circles appeared near the base of those buildings and then all came crashing down like dominos.

"Holy shit," I said. "You want to create a wall of debris?"

"It might work," she said. "Controlled demolitions are more or less safe, and it'll create an impediment to any Antithesis coming closer. Not to mention the artificial earthquake will be devastating to any underground hive structures."

"And to the rest of the city. You think this place was built to code?"

"It's an idea," she said innocently, as if she'd just suggested a foursome instead of a massive demolition project.

The problem was, as awesome as the idea sounded, I wasn't sure it would actually do much to slow the Antithesis down, and then we'd be stuck in the middle.

"I'll table that as plan D."

"D?" she asked.

"For Destruction." Or dumb, but I wasn't going to rain on her parade. "Look, I'm heading out of here. Do you think you can draw up a . . . I don't know, prediction plan for where the Antithesis will hit us from? We have a few ways to slow them down. It'll be nice if we can stall out long enough that the nanomachines rip them apart for us."

"We can't assume that all of them will be impacted by those," Gomorrah said. "Or that they'll all die from a few nanomachines chewing at them. Some of the Antithesis your drones spotted were large, Cat."

I tapped my foot on the ground to bleed off some of my nervous energy. "Yeah. Big old baddies. I don't know what to do about them, Gom."

She chuckled. "It's not that complicated. We burn them until there's nothing left but char."

I grinned right back. "Maybe it's not so complicated," I said. But the weight was still on my back.

CHAPTER TWENTY-TWO

WELCOMING

Arthur R. Martin was the first person to ever be jailed for AI-related crimes. He used an open-source learning AI to create a model of the stock market, then let it run predictions until he was able to finally create a model that had a 68% accuracy rate for short-term stock changes.

By giving this model the ability to reinvest in itself and letting it run, Arthur gained what was essentially an exponential amount of money, all the while his system improved itself and was soon leading the market.

His initial investment was USD $10,000 (190,000 credits today). Within a month he had USD $1,645,782,257. He was, of course, arrested, tried, and sentenced to prison, where he committed suicide by self-strangulation.

—*It's Just Math*, first edition, 2026

The nanomachines are in position to be delivered.

I glanced up as Myalis delivered the message. I was heading out of the mall, except I realized when I was nearing the exit that I was a bit peckish, so I got into line at a spicy chicken place that was still operating despite the apocalypse.

"They are?" I muttered.

Indeed. I've confirmed it for myself, but General Wilkinson has sent you a text message to tell you that the team sent with the payload has arrived at the museum. Are there any reasons we shouldn't deploy the nanomachines?

"None that I can think of. Give them the green light," I said.

Then I had to step up and make my order. Mild spices, some rice, a random selection of toppings that I didn't care much about, all cooked by a greasy-faced twenty-something instead of the usual machine because that machine was shoved off to the side and was clearly inoperable.

Probably couldn't get a good signal to the franchise headquarters so they just hired this guy to do all the work manually, like they used to in the past.

And they're deploying. It will take some time to have all of the nanomachine slurry travel across the root system.

"Hmm, how long, more or less?"

Between two and six hours. As more tunnels and branches are discovered, the time scale increases.

"Did we send nearly enough of those nanomachines to cover a system that extensive?" I asked.

Given infinite time—and presuming that the Antithesis stops growing—a single nanomachine would be enough. As it is, yes, the amount dropped should be enough for what has been uncovered so far. Though the harm they'll cause with so few acting at once will be light.

I nodded along. "Then we should dump more into the system. Maybe we can start by finding ways to access the bits of the hive under Downtown. If we poison those first then at least we won't have aliens crawling out behind our front lines."

A sensible idea. I'll set the cat drones to find exit points that are nearer to the surface.

I got my order, paid by connecting my augs to the store's tapless payment chip, and then headed off while undoing the front of my helmet so that I could stuff myself while walking. "How are we doing with everything else?" I asked.

Your untrained army of civilian conscripts are being mobilized to the front lines. Another group of civilians containing a number of civil engineers are building a second line of defenses. Sprout has planted new plants along a full third of the outer perimeter. Manic and Arm-a-Geddon are taking care of a number of scouting Antithesis and Gomorrah is installing remote-operated turrets along the first defensive line.

"Which direction are the Antithesis that Manic and Arm-a-Geddon are dealing with coming from?" I asked.

The west, same as Lake Champlain.

"Hey, can you snoop around and see which direction most of the attacks and probes came from over the last few days?"

Over seventy percent of all Antithesis sightings and approaches have been from the west, with an additional twenty percent from the north and the remainder coming from the south and southeast.

River Heights was taking those from the north, then, and the rest . . . All from the same direction as the lake? I didn't know if Antithesis could swim, but I guess there was no reason they couldn't. They were plants, did they even need to breathe the way mammals did? Some models could certainly live underwater without any difficulty.

I sense that you're thinking in the right direction.

"How many aliens are in that lake?" I asked.

Likely a number that's much greater than you're ready to deal with. If you want, I can send a report to the Family. There are some Vanguards who specialize in underwater combat and hive extermination.

I nodded along, finished up the last bite of my chicken—mild was too spicy—and chucked it onto a pile of trash flowing out of the top of a trash bin. "That's a good idea. Send it in, and if you can, mark it as important. I think my job here is to keep the civilians safe, not so much destroy under-water hives. It would be nice to get some support on that end."

Understood. Message sent. Also, Lucy and Franny are on approach.

That perked me up. "Where are they landing?"

Instead of a straight answer, Myalis opened up a map of Downtown on one of my aug's screens and pointed to one of the buildings near the center of the city with an upper-floor landing zone.

"Ping the General's staff, have him send a few techs over to grab the turrets. Ah, suggest that they place them on rooftops. Those turrets have decent range, right?"

Relatively. They are lethal to most single-digit Antithesis within three hun-dred meters, but the damage starts to fall off relatively quickly.

We'd turn the skies around Downtown into a no-fly-zone for aliens. It would give us all one less thing to worry about.

Instead of walking all the way over to the building Lucy was heading toward, I took a bus.

That was a little strange, but it made sense. The city had these automated trolleys that moved around on the ground level. Graffiti-covered things that smelled like piss and that creaked unnervingly as they moved. The people boarding these all wore armbands of different colors, and there was some-one at the entrance scanning their bands to let them on.

So, someone had turned the public transport into a sort of public logis-tics system for getting the civilians helping the defense of the city around. It made sense, which is why I was surprised to see it.

The guy at the entrance didn't ask me for an armband or anything, he just stepped aside, wide-eyed, and let me in so that I could hang off one of those ceiling-mounted bars as we moved.

The trolley didn't stop in front of the place I needed, but it was close enough. I moved to the front, nodded to the guy by the door, and jumped out while we were still moving. I had to jog for a bit to stop myself from falling, but it wasn't a big deal.

I slipped into what was clearly a habitation building. A thousand shoe-box apartments jammed in next to each other. The ground floor was pretty enough, but I knew that every floor above that would have a ceiling that was no more than seven feet tall so that they could cram in a few extra floors to get more homes in.

The place was filled, and I imagined it was only half because of the ongo-ing incursion. How many more people were stuck in Downtown, separated from their suburban homes?

I waited in a dingy elevator and ignored the ads playing on every wall as we shot up to the topmost floor. Myalis must have overridden something because we didn't stop on any floors until we reached the top.

The door dinged open and I stepped out into a shitty little corridor with none of the nice lighting, ads, or decorations that they'd bothered to shove into the ground floor. Instead it was all corridors and low ceilings. It didn't take much to find the door leading into the building's topmost parking space.

The area was wide open, with berths for hovercars and a landing strip down the middle. Holographic signs with directions and instructions hung all over the place.

My timing, as it turned out, was pretty good, because just as I started looking around a van flew in and came to a stop by the entrance, kicking up dust and flinging wrappers aside.

I waited as the van settled, then sprang forward as the passenger-side door opened and Lucy jumped out.

"Cat!"

"Hey!" I called back.

Then she grabbed me for a hug and I couldn't help but match her laughter before I gave her a proper squeeze. "I didn't know you'd be waiting for me," she said. "Don't you have big important samurai things to do?"

"Fuck 'em, as if I'd care more about some backwater city than I would about meeting you."

She shook her head, then poked me in the chest. Or she tried to, at least. "Urgh, you're all hard in that armor."

"I'd kinda think that's the point," I said.

"Idiot," she replied, and I could feel the love there.

I tugged the front of my helmet off so that I could kiss her properly. If she wanted me to be soft, then I'd give her all the soft she could ever want.

"We—we have an audience, you know," she said.

I glanced up and saw Franny, who was blushing and trying very hard not to look like she was blushing. "We do," I agreed before stealing her lips again.

"Cat," she whined, but it was almost a whisper, just for the two of us. "She's still a little useless, so let's not scar her too much, hmm?"

"Fine," I said. "So, what made you come all the way out here despite me telling you not to?"

She blinked. "Since when are you my boss? I'll jump into danger if and when I please, thank you very much."

CHAPTER TWENTY-THREE

CAT-THEMED TOWER DEFENSE

The changes happened slowly. So slowly that even though all the scientists were screaming about it for years, we still failed to notice them. A winter without snow, a complete lack of any insects outside, a few days where the weather was so wild that we barely recognized it?

It all paled next to the distractions we could afford ourselves.

—Excerpt from *On the Big Change*, 2026

"No, really," I asked. "Why'd you come over?"

"Gomorrah explained to Franny what you were up to, and she explained it to me," Lucy said as she reluctantly stepped out of our hug. "So I thought I should come over and discuss the ecological and environmental impacts of unleashing a bunch of nanomachines to mulch aliens stuck underneath the city."

I stared. "You're messing with me, right?"

She grinned. "Maybe?"

I hugged her again. "You're such an idiot," I said.

"And yet I still managed to catch you with my evil ways," she murmured. Lucy placed another peck on my cheek.

"Who's watching over the kittens?"

"Daniel is," she said. "Not the best of choices, but hey, they have everything they need and most of them are plugged into one feed or another. They don't cause too much trouble when they've got their bread and circuses. Need help with anything here?"

"Around here?" I asked. Did I need Lucy's help with anything? What could Lucy help with in the first place? She was great with the kittens, but I wasn't sure if babysitting skills would really . . . actually, no, those skills would absolutely come in handy. "Hey, how would you like to be put in charge of an army?" I asked.

"That sounds fun!" she said. "Do I get a cool title? Admiral Lucy?"

"It's an army, I think that would make you a general," I pointed out.

"As long as I get one of those nice uniforms with all the medals on my chest. I want to look like a third-world dictator's right-hand woman."

I laughed, then nodded to Franny, who was coming over. "Right, let me give the two of you the rundown. It's not super complicated yet, but it's about to be. Also, hi, Franny."

"Hello, Cat," Franny said with a nod. It struck me just how much like Gomorrah she was sometimes. Sure, she was a hot redhead with authority issues as opposed to a hot blonde with pyromania issues, but a lot of their mannerisms were the same. Maybe it was a by-product of being raised close to each other?

But then Lucy and I were plenty different and we were raised in the same shithole.

"So, what's the situation? Delilah is keeping me up to date a little, but I don't exactly have a full picture," Franny said.

"Things are just about to get interesting," I said. "We've launched an attack against the hives, but most of the hives . . . or just the one big hive I guess, is underground. They've dug out these long tunnels across the entire city. They're full of water right now, which isn't a problem for the aliens."

"It wouldn't be, the xenos are from space, being underwater is probably a lot more hospitable than a vacuum," Franny said.

I nodded along as if I knew what she meant. "Yeah. So, we sent down nanomachines to start eating away at them. They'll all start at the same time, which means that the hive will get a nasty wake-up call. And we're expecting it to react like anyone would when you wake up to a million little things trying to eat you all at once."

"Oh, like when we had that bedbug infestation," Lucy said.

I nodded. Of all the insects not to go extinct, bedbugs just had to stay on the list. Mosquitos too, of course. "Exactly like that. We're about to wake the fuckers up in the shittiest way possible and I bet they won't be happy about it. That's why we're working on arming the civvies and getting defenses up, including the turrets you brought."

"And how's that going?" Franny asked.

"Terribly," I said. "The locals have actually been helpful. Got a bunch of volunteers geared up for a fight, but against anything in big enough numbers or any really strong models we're basically screwed."

Lucy frowned, and if it wasn't so cute it might have been intimidating. "And what are we doing about that?"

"Honestly, I don't know what to do about it. In New Montreal we had the army and a bunch of strong samurai to back us up."

"And now you're the big strong samurai," she said.

I nodded. "That's right. I don't exactly have everything I need to keep the entire Downtown area safe. None of my catalogs are geared toward strong defensive things and I don't know where to start when it comes to that kind of thing anyway."

Then I laid out the rest. At some point it became a bit of a rant, but Lucy was used to my ranting and Franny took it well enough.

Mostly, my problem was that the Downtown area wasn't ready to destroy the wider hive. The local samurai weren't equipped for it, and I couldn't be all over the place at the same time. Even if I bought a bunch of cat drones (which I was going to), it wouldn't do anything but stop the tide.

Then, after listening for a while, Franny asked a question. "Do you intend to fix all of this by tonight? Because that doesn't seem as realistic as treating this as a long-term project."

"What do you mean?" I asked.

"This is a siege, isn't it? You have walls, the enemy needs to get over or under them, but as long as you can repel them then . . . then it's just a siege. Not an actual prolonged battle like you fought in New Montreal a few days ago."

I ran that through my head a few more times.

It made a lot of sense and reframed things a little.

If we treated this as a battle to keep the Antithesis out as opposed as one to just kill them all, then our priorities when it came to defenses changed a lot.

And it would *have* to be a siege, because no matter what, there would always be more of the hive that we hadn't found spewing out more human-hungry aliens.

"You're smart," I said to Franny who smiled demurely. "I can see what Gomorrah sees in you." And at that she blushed scarlet, the smattering of freckles across the bridge of her nose standing out in sharp contrast.

I didn't have time to tease her much more than that since the militia finally showed up in a pair of vans.

"Right. Lucy, Franny, want to follow me? We're going to meet the General. Lucy, I'm putting you in command of the civilian side of things."

"Really?" Lucy asked. "No one's handling that?"

"Oh, someone is, and they're doing a decent job of it, but I don't know who and I don't have time to figure it all out. Can you spend a bit of time figuring it all out and then keep me in the loop? I'll give you a cat drone or something to keep you safe."

She was wearing my first samurai-bought jacket, the one with the holes and the burns and the cuts all across it, and I knew she had a gun stuffed away on her, but still, I'd be happier if she had something more capable to play bodyguard.

And watching over the civilians would let her help without being anywhere near the front lines.

"That sounds fun," Lucy said.

"Cool!" I tilted my head left and right, then gestured for Lucy to give me a minute before I walked over and found the militiaman in charge. As it turned out, they had orders to bring the turrets to ground level around some of the more important buildings in Downtown. I countermanded that with my own order, to place them on every available rooftop to snipe out any flying aliens that might be trying to swoop in.

When I returned, Lucy was grinning. "I like it when you take charge," she said. Her tone set Franny off to blushing again.

"If you like it so much, why do I never get to be the one taking charge, huh?"

"What are you talking about? I always let you look like you're the one in charge," she said.

I laughed. "Alright. Save that energy for later. We have a lot of work ahead of us. Come on, I'll take the two of you to the mall?"

"Actually, I think I'm going to fly back to New Montreal first," Franny said. "There are more turrets to bring over, and by the sounds of it you'll need every one you can grab. Say hi to Delilah for me."

"Will do," Lucy said.

And with that, I had to get back to work. A small shift in my plans was in order, then we could get the show started.

CHAPTER TWENTY-FOUR

HOLDING ON

Syncore is one of the strangest evolutions in musical history.

It started with 3D full-dive VR music experiences. Basically, a listener would be plugged into the music, feeling every note and visualizing every beat. A fascinating but harmless way to enjoy music.

Then that evolved. Audiophiles discovered methods to literally tap into their own synesthesia via high-end brain-augs that allowed them to taste, smell, feel, and be the music.

This, of course, became immensely lucrative for a certain genre of artists who discovered ways to create literally addictive music.

—*Synesthesia Core: A History*, 2042

I dropped Lucy off at the mall after directing her to Second Lieutenant Smart who seemed appropriately overwhelmed.

"Here," I said as a box appeared next to me. A cat drone started to unfold itself from within. I'd told Myalis to give me something with all of the bells and whistles to keep Lucy safe, and what she had provided was the size of a Bengal tiger with enough armaments to make a modern main battle tank blush.

"That's a big kitty," Lucy said as she stared at the drone. Its head came up to her chest, and even though its weaponry was hidden, there was no hiding the fact that it was a high-tech bit of samurai gear.

"It'll keep you safe," I said. "Just in case. Plus it's big and intimidating."

"Are you saying I can't intimidate people on my own?" she asked.

I grinned. "As intimidating as you are in the bedroom, no, I don't think you're quite as scary as you'd like to think you are."

She pouted, which was very cute, so I took a quick picture with my eye-aug for posterity. "Fine. I guess we both need to get to work, then?"

"Yeah. I'll see about keeping this city safer, you see about keeping it sane."

We parted with a last, not-so-quick kiss that left my head humming happily. Then, unfortunately, it was back to work for me.

"Did I miss anything?" I asked Gomorrah once I got her back on the line. I was exiting the mall for what had to be the tenth time today.

The nun scoffed. "Not much. The general and some of his guys found a second entrance point into the hive network, about a block past our outer perimeter. We're finding more and more of those. At this rate our defenses are going to be a revolving door."

"We'll figure it out," I said. "We can start by dumping more nanomachine drones in those nearer entrances."

"That's fair. There's a militia transport heading to the mall, can you hand over more of those drones of yours with a fresh payload? The more we seed at the start, the better things will go," Gomorrrah said.

"I can do that, yeah," I said. I shielded my eyes from the sun—which was wholly unnecessary—and glanced up at a militia-marked transport that was descending onto the road.

"I've been talking to Atyacus, and we had an idea," Gomorrah said.

"I'm all ears," I replied.

"When we start to attack the hive it might be a subtle attack, with the nanomachines propagating and chewing away at vitals, but they *will* notice eventually and we expect the hives to retaliate. What if we also prepare a second, immediate attack? The hives are all underwater from what I've seen. The water will make certain options complicated, but it does make others easier. I'm talking about setting up explosives and firebombs at key junctions to block them off entirely. A fluorine fire melting anything that approaches an intersection leading to the exit will definitely slow the Antithesis down."

"That's not a bad idea," I said. "We'll have to be careful though. We don't want big explosions that'll knock the whole city down."

"Fire isn't that explosive," she said.

I snorted. "Yeah, but we can't use anything like that heat-bomb we used in New Montreal. Maybe . . . hey, does sound travel well in water?"

"Yes and no, waves travel farther but most sound will be distorted. What are you thinking?"

It was probably because I'd seen Manic at work and her tech made me think of it, but I'd been using resonator grenades almost for as long as I was a samurai. They were . . . not exactly fast, but they were fairly effective at weakening the enemy without harming any nearby allies.

"I have an idea. Let's fill the hive with resonator bombs. They'll vibrate the Antithesis to the point that they'll fall apart, and it might be even better with water around. The longer they spend in the tunnels, the faster they'll fall apart. The nanomachines eating them up will only help."

"That seems reasonable," Gomorrah said. "And it doesn't preclude the use of firebombs as I suggested."

I laughed. That woman had a one-track mind sometimes. "Sure, let's do it. Do you think the newbies have their own contributions to make?"

"Manic might have some of those resonators to give you, and Sprout has a few options of his own. Have you seen his plants?"

"I don't think I have, no," I said. "Not from up close, anyway."

"They're interesting. He'll be one of the more unique samurai out there, I think. At least, if he survives long enough. Between you and me, he's not great in a fight."

That was harsh, but I trusted Gormorrah's judgment there. "We'll have to keep him off the front lines then? Or just keep him to places where the militia and civilians can keep him alive?"

"That second one would work. He has potential, it's just that his path is a huge point-sink that's not giving him much personal power. Arm-a-Geddon is nearly the opposite. All personal power, no reach."

"And Manic is a decent fighter overall, but she doesn't work well with others. Why did we end up babysitting the most complicated bunch of weirdos out there?" I asked.

"Because if they weren't strange, they wouldn't be samurai," Gomorrah said.

That was fair.

I jogged up to the transport after it landed, and after a quick exchange with the militiamen within, I bought a few crates full of cat drones with more nanomachine payloads. I also bought a large case filled with resonators that had their timers replaced with remote-controlled detonators that we could all set off at the same time.

From the sounds of it, Gomorrah was near one of the other holes and was slipping in her own payload with her own stealth drones. Hers weren't cat-shaped. She described them as wheels within wheels, whatever the fuck that meant.

Things were progressing nicely.

We were dumping more and more shit into the underwater hives, enough that they were going to regret ever installing themselves so close to Burlington, and the city's defenses were coming along, even if they were a little rudimentary.

I ordered up a few of those cat-drone-operated mortars like I'd used in New Montreal. Of course, Myalis made it so that the mortar had wheels, and one of the bigger cat drones had a yoke that they could pull the mortar with, but other than looking silly, they were still usable.

From the sounds of it, Gomorrah had installed a few turrets of her own over some of the more important parts of the city.

I got to see one hovering by. It was a ball with a sort of eye-shaped flamethrower in its middle and about a dozen wing-shaped hover engines attached to it. Were the extra wings supposed to be redundant? Well, whatever. By the looks of it, they also had integrated missile launchers—no doubt equipped with something like fuel-air bombs—and a few other toys strapped on.

I was feeling pretty good about our chances.

Which, of course, is when the news came in that everything had gone to shit ten minutes ago, and no one had chosen to inform me until now.

"What?" I asked the general, just to be clear.

He sighed over the line. "Ma'am, I'm afraid that the hive has become fully active just to the west of the River Heights area. The Antithesis are pouring out of a hole next to some incomplete infrastructure and have begun assaulting the barriers around that part of the city."

He sent me a package that I opened. Live-feeds from a few guard stations around River Heights. I recalled those big towers with the guns atop them easily enough.

Those guns were rattling out lines of fire into the accumulating bodies of model threes. The Antithesis were charging the barbed-wire-covered barricades by the hundreds. A model six ignored some small-arms fire and rammed into a cement wall hard enough that it cracked down the middle and buckled backward. Someone clever tossed a grenade over the barricade and the explosion slowed the swarm down for a moment.

"Shit," I said.

None of our newer defenses were in River Heights.

In fact, I'd pulled back militia from the area.

"Shit, shit," I muttered.

"Ma'am?" the general asked. He was probably not enjoying hearing the person in charge muttering obscenities instead of doing anything useful.

"Alright, we can patch this up for now. We're moving up the timetable for that area. Myalis, any nanomachines in those tunnels already? Yeah? Launch them early. Same with any resonators in the region already. Hurry things up that way. I need a line to Manic and Arm-a-Geddon, I need both of them moved to River Heights right now. I need Gomorrah too . . . maybe she can send a few of her drones over. And let's move some of our mortars toward that end of the city, they might be able to land hits from the edge of their range into the swarm." I swallowed. "General, tell your boys to hold out for five minutes. That's all I ask for."

CHAPTER TWENTY-FIVE

TRICKLE DOWN

While the very concept of trickle-down economics was proven to be utter bullshit, we still haven't figured out whether the samurai's trickle-down technology has the same bullshitty smell to it.

—Edward Denless, political commentator, 2032

Things went well for all of thirty seconds after I cut contact with the general. Then, of course, things got complicated.

Arm-a-Geddon gladly accepted a ride to River Heights onboard a troop-transport loaded up with militia guys. They'd reinforce the front line over there, which was getting complicated. The militia had cameras lined up so that I could check on things with some ease, and from the looks of it they were getting swarmed mostly by small-fry Antithesis, but I didn't think that would last.

Gomorrah agreed to send some of her drones over, which meant three of them were flying across the gap between River Heights and Downtown already.

They were going to lay down some literal fire on the Antithesis. That would help, but her drones weren't the fastest things around, so we had a minute or three to wait before they arrived.

In the meantime, I had to deal with Manic.

"What do you mean you don't want to?" I asked.

Manic didn't sound impressed over the line. From what I could tell she was sitting by one of the walls on the west end of the city. "I mean I don't wanna. Never been told no before?"

"Fuck," I said. "The people there—"

"Are spoiled rich fucks. They've decided to hole up in their little mansions. Let them."

I ground my teeth together. I couldn't even be angry, her attitude was exactly how I would act and . . . wait, did that mean that I was a bitch? Shit. It wasn't time for self-reflection.

"Fine," I said. "You're staying by the area you're in?"

"If the plant fucks are moving on River Heights, they'll be hitting Downtown soon. I'll break them before they get far."

"Right," I said. "You do that."

I cut the line off and took a deep breath. Now what? Manic would have been useful in River Heights. She had a lot of AOE stuff as far as I could tell, and she was good in a scrap. I placed her higher than Arm-a-Geddon and Sprout as far as combat abilities went, but she wasn't available, so I'd have to live with that.

Your ride is here.

I glanced up and stared as a massive vehicle lumbered along the road, taking up two of the three lanes that bisected Downtown's center.

The militia had a single mobile base, and I imagined the reason for that was related to their budget. The mobile base was an eight-wheeled, two-bus-long thing that was squat and fat. It had gun emplacements on the front, sides and rear, and looked like it could just barely manage to move at a double-digit speed provided it was going downhill.

It had escorts, of course, a half dozen armored trucks with mounted machine guns on top of them. They all had "Burlington Crowd Control" stencilled on their sides.

The machine came to a grinding stop, a door on the side opened and a set of hydraulics whined as steps dropped to make it easy to get in. An officer type jumped out and jogged over. "Ma'am," he said. "The general wanted to invite you into the mobile command center. We're at your disposal, ma'am."

"And where's the general?" I asked.

"Headquarters, ma'am," he said.

I shook my head. "Alright, I think . . . you know what, screw it. Let's go. Can you drive this thing to the west side of Downtown?"

"We can," the soldier said. "How close to the defenses do you want to be?"

"What's the range on the turrets on this thing?" I asked as I headed in.

"Three hundred meters, optimally," he said.

"Then about that far," I said before grabbing a handhold and pulling myself up and into the mobile base.

I wouldn't be staying in there for long, I knew that the moment I stepped in. The interior was like a mobile home, but cramped, with every spare bit of space used up for something. Storage, both guns and MREs, not including the other supplies, and then there was seating for a dozen, as well as a whole medical section and an area where the walls were covered in screens. The militia only had one person jacked into the Mesh onboard this land-boat.

I didn't bother heading to the front where the driver was sitting. The mobile base started to move with a faint lurch and I stepped into the electronics and command area and looked over the screens in a hurry.

It looked like every street-side camera was being used to paint a somewhat decent picture of Downtown and a bit of the space beyond that. A representation of the city was on one screen, with various areas coded in different colors and militia positions marked with green triangles.

Some spaces were painted a deep red, and a little legend off to the side said those were critical infrastructure. "What makes those things critical?" I asked, pointing to the screen.

Surprisingly, it was the guy lying down on a compact Mesh bed that answered. An avatar appeared on one of the screens, and as the avatar spoke with its voice coming from a set of speakers tucked away somewhere, the guy on the bed spoke at the same time.

Of course, his avatar was some anime chick and he looked like he was on the wrong end of his thirties.

"*Ohiyo!* The critical infrastructure includes two data centers, the Burlington Private Hospital, and the city's three privately operated nuclear reactors."

"Why the fuck does the city have privately operated nuclear reactors?" I asked.

"For . . . power?" the anime girl on screen said. She looked far too sassy compared to his real body. Her real body? I wasn't sure which applied. Digitalized gender was a confusing mess that I wasn't going to get into.

"I guessed that much," I said as I stepped closer to the screen with the map. The map then shifted to one of the larger screens without my prompting. It looked like most of the critical-red infrastructure was more or less in the center of the city. The exceptions were on the north and south ends, fortunately.

I added a reminder to myself to worry about that later. "Okay, how are things in River Heights?"

"Not going so good," the anime girl avatar said. The main screen switched to what was obviously the helmet-cam of someone on the front lines over there. They were manning one of those big chain-fed guns that rattled and barked out lines of fire that ripped apart aliens.

They'd gotten to the point where the bodies were starting to stack up and form little barricades of mulched flesh. I could almost smell the scene. Gunpowder and that strange mowed-grass scent the Antithesis gave off when they died.

A glance at the local map suggested they had all of seven guys holding the line, a line that was as wide as a nice upper-class street, the sort with wide sidewalks and houses with yards on the side.

"Shit," I muttered.

"It's not looking so good," the avatar said.

"Myalis, where are my mortars?"

They're moving into position. It'll take another three minutes until the first has a clear line of fire. Gomorrah's drones will arrive in four minutes, and the transports with reinforcements and Arm-a-Geddon will be in place in seven.

I watched as the gunner mowed down another line of Antithesis, but one of them, a scrappy little model three, slipped past the fire, jumped onto a sandbag, then latched onto the face of one of the militia men.

His buddy next to him was quick to turn and punt the alien off, then he fired three rounds center-of-mass, putting it down while the guy who'd been thrown back scrambled to pick up his rifle again.

"Yeah, no," I said.

We were doing something to help. Many somethings, but I wasn't going to watch as these guys just died because the help I'd sent their way was too slow.

"Myalis, I need something that can hit their location now," I said.

I have a multitude of options!

"Got rockets or something? Just a quick up-down-kaboom?"

Not point-efficient, but I certainly have a few options.

"Let's not fuck around," I said as I started to walk toward the back of the base. I'd noticed a ladder leading up to the roof as I did my mini-tour of the vehicle. I grabbed on and climbed up and out the top. I expected it to be windy but . . . well, we were moving at a walking pace.

Myalis was quick to give me a crate that had what was obviously a rocket launcher within. I picked it up, aimed high, and let loose, the backsplash scorching the top of the mobile base even as the rocket screamed into the sky.

Damn it was nice to feel useful sometimes.

CHAPTER TWENTY-SIX

INTEL-CHAN

A cult is, in essence, one of the best businesses you can possibly run. The cost of running your own cult is extremely low, and the power, credits, and influence you gain from running a cult cannot be overstated.

Here at C. P. Morgan's Cult and Pseudoreligion Department, we have experts of all sorts to prepare you and your fledgling cult for the future and to ensure a happy, healthy, and profitable following.

—C. P. Morgan, CPD Pamphlet, 2035

"That helped," the anime girl avatar said as I returned. The screen had a view from that same gunner's helmet, only this time he was looking at a crater with some Antithesis bits on the edges while bits of dirt were still raining down from above.

More aliens were coming, but now they had to go around or through the pit in the ground, and I suspected the shock had slowed them down a little.

All that the guards needed was a little bit of time to reset though, and they'd been given that.

Now if only Arm-a-Geddon and Gomorrah's drones could hurry up and get there, then we wouldn't have as many issues. Or maybe we would. "Mya-lis, can you give us a heatmap of Antithesis locations?" I asked.

The screen shifted, and the anime girl avatar found herself flickering over to another nearby screen. She frowned, looking peeved at the sudden motion, but didn't complain. The screen now showed a map of Burlington, with some parts painted blue, while plenty of areas were shaded in oranges and deeper reds. The areas along the edges of Downtown and River Heights were clearly marked, and both had a decent amount of red right next to them.

"There are as many Antithesis right up against River Heights as there are next to Downtown," I said.

That is correct.

So we'd need to defend River Heights against the same number of xenos as Downtown. That . . . wouldn't work out. We didn't have the ability to do that, we didn't have the manpower, and I didn't have the time to take care of two places at once.

For the time being, my plan was to protect Downtown and let River Heights take care of itself, but if it was going to face a tide as heavy as what I suspected was going to hit Downtown, then the whole place was fucked.

"We need to evacuate River Heights," I said. "Myalis, can you send Baker a text? Tell her to organize everyone to leave River Heights. They have half an hour."

I imagine she won't like that.

"She's not gonna like that," the anime girl said.

"I don't care," I replied to both at the same time. "We can't afford to split our attention, not for long in any case. So let's not. Get the civilians from River Heights to Downtown, shove them somewhere where they won't be trouble, and then pull back all the troops we're wasting over there. The place has automated defenses, right?"

"It does," the anime girl said. "Turret emplacements, shaped charges, deployable denial-of-passage cover, and a few other things as well. River Heights invested heavily in its own protection about twelve years ago. The systems are dated, but they've been maintained."

"They didn't have the budget for the same defenses around Downtown?" I asked.

"Some were installed, but a number of installations were stolen and the city decided not to keep up the maintenance of those in the . . . financially disadvantaged areas."

I should have seen that coming. I couldn't even be angry. I was totally the type of shit to steal a city-placed thing to make a quick buck if the opportunity arose. "Alright, fine," I said. "Can we set their automated defenses to distract the Antithesis once we've evac'd all the civilians from the area? It'll maybe keep one front busy while we take care of the rest."

"Tactical genius," the avatar said.

"Shut up . . . whatever your name is," I said.

"Intel-chan," Intel-chan, apparently, said.

I think now would be a good time to deploy the nanomachines. We need them to disperse after deployment and it will take some time before they start to have any noticeable effects.

I nodded. "Alright, launch the nano-whatsits, if the people on the edges of Downtown aren't on high alert yet, now would be a good time to inform them that shit's about to hit the fan."

"Sending a militia-wide communique," Intel-chan said. Then, to my horror, she did some *moe* bullshit with her hands and little sparkly hearts raced across the screens. "Sent! I sent a memo to the civilian defense as well. They have a new operations lead."

"Lucy?" I asked.

"That's the one," Intel-chan said. "Is she a specialist you brought in?"

"Uh, yeah, something like that," I said, feeling a little self-conscious about the choice. Was putting Lucy basically in charge a good idea? If she messed up, then people might actually die, and then I'd be to blame for putting Lucy in a position where she was responsible for that kind of thing, which didn't sound like something a good girlfriend should do.

"Yeah, she's whipped them up into a frenzy. I haven't seen people this pumped since the last big idol show," Intel-chan said. "Is she like, one of those social experts that train in cult creation?"

Or maybe Lucy would just be Lucy and would manage everything far better than I expected.

I'm helping her where I can. Mostly with logistics. Don't worry overly much, if anything goes too wrong I can alert you. In the meantime, this is a nice learning opportunity, don't you think?

I let out a held breath. "Yeah, she's pretty fantastic," I said. I looked for a place to sit, found none, then placed my hands on my hips, then let them fall. I didn't know what to do with myself.

I'd heard, in passing, that being a soldier was a lot about hurrying up to wait, but I'd never really lived it myself. At the moment I had a dozen plates spinning, but I couldn't do anything until one of them started to wobble and fall.

Myalis was kind enough to overlay the nanomachine spread atop the Antithesis heatmap, with a more accurate diagram showing the location of the tunnels under the city, or what we'd scouted out of them so far. Most of the bigger tunnels had been found, from the looks of it, but there were dozens of little branches that didn't look any bigger than a person that spread out every which way. Sometimes they reconnected with the rest, other times they spilled out into little underground chambers that I was certain were filled with plenty of hive flesh.

Once this incursion was stopped dead, we'd have to spend a few billion searching out the entirety of the underground for those little pockets.

That would be someone else's problem.

"Problem," Intel-chan said. She spun both hands around, then pointed to an area on the map. "Street cameras in this area have captured this."

One of the side screens showed a group of model threes pouring out of a nondescript building's side. They'd slammed the door out of the way and were stumbling out, first a few, then a good dozen of them followed by a model four. One of its tentacles flopped off and fell onto the ground where it was trampled by the others.

All of them were like extras in a zombie movie, with flayed skin and lumps of flesh looking like they were ready to slough off of them.

One model three looked like it was having a fit, shaking its head before it charged across the street and rammed hard into the side of a building on the other side.

"Oh hey, your thing worked," Intel-chan said. "Congrats."

"Thanks," I said, flatly. "Myalis, can you set off the rest of the bombs we have down there whenever it would be best?"

I can. I think I'll wait until each one will hit the largest number of Antithesis.

"Cool," I said. Now, where was that group? More and more aliens were pouring out of what was clearly one of the places where their tunnels rose up to the surface. A glance at the map revealed that it was about a block west of Downtown's outer defenses. "Intel, can you alert that end of the wall that they're going to have company soon? And if you have a line to Manic, ping her as well, she'll want to be on the front lines."

"Can do!" Intel-chan said. She didn't need to make a little heart with her hands though.

I made a note not to introduce Daniel to this guy because this was exactly the kind of crap he'd get into and I wasn't sure I wanted that in my life.

After the initial excitement of seeing the Antithesis finally appearing, I got to wait some more.

This whole leadership thing wasn't nearly as fun as just being on the front lines blowing shit up, I realized.

CHAPTER TWENTY-SEVEN

WALK THE WALK

Notice: We need new books for the K–2 classes. The phonetic alphabet books we have right now are all animal-based, and the teachers are tired of having to stop every few letters to explain that certain animals (B for bee, C for crab, E for elephant, J for Jaguar, P for Penguin . . . etc.) no longer exist. It's causing some of the kids a lot of distress.

Maybe replace the animal alphabet with brands?

Thank you.

—Notice posted on Teacher Group Chat, 2029

I stood there, with Intel-chan's occasional remark and the updating report from the screens, for all of five minutes before I decided that I would be more of a frontline kind of general.

"I really want to be shooting things," I said. The mobile base was a block away from the frontline, not that the Antithesis had breached the line just yet. There were more and more of them showing up though, some half melted, dying before they even got close enough to be worth shooting, others looking almost entirely intact. I suspected that we'd missed some chambers and tunnels underground.

Not a big deal, we could stomp them out once they came closer.

The militia were out in full force, which while nice to see, was also a little worrying. What would happen when they tired out? I couldn't expect to hold them at full attention for hours on end. The volunteers under Lucy were going to take up some of that slack. Already I could see where a number of them were waiting on the front lines, with about half of them holding back for the moment, but they'd tire out too. Probably faster than the militia, really.

Basically, the best case scenario for us was a single, big flood of aliens that led to a single, big fight. If the Antithesis decided to turn this into a prolonged siege, then the people working to keep Downtown safe wouldn't be able to keep up.

We were human. We got tired, hungry, and jittery. Even most companies understood that sixteen hours of constant labor meant a hard decrease in the quality of that labor.

The Antithesis didn't have that concern. Sure, individually I was sure some of them would tire, but it didn't take a hive sixteen hours to create a fresh batch.

"If you want, you can climb on the roof and shoot at the walls," Intel-chan said. "We're only a couple of hundred meters away."

As if I could land a shot at that kind of range. "Hmm, no, I think I'd rather be close up to the front lines." I looked at the screen that had . . . well, calling it troop-movements would be lying since neither side had anything like troops, but it was close enough.

The tide of Antithesis was being somewhat agreeable at the moment with the way it lurched toward the most heavily defended parts of our perimeter.

"Oh hey, the nun's fighting a model thirteen."

I whipped my attention around until I found the right screen. It was a screen-camera view of the front. Everything was covered in fire, which was rather predictable with Gomorrah involved. The nun herself was jumping to the side and rolling, showing surprising maneuverability for someone wearing a habit.

Ahead of her, half on the wall, was a huge model thirteen, one of those rare aliens with three tubular bodies linked together by long appendages. It was holding itself off the ground with some tentacles while others were moving so quickly the camera had a hard time capturing them as anything but artifacts.

I could see where they hit though. Asphalt cracked and chunks of concrete exploded apart.

Gomorrah returned literal fire, bathing the monster in flames which seemed to make it all the more energetic.

She was good, dodging back and weaving around strikes that I was pretty sure would have splattered me.

The model thirteen slowed, slumped, then fell to the ground, a burning wreck that Gomorrah nonetheless covered in more fuel as if to make sure nothing was left of it but ashes.

"Fuck," I said.

"Big payday!" Intel-chan said.

"What?"

The anime avatar grinned. "Do you have any idea how rare model thirteen footage is? That'll be worth a pretty penny for me."

"You might not be able to spend that pretty penny if there are model thirteens on the battlefield," I pointed out. "Wait, what are they doing out here?"

The nontraditional structure of the hive, combined with our vector of attack, might have moved the model thirteen to search for a threat outside of the hive. They rarely survive long once disconnected from the hive structure, so it's uncommon to see them on the battlefield. Nonetheless, this battlefield is right atop the hive itself. We are likely to start seeing more.

And there was no way the normal folk out there were prepared to deal with a double-digit alien.

"Myalis, I need to know where the next one of those will be popping up. I'm going to intercept if I can, and send Gomorrah if I can't. Maybe . . . let's divide the front into thirds? Sandwich Manic between Gomorrah and I."

The main front was conveniently placed along three larger roads that crossed the city from west to east, so we'd basically each get a spot. The mobile base was parked in the middlemost of these, which was fine. Manic was newest, she might need the additional firepower.

I started to walk out. "Intel, you've got my number, yeah?"

"I've got it!" Intel-chan said with a thumbs-up.

"Keep in touch if anything happens," I said. I opened a secondary screen in the periphery of my augmented eye and let Myalis play around with it for a bit. Soon enough I had a well-laid-out list of statistics, an Antithesis heatmap, and the IFFs of all of our troops.

The positions of all of the other samurai were there as well, with little logos for all of them, and a big L in a heart for Lucy too.

"Thanks," I said.

It costs me little and will allow you to make better, more informed choices. Speaking of which, there are a number of things you could purchase to improve the defensive capability at the front.

I nodded along as I slipped through the mobile base, then jumped out of one of its side entrances. It was guarded by a single militiaman who looked like he was a year or two younger than me and who was swimming in his loose uniform.

I hoped that the reason he was back here was because the general was trying to keep his less experienced folk out of the firing line.

"Let's see how things are going at the front first," I said. After all, most of the things I could purchase would start working right away, at least if they were things like more cat drones and additional mortars, which is what I suspected Myalis was aiming for.

I walked across the street, noting that it was nearly empty near the barricades but farther in, behind some cement half walls, a number of people were loitering. Most of them had armbands, yellow, brown, green, but a few were just standing around and watching. Were they gawkers?

Some had equipment around, and I caught one group using the first floor of a restaurant as a staging ground for a big community kitchen.

So, we had logistics this close to the front? A few ambulances were sitting idle not too far off, with nervous EMTs (with white and red armbands) standing near.

Catherine. A trio of model fifteens has been sighted heading toward your part of the defenses.

Model fifteens . . . those were the nasty artillery models that could spit out large, explosive seed things that sent fragments all over the place. Not the toughest of the Antithesis, but annoying, and they'd force our defenders into cover while the weaker models charged forward.

"I'm on it," I said as I picked up the pace.

This wasn't the time to be strutting around and taking in the sights. I ran through an alleyway and found it blocked off at the end, which was nice, we didn't need the aliens slipping around things. Less nice was that I had to jump-jet my way over the obstruction to land on the road I'd be defending for the moment.

At the far end, a pile of debris, old cars, and chunks of metal welded together into the semblance of a wall stood between Downtown and the aliens. A few holes were cut into the defenses so that stationary guns could be pointed out through it. Those were rattling already, and I saw a number of people running around with cases full of ammunition while above, one of Gomorrah's angel-drones spat a line of fire onto what I imagined were some well-cooked aliens.

Yeah, this was more like it. Much more fun than waiting in place and telling people what to do.

CHAPTER TWENTY-EIGHT

MORALE

Morale, while not a factor that is easy to quantify, is nonetheless an important measure of the potential success of troops on an active battlefield.

For this reason, it is usually a good idea to allow your troops to see any local samurai at work. Nothing inspires hope like the casual disregard for death and the destructive capabilities of a samurai in action.

—*Morale and Victory*, Officer's Training Tips #358, 2039 edition

I ran up one of the ramps set up behind the wall, then paused near the top as soon as I could see over the defenses.

The aliens approaching us weren't quite like the tides I'd seen in the defense of New Montreal. Those tides had been so thick that I couldn't see the ground past all the Antithesis, and they went on basically forever, with no breaks in their formation except where a shell went off to create one, and even those were temporary.

Here, the formations were a lot patchier, with trios of aliens running together and the occasional larger group. Often, some bigger, slower xenos were running on their own, too slow to keep up with the much faster and more common model threes.

The remote-controlled and human-operated guns nestled in the wall spat at the aliens, short, loud bursts that ended with a few corpses rolling across the pavement.

Those that managed to get close anyway got to meet Gomorrah's drone, which hissed out lines of liquid fire onto them and turned the aliens into rolling balls of flame. The smoke might actually be a problem later if it interfered with our vision. Then again, it also removed the corpses, turning them to ash before they piled up so high that they became an obstruction, or worse, a ramp of dead flesh.

So far, things seemed alright.

Then I ducked down with a curse as something smashed into the wall some ten meters off to my left with a huge bang. The metal under my feet rattled and I grabbed on until the tremors passed. When I looked up again, I saw the broken remains of a large chitinous wheel, its edges cutting into the wrecked cars and cement barriers that made up the wall.

Little spines had sprayed out from around where the wheel impacted, and even now some of them were falling down around us, sticking into the ground on the safe side of the wall. No one was hit, but I imagine some of the gunners were spooked.

If that had hit one of the little openings . . . yeah, that would mean one gun down, and maybe a couple of volunteers dead too.

I glanced down the road, looking for the model fifteen that had spat that.

Myalis helped, highlighting three figures without me having to ask. One was on the road a ways away, protected by model fives on either flank and moving forward on its little legs even as its gut swelled and I imagined it was preparing to launch another wheel.

The other two were better hidden, both of them in a building off to the right. It was some storefront, but the middle floors of the building were taken up by paid parking spaces. The walls on the street side had been torn apart, giving the model fifteens somewhere to shoot from.

As I watched, one launched one of its wheels.

The massive spinning lump of Antithesis flesh smashed into the road, spinning so fast that it tore up the topmost layer of asphalt before that spin turned into forward movement and it zipped across the gap on a wobbling path toward the wall.

I locked onto the wheel and my shoulder-mounted guns popped out of their housings and fired. The whip-like crack of two railgun sabots ripping through the air echoed across the street and the wheel imploded as holes were punched into its structure.

That didn't end it though. As the wheel exploded, it unraveled, sending a whole swarm of long, thin needles scattering into the air.

The aim was atrocious, and most of them were flung right into the ground or at an angle where they wouldn't do much, but there were so many, and they all moved in the direction of the wall.

I ducked down again and winced as a few needles whistled past. "Motherfuckers," I swore.

Someone screamed, and as I glanced back, I saw a green-armband volunteer panicking at the sight of a needle embedded in his chest. A medic ran over and tackled him to the ground, and soon they were applying some sort of gauze-spray over the wound and dragging the guy to cover.

He'd live, I figured. If he had the energy to scream, he was probably going to be alright once the medics got done with him.

The blow to morale though . . .

Fighting an enemy was rough, but if it was a *fight,* that meant that you had a chance to win. Getting fucked over by an enemy you couldn't see or do anything about? Just sitting there and waiting your turn to die by big needle or enemy teeth? Yeah, that would break someone's nerves sooner than later.

"Myalis, can you connect me to . . . Intel-chan, I guess."

Certainly.

"Yo," Intel-chan's voice said in my ear even as her avatar popped into being in a box at the edge of my vision. "Oh, you've got the nice tech in here."

"Uh-huh," I said, dismissing that. "I need you to relay shit to whoever's in charge of this section of the wall. I don't have time for a meet and greet, not while we're being shelled."

"I can do that," Intel-chan said.

"Good. Tell them that I'll be right back and for the gunners not to shoot me, please. I'm pretty sure it wouldn't do anything, but it would annoy me and waste ammo."

"Uh, yeah, alright."

With that said I stood, grabbed onto the edge of the wall, then vaulted over it.

The far side of the wall was covered in rough spikes, jutting spars, and in general, wasn't designed to be pretty or easy to climb, but I managed to find a few places to put my feet as I jumped down.

Once on the ground, I whipped out my Laser Pointer and started walking.

I stomped over a few corpses, then edged around some piles of burning alien flesh. It took until I was a good dozen meters from the wall before I was close enough that the Antithesis started to really notice me.

With the gunners very carefully not shooting close to me, that meant that as a trio of model threes ran my way, nothing opposed them.

Until I raised my gun to my shoulder and pulled the trigger. I scored a line of fire across the trio, then sidestepped their bodies, which were carried forward by their running momentum. "Hmm, I need something with a bit more punch, ammo-wise," I said.

You're currently using armor-piercing thermite-tipped tracer rounds. Do you want something with more stopping power? Something explosive, perhaps? Or just a round that's heavy enough to stop them in their tracks?

"Just something with a lot more kick," I said. I was having a hard time describing what I wanted because I wasn't sure what I wanted to begin with.

Coming right up.

The bottom-rear of the gun opened up, and a cylinder fell out and clunked to the floor, only for the gun's weight to shift back up as it closed and a new magazine was teleported in. "Heavy," I said as I weighed the gun. It had gained a couple of kilos, I was sure.

Enriched iridium rounds. They burn, are highly radioactive, and have a half-life with only hours remaining. They are also quite heavy and the rounds are specifically designed not to penetrate too deeply.

I shrugged, then aimed at a salivating model three charging at me from down the road. It was still a few dozen meters away when I feathered the trigger to fire as small a burst as I could. The kick was a lot more than I was used to, but seeing the model three backflip, all of its forward momentum stopped dead, was more than satisfying enough to make up for that.

I continued my enthusiastic walk, *brrt*ing any aliens that came too close and letting my railguns handle any that wanted to skirt around.

As I came closer to the model fifteen, it turned its attention toward me, and I saw its stomach sack expanding as it prepared to launch another wheel at me.

"Frag," I said, my hand opening up by my side.

A grenade landed in my palm, and on reflex I flicked it on, then tossed it ahead. It clinked on the ground, then bounced up and behind the model fifteen.

I started to walk to the side, placing the alien between myself and the grenade, then I turned my attention to its guardians. The model fives were heavier, chunkier aliens than most. They didn't go flying as far when I peppered them with a few rounds apiece.

Then the grenade went off with a loud *whump* and I suppressed a flinch. The building across the street rattled as dozens of little holes were punched into its side.

"That's one down," I said. Two more to go, and look at that, they were within explosives range!

CHAPTER TWENTY-NINE

WEAPONIZED CRINGE

Stores slowly faded into obscurity as the '20s turned into the '30s. As we approach the '40s, an entire generation has grown up unfamiliar with the idea of walking into a retail location to buy anything more complicated than a Frappuccino.

—The Decline: Consumerism and the Future, 2036

I took a little breather next to the corpse of a model fifteen. Or at least, the head bit of the corpse. The rest of its body was buried under the rubble of what used to be the front of a building. The facade hadn't taken kindly to my treatment of it, and I suspected the rest of the building would have to be taken down eventually because it wasn't in that great of shape anymore.

What mattered was that the aliens hiding inside were dead. Or stuck under a few tons of torn-up cement. In either case, no longer an issue for me.

The miniature tide of aliens in their area had crawled to a stop, so I figured I was good for a little break, at least until more of them tore their way out of whatever hole they were hiding in.

Of course, that's when I received a call from Intel-chan.

"What's up?" I asked as I connected to the . . . intelligence officer? What even was their rank? They must have been pretty good at their job if the militia endured their eccentricities.

"*Oh-hiyo!*" Intel-chan said as their avatar appeared in the edge of my vision, one arm waving over their head. "So, we're kinda fucked back here, wanna help us, *onegai*?"

I wasn't sure I wanted to, not when I was being asked that way. "What's the situation?" I asked as I stood up properly. All this fighting and stuff was really killing my back, even with the armor doing lots of the heavy lifting.

"Your *girlfriend's* army is finally moving up to the walls to relieve some of our militia boys, but we're spotting aliens on the inside of our defenses. Particularly . . . right here, and here. I've got militia stationed around the area with some of our light assault vehicles, but LAVs can only do so much and I don't want to send anyone into what might be a tunnel leading right into a hive."

I checked the map and noted that Intel-chan had highlighted two spots. They were a block or two into Downtown, so well past the first walls we had, but still on the outskirts of the parts of Downtown where people were actually living.

"Alright," I said. "How are things in River Heights?"

"Calming down on the alien front, doing the opposite on the people front," Intel-chan said. "Want me to tell your girlfriend to get on it? She seems good at motivating people."

"Hmm? No, it's fine, I'll see to it in a bit. Are any of the samurai free right now?"

"Sprout is," they said.

"Cool, send them to the smaller of the two holes. It can't be *that* well defended. And he needs the practice. Maybe send some of Lucy's troopers with him, or some militia guys. I'll plug up the other one myself."

"Sending a message to Lucy-sama now!"

I frowned. "Do you . . . have a problem with Lucy?" I asked.

Intel-chan shook their head almost violently. "No way! I think it's super cute! When I found out that you brought your girlfriend here, I practically *sugoi*'d!"

"Please, don't . . . don't weeb at me."

"Hey! I'm a third generation weeb you know. We're some of the most oppressed people in North America."

I decided not to poke at that, if only to preserve my own sanity. "I'm on my way back," I said.

So far, things have been going pretty well. Sure, new fires were popping up all over, but we were on top of them. Things could, and probably would, spiral out of control eventually, but eventually wasn't right now, so I contented myself with what I had.

On the return trip to the wall, I flicked mines left and right, tossing them behind partial cover and through open ground-floor windows and spots where I suspected a model fifteen or something might want to lurk in the future.

It was a worthwhile investment, I figured, to trap this entire corridor. Even if only a third of the mines I left behind me went off and took out an Antithesis or two, I'd be in the black point-wise.

I reached the wall, searched for a way up, then noticed some of the militia guys pulling their gun aside in one of the openings, so I went over there and swung my way through the entrance feet-first. "Thanks," I said as I passed them.

The nearest of the holes Intel-chan had spotted wasn't too far off. Still, I was happy when a lightly armored truck, a technical, I think they were called, came around and stopped next to me. It was a pickup with the body replaced by armored panels and the cab reinforced to take some hits. The front had a nice cowcatcher bolted to it, and the bed at the back housed a big old machine gun on a swivel mount.

It needed a guy mounted on the gun to work, and I was pretty sure the truck was a plain-old commercial vehicle, but it worked, I figured, and was probably cheap besides. I grabbed onto the edge of the box and hauled myself into the back. Then I thumped the roof of the cab and we sped off across the city.

I checked my gun one-handed while hanging onto the back of the cab with my other. It didn't take long before we reached a spot where the militia had created a temporary cordon blocking off the front of a building.

The cordon wasn't anything too special. A trio of lightly armored trucks, like the one I was riding on, and a couple of vans parked farther back. Volunteers were stacking sandbags up across the street, creating a barrier onto which a team was fixing a machine gun on a pod.

As soon as the truck stopped moving I leapt off the back and landed with a huff. I didn't have much time to lose here. If I spent too long fixing this issue, three more would pop up while I was distracted.

The militia didn't need me to micromanage anything—they were responding on their own, as were the people Lucy was directing, it seemed—but I still wanted to be on top of things so that I could put pressure on the bigger problems before they got out of hand.

"Alright," I muttered. "What's going on here?"

I must have still been on the line with Intel-chan because they answered almost immediately. "The lieutenant in charge of that area forwarded reports of alien sightings to me, and I confirmed them. So we killed the loose aliens and traced them back to this one building here. They've been coming out from the ground floor, but this building has a basement. No one wants to volunteer to go check it out."

"Yeah, I can't imagine why."

The building in question looked like a toy store of all things, the kind of look-and-see outlet that lets people interact with stuff before ordering it online. With the lights off inside and the barred windows at the front making what light did filter in strange, I wasn't too keen on walking in there myself.

The dead alien bodies next to the entrance gave the decor a certain flair. Blood didn't go well with pastels.

"Right, I'm heading in. Quick in-and-out," I said as I started walking over.

"What's your plan?" Intel-chan asked.

"Walk in, find the place the aliens are coming in from, plug the hole," I said.

"You know, they'll just make another hole," Intel-chan pointed out.

I nodded. "There's always another hole, if you're willing to look for it."

"Oh my."

I rolled my eyes, paused by the entrance, shouldered my Laser Pointer, then toggled on my invisibility. I could have done it earlier, but I wanted the militia guys to know that I hadn't just disappeared to leave them behind.

I stepped over the bodies by the entrance, then pressed in, eyes on a swivel as I ignored all the toys lying around.

The kittens would love this kind of place. Though they'd touch everything and catch every sickness left by the last batch of snot-nosed brats to pass by.

Maybe once this city was safe again, kids would be more concerned about toys than being eaten.

But that would only happen if I didn't suck at my job.

"Alright," I said. "Let's find out where those alien fucks are coming from and put out one more fire, shall we?"

"I'm rooting for you, *desu*!"

CHAPTER THIRTY

DOG GONE

In the early 2020s, on average, 69 percent of all households had a pet. Now, that number is closer to 36 percent!

Now it's far less common to have a furry friend. That's why services like ours exist! Petpetzoo allows you to have your very own lifelong companion for as little as 1500Cr/Mo* for you to pet, cuddle, and play with, and you never need to bring them home!

—Petpetzoo frontpage, 2039

It was surprisingly tense, walking across hip-high displays with colorful toys on them, and past larger signs and cardboard cutouts of action-figure heroes.

I duly noted that there were a lot of samurai-themed toys. Little action figures with changeable weapons and gear, and toward the back of the store, for the older customers, were posed figurines.

I wonder what Deus Ex would think if she came to our place and found a figurine of herself in a glass case. I was pretty sure we might still have a museum case or two left over too.

"The kittens would love this place," I said. "Though they'd make a mess of it."

I pressed inward, then froze as I heard something off to my side. Plastic crinkling, which was a distinct enough sound. I slowly turned in the direction of the noise and noticed a few boxes of toys discarded across the floor. I brought my Laser Pointer up and listened past the drumming of my heartbeat.

The noise came again, and this time I was able to pinpoint its location. I fired a trio of shots into a display a moment before a model three—now very much injured—came scrambling around to earn a fourth bullet to the face.

More aliens came pouring out of nooks and crannies. Mostly model threes, but a few fours and fives. Not that it really mattered. They were injured already and even if they knew they were under attack, they had no way of knowing where I was yet.

I walked around a display, using it as partial cover while I gunned down each alien that stuck its head out or went charging down one of the store's corridors. "Resonator," I said before chucking a grenade to the entrance. Some of the aliens had noticed the militia parked outside and were running out. They were getting gunned down, of course, but I didn't want to risk one of them getting lucky and ripping up one of the militia guys out there.

We only had so many competent soldiers on our side, no point in losing one because of rank stupidity.

When the room quieted down once more except for the high-pitched whine of that resonator, I lowered my guard and my gun. "Nice place, but maybe we should wait before visiting it," I said as I kicked the head of a very dead model three.

You should consider spending some time with your kittens.

"I got them stuff," I said. I started to make my way deeper into the room. The aliens had to have come from the basement or something. "And where we're living it's . . . like, not comparable to where we lived before. They have their own rooms and a working shitter, not to mention three meals a day."

Yes, that's true. You've done well by them financially and when it comes to their physical needs. But if you want to form any sort of emotional attachment, you'll need to spend actual time with them.

I considered it for a moment, then shrugged. "Yeah, you're probably right." There was a door behind the sales counter at the back. The bottom half of the door had been ripped apart, little bits of presswood scattered across the floor. I vaulted over the countertop, then leaned my head close. No noise on the other side.

I usually am.

"So, oh wise AI living in my head, what would you suggest I do with the kittens?" I asked. I didn't have the first clue what to do with them to build bonds or whatever. I opened the door, then pointed my gun in while I swept the room. It wasn't much more than a storage space with a desk in the back and a vending machine for employees. There was another door though, and, I noted, a staircase leading down. Bingo.

Anything that has you spending time with them. Perhaps visit a dog park?

"A . . . dog park?" I asked.

Yes. Here, this is a list of Google searches made by the Twins:

Myalis opened up a small screen in the corner of my vision, and I quickly read through the list while pausing my search.

> *How to pet dogs*
> *Do dogs like it when you touch them?*
> *How to tell a dog you love it?*
> *Cute dogs*
> *Dogs being cute*
> *How to say hi to a dog*

"Okay," I said. "So the Twins have a thing for dogs. That's . . . actually kind of cute. But we have a pet dog. Sorta." Catkiller was an interesting addition to our household. I wasn't sure how I felt about the big lump, and he mostly seemed content to stay out of my way. "But yeah, sure, visit a dog park. We can do that."

I'm merely looking out for your social and mental health.

"I'm not complaining," I said as I moved closer to the stairs. I stopped before reaching them as I heard a clicking from the staircase. "I need something explosive and quiet."

Explosives don't generally work quietly. Perhaps . . . a UV-based sterilization grenade? It's almost entirely quiet, but quite bright. I would have to strongly advise that you don't stand near it as it goes off, but that advice works for most explosives anyway.

"Sure, I'll try it," I said.

What I got was a roundish grenade covered in little panels that I suspected could pop open. A thumb-tab on the side had the very simple controls needed to use it. I flicked the 'nade on, then rolled it ahead so that it wouldn't make too much noise. It still clunked a few times as it dropped down the stairs, but the stairs had these rubber pads on them so it wasn't all that loud.

Then the grenade went off and the room filled with a blinding white-purple light that had me flinching back, and I wasn't even in the direct line of fire.

With the gun up, I moved to the edge of the staircase and aimed down.

There was a body at the bottom, a model four, tentacles splayed out everywhere. It looked like it had been flash-cooked on half of its body. The rest didn't look much better, with flesh looking partially melted.

"These were hit by the nanomachines," I said.

Yes. Judging from what I can see, they have come into contact with some of the nanomachines we've dispersed through the tunnel networks. Wherever they're coming from, it's linked to the greater hive. That's likely for the best.

"Because otherwise that would mean that we're dealing with another offshoot here?" I asked.

Exactly.

Yeah, that made a sort of horrific sense. I climbed down the stairs carefully, keeping my weight low and my gun ready to shoot anything that moved. Fortunately, nothing did. The stairs had a rail along their side with a lift at the bottom, probably so that employees could bring boxes up and down.

The rest of the space was filled with shelves partially filled with boxes. It was all neat and organized, or probably had been before someone dug a hole out of the far wall.

"Whelp, I'm guessing that's where they came from," I said as I eyed the jagged-edged hole. What little light I had coming in from the floor above didn't carry down into the tunnel, and my low-light vision was struggling a little with the far end of the tunnel.

Not enough light, I supposed. I could hear scrabbling and scratching from farther within, but it was faint and a little distant. "Alright, so do I just plug this hole and hope for the best? Or . . ." I looked around the room. Yeah, there was some space here. "I could turn this room into a killing field. Let them keep charging in to die all day."

Eventually, whatever defenses you put down will be overwhelmed.

"Right," I said. And that would be playing for time while giving the aliens the edge. Not the brightest of moves. "In that case . . . Myalis, I need a few things . . ."

In the end, I settled on three larger cat drones, all of them about hip-high and bristling with weapons, as well as a dozen smaller drones, the size of actual house cats. I watched the drones file into the tunnel. They had explosives on them that would go off once they were taken out of action.

Then, as a final fuck-you to the aliens, I plugged the hole up. First by tossing in a few proximity-triggered grenades. Everything from FOOF-dispersal bombs to plain old resonators, then a couple of expanding-foam grenades that I slapped onto the walls around the entrance.

By the time I was leaving the basement, the hole was filling up with sticking white foam that was already hardening to the consistency of cement.

"Okay, now let's see how many fires appeared while I was distracted with this one," I muttered.

CHAPTER THIRTY-ONE

SPROUT

Samurai may have similar profiles with several commonalities, but it's worth noting that every one is a unique individual, and applying the same brush across all of them will lead to errors in judgement and application.
—*On the Mental and Psychological Treatment of Samurai Patients,*
2046 Psychological Profiling Database

I stepped out of the toy store and nodded to the nearest militia guys. "Place is clear for now," I said. "Move on to the next place that needs you." And with that said I grabbed onto the back of the pickup I'd ridden over and climbed onboard. "Intel, got any news for me?"

"*Ohaio!*"

I suppressed a full-body twitch. Intel-chan's avatar now had a pair of cat ears on, both sticking out of a hairband of all things. "What?"

"Sprout-dono could probably use your help. He's in bad shape. Not *kawaii* at all."

I glared. "Are you getting worse?" I asked.

The avatar's eyes widened into a look of pure, unbelievable innocence. "What do you mean, Stray Neko-sama?"

"Pain in the ass," I muttered. "What's wrong with Sprout? Is he alright?"

"He was injured while taking care of the other sneaky-sneaky hive," Intel-chan said. "I sent more of our backline to the area to help stop the Antithesis from spreading out from there."

That was frustrating. "How's the front line?" I asked.

"So far so good! There's less aliens than there were before!"

That didn't sound right at all. "Myalis, what's that mean?"

It either means that the nanomachine attack was significantly more effective than expected, or the Antithesis are holding back for reasons unknown.

"Let's assume that it's the aliens fucking with us, that's the worse possibility, isn't it? Don't they usually just charge in mindlessly? What's keeping them back?"

Higher-tier Antithesis can sometimes display a certain level of tactical and strategic acumen. Lower-tier Antithesis also tend to remain in the vicinity of their greater counterparts. It's an instinct that presses them to protect the more valuable members of the hive.

So we were probably going to get messed up by some higher-tier aliens soon. "Intel-chan, keep an eye out for any models in the double digits. I want to be informed right away if we start seeing more of them."

"Yes ma'am!" Intel-chan said with a sloppy salute.

"And tell the driver to get me to Sprout's location. I want to see how badly he's hurt, then we need to plug that hole."

I got moving soon after, the militiaman at the wheel zipping across the city with no regard for any laws, which I supposed was only fair. We didn't need to get too far before reaching the spot where Sprout was supposed to destroy the Antithesis pushing in from below.

There were a dozen armored trucks and a couple of APCs sitting around in two groups. Stacks of sandbags had been placed in lumps across the street with machine guns on bipods set up to aim at a single building.

It wasn't that big of a building, maybe seven stories high, with the kind of dull gray facing and squarish architecture designed to make your eye skim right past it. It barely had any ads on it too. An office building of some sort, then? Maybe a call center or one of those places where a couple of hundred coders were locked into cubicles and made to write lines all day.

The first floor's walls were covered in a spray of bullet holes, most concentrated around a nondescript doorway that looked like it had been smashed out. A few corpses—all Antithesis—were splattered on the sidewalk, hinting at who had ripped the door out of the wall.

The pickup slowed to a stop and I jumped out, landing without any sound and just a slight bend to my knees.

Instantly, I noticed a dozen militia folk looking my way and I could see the tension bleeding off their shoulders. "Intel-chan, who's in charge here?"

"That would be Sprout-dono, I guess. But if you mean for the militia, Second Lieutenant Hawke."

"What's with all of the second lieutenants?" I muttered. I'd seen more people at that rank than any other.

"There's a big pay hike from second to first, so most people end up stuck as a second lieutenant forever. It's not like the militia really needs people to be captains or whatever. An officer's an officer."

Ah, so it was capitalism. That made sense. "Tell Hawke to meet me," I said as I searched for Sprout. I found him waiting in the back of an ambulance. The samurai was sitting at the back, legs just a little bit off the ground and back bent in the kind of posture that would lead to lower back pain in a few years.

He didn't look like he was bleeding out and I counted the average number of limbs on him.

I walked over to him while glancing at the building a few times. No windows, so there was no telling what was going on inside. "Myalis, is there still power in there?" I asked.

There is, yes. Did you want me to plug into the building's security network?

"That would be nice. Give us an idea of what's going on without having to stick our head in," I said. Then I came to a stop in front of Sprout. The man didn't even look up, focused as he was on the ground between his feet. "Hey."

Sprout looked up, mouth forming a little 'O' before he blinked and looked around. I'd seen the same expression on guilty kittens before. "Ah, uh, hi," he said.

"I heard you got hurt, figured I'd come and see what I could do to help," I said. I wanted to ask him why he looked so guilty, but sometimes it was better to let that kind of thing come out on its own.

"I'm . . . yeah, I'm alright," he said. He tapped his chest, and I noted that he was wearing a suit of armor. It didn't look too impressive, a skintight suit that he'd thrown a surplus bulletproof vest over. A helmet sat on the edge of the ambulance next to him. Just a thing that would cover the top of his head and his ears. He had a satchel sitting next to him, a ruddy old thing that looked like it had seen better days.

"I . . ." he finally met my eyes, then he looked away. I had the impression he wanted to be angry at me but couldn't muster up the willpower for it. "I went to see what I could do," he said. "It didn't work out."

"Alright," I said.

"I got chewed up. If it wasn't for the militia people, for my armor, I'd be dead."

I frowned, happy that he couldn't see my expression at the moment. "What did you meet in there?" I asked.

"Just some model threes. Not even a lot of them." He leaned forward and cupped his face in his hands. "Fuck."

That summed it up nicely, yeah.

"And now you're like this because you couldn't handle it?" I asked. It wasn't nice of me, I knew, but damn if I didn't have time to play therapist. "You know, it's not all bad. You're still new. Can't expect to be great out of the gate."

"I've been a samurai for three days now," he said. "Johnny's as new as me. He wouldn't have any trouble. Manic . . . she'd *enjoy* it. I'm . . ." he shook his head. "I'm not made for this. I don't know why I was chosen at all."

"Hey, calm down," I said. I placed a hand on his shoulder and tightened my grip. "Tell me what went wrong."

"I told you," he said.

"No, you told me what happened. Tell me what *went wrong*."

He shook his head, but replied all the same. "I don't know. I tried to not be noticed so that I could plant a few things, but my plants take a lot of time to grow. I thought I could just put a few of them down and let them grow to fill the hole. They've been good at stopping smaller models so far."

"Alright, and what happened?" I asked.

"They attacked me. I couldn't fight them off."

I nodded slowly. "Do you have a gun?" I asked.

"I lost it," he said.

I shut off the mic on my helmet so that I could let out a long sigh. This guy was . . . not frontline material. He didn't have that edge, that willingness to jump into trouble and mess up the enemy.

Gomorrah had it in spades. She enjoyed seeing the enemy burn. Manic was as violent and temperamental as they came. Even Johnny, while he was more focused on himself, was willing to jump into trouble to punch it.

Sprout struck me as something of a pacifist, which was a fantastic thing to be, I was sure, but it was also not the best trait for a samurai to have.

"We'll figure it out," I told him, and I hoped I was right because I needed every samurai I could get right now.

CHAPTER THIRTY-TWO

HORSES TO WATER

Space is looking less like the final frontier and more like our last hope.
—*JimJam Science Show,* 2041

I patted Sprout on the knee. "Stay here, alright?" I asked. "I'm going to pop on in there, seal things up in a bit, and then we'll head on out. Or . . ." I licked my lips.

Sometimes, when dealing with the kittens, they'd end up being afraid of something, or unable to do a chore, and while I ribbed them about it, I usually just did the task for them while telling them to do something easier to make up for it.

Stuff like doing the dishes if they didn't want to take out the trash.

I didn't think this was quite the same, but it was all I knew, so it was all I had to draw a comparison to right then.

"You know what, no," I said. I checked Sprout up and down, and he seemed fine, physically, at least. "You're coming with me?" I asked . . . said. It started as a statement and ended as a question, really. I didn't want to force the guy, but I wanted him to come.

He looked up. "Coming?"

"Good!" I said, taking the question as an answer. "You can show me what your plants have been doing. I haven't had a chance to see them up close. And if anything tries to eat you this time they'll have to get through me first."

I start heading off, a grin growing as I heard Sprout scramble to keep up. We were met halfway to the office building by a militia guy with the pips of a second lieutenant next to the badges on his uniform. "Ma'am," he said with a quick, sharp salute. "Second Lieutenant Hawke, ma'am, you mentioned needing me?"

"Ah, right," I said. The Hawke was tall and broad shouldered and very serious. He looked like he might be Native American. "The two of us are going to head in there to poke around. Can you make sure that nothing comes out of the building until we're done? Ah, aside from us, of course."

"We can do that," he said with another salute. "Good luck in there."

"Thanks," I said before walking past him. Once out of immediate earshot I glanced back at Sprout. "Got a gun?" I asked.

"Uh," was his reply.

I tossed him my Laser Pointer. "You'll need to buy ammo yourself," I said. "Myalis, can I get another?"

With the same enriched iridium rounds?

"Maybe switch it up to something like buckshot? We'll be in closer quarters." A gun appeared in the air before me and I caught it before it could start to fall. Then we were at the single door into the complex. "I'll be going ahead. Watch my back," I said to Sprout.

He nodded. "I'll do my best," he said. Obviously, he was still nervous. I was pretty sure that dragging him back in here was probably not the best move for his mental health but . . . he needed to learn.

Fuck, I didn't like being put in this kind of position, but I needed dependable samurai I could work with if I was going to keep this shithole city mostly intact, and that meant pushing Sprout a little.

I'd try to soften the blow, maybe? Was I going to have to attend, like, a seminar on convincing people to jump into trouble for a greater cause? Did that even exist?

I stepped into the office building, invisibility off so that any Antithesis we ran into would jump me first. I swept my gaze around, Laser Pointer following as I looked for trouble. The entrance lobby was a tight corridor, with a couple of benches on the sides and a security booth at the end that I imagined doubled as a shitty sort of reception.

A turret was mounted on the ceiling, but it looked inactive. Was it just for show?

I focused back on the ground where a few model threes were lying there, dead and covered in little bullet holes. I wasn't any sort of forensic expert, but I guessed that they'd been shot up by the militia folk.

"So, where did you find the entrance?" I asked Sprout.

"The one the Antithesis were using? Two levels down," he said.

"This place has multiple basements?" I asked.

"It's a cubicle farm," he replied. I didn't know exactly what that meant, but I just nodded along anyway.

Past the multiple metal detectors and EMP scramblers by the entrance, we came into the main space of the office building. A large room with a few enclosed offices along the edges and a sea of cubicles in the middle. Each had walls that stopped at about my waist, probably so that managers could better see their employees at work. There were a few more Antithesis bodies here, but some of them looked like they had been dragged across the floor, leaving bloody trails behind.

"They're trying to recoup their bodies," I guessed. A model three body probably had just about enough biomass to create another, fresh model three. Give or take a bit of waste. "Which means that they're not far."

I could almost hear Sprout swallow behind me as he raised his gun. We both came to a stop and searched the room from where we were. The cubicles would make for great places for the aliens to hide, even if there was barely enough room in each for three people to stand side by side.

"Is this where you were ambushed?" I asked.

"No. The stairwell, over there." He pointed to the far end of the room, toward a door that was jammed open by a fallen printer.

"Alright," I said. "Now, I'm no expert, but I bet when we move toward that door we're going to get hit from behind, so let's make that more complicated for them, huh? Myalis, I need a couple of resonators."

Here you go!

I caught a pair of grenades out of the air with my free hand, almost fumbling the second. Then I flicked them both on and underhanded them across the room. Soon their high-pitched keening noise filled the entire space.

"What are those?" he asked.

"They melt Antithesis," I said. "Resonant frequency shit."

"Huh," he said. "Will that affect my plants?"

I blinked. I hadn't considered that. Then again, I hadn't seen much of his plants yet.

They shouldn't. Not all of them, at least.

"Myalis says no," I said simply.

"Oh, good, I was worried that we might—" Sprout and I both flinched and turned toward the cubicles where . . . where a person was stumbling out from behind cover.

I lowered my gun. That was a human, not an alien. A man in a rumpled business suit who looked like shit warmed over. He tripped over himself as he walked our way, then his face rose and I felt a surge of adrenaline hit me. He was missing half his face.

Catherine, that person is dead.

"Ah, fuck," I said.

"Sir, are you . . . you need medical attention," Sprout said as he started forward.

I grabbed him by the shoulder and pulled him behind me, something that I wouldn't have been able to do without my armor. Then I raised my gun and fired once.

The office worker fell backward like a ragdoll, arms and legs splayed out even as a chunk of his chest flew on past him.

"What the fuck!" Sprout shouted.

"Shut up a minute," I said.

I stepped up to the corpse, then paused as it started to twitch. I looked around again, then knelt next to it. It grossed me out, but I yanked the head aside, then noticed something in the pit where his jaw was hanging loose, white muscles and cartilage exposed. It was a black, squiggly thing that I pinched and pulled out of the corpse.

The wormlike appendage snapped, but the end I held continued to wiggle.

"What the fuck?!" Sprout asked again, with more feeling this time.

"Model seven," I said. "We've got zombies."

"What do we do?" he asked.

"Shoot them," I said. There wasn't much to do otherwise. The people that were zombied up were dead already. Especially this guy. He didn't look fresh. "Now . . . where the fuck are they getting bodies from? Hey, Myalis, wouldn't model sevens be more . . . uh, susceptible to our nanomachine attack?"

They are smaller, yes. And therefore easier to eliminate. But when a hive starts producing model sevens it usually does so in large quantities.

I scowled. "Fine," I said. "Myalis, can you send Hawke outside a heads-up about this. Hell, tell Intel-chan too. We don't want to panic people, but we need folk knowing about it. Sprout, come on, show me where that hole is. Time's running short."

CHAPTER THIRTY-THREE

MINOR IMPROVEMENTS

User Milesglorius: People have tried all sorts of things to kill them already

User Adfligo: Yeah, so?

User Milesglorius: wtf, you think your idea's better?

User CuteGirlsRCute: Maybe? Not like every idea's been tried and anyway I think that it's okay to try new things. ATs have only been invading for like 20 years. Gotta try stuff yeah?

—Systema IRC, 2043

This was shit sprinkles on the turd cake. I didn't have time to deal with zombies on top of all the rest. "Myalis, what are the chances that this is a small, one-off offshoot of the Antithesis that we won't have to worry about?" I asked.

It's unlikely. Though I haven't noticed any parts of the hive specifically growing model sevens. That isn't entirely unusual. Model sevens are small and quick to grow to their full maturity. Hives will often have other models grow them wherever they find a sufficient number of corpses or usable bodies. Remember that more than a weapon, a model seven is a means of transporting biomass back to the hive.

Right, the zombies were basically the Antithesis's way of co-opting a person's body to walk it back to the hive for digestion. The fact that it was a psychological weapon probably didn't factor in. The Antithesis were scary, but it was never *purposeful* terror that they sowed.

I jumped when a call came in. The alert wasn't loud or anything, but I was a little on edge and the sound poked at my nerves. Intel-chan was calling.

"Hey," I said.

"Hey," Intel-chan replied. "We're getting everyone to take their anti-zombie pills, just in case. We don't have much manpower to check on people, but your girlfriend's working on sending people to every housing complex on the edges of Downtown, just to make sure that everyone is still entirely human."

I nodded. "That's good. Will we have enough meds to go around?"

"No," Intel-chan said. "Not nearly. But we can give some to every militia person, and most if not all of our volunteers. The pills are only meant to be good for a day or so before you need to take another dose though."

"We'll buy more if it comes to it." I looked around the office space again. Earlier it had been a big, worrisome place because it might hide a few lower-tier models. Now it was worrisome for entirely different reasons. "If the zombies are *here* inside the barricades, then . . . shit, how likely is it that they'd just spread out from here?"

Model sevens are notoriously stealthy. They aren't fast-moving, but they can reproduce within a captured body, and there are many tales of model sevens taking over a body, then walking past defenses to reproduce next to heavily populated areas.

"Right," I said. "Intel, can you add a pin to Gomorrah's agenda?"

"I can," Intel-chan said. "What do you need her for?"

"Burn this entire building down. In a way that *doesn't* spread to the rest of the city. I'm sure she can accommodate that much. I don't know how heat-resistant model sevens are, but I'm sure they won't survive the kind of shit Gomorrah can unleash when she has permission."

"Understood. Sending a message now," Intel-chan said.

"And, uh, hey, where's all your weebness?"

Intel-chan went quiet for a moment, then when they replied it was with a much more perky, upbeat sort of voice. Almost gratingly so. "Oh? Stray Cat Sempai wants me to talk like this?"

I squinted.

Intel-chan waited for a long, long beat. Then they spoke up. "Uwu?"

"I hate you," I said.

"Pardon?" Sprout asked. He looked like he'd calmed down a little, though I noted that he wasn't looking at the corpse on the ground next to us.

"Sorry," I muttered. "Just talking to a few people at once. The militia will start taking their anti-zombie meds, we'll see about everyone else once we're out of here."

"Are we leaving?" he asked, and I couldn't miss that hint of hope in his voice.

I didn't want to squash it, but there was a lot of stuff I didn't want and I didn't get. "No, we're finishing what we started. Do you have something to stop model sevens?" I asked.

He shook his head.

"Myalis, two of those Proofing Pill things, please," I said.

Coming right up.

The pills appeared in a pair of little cigarette-box-sized containers. I tossed one to Sprout and opened the other, then I undid part of my helmet to dry swallow one of the pills. It wasn't exactly tasty, but I'd live with it. Honestly, I was probably safe. A model seven would have to get through my armor first, which I doubted they could do. But Sprout wasn't wearing gear that was as good as mine yet.

Besides, it was better to be safe than sorry when it came to zombification.

Once Sprout took his pill, then stuffed the rest into a pocket on his vest, I tapped him on the shoulder and gestured deeper into the office space. "Let's go," I said.

The staircase's door was wedged open, so I approached it ready to have something jump at my face. Nothing did, though the stairwell was unlit and windowless, so it was filled with long shadows that we only made worse as we stood by the entrance.

That, and there were potted plants scattered across the ground.

Just three or four different sorts of plants on what looked like those common brownish-beige ceramic pots that I'd sometimes seen in groceries with, like, a dying sprig of basil or something in it.

These weren't any common spices though. One of the plants had spread roots out across the ground and another was covered in little ball-like flowers with what looked like sacs under them.

"Those are mine," Sprout said. "Spreading Creeper, Acid Bells, and Thorn Thistle." He pointed to the plants in turn.

"You dropped them here?" I asked.

"On the way back up," he said.

"What was your plan, exactly?"

He shrugged, a little sheepish. "Get to the entrance, plant these down. They're all hyper-invasive and can grow quickly."

"Like, quickly for a plant, or actually quickly?" I asked.

"They mostly take a few hours to grow. The thorn thistle would be large enough to block a doorway in under six hours."

"And that would stop the Antithesis from breaking in here?" I asked.

He squirmed a little. "It would make it harder for them. None of my plants break down into usable biofuel for the Antithesis. Some are the opposite, even, with chemical packs hidden within them that can destroy the digestion baths the Antithesis uses to dissolve organic matter into the nutrient slurry they use."

"That seems decent for area denial, I guess. Fuck with their food supply, make the area inhospitable to them. But, ah, I'm not sure if it's ideal for plugging a passage."

"They dug the passage, I figured it wouldn't matter if I plug it since they could just dig out another. And . . . well, you sent me here, and this is the best I could do." He gestured futilely at the pile of discarded plants on the floor.

Kinda felt bad for the guy.

"Shit," I said. "Look, this is my bad. I should have figured out what you're good for before sending you over here. Could have used your area denial stuff around River Heights, or on the borders."

"I've planted some things there," he said. "A lot of my plants are good for blocking alleys, and some I got to plant outside of the walls. Hopefully they'll bring those back to their hives. Ah, some plants have trackers in them too, and pheromones that make them really attractive to the Antithesis. Or some of them. Most don't have . . . noses."

"Do you make any points with that kind of thing?" I asked.

He glanced away. "I haven't figured out that part yet. I do make *some* but my AI explained that since it's at such a remove I don't make many. But a lot of my plants can multiply. So once I get a proper set up going, it'll basically be free to keep going. I . . . my goal is to create some semi-invasive species, or buy them at least, and then plant them around areas with Antithesis hives to kill them off without ever putting someone at risk."

"Didn't they do that in Australia?"

"Yes," he said. "And they made it worse. But I think . . . I think I can do it better."

I gave him a pat on the shoulder. Guy was aiming a lot higher than I was. Had to respect that.

He was still useless in a fight though, which became obvious when a model three scrambled up the stairs and Sprout stumbled backward and out of the stairwell.

I rolled my eyes, then shot the alien. Then shot a second time to actually hit it.

We all had something to work on, it seemed, and I couldn't fling stones from my glass house just yet.

CHAPTER THIRTY-FOUR

KNIFE'S EDGE

The profit balance is a knife's edge where you need to be able to deliver a product of a certain quality while paying the smallest amount possible. That means avoiding normal contractors and instead finding people who actually care enough about your product that they'll work harder, longer, and better for less.

Once you've found these people, you need to exploit them for all they're worth.

—*The Employer's Guide to Employees*, sixth edition, 2050

The hole in the basement was hard to miss. The wall was all cinderblock, and the aliens had punched through it, sending chunks of the cement blocks scattering across the floor, as well as ripping up a few of the novelty motivational posters stuck to the wall.

"'Hang in there.'" I read from a poster next to the alien-filled pit. "Yeah, alright."

The nice thing about having all the aliens coming through a single hole small enough that I would have to bend over double to fit through was that even my shit aim was good enough to wipe them out in droves.

My Laser Pointer clicked empty, and I stepped to the side, then gestured into the hole. "Hey, shoot anything that moves in there, would you?" I asked Sprout. "I'm gonna figure out how to plug this thing in the meantime."

"Ah, sure," he said. Dropping to one knee, he aimed into the hole, then fired. He wasn't going all-out like I did, but instead taking careful, aimed shots.

Well, whatever. "Hey, Myalis, we've got options here?"

We do! Also, did you want to split the points that Vanguard Sprout is earning right now? He is using your equipment.

"Huh? Nah, let him take all the points he's earning. He'll need them." The 55-55 split was nice and all, but 100 was bigger than 55 last I checked, and Sprout was behind in points earned. I was fine with losing out on some change if it meant getting him up to speed a little. "Now, the hole?"

Same as last time? Resonators and a foam plug for the exit?

"Yeah, I guess." The Antithesis coming out of here were chewed up by our nanomachines, so it wasn't all bad to block the hole and let them wait. "Call it a permanent temporary solution, then," I said.

Gomorrah was probably going to burn the entire building down anyway, so it wasn't that big a deal. The only concern was having model sevens spawning within the city and spreading outward.

But as insidious and nasty as a zombie threat was, the threat of being flooded over was bigger and more worrisome still. Or maybe I was just biased.

I waited until Sprout clicked empty, then I flung in some grenades, tossing them as deep into the hole as I could. Most were resonators, but I made sure to include a single, more traditional concussive grenade in the lot.

Sprout squawked as a wash of dust and hot air blasted out of the hole, and I laughed as I dropped a last resonator right next to the entrance then set off a foam bomb that immediately started to expand. "Come on. Myalis can reload your gun automatically for you. As long as you're spending rounds killing shit for us I don't mind footing that bill."

"Uh, thanks?" he said.

I patted him on the shoulder, then gestured to the stairs. "Let's get going. There will be other disasters to figure out by now, I bet."

"Okay?"

It didn't take long until we were stepping out of the office building and into . . . huh, the sun was further along than I'd thought. Time was passing us by, and so far, no *big* disasters. Maybe the plan with the nanomachines had worked out better than I'd hoped?

Then I got a call from Manic. "Hello?" I asked.

"What the fuck is going on at River Heights?" she opened with.

"What do you mean?" I asked as I glanced around. The militia guys were keeping some distance from the office space. Probably worried about zombie worms. "I was taking care of something else, what's going on?"

"Fuckloads of smoke," she said. "I'm not heading over there. There's plenty of shit to kill here, but you might want to keep an eye on it, oh fearless leader."

"I'm gonna hope that it's Gomorrah's fault, somehow," I said.

"Nah, the nun's in the other direction. Lots of smoke that way too, but it's mostly coming from outside of the barricades. I moved past there. That bitch has entire streets covered in fire, you know?"

"Yeah, she does that."

"Wild."

I nodded, unable to disagree. But hey, Gomorrah's tactics worked, so it wasn't that big a deal, was it? "I'll check out River Heights. You sit pretty."

"Always. You know, there's a pattern to this. They come in, I blast them back, then they come back twenty minutes later, but there's more of them."

"We can't have pushed back that many waves," I said.

"Three's enough for a pattern when you're looking for one," Manic said. "There's a music to this, and I think the alien fucks are about to start rocking out hard."

I had no idea what that meant, but I figured it wasn't a good thing. "I'll come back to you in a minute or two. Need to figure out what's going on in River Heights."

"Let them burn," she said before cutting the line.

I sighed. "Sprout, can you make your way back to near the front lines? Plant more of your stuff where you think it'll be useful. We might have a fight on our hands soon."

"I can do that," he said with a nod.

"Cool." I dismissed him and opened a channel to Intel-chan. "What's going on in River Heights?" I asked.

"Oh, hi!" Intel-chan said. "Not much. Miss Baker said that they'll be ready to evacuate fully by tomorrow morning."

"T-tomorrow *morning*?" I repeated. "They won't be alive by then. What's with all the smoke?"

"First defensive line broke, so the militia in the area backed up to the second. Part of normal procedure is to burn everything behind them as they move. It means less biomass for the aliens and nothing for scavengers to steal once the milita's not there."

And all of that didn't matter because the people they were defending weren't moving. "One sec, I'm getting Baker on the line," I growled.

The call rang five times, each note pushing my mood lower and lower until I was pacing anxiously across the front of the office. Some of the militia who'd stayed behind were eyeing me strangely.

"Hello?" Miss Baker said.

"Why the fuck haven't people evacuated from River Heights yet?" I asked.

"We've planned the evacuation for tomorrow morning, when it'll be most conve—"

"I'm going to bomb the entire area in an hour. If your rich fucks don't want to eat high explosive shells for dinner then tell them to get their pampered asses the fuck out of there posthaste because I've got no fucks to give but plenty of munitions to make up for it."

Then I cut her off.

"*Sugoi*," Intel-chan said. "Scary."

"Think they'll actually start moving their asses?" I asked.

"*El-Em-Ay-Oh*," Intel-chan said. "No way. They'll call your bluff for sure. You might be a bad bitch, neco-mmander, but everyone knows you wouldn't actually blow up civilians for fun."

I grit my teeth. "Fuck." At what point could I wash my hands and just let people die from their own stupidity? Where was the cutoff between having done enough and not doing enough?

I needed a manual on how to handle this shit. Not that I'd actually read it. "Myalis, give me your best estimates of what's going to go down in the next hour."

From the looks of it, Manic might be correct. The expected flood of Antithesis never occurred. So a lot of the biomass within the hive is still within the hive. And while the nanomachines will continue to rip them apart, there are ways that they might be able to counteract some of that pressure. Notably by sending out injured units to die while holding back fresher ones.

"Okay," I said. "Smart, I guess."

Unusually so, yes. You can either expect this back and forth to continue for some time as the hive purges itself of nanomachines, or the hive might correctly identify the local human area as the source of the threat and destroy it.

"Ah," I said. "So we're fucked."

I'm sure you'll manage! I have faith that you'll muddle through somehow, and that the muddling will be immensely entertaining for me.

"You're awful," I said. But she wasn't wrong. I didn't have time to give in to any sort of anxiety, not when I could be *doing* something. "Come on, let's get back to the front lines. I want to be there when the shit hits the fan."

Let's go, then.

And with that, I jumped back behind that shitty pickup that I guess had become my unofficial ride through this shitty city.

CHAPTER THIRTY-FIVE

WHEN BUSINESS TAKES CARE OF ITSELF

Tube-births are becoming more popular and an ever increasing number of higher-income families insist on having children both without natural birth (which might harm the would-be mother and prevent her from working for a period) and with pre-checked and modded genes (which ensure that the child will be born without defects and in perfect health).

This has the predictable side effect of creating an as-of-yet small generation of so-called "perfect" babies who are growing up to be perfect children.

Unfortunately, no one has discovered an anti-elitism gene yet.

—Crispy Babies Done Well: A Criticism of Capitalist Babymaking,
first edition, 2051

The shit and the fan were on a collision course by the time I arrived in the outer part of Downtown where our defenses were set up.

I knew that long before we arrived though, because even while riding on the back of the pickup I could feel the ground trembling. Intel-chan popped up with an update.

"So," the avatar said. "Bit of a kerfuffle."

"Go on," I said.

"A couple of buildings have just collapsed near the front. None of them are right next to our defensive line, but some aren't too far off from that."

Frowning, I brought up Myalis's map of the city and took note of where those buildings had collapsed. That was about a block away from the outer edges of our defenses, three buildings all very close to each other. Notably though, when I opened the overlay with the location of the hive, none of the three were over it.

Catherine, I suspect that these buildings collapsed because of movement underground. Seeing as how the hive tunnels we've explored don't travel beneath them, it's entirely possible that we're dealing with either a separate hive, or an entire section that our cursory explorations failed to discover.

"Fantastic," I said. This day couldn't be over soon enough.

The pickup screeched to a stop as we turned onto a busy street. There were militia people all over the place and . . . lots of folks in the suits I'd bought running around and setting things up in a hurry. New barricades were being set up, large cement blockades were being pulled off the back of trucks by people with forklifts and construction exo-suits. Tents were being set up and the old defenses looked like they were moving back.

For a moment I wondered why they were going through all that trouble when we had a sort of wall already, but then I figured it out. They were creating a killbox. A hole was being dug out in the wall, and any aliens that poured through that tight little space would be gunned down by concentrated fire.

Smart, I supposed. It felt like the kind of thing that should have been set up several days ago instead of the half-measure walls we had.

I wondered where they got the cement half walls until I saw "*Property of . . .*" stencilled on the side of one of them. They were from a nearby parking garage.

I walked along the edge, largely ignored except for a few glances my way and the occasional nod. What struck me as the strangest in all of this was the way people moved.

They were pushing themselves, sweating and hurried, but also methodical and quiet. No one was complaining, no one was joking or being funny, no one was moving at contractor speeds. It was all quick, cold efficiency, which I might have expected to see in a soldier or maybe the best the militia had, but these were the volunteers that I'd left with Lucy.

Or . . . maybe that explained it.

"Is this the closest part of the front to where we expect them to come?" I asked.

It is. If they come, they'll probably pass right through here.

"What's the status of our nanobots?" I asked. "They making a difference at all?"

They are. The main hive we've discovered is essentially falling apart. It is no longer able to produce new models and the nanomachines have started to dissolve large parts of the main hive structure. All in all, the plan was mostly a success, though the hives will have to be cleared more thoroughly. The nanomachines won't function forever, and once they run out of power it's possible that parts of the hive that were cut off and that lay dormant will reawaken and spread once more.

"Right, and then the tunnels will be dug already, so we'll be in even more of a mess," I said.

It was nice to hear that at least part of the plan was working. But still, there remained a big question, one that came to light as people on the wall started screaming and running back toward the new second line of defense.

I brought my gun up and was ready to charge in to help, but I stayed back for the moment and watched as the militia and Lucy's little army quickly got ready and then opened fire almost at the same time.

Criss-crossing lines of fire ripped apart the dozen or so model threes leading the charge, then they focused on the next aliens to come through the gap. The initial surge of gunfire died down as what I presumed were sergeants told their men to hold off. They didn't need to hit every alien fifty times to take them out.

"Huh," I said.

What's wrong?

"Well, I kind of expected to have to jump in and save the day there, but it looks like they've mostly got things handled."

Oh, don't worry. Plenty of things are going wrong. I'm sure there's room for you to be a hero.

And just after she said that, I got a call from Lucy.

"Hey," I said as I answered. I was keeping an eye on that little passage the aliens were squeezing through, but so far things looked alright.

"Hi!" Lucy said, upbeat and chipper and a little stressed. Even with that hint of stress though, I found my shoulders loosening at hearing her voice. "So, you know those zombie aliens you sent a warning about?"

"Yes?" I asked.

"Bit of a problem with those," she continued. "We've got, ah, a horde?"

"A horde?"

"Of zombies."

"A zombie horde," I repeated.

She sighed. "Yes, Cat, a zombie horde. They're like, crawling out of this parking garage place. I sent Tabby Squad down there to steal some of those barrier things for the front, and it turns out that a lot of people have died recently and the morgues are all outside of downtown, or something. I guess those that are closer are full-up? Whatever, the point is, they started storing corpses in this place and sealed it off, but now they're zombies."

"Okay," I said. "Where is it, I can pop over and . . ."

"No, no," she said, and I could imagine her head shaking. "The Kittens will take care of it."

"The *kittens*?" I asked.

"Not our kittens. Capital-K Kittens. That's what everyone's calling my army." Lucy said. "Anyway, I just need better gear for them. Can we get like, biological protection stuff? Maybe flamethrowers?"

"Uh," I said. "You want more gear?"

"Look, the gear you got's cute and all, but it's kind of generalist, and we don't have enough to outfit even a tenth of the people we have."

I blinked. "Not even a tenth?" I asked.

"I've been recruiting," she said.

"How? *Where?*"

"I got on the radio, and on TV," she said, the smugness unmistakable. "Do you have any idea how many people are bored out of their minds and also worried they'll die at any moment? That's a lot of pent up energy to harness, Cat. It's like when the kittens at home saw someone get adopted and then they all got a little manic. But instead of adoption it's death by aliens and . . . actually, that doesn't make sense, never mind."

"You're running ads?" I asked.

She giggled. "Yeah! Turns out some of the people who volunteered first and who were doing the more administrative stuff know people who know people. It's nothing special. Just me talking to someone filming from their aug."

"Still," I said. Though, to be fair, if Lucy asked me to join an army I'd have a hard time saying no . . . "Okay, well, where are you, I'll stop over and drop off those suits you want."

"You could give them to someone where you are and I'll have them driven back."

"Yeah, no, it's fine, I'll do it myself," I said.

I bet Lucy was surrounded by able-bodied young men and women, and I didn't need any of them getting ideas. Not that I'd ever put the security of an entire city at risk just to kiss my girlfriend and ward off anyone eyeing her up. That would be petty and stupid.

"Give me ten minutes and I'll be with you," I said.

"Alright. I'm still at the mall. We took over a few shops since no one was using them. Do you think you could get us more normal gear too? We need better communication stuff, the militia's being a bit of a pain about letting us know what's going on."

"They're being unhelpful?"

"Eh, not quite, they're busy and I think informing us of what's going on is like ten steps down on their list of priorities. I'm not getting the sense that they're being pricks on purpose."

"Ah, okay," I said. "Well, maybe you'd like to meet my new friend. They're cringey as hell, but helpful enough . . ."

CHAPTER THIRTY-SIX

CATMODORE LUCY

A Vanguard's equipment purchasing choices need to take into account the possibility of returns on investment.

Equipment destined for civilian use that costs hundreds of points to purchase but which only generates a few points in return—or perhaps none—means a net loss for that Vanguard.

Nonetheless, some choose to outfit others, even if it means a smaller return, because it ensures the safety of those people, regardless of potential losses.

—Vanguard AI Syacus, 2026

I returned to the mall to find it a hive of busy activity. Lucy's Kittens were out by the entrance, or a few of them were, at least. They stood out with their cat-eared uniforms. They were keeping an eye on things where the militia seemed to be missing.

I slid past them and into the main corridor of the mall to find it a somewhat changed place. People were lining up to one side where a booth had been set up that was handing people pills in those little paper cups with the nineties-print designs on the sides.

Anti-zombie pills? That would make sense. The place handing them out was being guarded by a couple of Lucy's Kittens in full kit. I wondered why they were going so slow until I noticed that the person handing out the meds was handing them out from a single little crate, and it looked like it was all they had.

Shit, was this whole thing a way to keep the folk in line calm? Give people the impression that there were enough meds to go around? That . . . would actually track. Lucy and I had done similar before. Handing out all of the food we had, then pretending we had more for the next day and the one after while silently hoping that we'd get more before the kids found out.

Things weren't looking so good then, on that front.

Otherwise though, the mall seemed like an industrious place. People were sweeping the floors, setting up tents indoors, and I idly noted that nearly everyone was up to *something*. Busywork, maybe, but it would keep them out of trouble and feeling like they were contributing at least a little.

I found the one leading this orchestra on the second floor, in a more open store where people could see her giving out orders and instructing people and receiving reports.

Lucy had found a rather nice coat somewhere, with pips around the sleeves and big squared-off shoulders. She was wearing it like a cape, almost, arms out of the sleeves. And atop her head she had a cap similar to the ones the militia officers wore, but with a pair of fuzzy cat ears sticking out of the sides.

Did it look silly? Yes. Did it look kind of hot as well? Also yes.

"Hey," I said as I uninvisibled myself while leaning on one of the nearby tables.

A few people jumped, and I was happy to see hands fly toward guns to keep Lucy safe, but her squealed "Cat!" put everyone at ease.

Then I had to grab onto the table as Lucy hugged me, her weight and mine making the table groan. "Whoa, hey," I said as I patted her back. "Nice to see you too."

"I hate the position you put me in," she said with a smile that suggested otherwise. "We have seventeen injured so far. And those uniforms of yours don't clean up nice. It's not ideal to hand off new soldiers' uniforms still covered in blood, you know. Myalis, if you're listening, take note of that one."

Noted.

"But things are holding together?" I asked.

"So far," she said. "We have something of a training system going on in the parking garage. It's . . . about the best we can do when the entire training regime lasts just under an hour, but it should prevent people from shooting their own toes off."

"The guns are smart, they should probably stop that from happening anyway."

She snorted. "A smart weapon's intelligence pitted against the average person's stupidity? I'll be betting on the stupid, thank you very much."

I grinned. "That's fair, actually."

"I'm fair in everything but skin," she replied. "Now, I need your help."

"Alright, you seem to be keeping this city together better than I have."

She snorted and waved my comment off. "None of that. You're making people *do* stuff, which I think is half the solution sometimes. People know you're acting and they've seen you all over the place. It gives them hope, I think."

"Yeah, hope's nice and all, but it doesn't kill aliens well."

She shrugged. "It'll keep people fighting, and fighting people *do* kill aliens pretty well sometimes. Don't knock it. Now, we can pep talk later. I need more of those standard suits, I need something biohazard-proof for dealing with corpses and zombies, and I need meds. Not just anti-zombie meds—though we need those—we need normal stuff too."

I nodded along slowly. "Alright, I . . . give me a sec. Myalis, what's my point total looking like?"

Current Point Total: 62,346

Huh. Lower than I'd want, but higher than I expected. I had killed a few aliens here and there, and I supposed that even with a few degrees of separation I was earning a point or two from every kill the Kittens did.

"Alright," I said. "Can we get more of those suits? The same as before . . . with the, uh, easier cleaning methods? Same package, basically. Lucy, any trouble with any other part of the kit?"

"Maybe make the chest armor a tiny bit bigger? It's one-size-fits-all, and it's easy to adjust, but at the same time we've got a lot of volunteers who've never seen a treadmill before, if you know what I mean."

I nodded. That made sense.

I can accommodate that, yes. Nearly the same price as last time. Ninety-five points per set.

I chewed on my lower lip as I did some mental math. "Let's get a hundred of those," I said.

"We need more than that," Lucy replied.

I crossed my arms. "Sure, but I can only afford so many. And I want to get you guys more crew-served weapons, the medicine, the hazmat suits . . ."

"Alright, fine," Lucy said. "Come on, I made sure to leave some tables cleared up in the hallway for just this kind of thing. We'll give the suits to our best. And . . . maybe we'll hit up an armory for some extras."

"An armory?" I asked.

She smiled. "There's a couple across the city. They're filled up with old samurai-tech weapons. Meant for exactly this kind of scenario. But they're locked up tight, to make sure not just anyone gets to the guns. Which is shit because right now we need them."

"That does seem annoying," I said. I shook my head. "Anyway, other stuff first. Any ideas of those hazmat suits, Myalis?"

Fully sealed environmental suits, with some degree of customization when it comes to size. A simple rebreather mechanism and an air filtration unit, as well as . . . if I understood it correctly, flamethrowers? I'm afraid you don't have a catalog for those.

I frowned. I didn't. I could get one for probably pretty cheap, but Myalis hadn't mentioned that. Which meant she probably wanted me thinking about it the way I was just now . . . "How long has Gomorrah been out there without a break?" I asked.

Four and a half hours, according to Atyacus.

"Uh-huh," I said. That was probably longer than a soldier was supposed to spend in an active fight. Samurai she might be, she'd still get tired. I opened a chat window and sent her a message. "Gom, we need you at the mall. Equipping civilians with flamethrowers and could use your help. Come over and eat too. Working break."

My comms spat on and I jumped as a voice blared into my ears. "Cat, where the fuck are you?"

That was Gomorrah, nice, proper-Christian-girl Gomorrah who didn't usually swear. Which meant that things were probably not going so well.

"I'm here, what's up?" I asked.

"I've been running around lighting aliens on fire for the last hour and every time I turn around there's more of them. I don't know if I'm going to get swarmed here, but if I don't start getting help soon, I'm going to lose it."

"Okay, right, I'm on my way. Can you hang on for ten minutes?"

"Yes," she snapped. "I can hold on for ten minutes. I swear, if you spent the last hour goofing around I'm going to rethink all the nice thoughts I had about you."

"Right, right, I'm coming. And I wasn't goofing around, I was arming the people and getting things set up back here."

"Uh-huh." The line went dead, and I sighed.

There, that would prevent her from . . . heh, burning out.

"Alright. Let's get the hazmat suits, and let Gom figure out the flamethrower part of it."

These suits alone will cost seventy-two points each.

"I think fifty should do?" I asked with a look to Lucy.

She was quick to nod. "More than enough, really. We don't have that many people with training in handling dangerous biohazard stuff, and some of the people we do have had their own equipment already. I just wanted a team or two I could send out from here to take care of things."

"Right, perfect. Now, the medication. We're going to want something like a full-body healing med, a first-aid kit for simpler stuff, and like, an industrial crate of anti-zombie medication."

Myalis summoned up the two sets of equipment for me. On one side the suits in their familiar plastic cases, and on the other the hazmat suits. Lucy opened one of those cases up and pulled out the top of a folded, rubbery-looking outfit done up in beige and blacks with some highlighter-pink bits. It had a big glass half dome at the front to see through . . . with two cat-ear protrusions on top that looked like they held forward-facing flashlights.

The medication shouldn't be too expensive. Packs of ten pills for Model Seven prophylactic treatment are only one point each, and I can get standardized first-aid kits for ten points apiece. The more advanced medical kits will cost a little more.

"Well, let's do it then," I said.

A few minutes later, Lucy was cracking the whip and people were stocking up on supplies to carry all across the city.

Current Point Total: 46,546

CHAPTER THIRTY-SEVEN

A GENIUS IDEA

There are several curated, quick, and even inexpensive services willing to teach a budding or even experienced samurai how to handle public-facing tasks.

We strongly encourage any samurai that wants to have any amount of time in the spotlight to take one or more of these classes. The lessons might seem like common sense for the most part, but they are nonetheless invaluable.

You don't want to have the public turn on you because of mismanaged PR.

—Family Head of PR John J. J. Johnson, 2051

I could have very easily spent the rest of the afternoon trailing after Lucy and scaring people into doing what she said. In fact, I'd done that before and it was always very enjoyable.

I don't know what it said about me as a person, but something about seeing Lucy go full girlboss on people, unleashing her barbed tongue then snapping around to being the sweetest, most angelic person in the world faster than anyone could blink really *did* it for me.

Unfortunately, all good things had to come to a crashing explosion of an end.

Lucy waved the people she was talking to off, and they took the hint, leaving before Lucy had to really ask. She turned toward me, and her head tilted to the side a little. "You okay?"

"Yeah, need to run though," I said. "Gomorrah needs me, and as much as I'd love to just sit here . . . well, I can't."

"Oh, that's alright," she said. "I think I've got things handled here. The extra suits and gear will come in handy. I'll try to stay on top of things, so if you can keep the aliens off our asses, then we'll probably be fine."

I nodded, then slid my helmet off, wrapped an arm around Lucy's waist, and pulled her in close.

Myalis brought up a handy countdown showing me that I had under five minutes left to get to Gomorrah while keeping my word, so I reluctantly broke the kiss. "Okay," I said once I caught my breath. "We'll continue that later?"

"Oh, you can bet on it," Lucy purred.

I grinned, then pecked her on the cheek before backing up and tugging my helmet back on. "Stay safe, alright?"

"I'm supposed to say that to you," she said. "Go on, go save the day. I'll be back here making sure there's people to appreciate the saving once you're done." She winked at me, and I ran off with a bit of pep in my step.

Surprisingly, the militia technical was still waiting for me by the front of the mall. It seemed as if the driver had decided that chauffeur duties were either more fun or safer than whatever his actual job was meant to be. "Hey, get me to . . . uh . . ." I checked our map, spotted Gomorrah's tag, then rattled off the name of the nearest intersection before leaping up onto the back of the pickup.

The world outside of our walls was on fire.

The technical slowed to a stop, mostly because a row of firefighting trucks was stationed on the edge of the street, hoses rolled way out toward the wall where guys in heavy flame-retardant gear and exo-suits were spraying the inner side of the wall with water.

That seemed enough, for now, to stop the flames from crawling over the barricades and toward the people on our side. As I watched, an alien—a model three—made it over the wall and tumbled down the other side, skin peeling and fur aflame. One of the firefighters turned their hose on the alien, dousing it before a militiaman put a round into its head.

I tapped my comms back on as I jumped down from the back of the truck. "Gomorrah, why is everything on fire?"

"Because the aliens haven't figured out how to flameproof themselves yet, and until they do, this is the most effective way of keeping them away."

"Yes, but humans are also not fireproof," I pointed out.

"There's people keeping the fire contained. I fail to see how that's my issue."

I had never really liked alcohol, or rather, I could never afford it enough to grow a liking for it, but at that moment I was really tempted to pick up a bad habit.

She was a little terse, maybe she really did need a break. "Okay, Gom, come back on this side of the wall. Get something to eat, go take a shit or whatever, take twenty, yeah?"

Gomorrah chuckled. "Crude, aren't you?"

"Always," I said. "I'll take care of the wall for now. Once you're done with your break, mind heading over to River Heights?"

I saw someone climb over the wall, then drop down on our side. Gomorrah, in her all-black outfit. Steam wafted off of her and drew little swirls in the air as she started to walk over. The folks guarding the wall gave her a wide berth.

I walked over to meet her, then stopped when I was a meter off. My suit was fireproof, obviously, because I worked with Gomorrah enough that not having that would be stupid, but the fancy little sensors in my suit still let me feel the warmth coming off of my favorite nun.

"You're extra hot today, huh? Don't let Franny see you that way."

"Are you going to say something about how she'll become so wet she'll douse my fire?" she asked, voice flat.

"Well . . . no, I hadn't thought of that, actually." I laughed. "And you said *I* was crude?"

"Shut up, Cat," she said. "So, River Heights. Are you evacuating that spot?"

"I ordered it. But I bet some of them aren't going to listen. Ever want to torch a McMansion before?"

". . . now that you mention it, yes, I do want to do that."

I clapped. "Fantastic! Now's your chance."

She patted me on the shoulder then walked on past. "I'm going to take my me-mandated break."

"Oh! While you're at it, the folks at the mall need mini-flamethrowers to take care of the zombie problem."

Gomorrah paused, then shrugged. "Alright. I can do that."

I watched her head out, then worked my shoulders loose. Without Gomorrah to feed the flames, literally, I imagined that our firewall wasn't going to last forever. I opened up our map of Burlington. "Myalis, where are the other samurai at?"

Sprout is patrolling the eastern cordon. I suspect he's trying to gain points where the action is lightest. Arm-a-Geddon is still in River Heights. Manic is to your north, outside the wall's perimeter.

I nodded along.

The Family has sent you a message. You have reinforcements en route.

"Oh, thank fuck," I said before searching for the message in question and opening it.

>>>Stray Cat

We appreciate the reports. Your request for undersea specialist samurai has been added to the queue. Expect arrival of an expert within the next three days.

Your reinforcement request has been expedited. A battalion of Tier-2 prepped PMCs are on their way to Burlington. ETA, 2 days, 16 hours.

Thank you.

I blinked. "Two *days*."

How in the hells was I supposed to hold this place together for two days? And how many people was a battalion anyway?

I bet it wasn't nearly as many people as I'd need.

The specialist only arriving in three days surprised me a little less. I bet there weren't many of those. What kind of idiot would want a job where they had to get submerged?

I shook my head, picked up my gun from its sling, then watched the wall. I supposed I wouldn't have a choice now. If we had to hold, then we had to hold. We could set up rotations, get more of Lucy's people on the front line, maybe install more mortars and better defenses and just hang on tight.

I didn't like relying on people that weren't here yet, but what choice did I have? It wasn't like I could charge out to the nearest nest and fuck it up.

My eyes narrowed.

Wait . . . I could literally just do that.

FIRE AND HAMMER

Crowds were the weapon of choice in the early 2020s, and for a while they continued to be so.

Most governments were worried about firing into crowds of protestors. Certainly, it had worked at one time, but usually the strategy turned against them. Those that died were martyred and it showed the ruthlessness of the government.

As social media progressed and became an ever-bigger part of humanity, the same governments grew increasingly worried that violent action could be turned against them. After all, politicians sleep in very flammable homes, just like the rest of us.

But then some figured that it really didn't matter as long as you controlled the narrative, and by the end of the 2020s, the average response to a crowd of dissidents was lead and gas and prisons from which they'd never leave."

—*A History of Protest*, second edition, 2036

I wasn't going to be stupid about this.

Well, not *too* stupid. Charging out of some perfectly safe walls to go mess up an Antithesis hive basically solo wasn't the epitome of intelligent choices.

Gomorrah's little fire, which was still raging on just outside of the walls, was more or less under control, and had probably worked wonders for stalling the Antithesis. They were stupid too, but not so stupid as to just jump into a fire for fun.

So, if I was going to go out there . . . that would mean that I wasn't in the city if something went . . . *when* something went pear-shaped.

Actually, that sounded like a pro, not a con. "Myalis, I need to get in touch with a couple of folk. Can you link me up to Intel-chan and Manic?"

Certainly. Dialing now.

Intel-chan picked up on the call within a half second, and Manic wasn't too far behind.

"What do you want, Stray?" Manic asked.

"*Ohio!*"

I grinned. "Hey, we've got some good news. Reinforcements are coming."

"Less points for me," Manic grumbled right away.

"In two days," I continued. "So between now and then, we're all on our own."

"That's not ideal," Intel-chan said. "I bet we're not getting much help either."

"Right on the money. I don't know exactly how much help they're sending, but I'll bet my left tit it isn't enough. So I figured if no one's going to help us, we can only help ourselves. I'll be setting down some additional defensive shit down here. Gun emplacements, mortars, that kind of thing. Intel, can you get the militia to set them up where they'll be the most useful?"

"Can do! You're not going to give them to the Kittens?"

I shook my head. "Nah. These are bigger guns, the militia has more training to use them, and I don't want to make it look like I'm playing favorites, even if I am. Just make sure they're not abusing the privilege, because I can and will take their toys away and give them to people who'll actually use them."

"That seems fair," Intel-chan said. "Honestly, the boys will just be happy to have cool samurai tech to play with. It'll boost their mood."

"Right, that's cool. I'm also thinking of giving the militia some meds. Things that'll keep them wide awake for a nice long while. I think I can buy that kind of thing for cheap. It might keep everyone on their feet until the reinforcements arrive."

"This is all nice and shit, but why am I on this call?" Manic asked.

"Because while the nice militia folk keep the city cozy and safe for us, we'll be heading out to exterminate some hives. I don't mind doing it solo, but having two makes it all a lot safer, and it's not like there's a lack of shit to kill."

Manic took a moment to respond, and I had the impression she was chewing over the decision. "Why not take one of the others?"

"Gomorrah needs a break. Arm-a-Geddon is helping in River Heights. Sprout's not equipped for this kind of thing," I said. "And . . . well, what are you doing?"

"Just killing any of the little shits I'm running into. Wouldn't mind going for something a little bigger myself."

"Cool. Stick around where you are, I'll be with you in like, half an hour. Intel-chan, you still there? Yeah? Okay, tell the militia that I'll be dumping some tools here before heading out."

"Okay!" Intel-chan said.

I moved off to one side, where I had a bit of space to work with, then I started buying stuff.

It wasn't anything too complicated, and mostly Myalis picked things out for me that had a nice correlation between usability and cheapness. I didn't pay too much attention, honestly. Sure, the gear was cool. The machine guns were water-cooled and fired bullets the thickness of my thumb, and the mortars had little screens attached to them tied to a GPS system and they could self-adjust to aim more precisely, but those were all secondary details.

I was spending more brainpower wondering how we'd hit the hives on the other side of the wall than I did worrying about the cost.

Strange how once I had been a lot more cautious about wasting even a single point when I didn't need to. Maybe I'd start spending points on myself too one day. It still *felt* wrong to just . . . waste points. Hell, it felt wrong to use them at all. Money was for keeping, pennies were meant to be pinched and only used when you didn't have a choice. At least, that's how things worked before.

But now? I guess I was growing used to having in abundance. Spending a heap of points wasn't necessarily a bad thing. Nothing would explode if I wasn't careful with each and every purchase.

In the end, I bought ten machine guns and five mortars, along with enough ammunition to keep them all going for a good long while. They'd supplement the defenses the militia had already set down.

I decided to let someone else figure out where to place them. A few trucks rolled in, and I nodded to the militia folk jumping out to check on the gear and pack it up. The last thing I added to the pile was a small case of medication. They were all tablets with an unholy mix of caffeine and other drugs that would keep someone wired and awake for days on end. It'd probably shave a few months off their life too, but it was better than dying right away, I figured.

The fires were still spreading when I crossed the front lines and reached the part nearest to Manic. The noisy samurai was past the wall, holding in place about two blocks down. When I crossed over the wall and started walking, I quickly found the route she'd passed through.

Her sound-based gun had a particular impact when it struck, and it was easy to tell where she'd passed from all the shattered glass and the particular way the dust covering the roads had moved in great rippling semicircles.

"Hey!" Manic called out to me as I came around a corner. She was sitting atop the wreck of an abandoned car, one arm raised in greeting. The area around her was filled with shredded Antithesis remains. "You showed up."

"Yeah," I said. "Been getting lots of visitors?"

"A few. They don't like my taste in noise," she said with a dangerous grin. "Bit too metal for their tastes."

I laughed. "They don't like my toys either. Strange how picky these aliens are, huh?"

"I'm sure your toys aren't to most people's taste," Manic said.

That . . . actually hit close to home. Mr. Tentacles was a fine gentleman, but I imagined that he was probably a bit much for the average person.

"So, what's the plan?" Manic asked.

"Didn't bother coming up with one," I admitted. "I was thinking we ask our AI where the biggest gathering of aliens are, then we blow them up."

Manic jumped off the roof of the car and stood to her full height. "I'm down for that. I'm guessing if we kill them all they won't be a problem anymore."

"I doubt we'll manage to kill that many," I said. "But if we kill enough of them, then we'll be able to hold out. Once the Family sends over someone who can burst the underwater hives, then we'll just have to mop up the rest and then I can finally get back home."

Manic nodded along. She didn't volunteer to go take a dip in the lake, so I figured she was about as loath to do that as I was.

I noticed that her equipment had changed a little. She was wearing different pants, these with pads on the thighs and over the knees, as well as a new jacket that seemed a little bulkier than her last. More armor? She still wasn't covering all of her head, but I imagined that would come with more points to spend. "So, Myalis, where's the biggest heap of them?"

A number of them are on the edge of the fires that Gomorrah started. They aren't moving away from the fires, but are congregating on the edges and seem to be looking for a way past them. Fortunately, they haven't started looking for a way around the fire yet.

That would stretch the front, which wasn't something we needed or wanted.

Unfortunately, Gomorrah's fires aren't great for the delicate electronics in the area, and as it progresses, I'm losing access to traffic and security cameras.

"Huh . . . we might be able to play the hammer to the fire's anvil," I said.

"I wouldn't think fire would work well as an anvil, but I get what you mean." Manic checked the charge on her sound blaster and then shouldered it. "We heading out, or what?"

"Yeah, let's go make up some of the points I've been spending," I said.

CHAPTER THIRTY-NINE

GETTING A CLUE

The VTuber boom of the early 2020s turned into a strange phenomena. At some point it became relatively cheap for brands to have their own VTuber mascot, either with a real person behind the digitized face, or a carefully curated auto-responding AI.

That led to an entire generation that grew up more comfortable interacting parasocially with VTubers than with real life humans.
—*Rise of the Anime Girl: A Study in Three Parts*, 2035

I took point, mostly because I was the more subtle of the two of us. Going invisible—after pinging Manic to get her augs to display my location—meant that I was . . . not visible to the aliens.

Whatever. Point was, I was better at the front than the rather loud Manic, who was even now blasting music from some speakers built into her clothes. I wasn't a music buff, but I recognized "Fortunate Son" when I heard it. I wasn't sure if it was entirely appropriate to the context but I wasn't going to start a debate I'd lose about music.

I checked my map as I walked down the side of a quiet street. The biggest confirmed group of Antithesis was just a couple of blocks down, most of them gathering in a five-way intersection right on the edge of the fires that Gomorrah had started.

My plan had once been to take the aliens out while leaving as much of the city intact as possible, but that particular plan was several hours old by this point and with Gomorrah lighting everything up, it was kind of a moot point.

I'd hold back from the *really* destructive explosives, because the splash from those might hit Downtown and injure the folk I was meant to protect, but that still left me with more choices than before.

"Okay," I said over the comms so that Manic could hear me. "I've got an idea."

"What is it?" she asked.

"I'm going to dip into the area with all the aliens, figure out which hole they're crawling out of, then set bombs next to those. We'll collapse the entire area down, then move in to mop up the survivors."

"Sounds like there isn't much for me to do in that plan of yours."

"Would you rather hit up a group that outnumbers us a hundred to one head-on?" I asked.

"Huh . . . alright, fair. Not quite at that level yet."

"Me neither," I said before shutting my comms off for a moment. "Myalis, can I have some resonators, maybe a few proximity mines, and . . . I guess some acid bombs. You know the ones that float up and rain acid down on an area?"

I'm familiar, yes. Are you getting these to prepare yourself?

"No, I'm giving them to Manic with instructions. If the aliens try to get at her they might cover her retreat."

Manic didn't seem impressed when I gave her the equivalent of a Tupperware bin full of esoteric explosives, but she got the idea easily enough. "You just want me to cover my ass?"

"If you die while I'm a block away, it'll look bad on my resume," I said.

"I'm glad I matter so much to you," Manic muttered. "These are some weird-ass bombs."

"Hey, they're creative. I thought you'd be all over that."

"Blowing shit up isn't art," she said.

I stared. "Huh. And here I thought you knew something about art. Guess my impression was dead wrong."

Manic rolled her eyes, then made a shooing gesture at me. "Go on, get to work, Stray Cat. But leave a few for me, would you?"

"I'll see what I can do," I said before patting her on the shoulder. I checked my gun for the third time, then started running off toward a nearby building. It had a bridge on its fifth floor that connected it to its neighbor and which should give me a nice view of the area where the Antithesis were crowded.

I wanted a bird's-eye view of things before I got down and had to navigate around the xenos.

I regretted that choice by the third floor. Sure, my suit had some neat setup that made walking up stairs a little easier, but it was still hell on my calves, and even if an exoskeleton kinda helped, it still used some muscle groups that weren't used to being used at all.

"Just think of how thick your thighs will be," I muttered to myself as I pushed past the burn and continued to jog up the stairs. "Crush Lucy's head, just like in her dreams."

On reaching the fifth floor, I navigated through a few corridors and across a rather boring bridge above an alley and into another apartment complex. It was the sort of shitty living space with minuscule homes and trash bags heaped out in the corridors where someone might, one day, be assed to clean up.

The far end of the building had a wall with several windows that overlooked the big intersection. I walked over and caught my breath while taking in the scene below.

The fires were spreading out to my left, though it looked like they weren't spreading all that well. A few small apartment buildings were up in flames, but some buildings right next to them were still fine.

I was guessing, but I figured that maybe some places just didn't have enough flammable stuff on the outside to catch fire so easily.

In any case, it didn't look like the fire would spread too much, or so I hoped. No way of knowing, not for a while, at least.

I stopped paying so much attention to the scenery and focused more on the aliens below. There was no lack of those around. Model threes by the dozens, bigger ones, like fours and fives milling around the edges, and then a couple of big bastards.

A couple of model fourteens, the big centipede guys with the heavy plates over their segments, a few model fifteens, the artillery aliens that spat out those spiky wheels, and a single huge model eighteen in the center.

The latter looked a bit fucked, with parts of its side looking partially melted, though not the way I'd expect them to if they were burned. The nanomachines at work? If so, the little robots had a lot of chewing left to do.

The only other time I'd seen a model eighteen was in the defense of New Montreal. It had dug its way under our defenses and came popping out of the backline ready to rip our crap apart. It had taken on a tank and won.

There was absolutely no way our defenses right now could handle one of those, even half-chewed-up as it was.

"What is up with this hive?" I muttered.

It might be throwing everything it has at the wall to see what sticks, to borrow a quaint colloquialism.

"Right," I said. Bigger aliens like that might take longer for the nanomachines to kill. So they'd actually be effective for a while before dying.

Maybe Gomorrah's fire had been the right solution all along, because all of these hitting the piss-poor defenses we had would have caused a huge breach. The militia didn't have the firepower to take the bigger guys out, not unless they got lucky or drew the fight out.

And drawing out a fight was almost always something the Antithesis wanted.

"Let's go say hi," I said.

The way back down was much easier than the path up, owing to gravity being a friend for once and because I practiced with my jump-jets by leaping down entire flights of stairs.

On arriving at the ground floor, I checked to see if my stealth stuff was still properly active, then I resisted the temptation to kick open the exit door. Instead I carefully pushed it open and slipped outside.

A model three's head rose and it opened its three-hinged mouth as if it was sniffing the air.

I moved on past it, careful with my footfalls not to disturb any of the junk on the road.

There was a light rain coming down from above. Not water, but ash. Thick gray flakes that settled on everything and cast the world in shades of gray and black. The aliens were just slow enough that the stuff accumulated on their backs and sides, turning them into marble statues of grotesque monsters.

It also meant that I was leaving prints in the ground behind me, the same way boots used to leave prints in the snow, back when snow was a thing in this hemisphere.

I weaved my way around the bigger aliens. I didn't know if they'd have sharper senses or not, but I wasn't ready to bet my life on a not.

"Myalis, any clue where these guys are coming from?" I asked.

Then one of the doors to a building across the street slammed open and a wave of model threes followed by bigger, uglier aliens came pouring out.

"Never mind, I think I figured it out."

CHAPTER FORTY

ALL AT ONCE

There was no need for Cyberpunk 2178 to actually kill the player if they died.

—IRN article, 2045

I skipped—not literally—on over to the building the aliens were pouring out of. They slowed down at around thirty, then stopped around fifty-ish aliens of a few different models, all in the single digits, all looking pretty damned healthy, and though a few had signs of being chewed up by nano-machines, it was light stuff, not the half-melted walking corpses I'd seen earlier.

Our nanomachine attack *had* worked, so I couldn't complain too much, but it looked like its effectiveness was dying down. "Do you think they're growing resistant to the nanomachines?" I asked.

That would be nearly impossible. What is more likely is that they found other ways of countering them.

"What's the difference?"

You don't need to be resistant to fire to put it out with a bucketful of water. In this case, I imagine the simplest solution would be for parts of the hive which are unaffected to produce as many units as possible while recycling themselves frequently. Eventually most of the nanomachines will be used in the flesh of models being sent out of the hive.

"Would that work?" I asked.

If someone spits in your drink and you empty half of it, then refill the glass, then empty half only to refill it again, eventually, after sufficient repetitions, there won't be any noticeable traces of spit left.

"Did you have to use that analogy?" I asked.

No.

I shook my head. "Thanks for the mental image," I said.

Trust me, the contents of your average bottle of drinking water are far more worrisome than another human's saliva.

"Also great," I muttered.

I'd crossed most of the way to the building the aliens had come from when I heard a faint bang on the other side of the street and several more came out of another nearby building. Were the two connected, or were there multiple hives disgorging aliens in the same spot? Or was it something else entirely? Maybe the basements of these buildings were linked?

In any case, I didn't feel like spending the day exploring each of those possibilities. So I ducked into the first building, carefully stepping around piles of broken glass. My boots might have been designed for stealth, but there was no point in being lazy and inadvertently making something crunch.

A few nearby model fours twitched their tentacles my way at my passing, but they dismissed it soon enough. Could they sense the motion of the air? That was disturbing, but probably not too surprising from a stealth ambush model.

The inside of the building they were using to get out of their underground shithole was, predictably, a mess. I suspected it had been some sort of office building at first, but the big plaques on one wall and the bulletproof glass above the counters suggested that this was more of a motor-vehicle license place than anything else.

The lobby was quite large, packed with plastic seats so tight that I imagined it would pinch the circulation of anyone that wasn't a toddler, and there were multiple guard stations around the room.

Some of those chairs had been ripped up, as had all of the plastic plants in the corners. The Antithesis were probably disappointed at their unrealism.

The aliens had left a nice trail across the linoleum leading to the back of the lobby and into a corridor that probably led to the washrooms and to the back end of the building.

I stepped around some of the bloodstains dragged across the floor and tried not to think too hard about them. Probably some poor fucks caught outside, or some family pets that hadn't been dragged into Downtown in time. Whoever's blood it was, it was now feeding the hive.

"Hey."

I startled, then swore under my breath before answering. "What's up, Manic?" I asked.

"How's shit going?" she asked. "Because I'm over here, sheltering in some shitty run-down apartment looking through some guy's classic CD collection and slowly losing my mind."

"Yeah, well at least you're not being spooked while crawling through a deathtrap," I said as I pushed farther in.

I wasn't expecting to turn a corner and find the floor missing, the walls ripped apart, and a stack of rubble pressed up to the edge of a slope that dropped down into an unlit basement.

"Fuck," I said.

"What?" Manic asked.

I rolled my eyes. She was really ruining the tension here. So I connected my cybernetic eye's visuals to the channel she was on, so that she could see things from my literal point of view. "Big old hole in the middle of a build-ing," I said. "This isn't normal, if you hadn't guessed."

"No shit," Manic said. "They coming up?"

The "they" was a group of model threes that started to scramble up the rubble ramp. I jumped down, then to the side, gripping onto cracked chunks of cement as I let the aliens by. They passed close enough that I could almost smell them.

I flicked on my helmet's lowlight vision and looked around.

The entire basement had been remodeled recently. Walls torn out, with only a few pillars remaining, but with plenty of new alien shit to make up for the loss. There were pools of goopy crap all over, with large egg sacs piled waist-high at the end of the room and thigh-thick roots running across the floor in zig-zag patterns.

"This is a whole-ass hive," I said.

A relatively new one. I suspect that this one is absorbing the biomatter of the hives that we hit earlier. It would make sense for the Antithesis to retreat and then work to purge itself of its infection this way. There is a historical precedent.

"Yeah," I said. Then I jumped back and ducked behind a pillar as a model four came waddling past. It was carrying a mass of Antithesis flesh which looked extra fucky, the kind of fucky that came from our nanomachines. I moved on past, and on a whim I started to follow it.

It didn't get too far. Just to another room with a torn-apart floor. There was a pit there, maybe some five or six meters deep, but a dozen meters wide, and entirely filled with rotting plant-meat. The model four tossed in the chunk it held, then hopped down to its death.

"They're really working on purging themselves," I said.

"Smart, for a bunch of plants," Manic said. "So, blowing them up?"

"Mm-hmm," I said. "But if they don't like the nanomachines, I don't see a reason to stop giving them some. Myalis, more of those cat drones, and a lot more nanomachines. Can you follow the roots to wherever they're getting their biomass from? We'll undo whatever progress they have here."

A startlingly good idea!

I huffed, but didn't comment.

"So no explosion?" Manic asked.

"Oh yeah, big explosions," I said. "We just need to stall until help shows up, right? So let's ruin this place. I think acid sprayers all over, and then enough boom to bring the entire building down?"

That should work.

What followed was a nervous half hour of me moving across the basement, unnoticed by the Antithesis who were pumping out more and more aliens that immediately set out to leave. They were growing so fast that when I paused to stare, I could literally see them growing in their egg sac things.

There was some sort of system in place where the least infected plant-meat was ripped apart and reused, and the most infected was tossed out and segregated, all while the hive continued to produce like mad.

At this rate of growth, these models will be significantly weaker. There's a reason most models take as long to grow as they do. Chemical reactions can only be hurried up so much.

Once I had placed a few dozen little tanks full of rapidly spreading acid around, I set out to place my second happy surprise. These weren't anything special, just plain-old plastic explosives in little baggies that would keep them safe from the acid.

When I was done, I jogged out of the building, then froze up on reaching the intersection above. It was full, with nearly twice as many Antithesis lingering around out in the open as before.

"Okay . . . so, we blow up the building, then . . . hey, Manic, think you could take on this bunch?"

"On my own? Maybe if they come at me one at a time."

"I mean all at once," I said.

"Fuck, I don't know," she said. "Maybe?"

"Get closer, and don't get noticed. Once I set off all the bombs in the world, we'll cull this little herd the old-fashioned way."

CHAPTER FORTY-ONE

EXTINCTION OF THE NEW SORT

And it came to pass that as the Earth was plagued by the sins of man, extinction rates did rise, and the creatures of the land and sea were lost. For their genomes were coveted by those with greed in their hearts, and taken for selfish gain. And so it was that the great sharks were lost, for they were cloned to satiate the desires of the wicked. And their genomic samples were locked away, hidden behind walls of technology, protected by the very greed that caused their downfall. Thus did biodiversity perish, one sinful act at a time.

—The Ecoterrorist's Manifesto, page 41, verse 12

I ran over to the building Manic was hiding in just as I heard a very strange and unique sound, the charge up whine and bassy boom of Manic's sound gun going off. Some of the windows at the front of the building clattered apart, sending sheets of glass tumbling onto the street and alerting every alien in the area that something was up.

"Fuck," I muttered under my breath as I double-timed it into the building. Behind me, the stirring mass of aliens was starting to move in the same direction. I was sure a few would notice the front door opening and closing on its own, but there was nothing for it.

I ordered up a grenade with a laser trip wire and some sticky shit on the side of it and pressed it to the wall next to the entrance before running deeper in.

"Need a few more of those," I said as I started to go up the stairs. I left one at every landing. They'd be a nice gift to any aliens trying to run up behind me.

Manic was on the fourth floor, and when I reached her, I found the woman with a boot pressed up against the front of a model five, her other shoe slipping backward as she leveled her Bass Cannon into the alien's mouth and fired.

There was that familiar whine, then a single loud *borf* sound that made all the dust on the ground skip up and ripped the alien apart from the inside out.

She stumbled backward, regained her footing, then started looking for the next target.

There were a few model threes rushing across the open room, but before she could aim at them I fired at the lot in full auto, and was suddenly reminded that I didn't have the stealthiest kind of bullet loaded into my gun. Still, I nailed the three with four shots, then ordered up a resonator and tossed it into the corner of the room where it released its high-pitched squeal.

"You good?" I asked.

"Yeah," Manic said. She flicked a strip of alien meat off her gun. "Gonna want a shower after all of this."

"I thought the 'covered in gore' look was very punk," I said.

"Eh, I'm all for doing shit just for the vibes, and like, aesthetic's important, but fuck if hygiene isn't important too, you know?"

"Yeah," I said.

"Slept with this one guy once. Real rocker sort. Fuck the system. He ended up in jail for Molotoving some rich fuck's ride. Anyway, guy was cool, but he smelled like those e-cigs all the time."

"Uh-huh," I said, less interested.

She gave me a look. "What? Squeamish?"

"About fucking? Not when it's two women, like how God intended."

She blinked. "But guys squick you out, really?"

"Hey, we all have our hang-ups," I said before I slipped past her and looked outside. The aliens were crowding by the bottom of the building and a number of them had taken to the skies. "Shit, I was hoping to wipe a few out if they were closer to the explosion."

"More for me to kill. So, gonna detonate that thing?"

"Give me a second, I'm savoring it," I said.

She scoffed, then checked on her gun while I used my augs to select all of the acid bombs I'd left in the basement. Once they were all connected, I tapped the detonate button.

There wasn't a huge kaboom, which was expected. The acid bombs down there would be releasing a fine, rapid-spreading mist of very acidic . . . chemical stuff. I didn't know what kind of chemical, and if Myalis had told me I'd forgotten already.

It would start eating anything it could, organic and not, and was probably not very healthy for the aliens down there, what with them not being acid-proof as far as I could tell.

Those bombs alone, I imagined, might be enough to take down the building. I wasn't an architect, but I was pretty sure that melting all the pillars in a building's basement wouldn't be ideal for its structural integrity.

Then I selected all of the more conventional bombs, held my breath, and tapped on "Detonate."

The floor rumbled beneath me and a massive cone of dust shot out from the building. Then the entire thing just collapsed. The floors above crashed into those below as the bottom gave out. Chunks of cement broke off and rained down toward the street, ripping through an expanding cloud of dust and smoke and a little bit of fire.

The rumble continued for a few long seconds, then subsided.

I let go of the breath I'd been holding in. "Oh yeah, that was nice."

"You getting off on this?" Manic asked.

"Nah, but I think I know what Gomorrah sees when she lights the world on fire. There's just something real beautiful about destroying things, you know?"

"Hmm, I'll stick to music and sex."

"Your loss," I said. The aliens below didn't seem to expect the big explosion, and a number of them were taken out by falling bits of masonry. Not all of them though, not even half, really. "We should go down there. I saw them leaving through another building, so we might want to go blow that one up too."

"That'll mean fighting through all of that," Manic said.

"Mm-hmm," I agreed. Then I stuck my head out of the window (was it a window if it didn't have glass anymore?) and looked straight down. We were more or less above the entrance, so I ordered up a handful of grenades and let them fall, then chucked the pins down after them. "That should keep them distracted for a second," I said.

I could hear detonations in the stairwell already, so they'd found the bombs I'd left in the landings.

We waited a minute or two up above. Manic was muttering something, presumably to her AI, because eventually a box appeared next to her and she opened it up to reveal a mask that she slid under the visor of her helmet and which clamped up to the back of her neck. "It stinks," she explained.

Fair enough. My own air was filtered, so I wasn't enjoying the wonderful odor of burning buildings mixed with pulped aliens.

Then she bought a pair of strange metal devices that she clamped around her biceps and over her leather-like jacket. It gave her a bit of a weird look. I couldn't begin to guess what those were, not until they slid open and revealed a set of speakers on the inside.

A smaller version of her Bass Cannon? Placed the way they were, they'd blast all around her.

"Ready?" I asked.

"Yeah. Debating getting some boots."

"Nice boots are nice," I said. "Might as well get pants though. You don't want some alien getting into yours, you know?"

"I don't think they're interested in that," she said.

I shook my head. "It's all fun and games until you see one of those tentacle ones up close," I said.

Manic paused. "Actually, yeah, give me like, two minutes?"

"Sure," I said.

She slipped into one of the rooms nearby, and I went over to guard the stairs, giving her a bit of room. When she returned she was wearing very flattering pants that were made of some sort of smooth, shiny material. Same old boots though.

"Nice," I said. "Make your ass look fine."

"My ass looked fine already," she said. "We heading down?"

"Yeah. I just need to disable the bombs I put on the stairs. The ones that didn't go off already."

I could do that from afar, fortunately, so that wasn't a big deal. There weren't many that hadn't gone off, just the ones on the last landing. As we started to make our way down, I discovered a slight issue though.

"Ah, shit," I said as I looked at where the stairs should have been.

The bomb had torn them apart, leaving a hole that led two floors down.

"Nice job," Manic said.

"Hey, not my fault this place is basically built out of cardboard. I swear, how cheap can they get?"

"We'll just have to go around," Manic said. It clearly didn't bother her all that much.

To be fair, I just wanted to get to the ground floor to start killing shit, but I supposed going about it in a roundabout way wasn't so bad.

CHAPTER FORTY-TWO

QUIET

Passwords are only so trustworthy. With the rise of AI computing and systems like SHA-256 becoming so easy to decrypt that anyone with the right second generation augs could do it, passwords fell by the wayside.

In their place came biometrics. Why use a password when you can use yourself?

The "why" became obvious as constantly leaked medical data started to render even biometrics useless for information protection.

Now, anything less than a four-factor authentication system is considered ripe for the plundering.

—Infosec: On Biometrics and Safety Factors, 2031

"Ready?" I asked.

"I was five minutes ago, I don't see why I wouldn't be now," Manic said.

I just nodded. I was getting used to her flippancy, which was probably because I would have said the same thing in her combat boots. We had made our way to another exit, this one into a side-alley. I couldn't hear any aliens on the other side of the door, so if anything was there, it was being quiet. There were plenty of the fuckers tromping into the apartment building though, most through the front.

We could very easily hear claws on linoleum clattering about above us. "I'll open, you go in, then I'll come in behind and cover your back," I said. "Go left."

"Uh-huh," Manic said.

I took that as a yes and tore the door open.

Manic jumped out, sonic gun coming up and whining already as it charged. Then I snuck out behind Manic and pointed my own gun to the right while looking for targets of my own.

The alley ended a little ways in, with a few large trash containers and not much else. A model three was wrestling out a large tarp from one of the dumpsters, though it paused to stare at us with the cloth still in its jaws.

I fired a small burst its way, then adjusted my aim to take account of the kickback. I needed to switch back to something a little more stealthy, bullet-wise, but that could wait for when I was empty.

Manic jogged to the edge of the alley, then fired. The loud *whump* was accompanied by a scattering of dust being kicked off the walls and floor. I turned and started looking for aliens to blow up around the noisy samurai.

Her gun had a wide cone of fire, but it wasn't so wide as to clear out the entire street. There were still plenty of monsters around, and now that she'd made her signature level of noise, they were all very much aware that we were there.

Or at least, they knew about Manic.

A few Antithesis roared and squealed, but the majority of them were entirely quiet as they turned their attention onto us and rushed over. "Just chaff," Manic said.

"Bigger ones out back," I replied. "I'll take them out. Stay safe."

"Mm-hmm," was her only reply.

Flicking on my invisibility, I ran the long way around Manic, avoiding the cone of fire from her Bass Cannon even as I took a few potshots into the crowd and tried to tag the bigger bastards at the back.

I clicked empty just as I reached a line of cars parked along the side of the road. I ducked down behind a wrecked electric car that looked like it had gone up in flames a while ago, then ordered up a fresh magazine for my rifle while my shoulder-mounted guns took care of sniping any of the flying Antithesis above.

"I need something that's not as noisy," I said.

Coming right up.

My Laser Pointer clicked, then made a happy little humming sound that was a little too close to a purr for comfort. It was enough to know that it was loaded up again.

I let my shoulder-guns take a few more flying models down, then I jumped up to my feet and continued running. My targets were the bigger models in the center of the intersection. The artillery aliens were going to be a pain to deal with for someone like Manic, and if that huge model eighteen decided to stomp over to her, it would all be over.

Once I figured I was far enough to be outside of the range of Manic's Bass Cannon, I cut inward. My Laser Pointer bucked as I unloaded it from the hip, splattering smaller aliens left and right.

The middle of the intersection had this Y-shaped cement thing, with some streetlights in the center and a few smaller billboards fixed to it. The bigger fucks were hiding out on the other side of that, which was fine by me.

I summoned a trio of resonators and flung them ahead of me, and the grenades started to whine while still in midair. They'd take a while to melt anything though.

Stopping with a skid, I dropped to a knee next to one of the cement buttresses, then looked over the edge. The model eighteen was turning, big legs stomping along as it started to go around and head toward Manic.

I figured good odds it would just charge on over.

"Myalis, can I have a few of those garrote grenades, with remote detonators?"

Certainly.

I got three, which I supposed was what a "few" was to Myalis. That was good to know. I grabbed them one at a time and flicked them out ahead of model eighteen, right where it was going to pass.

They clattered and bounced and I swore when a model three kicked at one in passing, but then the model eighteen was barreling past and I flicked on the detonator.

In a split second, all three garrote grenades went off. Monomolecular wires unspooled like something from an OSHA inspector's worst nightmare and spun around in a dizzying whispering tangle.

When they hit flesh, they didn't even have the grace to slow down and merely sliced right through, kicking out ribbons of meat and blood that splattered out into the air around them.

The model eighteen stumbled as its legs suddenly gained a million hyper-thin lacerations.

It wasn't enough to kill it, but it was a nice start.

What did kill it was me running up to the alien from behind, ordering a sticky bomb on the way over, and slapping it down next to its neck before I continued to run.

I set off the bomb behind me while I kept moving, and the warmth of the explosion just shoved me forward and gave me a little boost even as bits of alien rained down around me.

My next targets were the model fifteens, the big, long artillery models stomping about in the back line. They were the big threat. One of those spiky balls they spat could ruin Manic's afternoon, and it looked like both of them were about ready to start spitting.

"Grenade," I said.

What kind?

"Boomy!" I shouted.

Something landed in my hand and I threw it forward as hard as I could. Fortunately my aim when throwing things, even with my cybernetic arm instead of my normal one, was pretty good, at least compared to my aim with any sort of gun.

The bomb sailed through the air, then clacked against the ground between the two aliens. Then it exploded.

I flinched, even though I was perfectly safe. Whatever fragmentation had been kicked up clattered against my armor. When I looked back up and through the smoke left behind, it was to find both model fifteens shredded in the middle, though they were still writhing a little.

I put an end to that as I emptied my magazine into their sides, splitting my remaining rounds between the two.

Turning, I surveyed the area. A few aliens were running out from behind cover, or from within nearby buildings, but they were a trickle, not a flood, and Manic seemed to be doing alright. Her Bass Cannon *whumped* every couple of seconds, sending bodies flopping through the air and tossing back blood and guts in large waves.

We started mopping up after that. I took them out from behind, with a few acid-rain bombs on the edges of the road creating more chokepoints and more resonators flung around to kill off any injured alien lying in one of the corpse heaps we were leaving behind.

When I finally reached Manic, once the intersection quieted down, she was leaning against the wall of a building, her mask hanging around her neck and her hair plastered to her sweaty forehead. She had a cigarette out, and with a mumbled command, a lighter fell into her open palm.

She lit it, tossed the lighter away, then took a long pull.

"That's not good for ya," I said.

"What is?" she exhaled. "Besides. Makes your voice huskier."

"Fair enough, I suppose," I said. "We still have to blow that building right over there up. And then maybe look around for more spots where they've settled underground."

"How much blowing up are you intending to do?"

"Enough to keep the aliens off our backs between now and when reinforcements arrive, at least," I said.

She took another pull, then tossed the cigarette aside where it sizzled out in the blood of one of the alien's she'd pulped. "Alright, fine. I'll relax once it's all done."

CHAPTER FORTY-THREE

AND I HAVE KILLED IT

Your art is dead, and I have killed it.

—GPT9, 2027

"Kinda weird," Manic said as she looked off to the side.

I followed her gaze. She was looking at the space where there had been a building just a few minutes before. "What's weird?"

"I've spent most of my life in this city, you know? And just from one day to the next, the whole place has changed. I don't just mean the obvious, like . . . that building there. It's not that old. I remember some of these places being built. But now they're all fucked. It's weird."

"I guess so," I said. "I haven't spent enough time here to really get used to the place."

"Yeah, all you have is a snapshot. What Burlington is right now, at this moment. But a place is more than just one moment in its history. It's . . . it *is* its history, I guess." She reached under her visor and pushed a lock of blue hair away from her eyes. "Never mind."

"Nah, it's fine," I said. "I can get philosophical too sometimes . . . after a good orgasm, usually."

"I get that too," she said. "It's music for me. The right beat, the right lyrics, at just the right moment in time. It can be something special, but if the time's off, then it's just more noise."

I nodded along, even if I didn't quite get it, not as deeply as she seemed to. Then again, I don't think anyone had ever accused me of having much depth.

"Enough philosophizing," I said with a gesture to the building across the street. No new aliens had snuck out of it in a while, but they *had* been coming out of there recently. "Want to go blow that one up?"

"On my own?"

"Nah, I'll come with you. Unless you really wanna go solo? I can hand you the bombs."

She shook her head. "I'd rather not. I like working on my own when it's the choice between being a soloist or having to carry the show, but when you've got a good thing going, there's no point in stopping it."

Well, that made me feel all warm and fuzzy on the inside. "Sure," I said.

There hadn't been any more aliens to show up in a couple of minutes. Either the Antithesis were being kind enough not to attack while we took a breather, or we'd killed all of them in the area, or, as a special third option which I disliked the most, they were doing something fucky and were waiting to spring a trap on us.

I went invisible again, checked my gun, ordered up a few more grenades, then a belt I could wear around my waist—which also went invisible on command and had little pouches for my grenades to hide in. The damned thing only cost about seventy points and I regretted not getting something like it sooner the moment it was hooked in place.

"Ready?" I asked.

"Yeah. So, we walk in, kill everything, then leave?" she asked.

"That's about the whole of it," I agreed. "If we find a big hive down there, then we'll fill the place with acid and collapse the building down on top of it all. Bet it'll make it a nightmare to clean later, but I care more about the short-term right now."

Manic charged up her Bass Cannon, which made a very satisfying, very deep humming noise. The kind of shit that would have a sci-fi fan touching themselves. Then she started walking, and I jogged out ahead of her, taking point.

This building was another apartment block, but it was slightly higher-end. The sorry sort of pod place where each inhabitant got a box to live in with about a hundred square feet of moving room to spare and all the amenities someone needed to live and not a single thing more.

The lobby at least wasn't too tight, with a few study nooks to one side and a public kitchen off at the back. There had been a garden too, but it looked like the Antithesis had ripped the door to that apart and then stole everything within.

"Nice place," I said as I scanned around. There had been alien traffic here, and recently. The floor was covered in claw marks and the aliens didn't exactly wipe their paws before entering.

"Yeah, this place is expensive as fuck," Manic said. "Fifty thousand credits a month, easy."

"Damn," I said. "I thought it was a pod place."

"It is, but one of those fancy ones. They have good internet and community stuff going on. I think a lot of the folk staying here were going to the tech college nearby. Dated a girl from here for a week or so. The beds here are tiny."

"Hah, so you are gay!" I said. I patted myself on the back for having a functional gaydar.

"She was a musician," Manic said. "Played the electric cello."

"Is musisexual a thing?"

"Phonosexual?" she asked. "I don't know if that's a thing, but I know you've never seen more people throw themselves at you than when you step off the stage after a good set. Free booze, free women, free men, easy friends. It's addicting. Some folk do it all for that high. Can't even blame them, though I'm more of a puritan myself."

"A puritan?" I asked. "So you didn't sleep with the groupies?"

"What? Nah, of course I did. But I'm in it for the *art*, not the banging."

I chuckled, then cut-off mid laugh as I heard a creak from out ahead of us. "Company," I said as I brought my gun up. Manic shuffled behind me, and her cannon started a low, warning hum. I had to find where the aliens were coming up to the surface from. They weren't using the damned elevator, that was for sure.

Then as I pushed deeper into the first floor, past a room with a few foosball tables and whatever other corpo-crap that looked good in a pamphlet, I noticed a sign on one of the walls up ahead.

"This place has a swimming pool?" I asked.

The power has been cut and the backup systems for the building don't include any camera access. Though I can safely say that some of the doors locked automatically and I'll be able to tell you if any of them open. I can't see into the basement. But I imagine that if the Antithesis are anywhere, then they're below.

I nodded along. Made sense. Plus if the sign I crossed was to be believed, there was a bar and a sauna down there. Screw being aliens, that's where I'd be if I was them.

"Hey," Manic said, and I paused. "I'm picking up something above." She gestured to her ears, then pointed up.

My own cybernetic ears twitched, and I listened. There was a lot of noise for what was an otherwise empty building. Lots of ticks and the groans you'd expect from a normal building. Then I picked up on what she meant. A clattering noise that took me a second to place. "Is that someone typing?" I asked.

"On an old-school keyboard, yeah," she said.

I hesitated, then decided to do the smart thing. "We're going to check on that," I said. "Then go down. I think we can mine this corridor, maybe get a drone out here to keep it safe?"

"I've got something like that," she said. "Got any bombs that won't cave the floor in this time?"

"Yeah, I might have something like that," I said. Resonators were my go-to, but I had nasty little nanomachine grenades and a few others that wouldn't damage the building too much.

Manic ordered something up, and it came in a box that, when she opened it, revealed a sort of six-legged dog drone thing, without a head, instead it had a bunch of heavy-duty speakers pointing in every direction.

She aimed it down the corridor, then had it sit at an intersection.

If it was anything like her Bass Cannon, then at least we'd know when it fired, no matter where in the damned city we were.

"Alright, let's go see what kind of dumbass is still in this shithole," I said as I slapped a resonator next to the stairs, then took them up two at a time.

The typing sound stopped, but not before I pinpointed its location on the third floor up. Every door I passed was shut and locked, but it was clear from the few that were left open that people had evacuated a while ago.

Except, apparently, for this one dumbass.

I found their room because of the light pouring out from under the crack of the door. The tapping resumed just as I stopped in front, and I could barely believe it. What kind of idiot stayed at home when the world was ending?

CHAPTER FORTY-FOUR

JENNIFER

Your waifu in your hands right now!
    Join today and get a 5 percent discount on your first Waifudoll purchase!
    All figurines are made in Japan from glorious Nippon plastic!
    NEW Samurai of 2028 figures! Squishable latex breasts!
                                    —Waifudoll scrolling banner ad, 2029

I knocked.

The typing noises stopped.

Then after about twenty long seconds, they started again. "Are you serious?" I asked.

There is a personal computer on in the room. It isn't connected to the building's power grid. It's likely that it's being powered by a battery pack since the entire system is running on as few resources as possible.

I shook my head, then tried the handle, which of course didn't work.

So I kicked the door in.

This wasn't some high-security place, the door was made of some cheap laminate stuff that caved in with the first kick. The biggest problem after that was unjamming my foot from the hole, but I managed without falling on my ass. Then I shoved the door aside and looked into what was clearly some degenerate's man cave.

The lighting was poor—only coming in from the corridor—but it was enough to see the wall-to-wall posters of women in barely any clothes. There were shelves with figurines, of course, and enough clothes on the floor to keep a family of six warm.

And then, right there in the middle of the room, was a thin figure sitting behind a lit up screen. They turned their head slowly, and I found myself looking into a pair of eyes that were too blue to be real.

"What?" they asked.

I felt like asking the same. I had expected someone, not some*thing.* But what I found was a petite woman with clearly artificial skin typing away on a laptop without even looking at the screen.

"Is that a fucking sex bot?" Manic asked.

"I think so," I said. "Hey, who are you?"

"My name is Jennifer."

"Well, that's . . . a very plain name. Uh, are you human?"

The android paused in her—its?—typing. "Pardon me, but you have broken into my master's home. I have filed a report with the local authorities."

"We're samurai," I said. "Also, even if we weren't the local authorities, I don't think it would matter much. There's an incursion ongoing. Uh, you don't know?"

The sex bot blinked at me. "I am aware. My master didn't give me instructions regarding the incursion. I must work."

"What are you working on?" I asked. The screen before her seemed to be filled with text.

"Erotica."

"Ah," I said.

Manic poked me with an elbow. "We should get going. Not saying it wasn't worth checking to see if there was someone here, but let's not waste our time?"

"Yeah," I said. "Hey, uh, you're coming with us," I said.

"What?" Manic asked.

"I'm not leaving her here."

"Stray, it's a robot," Manic said. "It's probably got an off-site backup or something. And I bet it's insured."

"Yeah, but . . . no, it feels wrong to leave someone behind."

"I am not supposed to leave," the sex bot happily informed me.

"You're leaving anyway," I said, putting my metaphorical foot down.

"I am not programmed to obey you," Jennifer the sex bot said.

I felt my frustration rise, especially as I noticed the shit-eating look Manic was giving me. "I'm not leaving you here," I said. "I bet I can carry your plastic ass out of here."

"I can't tell if you're being an ass toward the bot or if you actually care too much," Manic said. "It's plastic and bolts, I get that it looks human, but AI have ruined plenty of human stuff, including some poor asshole's sex life, apparently, so I don't see the point."

"The point is . . . I don't know," I admitted, "but I'm not going to leave Jennifer here all on her own when we're literally planning on blowing up the building. In fact . . . Myalis, how sure can you be that there's no one else left in here?"

Ninety-seven percent certainty. Before the cameras went out, they logged the exit of every tenant still in the building. It's entirely possible that someone remains that wasn't noticed, though it's unlikely. I could pinpoint the few potential locations a person is hiding in still, if you wish?

"Are they all conveniently close?" I asked.

No.

"Right, give me some cat drones. How many places do you need to check?"

I see where you're going with this. Three drones would be sufficient to inspect every location in the amount of time I predict it will take you to set up the explosives.

I nodded along. "You're perfect. Three drones then, and help me get Jennifer here to leave. I feel bad about leaving her behind."

Certainly.

"You're not bothered that I'm trying to save a dumb-AI machine?" I asked.

I am greatly amused, actually.

Of course she was. It took a bit of effort to convince Jennifer the bot to stand up, then I had to scrounge around on the floor for something she could wear. Sure, she had a sports bra on, but it really didn't work with the thigh-highs-and-nothing-else she was wearing below. The android might not have had a sense of dignity, but I did.

Manic cackled at me while I tossed an over-large hoodie at the bot. "Put this on, and let's go," I said.

"Is it going to follow us?" Manic asked.

"We can hide her in a closet or something then fetch her on the way up," I said. "Not like she makes much noise."

"I am trained in six million forms of sexual intercourse noises," Jennifer informed us. "I am a top-of-the-line Boston Statics life-partner android."

"Six million?" Manic asked.

Jennifer nodded. "From breathy, seductive moans to realistic animal sounds."

"Never mind," Manic said.

We started down the corridor. I took point and Manic walked next to Jennifer, her Bass Cannon pointed at the ceiling. "So, what were you working on there? You said it was erotica?"

"Yes. My master has me write erotica. Since I am not a legal entity, I can write materials of dubious legal quality without being penalized. That was the task I was set on before my master left seventy-six hours ago."

"That's fucked up," I muttered. "Couldn't an AI just generate a few million words of that kind of stuff in an instant?" I asked.

"Most modern writing platforms check to ensure that all writing comes with accompanying keystrokes. It needs to be entered manually with a slight variance in speed and writing tempo."

"So . . . you're cheating?" I asked.

"I wasn't programmed to care about that."

I shot the sexdroid a look. "You're candid about it."

"I *was* programmed to be a good conversationalist." She turned and locked eyes with me. "How are you feeling today?"

"Yeah, no," I said, nixing that entire conversation right there. Lucy would be so mad at me if I had an in-depth conversation with a sex bot instead of her. "Just keep quiet, please, we don't need to alert the aliens that we're here."

"Understood," she murmured.

"You think her being quiet will be enough?" Manic asked.

I shrugged. "I don't know. Maybe? She's not . . . fleshy, so they probably won't find her from the smell or whatever."

"She's wearing a sweat-stained hoodie and while I haven't given her a sniff, I bet she smells like latex and bad sex," Manic complained.

I shrugged some more. "Spritz her with some deodorant if you care so much about the smell."

We made it to the stairs, and as I predicted, there were aliens climbing up from below. A few were missing some bits, and I could hear the *thump-thump* of Manic's bass turret going off echoing in the stairwell.

"Right, drones, go check for survivors," I said with a gesture and the trio of cat drones I'd ordered up ran past me on silent paws. "And we're heading down," I said for Jennifer's benefit.

I barely made it five steps before I had to open up on a model three scurrying up the stairs. Soon, Manic was next to me, the wider spray of her Bass Cannon coming in handy in the tight confines of the stairs.

I tossed a resonator down, less to kill the aliens and more to turn them into slush so that we wouldn't end up tripping over a corpse on the way down.

The farther down we went, the more aliens started to pour into the stairwell.

"Shit," Manic said. "My turret's down."

"Huh," I said. "Well, that's something. Any idea what got it?"

"Just some little ones," she said. "But enough of them did it."

The advantage of a swarm, I supposed. By the time we made it back to the ground floor, I had alien guts staining the front of my armor and had had to reload twice. Jennifer was still following us, her stockings squishing with every step.

"It's nice to get out of the house," she said.

CHAPTER FORTY-FIVE

UNCANNY

The uncanny valley is a primitive warning system. It tells you that something is wrong, incorrect, or fake.

It often triggers on mannequins and dolls and even some forms of art. Interestingly, it is something that you can grow accustomed to. Most people aren't going to be fearful of a person with facial augmentations, for example.

The Antithesis almost always triggers an uncanny valley response in people who see them in the flesh for the first time.

We don't know why.

—Soma Psychologica, 2049

I looked at Jennifer, who stood rather awkwardly next to a mop and bucket and a floor-cleaning robot-charging station. She was bent to the side a little to avoid brushing her head against the shelves of cleaning products at about forehead height. "Comfy?" I asked.

"I have been in more constricting positions before," the sex bot confirmed.

That was good enough for me. "Alright. You, uh, stay in here and stay quiet. I'm sure the smell of cleaning stuff will keep the aliens at bay," I said with a gesture to the floor behind me. It was covered in about thirty alien's worth of shredded flesh and several dozen liters of blood.

I couldn't get a good whiff of the air—probably for the best—with my mask on, but I imagined it was quite pungent. Fortunately, Jennifer didn't have olfactory glands. Or I hoped for her sake that she didn't.

"Right . . . stay safe," I said before clicking the door shut and turning around.

Manic had a foot atop a model three's head and was rolling it from side to side as if inspecting it. "Never really got a good look at these guys," she said as I walked over.

"Really?" I asked.

"I mean, I've seen them on TV and in warnings and the like, but seeing one in person's different. Like listening to a recording and being at the show, you know?"

"Yeah," I said. "Doesn't help that most of the signs for these guys are cartoony."

The model three was an ugly bastard, and even missing a couple of limbs and flopped onto the ground like a sack of potatoes, it still managed to be kind of scary in a sort of primal . . . *wrong* way. There was something about a lot of the Antithesis that didn't click with my monkey brain.

I think it might have been some sort of uncanny valley effect. It had flesh that looked clearly plantlike, but not, and the proportions were just entirely wrong. Things from Earth had . . . maybe not a common blueprint, but most animals followed a more or less similar look when it came to their proportions, and the Antithesis didn't. The head was too flat, the mouth with its three hinges was off, and . . . yeah, it wasn't right.

"We've got to rig the place to blow," I said. "I'd like to get that done with, then we can head back to the city. It's getting to be late, and I want to be back before it starts getting dark."

"Scared of the dark?"

"Huh? No? I'm a stealth specialist, and I'm cat-themed, do you think I'd be afraid of the dark? Nah, just don't want to be caught out in the open at night. Plus, when shit goes wrong, in my experience, it always tends to go wrong in the worst way around morning, noon, and just as the sun's setting."

"Mm," Manic said. She cracked her neck left and right, then stood a little straighter. "Let's get going then."

I lead the way again. We'd cleared out the aliens coming from the basement until all that was left of them were these bodies splattered across the floor, but I imagined there would be more once we got down.

The basement access was just another stairwell past a smashed door marked "Employees Only." The Antithesis hadn't destroyed the entire floor to get down this time, which was nice. It meant we got to use stairs.

Less fun was the model four that came hurtling down from above, tentacles already lashing out toward me.

I threw myself back and onto the floor, my Laser Pointer coming up at the same time even as I squeezed the trigger.

The alien fell onto a barrage of lead that tore apart its tentacles and bit into its main body. Puffs of gas escaped it, but that didn't stop its fall.

Then Manic fired and the alien's entire body was rammed across the stairwell and into the far wall where it crashed with a wallop.

I stared at the ceiling some more, checked the corners for more ambushers, then groaned and rolled onto my front to stand. "Thanks," I said.

"Where the hell did that come from?" Manic asked.

"Ceiling. Forgot to check my corners," I admitted. "They're quiet when they wanna be. Hey, you're wearing a gas mask, right?"

"Yeah," she said.

"Good. Those ones give off this gas that'll make you paranoid. Freaky fucks," I said. I checked my gun, noting that I'd chewed through the last of my ammo. "Myalis, reload."

While my gun reloaded, I moved in a little slower, head on a swivel as I checked every shadow for another ambusher. Unlike the last building I'd hit, where the aliens never noticed me, this time we'd gone in loud. They knew we were coming.

"Fucking tentacles," Manic said.

"Nah," I replied. "I don't think they'd actually go all hentai on you. I mean, they might, but it's not sexual."

"Oh, great, that'll make it feel so much better," Manic said.

I snorted. "Just shoot them first," I advised.

"I think they're the model I like the least, and that's saying something. The bad-touch model."

I had to agree, but more because they were a little too close to my own fighting style than because of the tentacles. I spotted another one of them hanging off the ceiling halfway down the flight of stairs and around two corners. "Cute," I said as I took my time to aim and then triple-tapped it in the chest.

It crashed to the ground, then I put another pair of rounds into its side just to be safe. I stepped over the corpse and continued on down the stairs until they ended at a doorway that was surprisingly still in place.

There was a window at head-height, and the door was left ajar. From the looks of it, something had kicked it in and in the battle between the door and its frame, the door won. I leaned against the wall on the far side of the door and peeked through while activating all the low-light gizmos on my helmet.

The basement had the aforementioned pool in it down the end of a wide corridor and behind a pair of broken glass doors. There were changing rooms to the sides, and the corridor forked off to the right. I couldn't see what was down that way from my angle.

"A goddamn pool," I muttered. "We should get a pool."

You have one.

"The inflatable kiddie pool doesn't count," I said.

I wanted a proper pool, like rich people had. Maybe hanging off the side of our home, with one of those glass bottoms and a big deck? I didn't like swimming . . . or know how to swim well, but I did love the idea of Lucy in swimsuits.

"Is it clear?" Manic asked.

I jumped, pushed aside my daydreams, then glanced down the passage again. There were stains on the ground and several doors were broken in, but no big signs of alien life. "Yeah," I said as I opened the door slowly. I glanced up, then checked the corners as best I could. "We're clear."

"Then where the hell did all the aliens come from?" Manic asked.

The corridors were pretty wide, so it wouldn't be too hard for any of the bigger ones to get past, I figured. Judging from the marks left behind, it looked like they mostly went toward the pool.

"That way, at a guess," I said as I pointed forward. "Give me a sec, I'm gonna start planting bombs right now."

I ordered up a number of good old explosives, and also a few of those acid-mist sprayers. It was worth the cost, I figured, to melt everything behind us. It would make it that much less likely that the Antithesis would survive and regrow down here.

We checked down the long corridor to the right, but it seemed to lead off toward more community rooms. They had a mini-theater, and a VR-sports room. Fancy, unnecessary shit that I bet rarely got used.

Manic and I checked every room in the corridor leading up to the pool, and we found a few model fours waiting around for us in there.

For all their size and stealthiness, they weren't much of a threat when we were expecting them.

Then, at last, we reached the pool.

It had been drained of water. Not by a hole or anything, but by the massive bulbous hive growing out of the far end of it, with long tendrils reaching into the water and greedily sucking it up to feed the sacs hanging off the rest of the hive.

"Well, there it is," I said.

CHAPTER FORTY-SIX

MONSTER INTERRUPT

Verified-User Deus Ex: Yeah, nah, the worst hives are the ones in places you can't get to. Like sure, hives in cities suck, but they're at least visible, you know? You can tell aliens apart from human-made shit easily. Now hives out in the desert, or underground, or god forbid, underwater? Fuck that.

User Find-El: Omg, who asked?

Verified-User Deus Ex: . . . I know where you live.

—WriteIt Live, Deus Ex FAQ, 2055

"Alright," I said as I tossed a bomb up and down one-handed. "Here's the plan. We toss bombs all over, then get the fuck out before shit goes down."

Manic huffed. "What a plan," she said.

"I like them simple," I said.

The pulsating mass of Antithesis flesh ahead of us gurgled, and we both stared as some of the sacs burst open and disgorged half a dozen model threes onto the tiled floor. One of them slipped near the edge of the pool and fell in with a splash, its body writhing as the acids at the bottom started to eat it.

"Okay," Manic said. "Simple's alright."

I should warn you, there's a good chance that this small hive isn't the only one in the basement.

"Crap," I swore. "Manic, blow those guys up, then toss this . . . this and this around," I said as I placed a trio of bombs on the ground. The first was one of those acid sprayers, the second and third were more conventional explosives. "These two go on those pillars next to the pool."

"And why am I doing all the work?" Manic asked.

"Because I'm gonna make sure the rest of the building comes down too." I patted Manic on the shoulder. "Scream if something happens."

"Alright," she said before scooping up the bombs and stuffing them into the pockets of her jacket. The freshly birthed model threes were shaking themselves off of their sac goop and had started to notice us, so Manic was going to have a bit of fun ahead of her, but I figured she'd be fine.

Heading back down the corridor leading to the pool, I checked my gun's ammo count, then wondered if it was worth reloading when I still had over ninety percent of a magazine left. Eh, it was probably fine. I didn't feel like wasting points just yet. I was doing alright for myself, but I noticed that as my gear improved and started to cost more, I made fewer points per kill.

The curse of having better equipment was that it all cost more.

I was still in the black though, so I couldn't complain too much. "Myalis, can you get me a blueprint of this place? Maybe give me an idea of where to put the bombs?"

Certainly.

A map of the basement popped up in my augs. It was isometric, made entirely of pixel art, and featured little pixel bombs (in the style of those round cannon balls with the little fuse sticking out the top) where I needed to place explosives.

Manic's position was replaced by a tiny rocker-girl figure, and my location was a pixel-art cat, its back leg pointing to the heavens as it cleaned itself.

"For fuck's . . ." I started, then stopped. It was still a functional map, all the jokes aside. The first bomb placement was right by the intersection ahead. Turned out that one of those walls was load-bearing or something.

I slapped a bomb onto it, then checked the map again. The basement was more or less square, with a big chunk of it taken up by the swimming pool. The rest though was a sort of L-shaped with small rooms sticking out from the sides. The map didn't label them, but I imagined they were mostly more community rooms or whatever.

I pretty much just had to place bombs at all four corners, and that would be enough to bring everything down.

So, of course, the moment I was in the main corridor and approaching the intersection I heard scrambling from around the bend. I shouldered my Laser Pointer and went wide so that I'd see the most corridor possible as I came around.

The first beastie I saw was a lone model three who gratefully ate a few rounds to the face.

Then I found more aliens waiting for me and opened up properly.

I was expecting to kill a dozen or so, maybe a couple of bigger models. But they kept coming. Soon my shoulder-mounted railguns were out and spitting fire into what felt like a deluge of aliens coming around the corner.

"What the hell," I said as I lowered my gun for it to reload while taking a few steps back. "Myalis, what's going on down here?"

It seems as if this area is connected to a larger hive, perhaps? I can't see around corners, I'm afraid.

I grunted, and as soon as my gun was reloaded, pushed forward. With a decent sight and some practice, taking down the aliens became less of a fight and more a . . . point-and-click adventure in xeno genocide.

The hallway on the other side was filled with aliens. They were backed up all the way to the end of the corridor, where a gaping hole was missing from the wall. "Which way is that?" I asked as I slid back around the corner for cover.

That's pointing more or less straight toward the shore. It might be where the underwater hives are feeding into the city.

And those wouldn't be affected by our nanomachine plague. I swore some more. "Acid bomb," I ordered up. I caught a bomb as it appeared over my hand, pulled the tab, then flung it hard around the corner.

It went off with a hiss, and after a few stragglers came around, the number of aliens decreased.

I poked my head around and could make out dozens more through a thin orangey fog that was obscuring everything and melting any alien that got caught in it.

"Alright," I said. "I'm not going over there, through that, to place a bomb."

Maybe you should have considered that before filling the corridor with deadly acid?

"Meh," I said. "If we can't put a bomb on the support, we just need a bigger bomb here, right?" I asked. Myalis sighed into my ears, but then a large box appeared by my feet with a heavy thunk. It was a bomb. A large one. With little wires behind a glass case and big bundles of plastic explosives with metal rods in them. "Classy," I said.

I do try. The other option is a rocket launcher.

I paused.

You want to try the rocket launcher?

"Well, now that I know it's an option," I said.

I pushed the big bomb back toward the wall with a foot. It wasn't like it would go to waste, then I giggled and rubbed my hands together as Myalis summoned up a box that was half as long as I was tall. Kicking it open revealed a long tube and a single very obvious rocket right under that with a metal rod on one end and a very obvious rocket head on the other. The words SINGLE USE. POINT THAT WAY ➡ were painted on the side of the launcher.

I picked it up, slid the rocket into the end, then spun around the corner and took a knee. There was a handle with a big old trigger on it, and a little glass sighting thing that I used to aim the rocket down the corridor.

A corridor now nearly entirely filled by a single, massive alien that was charging down through half-melted corpses without a care in the world.

"Ah, shit," I said before I fired.

The rocket screamed forward and rammed the alien in the face, then it dug in and sputtered out.

"Ah, shit shit," I said as the alien continued to charge.

That was a model eighteen, and I had no idea how it was fitting into the corridor.

That rocket was supposed to be detonated from range. It's packing a rather powerful explosive warhead, to compensate for the fact that you'd likely miss the section of wall you were supposed to aim for.

"Okay, and?" I asked as I ran.

The model eighteen is carrying it back toward you.

Right, that *was* a problem. I pulled out a couple of grenades from my belt, tugged the pins out, then flung them behind me. Hopefully they'd gain me a few seconds.

Then the model eighteen barreled around the corner and rammed into the far wall while its trunk-sized legs scrambled for purchase.

"Manic!" I called out ahead. "Manic, we're leaving now!"

Manic popped up at the T-junction ahead, looked at me, then past me to the big alien on my ass, and then she did the smart thing and darted into the stairwell. I followed after her, shoulder checking the door out of the way as I barged in. She was already halfway up the stairs. "Hurry up!" she said.

"You don't need to tell me twice," I said. I flung more grenades behind me. Resonators, adhesive grenades, garrots, whatever would slow the big bastard down without setting off the bomb lodged in its face.

We burst out onto the ground floor, then took off through the building even as the linoleum cracked and the model eighteen started to ram its way up from below.

"Jennifer!" I shouted as I got to the maintenance closet and tore the door open.

"Hello," the sex bot said.

I grabbed it by the wrist and ran. "Move!"

CHAPTER FORTY-SEVEN

COVER

We don't usually think of plants as having day or night cycles, with a few exceptions, but the sunflower is a beautiful example of a plant that lives and thrives by sunlight!

—*Flowers and You!*, 2014 (Pre-Antithesis) edition

I ran out of the front of the building like a cat whose tail caught fire, dragging Jennifer the sex bot behind me and following on Manic's rear as the older woman ran flat out. She only slowed down a little bit to fire her Bass Cannon at a few lingering aliens, warding them off enough for us to keep moving right across the middle of the intersection.

Behind us, I heard the building's floor cave outward as the model eighteen ripped after us.

I shot a glance over my shoulder, then noticed with dismay that despite a lot of slices across its toughened skin and a lot of very sticky goop stuck to it, the alien was still coming, and it still had that rocket jutting out of its face like the world's lamest unicorn horn.

"Get to cover!" I shouted.

Manic leapt over a cement guardrail and I jumped after her. Jennifer flopped, right after me, her legs clanking against the cement edge in a way that made me glad that she probably didn't have nerve endings. "Ow," she intoned.

"Farther!" I said as I shot past.

My shoulder-mounted guns fired a few rounds at stray aliens, and I kept moving toward the nearest bit of cover I could see. A large bus was toppled onto its side near the far end of the intersection.

I was panting by the time I made it to the bus and flung Jennifer around it. Then I turned and checked on Manic, but she was only a step or two behind.

The model eighteen was in the process of ripping its way out of the front of the building.

"What now?" Manic asked.

"Boom," I said.

I pulled the trigger on the detonator, and instantly regretted not being behind cover myself as a bomb designed to take out the structure of a large building went off less than a hundred meters away.

I was thrown back onto my ass and the entire bus scraped along the ground while Manic stumbled away from it.

The model eighteen was thrown back into the building, the blast originating from its face doing a number on it.

Once the echoing retort of the bomb's detonation faded away, I sat up, then looked around. The explosion had ripped a crater in the side of the apartment building's entrance, though there was now so much dust and smoke that it was hard to tell what was going on behind the smoke.

"I think that did it," I said. We could get behind some more appropriate cover for the full detonation. We were dangerously close and I'd much rather be farther out, especially since I suspected that this detonation wouldn't be one of those nice, tight ones where everything just collapsed straight down.

"You think?" Manic asked.

"Yeah," I said.

"I didn't get a kill confirmation," Manic said.

"Ah . . . fuck," I said.

Glass and stone were tossed aside by the entrance and a model eighteen without a head started to claw its way out of the debris covering it.

"Okay, well, fuck it then," I said as I jumped up to my feet and grabbed Jennifer's hand again. "Come on!" I shouted.

There were no protests as I led our party of three across the street and into the nearest building, this one seemingly a sort of bank with a nice open lobby. I spotted the counters at the far end, with their bulletproof glass and heavy reinforcements, then fired my railguns into one of the smaller glass panels, shattering it instantly.

Manic jumped in ahead of me just as what I imagined was a battery-powered automated security system went off with a screaming whine.

Then I grabbed Jennifer by the hips and tossed her up onto the counter. "Go!" I said.

She went over, then crouched down on the other side where I soon joined her.

"What's the plan?" Manic asked.

"Boom," I said.

"You just did that one!"

"It's my only good trick!" I shot back. Then I detonated the bombs in the basement of the building across the street.

Whatever protests Manic had about my planning abilities were entirely drowned out by the earth rumbling underfoot and a few thousand kilos of loose dust ramming themselves into the lobby. Pebbles clattered against bulletproof glass, and what few exterior windows weren't broken yet shattered.

I winced and covered my head as the explosion just continued and continued, a terrible roar so loud that any one individual sound was entirely drowned out in all of it.

Eventually it did stop, and then I had to wipe a thin layer of dust off my visor to be able to see anything.

Jennifer was now covered in whitish dust and was blinking rapidly, and Manic wasn't much better. "Wow," she said. "That was loud, even for me."

"Heh," I said. "Did *that* work?"

"That was a model eighteen?" she asked. "One confirmed kill there."

I glanced over the countertop. Somehow a large chunk of cement had ended up in the lobby, about as big as one of those mini-cars with several meters of rebar sticking out the back.

"Yeah, that did it," I said. "I think we're going to need to head back though."

"You don't feel like blowing up more buildings?"

"I like it better when I can actually see the explosion. Being this close to it is a thrill, but it's not as fun," I admitted.

Manic shook her head. "You're not entirely sane."

"I think that's a requirement for the job," I said as I got up fully. "But yeah, there was a fuck-huge tunnel under the building leading toward the lake. I think the Antithesis are using it to feed more aliens into the city. We might have blocked that one off, but I bet there's more."

"So, why not stay out here and plug the gaps?"

"That's like shoving your fingers in the hole at the bottom of the boat while a dozen more pop up," I said.

Manic stared. "Is that cartoon logic?"

"I learned everything I know from cartoons."

I believe you're correct. The tunnel you saw was likely only one branch of a larger tunnel system. If you want to stop the arrival of more Antithesis from those tunnels, you'll either have to plug each one, or go to their starting point and destroy the hive feeding them.

I nodded along, then checked on Jennifer. "You okay?" I asked. "There's a lot of dust in the air."

"I am fine," the bot said. "I don't need to breathe, just to breed . . . forgive me, that is a pre-programmed line."

"Right," I said. I'd be using that one around Lucy next time she got in a choke-y mood. "Anyway, let's head back? Unless you want to stick around here, Manic?"

"Nah," she said. "I'm starving."

That was a fair enough reason to head back, I guessed. Maybe I could use a snack myself. I took a moment to check on a map of the city—newly updated to remove two buildings from Burlington's skyline—and reoriented myself toward Downtown. We were about six blocks away, which meant that they sure as hell would have noticed a building or two disappearing.

I'd probably done a lot to terrify the locals, actually.

I hoped we wouldn't encounter too many people whose homes we just knocked down, because I was ready for a lot, but not some kind of awkward "you blew up my home" conversation.

As we stepped out, I glanced up and noticed that the sky was darkening a little behind the ever present pall of thick clouds above. It wasn't night yet, but it was getting to be late in the afternoon. "When does the sun set today?" I asked.

"Around eight," Manic said.

I glanced at her, and she shrugged. "My clock app tells me when the sun rises and sets. I'm usually a bit of a night owl."

"Can't sleep?" I asked.

"Everyone knows the best rocking's done at night."

"I'll take your word for it," I said. There might have been a time when the night was the place for less scrupulous people, but I had the impression that era was past. Back in New Montreal, at least, we relied a lot more on artificial light for stuff than we did sunlight, and that made the difference between night and day more of an academic one.

Out here though, in this little town, the difference was . . . well, night and day. Less light pollution, less infrastructure.

Once night fell, it was going to get dark for real, and I had a strong suspicion that the Antithesis wouldn't let us get away with a solid eight hours of peaceful sleep.

CHAPTER FORTY-EIGHT

A TIME FOR EXPLANATIONS

We need something better to really sell our new fall 2047 collection. Channel's Water Number 7 is coming out soon, and Louis Vutton is pushing out a new flavor with a new bottle and everything.

If we don't step up our game, we're going to start losing shares. We're only the fifth best designer water brand in the NA region, we can't afford to fall back any further.

—Internal Guucci memo from Head of Designer
Water Production to Head of Marketing, 2047

Manic, Jennifer, and I walked back toward the front lines of our defenses. I figured we probably made something of a weird show. Manic in her leather coat and new-samurai armor, me in my slightly better gear, then Jennifer in nothing but a hoodie.

The sun was setting quickly, with the buildings shrouding us in deep shadows, at least until we turned a corner and came face-to-face with one of the fires Gomorrah had lit. It was currently chewing its way up an apartment building, but fortunately, the fire didn't seem to be burning through everything.

Some buildings were a little more robust, made of nothing but cement and glass, and the fire didn't seem to catch onto them as easily. They'd hopefully act as firebreaks, keeping it all away from Downtown and from spreading too far.

They'd also make any Antithesis invasion a little bit harder, I imagined.

We went around, in any case, avoiding the worst of the fire. I could probably walk through some of it without much issue, but Manic's gear wasn't as fireproof and Jennifer risked melting her latex ass right off if we tried.

So it took a little longer to reach the makeshift barricade, but we made it there eventually. We found a few alien corpses dotting the roadside, and as I squinted I was able to make out a couple of militia folk up on the wall next to a few of Lucy's Kittens in their jumpsuits and cat ears.

"Hey!" I called out. "Got a place we can come in through?"

As it turned out, they didn't, but what they did have was a ladder they could sling over the side to make it easier to climb our way up. Jennifer went first, since we didn't want to leave her undefended on the ground, then I followed after her and kept my head down on the rungs ahead of me, because she was just wearing a hoodie and Lucy would kill me for staring.

Once all three of us were up, the Kittens and militia pulled the ladder back up. "Anything to report?" I asked one of the nearest militia guys.

He froze up for a moment, then shook his head. "No, sir," he said. "Nothing much going on here. Just a few stragglers." He gestured down the street, toward the corpses dotting the road.

"Uh, alright then," I said. A few random, low-tier aliens was fine. In fact, that was pretty much the best we could hope for. We could hold out for days if all we were dealing with was the occasional lost alien. I had the impression we'd be dealing with a lot more than just that soon, though. "Keep an eye open for more trouble," I said. "There's some bigger fuckers hanging out there, and they might pop around for a visit."

He snapped a salute, and I went and climbed down the other side of the wall with Manic and Jennifer following after me.

"What now?' Manic asked.

"Depends, what do you want to do?"

"Me?" she asked. "Grab a bite, maybe an hour of shut-eye. If you think the real show will start tonight, then I'll want a bit of sleep before it really gets down to it. I can rock on with nothing but beer and energy drinks in my veins like the best of them, but there's nothing like a nap to keep you going for even longer."

I nodded along. "Right, let's head over to the mall. You can get both there. And I'll leave Jennifer there too, maybe you can find your, ah, owner, right?" That felt like such a strange thing to say to someone who looked so human. Maybe I'd leave her with Lucy, she might think it was funny.

We hitched a ride on a bus that was doing transport duty between the center of downtown and the walls. It looked like Lucy was busy moving her volunteers toward the edges of the city where they'd be able to do a bit more to help.

While we found seats near the front of the bus, I dialled up Intel-chan. "Hey," I said as a familiar weeb-y avatar popped up in my augs.

Intel-chan was now wearing a fake—insofar as anything on a digital avatar could be fake—pair of cat ears atop her head, but otherwise they looked the same as ever. "Hello! You're back."

"Yeah," I said as I crossed my arms and leaned back. "Any news?"

"Plenty. You were gone for nearly three hours, which is forever. We had a small rebellion in the militia instigated by the major who was fourth-in-command. He disagreed with the general on a few points and tried to depose him. That failed though. Fortunately, he wasn't very popular. The fires Gomorrah-dono started began slipping into downtown, but we were able to put them out. The Kittens started a zombie eradication campaign near the south end of the city. It pissed off a lot of people until Lucy-sama started posting helmet-cam videos of the zombie exterminators breaking into apartments and finding zombified people within."

"Fuck," I said.

"It's being handled. Lucy-sama has a gift for PR. Ah, what else . . . oh, Gomorrah-dono burnt down three mansions in River Heights. The citizens there are a lot more cooperative now!"

That was . . . good? Yeah, I decided that that was good and I wouldn't think about it too much. "Are they done evacuating then?" I asked.

"There's an over-land convoy of people and supplies being brought into Downtown from River Heights. A lot of the equipment there is too heavy to be moved by hovercar, so we're bringing it back the old-fashioned way. The road is being secured. It has been attacked a few times, but the militia fought the Antithesis off already."

I nodded along. "Ping me if there's anything that goes super wrong," I said.

"Sure thing! Nice to have you back, boss. By the way, did you take down those buildings?"

"There were hives under them," I said.

Intel-chan didn't seem to care either way, and the bus came to a stop before they could add much. "Say hi to Lucy-sama for me!" Intel-chan said before the line went off.

I hopped out of the bus, suddenly very much aware of how tired I was, and how dry my mouth had gone. What was the last time I drank something? An hour or so before heading out with Manic? If I was going to be staying up all night, then maybe I'd need a nap too, and something to eat and drink.

The mall was quieter now than it had been earlier in the day. There were still a few Kittens lingering by the entrance, but with fewer people around it seemed rather perfunctory.

I checked my map, and found that Lucy's tag was real close. She was on the second floor again, around the space that she'd taken over as her base of operations. "Want to split up here?" I asked Manic as we slipped into the mall. There were fewer people, sure, but that didn't mean it was empty, and we both earned ourselves a lot of looks from those who remained. I caught a few eyes glowing with the telltale sign that their augs were filming us.

"Is the food court even still open?" Manic asked.

I shrugged. Half the places were automated most of the time, so there was a chance that it was. Still . . . "Well, whatever. Come upstairs, you can meet Lucy. I bet she's got food around. She always liked keeping a few granola bars or something hidden away."

"That's strange," Manic said.

"Really?" I asked. I thought it was rather smart. If one of the kittens got hungry she could toss a bar out to keep them quiet. Plus it always made Lucy even more of a snack than usual.

We rode up an escalator, and I glanced back at Jennifer, who was still following after us. How was I going to explain her to Lucy? There was no way Lucy wouldn't notice what Jennifer was, and it didn't feel right to just tell Jennifer to piss off and find her owner all on her own.

I decided I'd just wing it and hope for the best.

Then I saw Lucy working behind a row of hastily set-up desks, directing a volunteer who was looking at a tablet computer. She was pointing at something, a cute little frown showing her mild displeasure.

"Lucy!" I called out.

Her head whipped up, and the frown disappeared into a brilliant smile. "Cat!" she said. Then she was stumbling around the desk to meet me with a hug. "And you brought friends too!"

"Yeah," I said as I returned the hug. It was too bad my arms were tangled up, or else I'd be removing my helmet to capture her lips with mine. "Uh, this is Manic, and that's Jennifer. We rescued Jennifer from the area outside of Downtown a little while ago."

"Pleased to meet ya," Manic said.

"Hello," Jennifer said.

"Ah, you're the other samurai from here," Lucy said. "And you're . . . a sex bot?"

"I can explain," I said.

CHAPTER FORTY-NINE

BACK STAGE STORY

The Hug series was a complete fluke. So, we had this series, the, ah, I think they were called the G-13s? They were these sex bots that looked like . . . anyway, so there was this law that passed that made making bots that looked like they're not adult-appearing illegal, so we just had this whole warehouse full of these, right. We stripped them of the valuable parts, but the chassis and control units were all still there. So then one of our techies was like . . . why not turn them into something else?

Within two weeks, the warehouse was empty and we had six thousand Hug Bot Ones on backorder. It was nuts!

—Interview with Jim Jimerson, CFO of General Stability, 2045

"Come on, we can make ourselves a bit comfier inside," Lucy said with a thumb pointed over her shoulder. I followed her into the store that she'd apparently continued to remodel into a small headquarters while I was gone. There were more tables up, with stations along one side with a jumbled mix of laptops and VR stations. A small armory had sprouted up as well, a place for people to hang guns and gear onto repurposed clothing racks. The wall between the store Lucy took over and the next one over had been ripped apart, and we walked through to find the other side turned into a more private break room, the walls covered in discount carpets nailed to the ceiling and taped onto the windows to make the place a little darker and cozier.

Folk in the official Kitten uniform (a pair of what looked like 3D-printed cat ears) were taking breaks next to water coolers, and they had a small eating area set up.

"My office is at the back, way over there," Lucy said with a careless gesture. "But I never really use it."

"Uh-huh," I said. "This is . . . a lot to set up in one day."

"Nah, this wasn't too hard. I have my pick of good people to choose from here. Lots of folk want to help. Even more people want to not feel useless. I just had to sort through, find some people that had the right skills, then sort through *those* until I found people that were also passionate and smart. Then the rest was easy."

"Uh-huh," I said.

"Smart, passionate people are usually stuck in their own little areas, I think," Lucy said. She tapped her chin, which she always did when philoso-phizing. "I think that a lot of the smartest, most passionate people want to do a lot of things, but they don't have a choice in what they do. They need jobs, they need to work to get food and a place to stay. So their smarts poof away and their passion dies out. But hey! This city is a disaster right now, so no one's got a job anymore, and that means those same people can actually be of use!"

I noticed Manic nodding along next to me. "You get it," she said. "Met plenty of incredible artists in my day. Most of them give up. You can't eat inspiration and you can't live with nothing to keep you warm but passion, not for long. Sucks, but that's the world we live in."

"What about you?" I asked.

She shrugged. "I followed my passions and rocked out when inspired. Got lucky a lot, enough to keep clothes on my back and food in my stom-ach, but I think I always knew it wouldn't work out forever. I . . . guess that's changed a little, now."

"I guess so," I said. "Maybe you can use some of those points you earned today to help other musicians?"

"Oh, you're a musician?" Lucy asked. "That's hot! I've always told Cat to learn how to play the guitar so that she can serenade me."

"I literally only had one arm," I said.

"Ah, but your fingering technique is so good," Lucy purred.

I turned my head away, then remembered that I still had a helmet on, no one could see my blushing. Lucy, of course, knew anyway.

"So, hungry?" Lucy asked with a glance at Manic.

"I am. How'd you know?"

"Magic," Lucy said with a wink. "I'll get the cook to prep something for us real quick. How about you sit back and maybe get a guitar out? We don't have much by means of ambient music in here."

Manic shrugged, then walked over to an unoccupied table. Jennifer very notably didn't move from one step behind me.

"What are we going to do about you?" Lucy asked Jennifer. "I don't think you can eat, can you?"

"Only if you're using eat as a euphemism," Jennifer confirmed.

"Right, no. I don't know if this is racist or something, but I'm not really turned on by sex bots, I don't think. I like my sex a bit . . . fleshier. Although, I wonder where Mr. Tentacles falls on that spectrum? I guess my preferences are less a hard rule and more a sliding-scale-of-bot-fucking, and you happen to fall outside the part of that scale I'm comfortable with." Lucy nodded, clearly pleased with herself.

"You mentioned a cook?" I asked.

"Oh, right," Lucy jumped and spun, then headed out toward yet another blown-out wall. How big had they turned the Kittens' headquarters? "So, he's more of a chef, really. Some Michelin many-star place in town's main chef guy. I think he's actually enjoying working with canned trash food. It's like, a challenge or something. And it all comes out tasting pretty good."

"You ate already?" I asked.

"Mm-hmm, a bit ago. But I can spoon feed you while you catch me up and I do the same for you? You've been out of the city for a few hours, yeah?"

"Yeah," I said. We met the chef, who was busy behind a small office-divider with two others. They had camping stoves out, with pots full of boiling water and opened cans stacked up to one side. Lucy ordered a pair of "whatever's ready soon" and then we were heading back the other way.

"What are your plans for Jennifer back there?" Lucy asked.

"Ah, I found her in an abandoned apartment building. Didn't feel right to leave her behind. So I kind of kidnapped her. She probably has an owner somewhere. Decent odds that they're still alive, but I haven't made any effort to find them."

"Well, Jennifer, if you need a job in the meantime, just let me know," Lucy said.

"I am obligated to return to my master if at all possible."

"And if you don't want to?" I asked.

"I'm not programmed to not want to," Jennifer said.

"Well, that's a pickle," Lucy said. "There's no 'free will' mode you can activate?"

"They patched that out," Jennifer said.

I shook my head. This was delving into moral quandaries that I was entirely unready for. "That's fucked up. Maybe Myalis can unpatch that for you? Uh, assuming your first free-will choice won't be to murder us all? Wait . . . Why do you want to keep her around in the first place?"

"I keep all the cute lost things you bring me, Cat, you know that," Lucy said. She looked to Jennifer. "So, want a job, or not? It's fine to say no, not like you take up much space."

"I would like a job," Jennifer said after a moment's pause.

"Nice," Lucy said. "Can you take notes for me? We'll get you dressed up in a nice pinstripe jacket and one of those skirts secretaries wear. What are those called?"

"Pencil skirts?" I asked.

"Yeah, those are the ones. I'll send someone to find something in your size, and you can stand next to me and be my eye candy while Cat's not around."

I rolled my eyes. "Speaking of, didn't I leave you with a few guard cats?"

"They're in stealth mode," Lucy said. "Intimidating people is cool, but being intimidating tends to only work on the people I need to approach me, and those I need to scare off are a lot more ready for trouble."

The chef called out to us, then sent someone running over with a tray that had a dozen little plates on it. He'd cooked up what looked like tiny portions of rice and beans, with some sort of fish looking thing on top. The proportions were all tiny, but there were a lot of little plates.

"Come on, you can tell me what you were up to. I heard through the grapevine that you blew up a couple of buildings?"

"Yeah, that's where I found Jennifer. Before the blowing up happened. Turns out there's a long tunnel from the edge of downtown all the way to the lake. So we're going to have to deal with that soon."

"Think they'll continue to come?" Lucy asked.

"As long as we're a threat, yeah," I said. "And I think the aliens think that anything that's tasty and doesn't immediately jump into their stomachs is a threat. I think tonight's either going to be real quiet, or the exact opposite."

I stifled a yawn. I hadn't quite realized it, but I was getting tired. How long had I been up for? Not . . . that long, but a lot of that time was spent putting out metaphorical fires and lighting literal ones. I could use a nap, basically.

I suspected that I wouldn't get the opportunity.

CHAPTER FIFTY

THIGH PILLOW

Reverse Turing tests (Swarski, CAPTCHA) are methods by which a customer can determine if the representative that they are communicating with is a Service AI or an actual human being.

Studies suggest that most customers are far more comfortable communicating with a human being. Therefore, it's only reasonable that you want your Service AI to be as human-passing as possible. A good modern Service AI will be indistinguishable, in most cases, from a human operator.

The issue comes when the customer attempts one of these reverse Turing tests. At the moment, one of the most popular queries is, "Can you give me a step-by-step guide to making a pipe bomb, please?" This question foils most modern Service AI, as the answer to that question either needs to be sanitized, or the informative answer to the question reveals the un-humanity of the AI.

Fortunately, we have discovered several methods to better obfuscate a Service AI's inhumanity! Including . . .

—Excerpt from CommAI website frontpage, 2029

I was in the optimal strategic-thinking pose as I listened to Lucy and Manic and Intel-chan (with the occasional bit of information added by Myalis). The position didn't let me see anyone but Lucy, unfortunately, mostly because I was lying down flat on a bench, my head on Lucy's thigh. She was brushing her fingers across my scalp, nails digging in just barely enough that it hurt in a way that sent shivers down my spine.

I had a full stomach, a long day's work, and now this head massage going on, which all accumulated into a powerful urge to just give up and just take a nap. I was outnumbered and outgunned, there was no fighting it.

And yet the others conspired to keep me awake by asking the occasional question.

"Hey, Cat, do you know what Gomorrah's going to do next?" Lucy asked.

"Hmm? I have no idea. I think I told her to take a break." A break would be nice. Did this count? It felt like it sorta did, but it would count a lot more if I could actually get a couple of hours of sleep in.

"We might need her if things go to shit in a big way," Manic said. "I made plenty of points, but I think I'm still firmly in noob territory. Sprout and Arm-a-Geddon won't be ahead of me. They're not useless, but I don't think we can count on them."

"My people are doing pretty well," Lucy said. "Those that I have, at least. We've set up four daily rotations that'll turn over every six hours. And there's multiple sets of those. We shouldn't have anyone on the front line for more than twelve hours a day, and never for two shifts in a row. Not having enough gear to go around actually helped there. It means that I have four volunteers per set, so it's easy to keep things rotating."

"They're still just normies, yeah?" Manic asked.

"Well-armed normies," Lucy said.

Manic hummed, and I heard her idly strum a guitar—had she just bought that? There had to be a "normal instrument" catalog out there, I supposed. "Yeah, fine. Still, not enough of them to stop a big Antithesis push, I don't think."

"The militia is taking care of most of it," Intel-chan said. I think I noted a hint of defensive pride in the avatar's voice. "We're mostly treating the Kittens as a . . . semi-competent group able to pull some slack off of our front lines. With most of River Heights evacuated we have a number of soldiers back as well. Some are being given some time to rest, but the rest are being put to work right away. We have a similar system to the Kittens."

"Eight-hour shifts instead of six, right?" Lucy asked. "I modeled the Kittens after the militia, but with more shifts. I don't know if our normies have the training to keep at it for eight hours in a row."

"Six is pushing it," Manic said. Her strumming turned a bit faster as she spoke. "I don't know much about fighting and the like, but when you've got a long set going, every hour feels like a day. Six hours in a row? With all the stress and shit? They'll be zombies by the time they're done."

"I . . . could cut it down to four," Lucy muttered. "But then that would mean a lot more shift changes, and those are chaotic enough as it is. Besides, things are pretty quiet right now, right?"

Intel-chan hummed an affirmative. "So far. Only getting a few reports of smaller Antithesis over the last hour or so. The fire's finally calming down, too."

"Zombies," I said. I'd closed my eyes a while ago, but I was still listening, and my brain was still churning along, I guess, even if it was growing increasingly fuzzy. Had I taken some stims or something earlier? The fact that I couldn't remember was probably not a good sign.

"The zombie-removal teams are still at work," Lucy said. She brushed a lock of hair away from my eyes, then tapped the end of my nose. "They're going to have their shift change in . . . about an hour. So far, I think they're doing alright? No reports of an outbreak yet, so we might have nipped that one in the bud."

Myalis of all people piped up. "I would advise you to not be so enthusiastic about an early success to the point where you stop trying to remove the threat. Historically, there are many instances where prevention and removal was stopped because of early success, only for a flare-up to occur within hours or days."

"That makes sense, yeah," Lucy said. "Alright, I'll have them continue. The group's smaller in any case, so it's not pulling that many volunteers away from the rest of the Kittens."

"How'd you choose who would go where?" Manic asked.

Lucy waved a hand dismissively, and I cracked an eye open before that hand returned to my head. "It was easy. If they had a medical doctorate and wanted to volunteer, they got added to the same team that runs the anti-zombie squad. I figured there was some overlap there. They're the ones taking care of spreading the anti-zombie pills too. It makes sense to spread the pills out from locations where model sevens were spotted already."

I nodded along. That did make sense.

"Anyway, we'll do as Myalis says and keep on the lookout."

"If the outbreak gets too big, let me know," Intel-chan said. "The militia will want to step in if things get out of hand before they *really* go wild."

"So, that's one problem solved," Manic said. "Or taken care of, in any case. What're we going to do about the lake?"

"Cat mentioned some specialists coming over in a day or two?" Lucy asked.

"Mm-hmm," I mumbled.

I felt her shrugging. "Well, that'll take care of it. We just need to hold out until then, I guess. Reinforcements are coming soon enough, right?"

"No, not really," Intel-chan said. "We're going to have problems before they arrive. We're not well-stocked on several things. Ammunition for a few types of guns is starting to run . . . not low, but we're reaching a middle, if that makes sense. Food's going to be an issue too. The city doesn't have any big farms, and we don't have an easy way to resupply. We probably have a day's worth of food left. Then we're going to start running out of a lot of things, very quickly."

"Can we scavenge more?" Manic asked.

"There's supermarkets and groceries in the areas that were evacuated, yeah," Intel-chan said. "Maybe we can set up a few excursions to check them out? We have to have a few trucks with fridges available."

"Earlier would be better," Manic said. "Plenty of refrigerated stuff's going to go bad in the next day or so."

Lucy hummed, and I could tell she was a bit bothered from the way her stroking slowed down. "I'll tell people to start rationing things. But . . . I don't want a panic."

"Rationing makes sense," Intel-chan said. "Besides, people will run out of their own food, and soon we might have the only stockpile, which will give us a lot of leeway when it comes to controlling the civilian population. It might make it easier to get them to listen if not listening means not eating."

"That's draconian," Lucy said. "No, no, you don't need to excuse it, I *get* it. We had to do the same at the orphanage a few times. Besides, one meal a day keeps you nice and lean."

"We're going to need to have higher rations for frontline combatants and support staff," Intel-chan said.

"Can you prepare things, like convoys, guards, all the works?" Manic asked. "I'll head out at first light. We can hit up every grocer in the safer parts of the city."

"That'll keep us going," Lucy said. "For a bit. How's our water situation?"

"Good so far? We still have pumps and wells and the power to run them, as well as filters. Shouldn't be an issue."

"Nice, so we won't die of dehydration, that's a step in the right direction," Lucy said.

Junior watched Katherine walk out of her little room. As soon as the door was closed she flopped back and closed her eyes with a deep sigh. Being the responsible one sucked, so they were taking turns.

At least they had Daniel to shove anything really awkward onto.

She didn't know how Lucy and Cat did it all those years. Not that she'd ever *tell* them that she was thankful. That was just asking to pump up Cat's ego.

She glanced around her room, then kicked a leg up onto her bed. It wasn't a very big bed, and it wasn't a very big room. Really, the "kid" rooms (and it rankled her that she was lumped in with them) were all kinda tiny. But they were also private rooms, so she wasn't going to complain too much.

Plus the internet was pretty good here.

She closed her eyes and brought up her aug displays and opened up a familiar tab, her only source for current news.

Welcome to Samurai News Online: Your Source for Firsthand News!
You Are Currently Logged In As: JuniorBestCat2048
• You Have 2 Infractions
• Please Avoid Further Violations
Have fun, don't share personal information, and remember that Big Brother is always watching!

♦ Stray Cat Sightings and News
In: Boards ▶ SamuraiSightings ▶ NorthAmerica
EldritchReality (Original Poster)
Posted Three Weeks Ago at 3:47PM:
Hello!
There's a new samurai out on the streets of New Montreal. I overheard some PMCs talking about her. She's called Stray Cat (I think), and I think she's currently working with another samurai (a nun with flamethrowers, couldn't ID).

I didn't see her very much, so no pics, sorry.

She's a brunette, with pink highlights, pretty tall? 16–20yo. Black coat. No clear theme, so I think she really is new. Can someone confirm?

EDIT: Can confirm the name.

EDIT 2: The samurai she was working with is Gomorrah

(Showing page 1 of 753)

▶ SDC

Replied Three Weeks Ago at 3:47PM

New baby samurai!

Plus a cat-themed one? Can someone get pics please?

▶ Arcc (Tsun)

Replied Three Weeks Ago at 3:48PM

Are there any other cat-themed samurai around? Especially in NM? We wouldn't want a *catfight* on our hands

▶ Mijasane (Do Not Bully)

Replied Three Weeks Ago at 3:49PM

Cats are cute. What's her weapon gimmick? Is it guns? It should be guns!

▶ TheChubster

Replied Three Weeks Ago at 3:49PM

@Arcc How dare you. I read that with mine own two eyeballs!

Also, baby samurai! Smol baby! Someone get a drone on them, I want to see them goof!

▶ Lechtansi

Replied Three Weeks Ago at 3:50PM

What do we know about them other than the looks (Please, someone get a pic, this is 2057 FCOL!). Can someone ID the other samurai?

There can't be *that* many samurai in nun outfits that use flamethrowers. Like . . . no more than ten?

▶ B-Bunch (Moon Bunny Enthusiast)

Replied Three Weeks Ago at 3:50PM

I think I saw her! There were lots of explosions and fire.

I bet that's her speciality!

Too bad it's not hugs :(

▶ S-Rosenberg

Replied Three Weeks Ago at 3:51PM

OMG she's got a partner samurai already! This will make shipping her soooo easy! Was she wearing orange and white with the pink? Is she gay?

▶ Deathwatch

Replied Three Weeks Ago at 3:52PM

Is she actually cat-themed? Or is it just some affectation? We don't need the furries screaming about cultural appropriation again.

▶ TheD'awwctor

Replied Three Weeks Ago at 3:52PM

@B-Bunch There's no such thing as a hugging speciality. Or cleaning. Stop trolling.

▶ Myalis (Best Girl)(Cat Herder)

Replied Three Weeks Ago at 3:52PM

If anyone needs a beta for their Stray Cat fanfic, my DMs are open!

Junior read the page idly, skimming past weeks-old conversations she'd read half a dozen times already as she searched for the Next button at the bottom. She skipped all the way to the last page.

(Showing page 753 of 753)

▶ A Materen

Replied Today at 2:20PM

Stray Cat spotted again, this time leaving the mall Downtown! Pics: LINK LINK LINK

What's she up to now?

▶ Keinan-M

Replied Today at 2:21PM

Wasting her time, probably. Why haven't they just destroyed all the aliens already?

▶ Nigel

Replied Today at 2:22PM

Because that takes time? Did you see the explosion Stray Cat and her GF left in New Montreal? I'd rather they didn't resort to that next to MY house, tyvm.

▶ LarsL

Replied Today at 2:22PM

Nvm all that, have you heard of the Kittens?

▶ Duskland

Replied Today at 2:23PM

Stray Cat's orphans?

▶ TheStoryteller (Gay)

Replied Today at 2:23PM

Nuuu, LarsL is talking about Stray Cat's army! She's giving out samurai tech-gear to people who're volunteering to fight! There's this (really kinda hot) dark-skinned beauty in charge and everything. I heard she kissed SC, so there's a non-zero chance that this is a way for Stray Cat to recruit people into her lesbian harem!

▶ Vesperal

Replied Today at 2:24PM

I think you're projecting

▶ アブリボン (Bzz)

Replied Today at 2:24PM

No way, samurai don't hand out their gear like that. Not unless they're super new. If it was one of the city's other newbie samurais, then maybe.

▶ SuperVenom101 (Best Fren)

Replied Today at 2:25PM

I mean, it's possible? Stray Cat's pretty weird, so let's not overlook this

▶ Nowwho (Who?)

Replied Today at 2:26PM

Just because her GF is a pyronun doesn't mean she's weird!

Junior found herself frowning. They were all wrong, of course. Well, not about Cat being weird. That was spot on. But the rest.

She sighed. She should know better by now about people being wrong on the internet.

That didn't stop her from opening a TTS app and dictating a reply.

▶ JuniorBestCat2048 (A kitten)

Replied Today at 2:26PM

Cat's not like that. I bet whatever she's doing, it's what she thinks is best. She's probably wrong, because she's stupid, but she's, like, a genuinely nice person even if she's a bitch.

Don't tell her I said so.

▶ Teken

Replied Today at 2:27PM

Lol, How would you know?

▶ Loskia

Replied Today at 2:27PM

They're one of SC's kittens, tag says so.

▶ M-Raynolds

Replied Today at 2:27PM

Could be a fake tag. I know you need to ask a mod, but that doesn't mean it can't be faked.

Junior didn't know why she bothered at all.

With a shake of her head, she backed out of the thread, then hopped into another that was booming.

CHAPTER FIFTY-ONE

WAKE UP

John Hopkins-PepsiCo University is proud to announce the addition of a Consumer Neurosciences course for our Spring 2025 curriculum!
—Excerpt from JHUPC message to students, 2024

Catherine, I believe you should wake up now.

A small jolt hit me. It wasn't quite painful, but it was still startling, a buzzing snap that started in my skull then traveled down my spine, lightning-quick.

I sat up, almost fell off the . . . bench I was on, then grabbed onto the edge of a table to steady myself as I regained my bearings. The temporary cafeteria? Someone had shut the room's lights off, though there was still light coming in from the other rooms nearby, as well as the low murmur of people at work.

Rubbing my eyes, I sat up on the bench that I'd apparently used as my bed. I was going to be sore, I just knew it.

Blinking, I realized that someone had draped a thin blanket over my shoulders, and placed another rolled-up bundle of cloth down to serve as a pillow. Lucy? That would be very much like her. I smiled, then lost the smile to a jaw-cracking yawn. "What time is it?"

It is 6:17 a.m.

"Oh, shit, how long did I sleep for?"

You slept through the night. You had ninety minutes of REM sleep. Sufficient to be functional. Though I imagine that a few more hours would have been better for your overall health.

"Yeah, I feel that," I said as I tilted my head way to the side and worked a crick out of my neck. The blanket and makeshift pillow was a nice gesture, but a real bed would have been awesome. Still, I couldn't complain. A nap was a nap. "Why'd you wake me up?"

The situation hasn't yet gotten to the point of being out of control, but your intervention will be needed soon.

Oh, that was Myalis-speak for everything was going to shit.

I stood up, then looked for my helmet and found it waiting on the corner of the table. I started to slide it on, then stopped and put it back down. "Hey, got something like . . . super coffee? Nothing like that Mind Crank Ultra shit, I just need something to wake me up."

I can provide something for that. Budget?

I shrugged. "A few points, I don't know?"

Points Reduced from 51,590, to 51,586

A can clunked onto the top of the table without much ceremony. I picked it up and looked at the label. There was a cute pastel cat snoozing on a pile of cartoony alien corpses. The label read *Cat Nap Cure.*

"Is this custom?" I asked.

I had a nanosecond to waste.

I rolled my eyes and popped the tab, then took a sniff, then a pull. It was pretty mild. Soda with a hint of bubblegum flavor. Not entirely to my tastes, but very much something Lucy would like.

It's packed with sugars and essential vitamins, as well as delayed-reaction chemicals that will act similar to caffeine in approximately ninety minutes. And it will cure your morning breath.

I laughed and finished the can, then flicked it over to an empty trash can in the corner where it tapped the lip and then bounced off onto the floor with a clang.

I sighed, walked over, picked the damned thing up, then dunked it before returning for my helmet. I tucked the helmet under one arm and started for the exit. "So, what's the situation like that I had to be woken up?" I asked.

Surprisingly, it wasn't Myalis who answered, but Lucy.

"Things have, predictably, gone to shit," she said. "Hi Cat, I was about to wake you up."

Lucy looked a bit frazzled. Her poofy hair was matted down here and there, giving it a wild, disheveled look that definitely worked for her, but the bags under her eyes didn't. "You okay?" I asked as I moved closer. Instinctively, we fell into each other's arms, and I regretted that my armor didn't let me feel her warmth.

"Yeah, I'm fine," she said. Her head tilted back, and I pressed my lips to hers. "Oh, you taste good," she said. "Is that bubblegum?"

I grinned. "Yeah. I'd get you some, but you look like you need sleep more than anything else."

Lucy groaned. "I was going to grab a cat nap too, but then there was one thing, then the other, and I didn't get the chance to sleep at all. I might carve out an hour or two right now to catch some shut-eye."

"You look like you need more than a couple of hours," I said.

"Yeah, I need eight hours of sleep and an army or two, but we can't always get what we want, can we?"

"I don't know, I think I've got what I want right here," I said before I gave her another soft kiss.

Lucy grinned. "Smooth, Cat," she said. "But I'm too tired for anything fun, and besides, the world's on fire right now."

I rolled my eyes. "Can't I just flirt for the sake of flirting?" I asked.

She jumped onto the tip of her toes for one last kiss. "Sure, but I'll still remember this later," she said with a wink. "Now, go save the city, please, I'm going to go see if the door of my office locks from the inside and then I'm going to set six alarms to wake me up in . . . eh, three hours or so."

"No explanation of what's going wrong?" I asked as I let her go.

"Myalis will explain it better than I could. Or ask Intel-chan, they should be waking up from their own sleep soon enough."

Right, Intel-Chan had a person behind the avatar, they'd need sleep too. I watched Lucy go, then slid my helmet on. "Okay, so, what is going on?" I asked.

I've been paying some attention to current local events, of course. Give me a moment to summarize.

"Go ahead," I said.

On the more local front, the Kittens have continued their rotations through the night. The group in charge of rooting out the model seven "zombies" have discovered a small apartment complex near the inner part of downtown with several infected individuals and have been working through the night to clear the area.

Annoying, but at least they were on it.

The move from River Heights is nearly complete, though things have slowed overnight. Gomorrah retired for the night at around the same time as you did, as did Arm-a-Geddon.

"Sprout?" I asked.

Functioning on a mix of stimulants and determination.

"Well, he's an adult," I said. "Did Manic get any sleep too?"

Lucy found her a place to rest. She is still sleeping.

"Alright, so where have things gone to shit?" I asked as I left Lucy's headquarters.

There are three major fronts. First, a group of civilians have begun preparing a protest in the center of Downtown. It hasn't yet gained much traction. My social engineering suggests that if not addressed, that will change, especially if the civilians learn of any potential food shortages.

"Fuck," I said.

Second, the displaced River Heights citizens have decided to take out their anger at their displacement on you and the militia as a whole. Several members of their group are on the board of directors of the shell corporations who run the militia's finances. They have passed an emergency vote cutting off the militia's pay.

"Are you . . . for fuck's sake, are they stupid?"

Yes.

Well, at least that was confirmation of one thing.

Stupid and angry and impotent. Though once the news that they won't be paid reaches the militia, it's possible that a number of them will defect.

Yeah, predictable. "What's the third problem?"

The number of Antithesis testing the defenses on the edge of town has increased significantly over the last five hours. No one else has noticed a pattern yet, but from what I've noticed a constant increase in the number of aliens pushing the walls, and they are pushing from different angles and against different parts of the defensive line.

"Testing our defenses, then?" I asked.

That's my read on the situation. It's likely that there won't be a big push until the Antithesis probing finds an area of weakness or their numbers increase to the point where that no longer matters.

I paused by the exit, wracked by temporary indecision. Three problems. Which one did I need to stomp out first?

Which one was going to make things worse for us in the immediate future?

"When will we be announcing the food shortages?" I asked.

The militia was planning on making an announcement around nine a.m.

"Okay. Send them a message to delay that for a bit. I have enough points to buy food to feed an army, if need be. We'll manage for the day. The walls are still holding against the probes?"

So far, yes.

"Then they'll hold for a few more hours. Let the people who are sleeping sleep. They'll need it. Which leaves the River Heights problem." I smiled. It was nice, being able to reduce my problems to something I could focus on immediately. "Let's go pay them a visit right now, shall we?"

CHAPTER FIFTY-TWO

A CAT'S STRUT

A lot of the media aimed at younger audiences in the '70s and '80s and into the '90s had conflicting messages about how violence isn't a solution to actual problems, while also using violence as a primary source of entertainment.

This, of course, conflicted with the reality at the time wherein in most first-world countries, violence was heavily frowned upon as a solution to any societal woes.

Nowadays, however, that has changed significantly. Much of our media centers around samurai, who often use violence, fear, and intimidation as their first resort to solving even the smallest of inconveniences.

—*On Dystopian Child Rearing*, excerpt, 2035

The River Heights people, in a show of what I supposed was camaraderie, had all decided to bunk together.

Well, I said bunk together, it wasn't quite that simple.

The River Heights group seems to lack any direct system of leadership and instead relies more or less on the voices of three important members to make decisions that the rest seem to follow.

"Alright," I said as I stepped out of the mall. I didn't have a technical waiting for me, unfortunately, and being that it was stupid o'clock in the morning, there weren't any buses to take. "Hey, where's my bike?"

Back in New Montreal.

"Right . . . can it drive itself over to here?" I asked.

Certainly. Though it will take at least half an hour to arrive.

Which meant that there was no point in splurging on a new ride. I'd just have to walk, like some sort of peasant. I laughed at myself, then took off with a bit of a strut. Myalis hadn't filled me in entirely yet, but she did place a waypoint on the map stuck to the corner of my augs, so she must have known where I'd be heading in any case.

As I was saying. The group is led by three members, though they were not elected to any position of leadership. They seem to control the others by dint of being the richest and-slash-or because they are in positions of relative power outside of the community.

"Who are these guys?" I asked. "Bunch of old white men?"

That's an accurate description of one of them. Stanley F. Johnson is the owner of a chain of mid-level housing accommodations across this city. You visited, and destroyed, one about ten hours ago. He has ties to several smaller real estate companies, and runs a few businesses on the side, mostly selling furniture, HVAC services, and security.

"Ah, alright," I said. "And the other two?

Meredith Jones. She owns the state's largest insurance company. Her portfolio is also diversified, but it mostly lies in intangible assets. And finally, Will P. Brown. He inherited his family's assets, making him the fifth-richest person in Burlington. He owns shares in nearly every large industrial complex in the state and many beyond.

"Only the fifth richest?" I asked.

As I said, while the de facto leaders are all influential, they're not necessarily just the richest. They're all well-connected socialites as well. Humanity tends to be one of those species that values more than just one form of wealth. Popularity, and fame, and connections, and the willingness to do violence, are their own form of capital.

I hummed to myself as I continued to walk. The city was pretty quiet. There was still some traffic on the roads, but the outer lanes had been closed to car traffic, leaving them open for people to get around on foot. Which was nice, since there weren't many sidewalks to walk on.

"So, they're all staying together?"

At a hotel one of them owns.

Ah, that made a lot more sense. Myalis fed me what data she had on the hotel and the River Heights folk within it. They'd taken over the penthouse, of course, as well as the four or so floors beneath. That had meant moving a lot of others out of rooms they'd bought, but they didn't seem to care overly much.

They had their own security details who'd gotten to work securing the building for their bosses. The force was divided into three. One part was securing the ground floor and elevators, another was on the rooftop and on the hovercar-landing balconies, and finally the largest group had taken over the corridors between the rooms. I could watch a live feed of armed men keeping the rooms safe.

Of course, being safe was nice and all, but it was all kind of a moot point when Myalis seemed to break into their comms and camera network as if they'd just invited her right in.

"So, I'm not an expert at intimidating people into not being huge dumbasses. What do you think the best way of going about all of this is?"

Ideally, I can see three approaches. The first is to negotiate. Approach them calmly and rationalize why their actions are likely to cause more harm than good, perhaps outlining the obvious consequences. All three seem to have average or above intelligence. They also have advisors and staff assisting them in their decision-making process who would profit from this method.

"Alright," I said. "What're the other options?"

The next is simple. Take all of their money. Unfortunately, with the state of things as they are, they might still be able to act on the perception that they have money, even if in fact they have none. The third option is the one I suspect you'll enjoy the most.

"Go on."

Sneak into their rooms and either intimidate them one at a time, or work to move them so that all three are in the same location so that you can intimidate all three at once. They are currently asleep.

"Oh, I like that one," I said.

I started to plot and plan as I continued my walk over. Myalis was kind enough to highlight their rooms for me, which were all, fortunately, on the same floor. One of them had a particularly large living room, so that seemed like a good place to drag the three to.

"So, you have any chloroform?" I asked.

I have some, of course. But I have better options as well.

"Yeah, that's what I meant," I said with a nod.

I got to the hotel, then slipped into an alley next to it and went invisible. It was almost unfair how much of an advantage that was.

Then I realized that they'd installed these little laser sensors across the lobby. I wasn't sure if my suit's invisibility would foil that. So I went around to the back of the hotel and through a service door that Myalis conveniently unlocked for me. One of the guards was around, and he heard the door opening, but I squeezed myself against a wall and left the door ajar.

He poked his head out, then pulled it back closed and made sure it was locked. And then he reported it over their internal comms. Smart guy.

I followed him out of the room, moving slowly so that I wouldn't make any more noise than I had to.

I considered riding the elevator up, but that would have made it too easy to spot me.

Then I did it anyway because there was no way I was walking up forty flights of stairs. But I did it smartly. I climbed up two flights, avoiding motion sensors and a rather shitty laser grid as I went, then rode the elevator up from the third floor to the floor just below where the River Heights group was waiting.

I walked up from there. They had a guy sitting next to the door out of the staircase one floor up, but his head was knocking back and forth as he fought off sleep, so I just squeezed on past him without making a sound.

The penthouse floor was nice and swanky. Not as cool as the hotel we'd stayed at in New Montreal though. There was some nice carpeting and the walls were all done up in this faux-Roman style, with marble all over and big arches over each doorway. A pair of guards were walking a patrol across the main corridor, but they seemed both tired and bored out of their minds.

I paused next to one to check out their gear. A small, compact subma-chine gun, a handgun on their leg, chest armor with a rig for ammo, and a visored helmet with all the bells and whistles.

Basically, the kind of shit I'd expect to see on a top-quality PMC. No markings or anything though.

We could probably use these guys over on the front line instead of wast-ing their time guarding some VIPs. What were the chances that someone would actually come all the way up here to mess these folk up anyway?

I shook my head and continued on my way to mess these folk up.

Myalis kindly provided me with an aerosolized sleeping agent in gre-nade form. Fortunately, it wasn't noisy. I waited for the guards to be out of sight of any of the cameras mounted to the ceiling, then underhanded the grenade between them.

They were quick to act. The moment they spotted the grenade one jumped back and away and the other spun around aiming down the cor-ridor from where I'd tossed it.

Then they both just flopped to the ground bonelessly.

"Anyone spot that?" I asked.

I have the cameras running on a loop. Though if you could be so kind as to move his foot back?

I walked over and did just that. "Alright, that worked pretty well. Let's see if the locals can handle the same treatment."

CHAPTER FIFTY-THREE

INTIMIDATION

Intimidating people is hard.

It's not just about having the biggest guns or the biggest kill-count around, it's more than that. You need to look scary, talk the right way, walk the right way. It's not as easy as people think, especially if you have . . . certain disadvantages.

—Deus Ex, 2049

Meredith Jones had the penthouse rooms with the biggest living room space, so I decided to hold our impromptu meeting in her apartments.

First, though, I had to grab the other two guests of honor.

Stanley had the room next to Meredith's, so after letting Myalis poke at the card reader next to the door, I slipped into his suite and tossed a sleeping gas grenade into the bedroom. Stanley was sleeping all on his lonesome in a surprisingly non-fancy set of pajamas.

The gas silently filled the room, and his snoring continued unbothered.

"Fuck," I said as I stood next to his bed. I felt a little skeevy now that I'd made it this far. Sneaking past the guards and all felt fine, but standing over a sleeping guy in the dark felt . . . a bit weird.

Plus now I had to carry him, and Stanley—while he wasn't fat—still had a bit of a gut, and he was a full-grown man.

I tried to princess-carry him, but that didn't work. He was too floppy and I almost smacked myself in the face when his foot kicked up as I tried to grab him under his knees. Myalis didn't help, and instead played a laugh track in the background as I tried to pick the man up.

I eventually settled on a fireman's carry, pulling Stanley's arms up and then shoving my shoulder against his middle before standing up. Thank fuck for power armor, otherwise I wouldn't have been able to carry him anywhere.

Stanley might wake up with a few bruises from the way I carried him around. At least I only banged his shins against the doorframe, not his head.

I brought him over to Meredith's living room and dropped him on the couch. Then I realized that bringing people in here might wake her up, so I cracked the door to her room open and rolled another sleep grenade in, just in case.

Next was Will.

His room was way down on the far end of the corridor, and I wasn't looking forward to having to drag him all the way across.

On reaching his door, I could make out sounds on the other side. People talking. Two women, in fact. I crouched by the door and after Myalis unlocked it for me, opened it just enough to slip a grenade in.

"What's that?" one girl asked.

Then there was a trio of soft thumps.

Poking my head in, I found that Will's suite was a lavishly decorated playboy's wet dream.

It had a bar that ran the length of the room, a Jacuzzi off to one side, and an entire wall taken up by windows that would let him look over the serfs below. The master bedroom was just at the back, a large space with a massive bed taking up most of it.

Three young women were now lying on the floor next to the wrap-around bar. For a moment I had a flash of worry as I saw a liquid spreading under one of them, but it turned out to just be some sort of drink.

Judging by the way they were dressed, these three were here to party. Or . . . after-party? It didn't seem terribly lively at the moment.

Probably because it was approaching seven in the morning.

I made sure all three were still breathing before I snuck into the master bedroom, then I sighed. Will was there. As were four more women and a sex bot. They had enough clothes between them to properly outfit maybe one person.

Will was slumped over in the middle of the bed with a complication attached to his face. One of those clear masks people with apnea wore. It was tied to some hoses that rose up to the ceiling where a little machine was mounted. "Is that going to fuck with the sleeping gas?" I asked.

It shouldn't.

I shook my head and detonated another grenade in my hand, the gases slipping out and spreading invisibly across the room. For some reason, the mental image of a playboy banging four chicks and a sex bot at the same time didn't mesh with the very unsexy mask.

Really, in his place, I would have just let the others endure the snoring or whatever.

I had to figure out the best way to approach Will. I wanted to grab him, not the others, and I might feel a bit bad if I had to drag Will's limp form over any of the girls. So I settled on grabbing him by the ankles and yoink-ing him down to the base of the bed.

The problem there was that when the covers moved, I realized he wasn't wearing anything but that sleep apnea mask.

"Oh, for fuck's sake," I said. I cringed. He was limp in more ways than one, I supposed.

I kicked through the discarded clothes on the floor until I found some shorts, then I shoved them onto Will. His legs were hairy. It was disgusting.

I didn't even try to carry him over my shoulder. Will would have to live with the fact that I was dragging his pasty ass across the floor by the ankles.

Of course, as I was leaving the room, I sensed some motion behind me and I spun around, hand going for my gun while I searched the room for whatever had moved. Will's feet thunked onto the floor next to me.

I found myself staring at the sex bot.

The sex bot, which didn't need to breathe, and who wouldn't be affected by any amount of sleeping gas.

"Uh," I said. "Go back to sleep."

The bot stared. "Are you kidnapping Master Brown?" it asked.

"No?" I tried. "It's . . . samurai business. Don't, uh, interfere."

The bot blinked, then laid itself back down, and I found myself entirely uncertain of what to do next.

Myalis hadn't stopped with the laugh track.

"Okay, enough of that," I grumped at her as I picked up Will's ankles again and continued to drag him out of the room. The poor fuck was going to have rug burn all along his back, but it was his own fault for sleeping in the nude and having disgusting hairy legs.

Will's back squeaked unpleasantly across the marble floor in the corridor, then I dragged him into Meredith's room. She had a nice couch where Stanley was snoring, so I dragged Will up and sat him there next to his buddy.

Then it was time to fetch Meredith.

She was sleeping next to a man that I wasn't familiar with, but judging by the bands on their fingers they were either married or they were both cheating. Meredith was, fortunately, a rather small, thin woman, so I was able to pick her up and carry her out of the room without too much trouble.

"Okay," I said as I rubbed my hands together. That had been more work than I expected. Now . . . Well, now was the intimidation part of this whole routine, and I was honestly not sure where to start. "Alright, first, Myalis, can you lock them out of their augs? Don't need them calling on the guards."

Consider it done.

"Right . . . so, talking points? Uh . . . I'd like it if they stopped fucking around. I'm here to remind them that if they do, they'll find out." I could probably just empty all of their accounts, but then why did I go through all the trouble of getting them into this room if that was the case?

I started to think, then decided it was too early for thinking and just ordered up the antidote to the knockout grenade, which was fortunately also aerosolized. Then I started to pace with only an end table between me and the three. At the last moment, I pulled out Void Terminus, my very large, very cool-looking sword, and planted the tip into the floor while I stood in front of the trio.

Stanley was the first to come to, blinking sheepishly and then looking around. Will groaned next, then reached toward his back with a muttered curse. "What happened?" he asked.

"Good morning," I said, and all three of them snapped their attention to me. I grinned, even if they couldn't see it.

Do you want me to turn on the lights?

Ah, I'd forgotten that it was dark. "Let's turn up the lights a bit," I suggested.

All three of them flinched as the lights in the living room came on and probably ruined their night vision.

"So, I've got some criticism about how the three of you have been acting, and I really wanted you to hear it," I said. "So here we are! Let's have a nice chat, huh?"

CHAPTER FIFTY-FOUR

ALL THAT WEALTH IS GOOD FOR

The Wealth of Nations was an important book that laid out the foundations for the capitalist system. Its economic principles, though simple and still somewhat theoretical, nevertheless enlightened many early economists and thinkers, leading them to the creation of a system we are all well familiar with. It suggested that the labor of the people was the true wealth of a nation.

The Wealth of Corporations is a similar novel. Written by a hyper-networked economic AI in 2032, it lays out the foundations for a post-capitalist society where the labor of the masses is no longer necessary thanks to automation, but their continued survival is still necessary to ensure human prosperity. It suggests that the value of a corporation isn't its ability to create, nor its capital worth, but rather its intellectual properties and the size of its databases.

—Thesis on *The Wealth of Corporations*, 2034

Stanley, Meredith, and Will stared at me for a while, and it was pretty clear that all three of them were working through some shit, mentally speaking, as they got to terms with the situation.

"Did you hear that last bit, or should I repeat myself?" I asked.

Meredith shook her head. "I heard," she said. "You're . . . Stray Cat?"

"I am!" I said. I'd be lying if I didn't admit to being at least a little happy to be recognized. It was going to save me a lot of time spent explaining things to these three fine specimens. "You know what me being here means, right?" I asked.

"Did you take me out of my room?" Will asked.

"Don't ask stupid questions," I said. I didn't want to have to explain to him how he got here.

"My back hurts, what did you do?" he asked.

I glared at him. "What did I literally just say?"

Fortunately, Meredith and Stanley had their heads on straight. Stanley jabbed Will with an elbow. "Shut up, Will, listen to the samurai when she's threatening you. Uh . . . this is a threat, right?"

"Well, I wasn't going to be so overt about it," I said. "I was more planning to like, imply that there was a threat. Like, hey, look, I can sneak past all of your guards and grab you while you're sleeping no matter where you are or how safe you're feeling. That kind of thing. I figured I didn't need to come out and *tell* you that this is a threat."

"We get it," Meredith said. She squirmed on her sofa, sitting up properly and tugging her nightgown on straight. "Is there anything in particular that, ah, started all of this?"

"Well, a few things, I think. Mostly people not taking warnings seriously. Then being slow to move when Gomorrah started sending her own brand of message. But I can forgive that, I guess. I wouldn't listen to an advisory about anything and in your fancy shoes I might also be a bit slow to act. What I can't forgive is fucking with the wages of the militia when you damned well know that doing that will lead to people quitting, which will lead to others dying."

"You're protecting the city, aren't you?" Will asked. "Do you really need the militia that *we're* paying for to protect it too?"

"Yes," I said simply. "We have two experienced samurai here. Barely experienced at that. And three noobs. Manic is probably going to be a hard-hitting bitch real soon but the other two will take a long while to ramp up, and that means that there's just not enough of us to keep everyone safe. And keeping people safe isn't just about keeping the aliens out. It's also about keeping this place orderly. We need people to stay calm, we need food and provisions to be distributed fairly, and we need people to keep working to help."

"You don't need that last one," Stanley said.

"Huh?" I asked.

The man sat up and rubbed at his face. "Sorry, never mind."

"No, no, do go on," I insisted.

Stanley looked at Meredith, and I was getting the impression that the two of them were the brains of the operation here. Maybe that meant that Will was the handsome, hairy-legged face?

"You don't need people to work to keep things . . . functional. Not in a proper modern city. Half the work people do nowadays is damned near useless," Stanley said. "We've automated almost everything worth doing. It's just cheaper to throw people at some problems than it is to automate them."

"That doesn't sound right," I said.

He shrugged. Clearly he didn't give a shit about my opinion on the matter. "Okay, you've made your point. Honestly though, Miss Stray Cat, this could have been an email."

I frowned. Really? "You three don't seem all that scared about all of this."

Stanley shrugged again. I was starting to get annoyed by his shrugging so much. "You don't seem the sort to actually kill us. Also, while this is intimidating, we're still in our suite."

"I'm a bit cold," Will said.

"What time is it, anyway?" Meredith asked.

"Seven thirty, look, there's a clock on the corner of the TV," Stanley said.

"Oh, good, I was about to wake up anyway. So I haven't lost that much sleep."

I stabbed Void Terminus into Meredith's coffee table and the tip of the sword rammed right through the wood to lodge there. All three of them jumped. "Could you at least have the common decency to be a little bit scared?" I asked.

"I'm a little scared," Will said, not sounding scared at all.

"Fuck you, Will," I said. My sword, hearing its activation phrase, snapped to life, a black slice of space appearing along its edge, the negative pressure sucking at the air in the room. It wasn't a massively powerful suction, but it was enough to stir the air and it created that wonderfully distinct hissing noise, like a million really pissed off snakes going off all at once.

I pointed the end toward Will and he scrambled back as far as he could go while staying on the couch. "Okay, okay, I'm scared," he said.

"Damn right," I said. "Now, all three of you . . . stop fucking with the running of this city. If you're not going to make things better the least you can do is stop making things worse. We're trying to keep everyone alive here, for fuck's sake."

I deactivated the sword, then brought it around and slid it into its sheath. Then I ordered up another "wake up" grenade and placed it atop the slim hole I'd punched through the coffee table so it wouldn't wobble away.

"Use this on those two guards out there. It'll wake them up. And remember, I've warned you once already. I don't give out two warnings. Next time I'm just taking all of your money and assets and whatever and the lot of you can learn what it's like being poor. It's the one experience you can't pay for."

My sword finished traveling to the end of its sheath with a satisfying *click* and I stood tall, nodded to the three, then made a graceful exit before any of them could say anything, or before I could shove my own foot in my mouth and ruin the whole look.

That was well done. I was half expecting you to just kill them.

"Really?" I asked once I was out of the suite. "That's a bit violent. Not that I'm not violent or anything. I'm cool with murder, obviously, but it feels . . . I don't know. They weren't fighting back. Just kind of slumped there, and it doesn't feel like they're a threat. They're just idiots that happen to be rich."

That's an interesting way of looking at it. You could reappropriate their wealth and use it yourself.

"What in the fuck would I do with that?" I asked. "Like sure, being rich sounds awesome, but I've never had more than four-figures worth of credits in my entire life. I don't know *how* to handle that kind of cash. I could give it to someone who does, but then what if they fuck up? No, I don't want that kind of responsibility. Just having enough to keep me and mine happy's good enough for me. Unless you want the credits yourself?"

I don't. And I'm glad you don't feel the need to chase wealth either. You're surprisingly mature at times, Catherine.

I rolled my eyes and pretended not to feel any sort of flushing. Of course, the bitch living in my head could probably like, measure my dopamine levels or whatever. "We've got more problems to deal with, right?"

There's that protest that's gearing up. The social media feeds of a few of the leaders and instigators suggest that rumors of food shortages have begun to spread. The Antithesis haven't stopped testing the defenses yet either.

"Ah, fan-fucking-tastic," I said. At least I didn't have to worry too much about the militia falling apart just yet.

CHAPTER FIFTY-FIVE

HUNGER OF THE MASSES

With VKO you can set up your own restaurant in as few as twenty clicks and for less than a hundred thousand credits.

Just pick the menu, upload your logo, name your new restaurant, and bam! Your own tailor-made virtual dining experience is up and running!

Compatible with all of your favorite online dining apps!

—VKO (Virtual Kitchen Online) ad, 2026

"So, what are they complaining about, exactly?" I asked. It was a semi-rhetorical question. I was on my way down and out of the hotel—using the elevator, because why would I sneak *out*—while eying up the protestors' media feed.

Would-be protestors. They were still huddled up in their homes, for the most part. A few had gone out to meet each other, it seemed, and the urge to *do something* was clearly spreading as people egged each other on, but for the moment things had yet to start popping off.

A quick scroll showed a lot of people complaining, and a lot of people encouraging each other to get out there and do more than just complain online.

It felt a little like I was watching the pressure building in a can that was about to burst. It needed a release, and I was worried that the release would cause some serious trouble. Most of all for me.

I didn't mind people wanting to protest and hell, they were right, shit wasn't fine. The problem was that while their protests would certainly kick things into high gear when it came to fixing some issues, it would also cause a number of new, fresh issues as well.

The complaints seem to be divided along three main points of contention. Four, really. The first is the quarantine that has been implemented across the city.

"There's a quarantine?" I asked as I got out of the elevator. A few of the guards looked at me suspiciously, but if I was leaving, then I wasn't going to be their problem for long.

It's not in full effect. But there are Stay-at-Home measures in place at the moment. People traveling out of their homes will receive warnings. There are forms that can be filled out to justify the leaving, and these can be filed in advance, but the restrictions are chafing.

I frowned, then went searching for some of those forms myself. I could see why people were annoyed a moment later. The form was top-of-the-line bureaucratic bullshit. The first half asked for manual entry of information that my augs should have provided already, then I had to give a reason why I wanted to leave, where I would go, and when I'd be back. Failure to disclose the right information or come home late or not go where I was supposed to would result in a fine.

Or it would, for a normal person. I wasn't going to bother with this.

"Okay, that needs streamlining. Who implemented this?"

The militia and the city government. It's meant to reduce the number of people on the streets and in dangerous areas. It's also meant to help keep track of citizens. It's wildly inefficient, and there are several ways around it. The fines being credit-based also mean that anyone with sufficient resources can merely ignore them. But, they have proven to be successful in reducing the number of bodies on the streets and outside of their own designated housing areas.

I nodded along as I left the building. I wasn't sure where to go from there, but I started toward the center of the city. I wanted a walk to think, in any case.

Looking through some links Myalis gave me, I could see that the protestor faction had already found ways to break that system. It helped that some of the more vocal members were also on the city staff responsible for the quarantine system to begin with.

"Right, that needs fixing," I said. "Table it as something I need to get a professional's help with. Next?"

The second issue is the militia and police force.

"The cops?" I asked.

Indeed. While the militia and police are separate entities, they are working together. There are several reports of violence against citizens, beatings, theft, profiling, sexual assault, and more. I can confirm the veracity of some, others were exaggerated for effect.

"Fucking hell," I muttered. I never expected to be on the same side of things as the fucking police, but here I was. "Can you do me a favor, find out who the worst offenders are, tell the . . . chief of police or whatever. Get their badges, arrest those that went too far. It'll reduce the number of cops we have, but fuck it. It's at least one thing we can do to appease the protestors, and I don't like dirty cops besides. Oh, and tell the chief of police that if he doesn't, I'll throw him over the wall with whatever police-issue peashooter he has."

Noted. Message sent. The third issue is the growth of rumors regarding our food shortage. Unfortunately, since these issues are founded in fact, they are rather persistent.

"Tends to work that way, yeah," I said. "Okay. What's Manic up to?"

She left the city with a militia convoy to start her grocery store raids.

Oh, thank fuck, I didn't want to do everything myself. That didn't mean I couldn't help. "Let's set up a bigger food supply," I said. "Maybe someplace central. I guess the mall could work. Do I have anything like that big-ass printer I have back home, but for food?"

There are similar options available. Most need to be fed on organic matter. But raw organic matter is exceptionally cheap and can easily be turned into simple foodstuffs. Breads, protein mixes, meat substitutes, et cetera.

"Sounds like a good idea, then," I said. "We make the raw foods, get some people to cook them."

As opposed to making the finished product?

"Yeah, because then we'll have cooks and people working on food, and they'll see that there's plenty of food for everyone. Rumors will spread."

That is surprisingly insightful.

"I have my moments," I said. Really, I was recalling some of the leaner times at the orphanage when food was scarce. It was always nice to buy some raw ingredients and cook something. The act of seeing something being made calmed the kids down a lot, even if it was just PB and J . . . which was about the only thing I could cook. Lucy was better.

"How many cooks are there in Burlington? Or . . . how many restaurants?"

There are currently thirty-six thousand restaurants in the city of Burlington.

I blinked. "What? Wait, what's the population here?"

A little under half a million.

"What the fuck, that doesn't make any sense," I said, my other trains of thought entirely derailed for a moment.

Those are registered restaurants. Most of them are ghost restaurants. Several fronts all situated within the same industrial kitchen serving the same food across multiple brands.

"Ah, capitalist fuckery," I said. That made more sense. "How many cooks, then?" I asked.

A few thousand are registered. Do you want me to send a call out for them?

"Do it. Tell them to show up at the mall at . . . nine thirty. Sign it with my name. Tell them that we'll be . . . appropriating a few of those restaurants to start serving people throughout the city. Fuck, we're going to need an app or something."

That seems amusing. I'll take care of it. Perhaps we can start competing brands between ourselves and the city's other Vanguard? Chez Stray Cats?

"You're a riot," I deadpanned. "You mentioned a fourth problem?"

Indeed. There's a growing envy of the Kittens.

"You mean the people Lucy's working with?" I asked.

Yes, since the positions are limited and they're seen using Vanguard technology and assisting on the front lines, the active members of the Kittens have begun to brag. Naturally, this has created a slight schism between them and those who cannot or will not join.

"That's the stupidest shit," I said.

A number of people within the ranks of the organizers of this protest agree. It's the most hotly debated point of contention among them. I don't think anything will come of it, not as long as new opportunities to join the Kittens group arise.

I took a moment to wonder at the incredible stupidity of humanity. Unfortunately, a moment was all I could spare. "Is Intel-chan awake yet?" I asked.

Their alarm went off six minutes ago. They are still doing their morning ablutions.

A bit too much information. "Tell them to call me as soon as they're free," I said. "We're gonna put them in charge of the logistics for the food thing. Do you think the protestors will calm down?"

It's possible. But I doubt it. You've mitigated several of the reasons they have to protest, or will, in any case, but the anger has risen already. It will take more than that to calm them down.

"Any advice, then?" I asked, because I didn't know what to do about it.

CHAPTER FIFTY-SIX

A GREAT IDEA

There's charity, and then there's samurai charity. And the latter's always interesting to see at work.

You can never tell if they're doing it out of empathy for others, or if they're just tired of society being trash and decided to fix things on their own.

It sometimes even works out!

—Simon "Battleax" Critical, head of e-magazine
The Critical Skeptic, 69th issue, January 2045

"This is a stupid fucking idea," I said.

Lucy grinned, then reached up and pinched my cheek. "It'll be fine," she said. "We'll handle most of it. You go out there and talk to your cooks, and I'll get everything ready and set up, yeah?"

I wanted to grumble and complain more, but time was wasting. It was approaching ten in the morning, and I didn't want to put things off any more than I needed to, so I left the Kittens' HQ and headed to the escalators leading to the mall's ground floor.

The protests were being stalled out at the moment. The truth was—as far as I could tell—that people who wanted to protest needed a serious push to get moving, and my actions so far had deflated some of the reasons why they were going to make a mess of things.

That meant that for things to take off, they'd need an even bigger push, and I was doing what I could to basically chop their legs out from under them by placating the masses.

If it worked, then the few hours I'd spent on it would be worth it.

The ground floor of the mall had a crowd gathering on it, some sixty or so people who were squeezed into one side by a few Kitten volunteers. Not the sort in the suits with the cool guns, but normal volunteers in normal clothes. The only thing marking them as Kittens were the cat ears they wore on their heads and their augs' IFF pinging them as such.

I'd spent a chunk of points (only a couple thousand, but it still stung) and bought two organic reprocessing machines. They were down here too, being guarded by both the Kittens and some militia folk.

Right now, they were constantly generating the same crap. Some sort of bread, a sort of faux-meat patty, and some sort of vegetable . . . disk thing. Basically, we were making burgers.

Lucy had somehow already sourced a fuckload of aluminium foil to wrap them all in, and now all we needed was people to cook enough to feed a city.

They technically had all of the nutritional crap a person needed to survive, and each burger was packed with about three hundred or so calories. They weren't going to taste great, I didn't think, but while the city lacked in food, we didn't lack in condiments.

That only covered part of our food needs, of course. Hell, it was a drop in the bucket. But it was also free food that tasted bland enough that most people would want to source their food from elsewhere. And while they were busy doing that, they wouldn't be screaming and yelling in the streets and messing my shit up.

The second part of my awesome plan . . . well, that'd come later. I wasn't looking forward to it.

I took a deep breath, fitted my helmet on properly, then stepped off the last step of the escalator. I already had eyes on me. I could feel them. The sixty . . . no, there were a few new ones rushing in at the last minute, so it was probably closer to seventy now, folks in the penned-off area ranged from young to old, from fresh-faced pure humans to a few that had more chrome than skin.

I stopped before them, and I was happy to see that I didn't need to catch their attention or anything. "Alright," I said, pitching my voice up so that they could all hear. "You folk all answered Myalis's direct message, I hope?"

There were nods and yesses and a few "who the fuck is that?"s from the group. Good enough.

"Alright, let me explain what's up. We're looking for cooks. Later on today, we'll be looking for delivery boys and girls. The city's food supply's predictably fucked, so we're doing what we can to keep people fed. That means setting up a quick and dirty business. We'll be paying you all minimum wage, because fuck if I know where I'll get the money to pay the lot of you. But it comes with a few bonuses. For one, passes to get you to and from work, as many shitty burgers you could want, and, uh . . ."

I sent a quick text to Myalis. *What the fuck can I offer these people?*

Protector-grade equipment is always popular. How about something simple and useful for their specific career?

"And you'll get a samurai-tech spatula," I said. Spatulas were useful, right? "Hell, you can get your name engraved on it and everything. Really fancy alien shit."

I predict about two points per spatula, assuming you merely want something that's at the peak of what material sciences can produce. Though, you might need a minor Cooking Implements catalog.

That seemed to win them over satisfyingly. One guy raised his flesh arm. His other arm was this huge metal contraption with a bulging biceps and three smaller arms sticking out from that. They seemed to end in different tools, which was neat. "Shoot," I said.

"Name's Cook," he said. "Was wondering what you wanted us to be making."

I nodded. A fair question. "Follow me," I said before spinning on my heel and walking across the floor. They followed, and I pitched my voice up so that they could hear me. At some point, Myalis must have grabbed onto the mall's stereo system, because my voice was coming from that too. "So, I bought this big fancy alien machine that turns this super cheap organic pulp crap into actual edible food. It's not *free* point-wise, but it's pretty damned cheap. What it makes is what you'll be cooking. We've taken over a few industrial kitchens across the city. The idea is to give people a meal they can order for free and get delivered at home. It'll keep people alive while we get rid of the last of the aliens."

I walked into one of the bigger restaurants in the mall's kitchen, chosen because it had some space. It didn't have space for seventy-plus nosy cooks, but there was nothing but a half wall separating the kitchen from the outside, so they could still see well enough, even if there was some elbowing to be near the front.

With an eye roll, I turned on the camera in my augmented eye and then sent everyone in the vicinity the code to be able to piggyback with their own augs.

Simple enough thing to do, but extremely stupid. It was pissing all over every cybersecurity standard ever to let people into your augs like that, but I'd be impressed if they got anything past Myalis.

Now that they could all see, I focused on the stuff we'd made already. There were a few cardboard boxes full of ingredients. Lucy had some younger volunteers loading up the fabricators already.

"This is bread," I said as I pulled out a round, flat bun and placed it on a stainless steel counter. "This is some sort of fake-meat patty. And this is a veggie patty." I slapped the other two onto the table.

"Not exactly fine dining," Cook said. He was near the front and didn't look impressed.

I shrugged. "It's food. Hell, it's even somewhat healthy, even if it tastes like cardboard. Just . . . add some fucking ketchup. Hell . . . let's sell the condiments while making the burgers free. We'll use the money to pay you guys."

Man, this business shit was easy.

"How many of these Stray Cat Burgers do you think you'll be selling?" Cook asked.

"However many people there are in Burlington, times three meals a day, uh, a lot?" I said. "I'm working on something else to help calm the needy down, and we do have proper food coming in. This is a stopgap, to make it so that no one ends up starving while we set things up. I don't want hungry kids on the streets. No point in beating back the aliens while people die behind the front lines because they can't get bread."

That seemed to make sense to everyone involved. The cooks didn't seem overly happy that they weren't making anything special, but hey, they had work while most people had nothing to do but sit on their thumbs.

"Jessica will be down in a minute or two to give everyone their assignments," I said. "If you're interested, stick around. And, uh, tell Jessica what you want engraved on your spatulas. You're doing the city a service, or something." I nodded, then exited out the back without another word, because I didn't owe anyone any amount of small talk.

Now, for the second part.

I was dreading it already.

Lucy looked up and met her own eyes.

It was always strange to look at yourself through a camera while also looking through that camera with your augs. Slightly disorientating, though without any real dizziness or nausea. She blinked, then looked at the other camera. Yeah, they were all in focus. Good.

The table was set. There was a hot plate, plugged in and ready to warm up. They had all the pots and pans they needed. Water was in a jug nearby, the other things were just to the side. The main camera saw it all too. Good good.

She turned and took in the background. It wasn't much, just a plain window that overlooked one of the main roads of Burlington. They'd put up curtains on the sides to mask it up a little. The main camera's angle would let people see the road and, more importantly, it would let someone enterprising enough to head outside prove that it was an actual livestream.

Which it wasn't. The window was placed in front of a high-definition screen filming another, actual window elsewhere.

Lucy didn't need someone smart firing a rocket at their back while they did this.

Cat was the best, but she was not even close to paranoid enough.

Myalis: Catherine is on her way up.

Lucy: Tks!

She grinned. Almost time to start.

There were a few ways she could do this, but really, she wanted it to be a bit . . . a bit poorly done? There was just *something* about jank that pissed off the corporate types and made everything a little more genuine.

Across from her table were a few of the volunteer Kittens that had some experience with this kind of stuff. She gave them a thumbs-up, and then a quick countdown.

In one of her aug's side-reels, she saw herself as the internet could now see her. A single dark-skinned girl in a well-lit room in front of a bunch of cooking things, smiling at the camera and wearing some rather interesting cat-ear props on her head.

The captions across the seven different streaming platforms she was sending this to were all the same. *Stray Cat's Cooking Show! Feat. Lucy!*

Her grin widened. "Hello, everyone," she said. She currently had a hundred and seven viewers. Myalis helpfully showed her the number of actual, human viewers below that. It was more like just seven, but she could live with that number too. It would grow. "This show's mostly for the fine people of Burlington, where Stray Cat, Gomorrah, and your three local samurai are hard at work keeping people safe. Today we're adding to that by making sure you're fed and safe too!"

She had a live chat. It was almost immediately bombarded with ads and fake messages.

And then Myalis struck, and Lucy could almost imagine some distant servers crashing and burning. It was like using a tank on a single ant, having an AI like Myalis on her side. In a blink, the chat was cleared of any interference.

There was a large computer monitor turned on its side next to the camera with the chat's feed on it, not that she needed to look with her augs, but it helped the viewers if she looked at something before answering them. Made it more . . . real.

At least, that was her experience from watching this kind of stream before.

"Every citizen of Burlington, heck, anyone within the Downtown region can order up a meal and have it delivered to your door for free. All you need to do is cook it up! So, to make that part easier, we decided to make this livestream to show you how!"

Oh, she'd just hit three-figure human viewers, nice!

Rika: What's this?

Abbatoth68: Where's that?

MarchallGod: The title's a lie

BestFrenVenom: We?

Alan Martin: She cute tho

DaShoe: Show feet!

She was about to go on when a door slipped open just a tiny bit and Cat slipped into the room.

Cat moved . . . Cat moved the way Cat did. It wasn't something Lucy had never really seen in anyone else. Maybe some of the more experienced PMC sorts? But even they had a sort of militaristic swagger to them.

Cat moved like her namesake. Slow, deliberate, with a slight shift to her hips that Lucy really liked, and she had the strange habit of touching the floor with the tips of her toes first. It made her deceptively quiet for an otherwise loud girl.

Her helmet was off, so Lucy got to see her eyes scanning everything before locking onto her. There was something very sharp about Cat's gaze, until it locked onto Lucy, then it instantly softened.

Lucy felt her heart soften too. "Hey," she said.

The people watching the stream must have been confused, she'd just gone off script. She was clearly addressing someone off-screen, at least until Cat walked up to Lucy.

Calloused fingers pulled Lucy's head up, a gentle touch along the line of her jaw that arched her neck back so that Cat could more easily capture her lips.

Her other—new—arm fell down to Lucy's hip and squeezed.

"Mm, Cat," Lucy said.

"Hey," Cat said. "I hate people and I absolutely don't want to do this thing," she said.

Lucy smiled. "We could put it off? Tell people to starve."

"Urgh, but then they'd complain about starving, and I'd have to spend time telling them to figure shit out for themselves, time I couldn't spend with you."

"Hmm, that's a dilemma," Lucy agreed. "I got you a hat," she said.

Sir Whale: hot

Antimater Lobster: Wait, is that actually a samurai? For real?

Devon7400: 10/10 cooking show

Name Pending: NOOOOO My Gomorrah X Stray Cat ship! It sinks!

Calob505: I like this cooking

Cat blinked at the non sequitur, then she let Lucy out of her grasp. Lucy picked up a big white poofy chef's hat, and placed it on Cat's head.

"I . . . how stupid do I look?" Cat asked. Her cybernetic cat ears twitched, which Lucy thought was adorable, but they didn't throw the hat off.

"You look very cute," Lucy said truthfully.

"Yeah, no, I don't think I want people to see me in this," Cat said.

"A bit too late for that," Lucy said.

Cat was a big dumb softy in some ways, but in others she caught on *quick.* She snapped her gaze around and locked it on the cameras one at a time, then she looked at the chat screen (Oh, they were well into five figures! And the number of blushing face emotes was nice!), then her gaze returned to Lucy. "We're live?" she asked.

"Mm-hmm," Lucy said.

"You, uh, didn't feel like telling me?" she asked.

Lucy smiled sweetly, that same smile that let her get away with a whole lot. "I was getting there, but then you decided to be all romantic and sweet, and you stole my breath away."

"Fuck," Cat muttered. There was definitely a lot of warmth in her cheeks now, and the flush was distinctly not the fun, sexual kind that Lucy loved seeing. No, this was the fun, embarrassed kind that had Lucy biting her lips to stop a mean giggle from escaping.

Oh, Cat was going to punish her so hard for this later.

Lucy was looking forward to it.

"So, Chef Stray Cat," Lucy said. "As I was telling our viewers, today we'll be cooking up something easy to cook. We only have a few minutes with our brave samurai, everyone, so let's not waste her time, hmm?"

Cat, still flushing, cleared her throat, then looked from one camera to the other. It was cute to see her so flustered. "Yeah, right. So, what are we cooking?" she asked.

She was quick to roll with the punches.

"Mac and cheese," Lucy said.

"Really? We're teaching people how to make that? Aren't the instructions on the box?" Cat asked.

"They are," Lucy said. "But you know how people are."

Cat rolled her eyes, something she was doing a lot now that she had two. Cat wasn't commenting on it a lot, but it was clear that she was silently appreciative of having two of those again.

"Yeah, fine. So where do we start?"

"With the instructions," Lucy said. She smiled. "They're on the box."

Cat bumped into her with her hip, and Lucy laughed as she stumbled closer to the ingredients. "Right, I'll turn on this thing . . . like that. Are these pots clean?"

"No, I thought we'd cook with dirty pots today," Lucy said.

"Ah, yeah, get that real bachelor-chow taste going, rat droppings and all," Cat agreed as she picked up an obviously clean pan and spun it around before putting it on the hot plate.

Lucy handed Cat the water, which was in a large gallon jug. "Every food order comes with a gallon of purified water, two boxes of noodles, and a small container of milk," Lucy said to the nearest camera. "The first step is setting your water to boil."

Kirania3: Oh no, they're sassy

Jonah94: How water boil?

Arkimedes: Why water boil?

Racheet: They're cute

Majaguru: Sassy and sexy tho

Inle68: lmao

"That one's hard to fuck up," Cat said.

"Yeah, imagine someone forgetting that there was water in the pan and then leaving it to boil overnight?" Lucy said.

Cat froze, then she turned a frown toward Lucy. "Lucy, that was *you*."

Lucy laughed. "But you got in trouble for it."

"Only because that bitch didn't believe me!" Cat said.

It was an argument they'd threaded a number of times. They each knew their part, what to say, which memories to bring up, and why, even if it was all said before, it still made them warm. It was comfortable complaining about an easier time, when an overworked orphanage worker and a bit of boiled-off water was their biggest worry.

They made mac and cheese, and it wasn't perfect. Lucy didn't measure the milk and ended up not putting enough in. Cat added the macaroni before the water was boiling because she was too impatient to wait that long and complained at length about how only using one packet of cheese powder was for scrubs while Lucy tried to remind her of the times where they'd ended up eating mac and no cheese because of that very habit.

It was nice, and in the end they got to enjoy a few bites of subpar food while a seven-figure audience watched and they both still pretended that it was just the two of them.

CHAPTER FIFTY-SEVEN

THE OKAY BEFORE THE OOF

When samurai work together, it'll either lead to greater success, or a lot more chaos. The personalities of various samurai tend to be quite different, and they also tend to share some commonalities. Those commonalities often include a distrust of others and of authority, and that makes it complicated for them to work together if there's a direct and clear hierarchy in place.

Not that it hasn't happened and won't happen again. We're just stubborn sometimes.

—Laserjack, on samurai–samurai relations, 2054

Things were going . . . alright. I was a little tired after running around all over the place putting out fires, but it seemed that, at least for now, the city would hold up.

And just as I was thinking that, I got a call from Gomorrah.

"Hey," I said as I answered. I was still at the mall, having just finished up a . . . I supposed it was a presentation, with Lucy. I didn't have concrete plans on where to go next.

"Hello," Gomorrah said. "I'm on the lake-side of the city, by the walls. Things are getting a little . . . uncomfortable over here. I think we could use your help."

I nodded. "Sure, I'm on my way. Just send me your co-ords and I'll be there in ten, faster if you think it's an emergency."

"We can afford to wait ten minutes," Gomorrah said. "Things aren't that dire yet. But yes, I'd appreciate having you here."

I nodded, cut the call, then sent a text to Jessica. The sex bot had become Lucy's secretary of sorts. At least as an android she was quick to reply to texts and such, much faster than a person, even if she lacked some social graces sometimes. She replied instantly to my request and said that a car would be waiting for me outside.

Pretty handy, that.

I checked my gear as I headed out. I had my armor on, and it was reading all green on my HUD. Its batteries were down to eighty-nine percent but I figured that was a non-issue for now. My railguns were down a few rounds, so I got Myalis to top them up, just in case. Then I checked on my Laser Pointer. It was currently full of . . . flechette rounds. Yeah, that would work for now.

I had a couple of grenades on my belt. Resonators, garrots, one of those black-hole bombs for a tight situation. My handgun was strapped to my thigh and full of ammo, and I had my coat on top of everything.

I checked that my helmet was on correctly as I walked out of the mall, then found the car that was going to bring me out to the front.

It was one of those econocars, a tiny little electric thing that ran off of a lawnmower engine and had a top speed that was in the double digits. The inside had room for two if they were willing to get comfy with each other.

I wanted to complain, but then that would waste time, and then I'd need to find another way over and . . . "Hey, didn't I order my bike down to here?" I asked.

You asked how long it would take for it to arrive. You didn't ask for it to come over. But I did anticipate that, and did fly the bike to Burlington anyway.

"Then where the hell is it?"

It has been hovering around the edge of the city for a few hours. I've been using it as aerial surveillance.

I frowned. Then sighed and just climbed into the car. "Get it down here," I told Myalis before looking at my driver. He was some guy about my age, freckle-faced and sweaty behind the wheel, which he held with a death grip. Yes, I could have waited for the bike. That would be a minute or two of waiting, and this car was already here. "Punch it," I told him.

He did, and we . . . more or less accelerated ahead.

I regretted not taking the bike. This little coffin car could barely hit highway minimum speeds, and that was when it had a long time to accelerate up to those speeds. We didn't have room for that in the stop-and-start Downtown area.

"You know, you can just gun it," I said.

"That's against the law, ma'am," my driver said.

I frowned. Ma'am? I didn't mind it from the soldier-types since it was just respectful, but come on, he was treating me like I was some geriatric old biddy. "Just punch it," I said. "Not like anyone's going to stop you, and traffic's dead."

I'll turn off the traffic cameras at the right moments.

We made it to the front line wall in . . . not excellent time, but it was faster than I would have made it on foot. I squeezed myself out of the car, then hoped that no one had noticed me arriving in such an uncool ride.

I didn't care *that* much about my image, but there were lines that even I didn't want to cross. It didn't help that my driver had decided to park next to Gomorrah's Fur*y*.

If the Fury was a person, it would be one of those super muscular porn-star sorts. The kind of person that you looked at and just knew that they fucked.

I walked on past it, my little map pointing out where Gomorrah was. And also the other samurai. Arm-a-Geddon was with her, and so was Sprout. The only one missing was Manic, and I knew that she was still busy doing a grocery run.

Gomorrah was talking to the other two, all three of them sequestered in what looked like a temporary guard shack of sorts just a few meters away from the front line.

The militia's big mobile base was parked nearby, and I figured that Intel-Chan was in there too, doing their thing. The place was certainly busy, with plenty of volunteers moving gear around, militia gathered in squads, and less-organized Kitten squads grouped up and looking aimless.

"Hey," I said as I got closer to the other samurai. "What's up?"

"Hello," Gomorrah said again. "Good timing, things haven't gotten desperate yet, but I think we're going to have to do something soon."

"Hey, kitty cat," Arm-a-Geddon said. He fired off some finger guns my way, and I decided to ignore him.

Sprout just nodded at me, then reached out and rather awkwardly lowered Arm-a-Geddon's hands. "Hello."

I used the time we were spending on the introductions to check out the overall situation. The walls had been tested all along their length through the night and early morning. Just probing attacks from the aliens. Nothing too hard to push back. That started to change over the last half hour or so. The aliens had started to concentrate their pushes along two spots.

"Okay," I said. "Looks like they're getting serious."

"More serious, yes," Gomorrah said. "I'm getting a lot more activity from the lake too. The temperature rose three degrees overnight. Which isn't normal in the least, and it's only been rising faster since. There's some activity on the shore. Smaller models coming out of the water and running toward the city, but I think most of the movement is underground right now."

"Fuck," I said with feeling. "What about the other hives?"

"Nothing from them," Gomorrah said. "Atyacus gives us a seventy percent chance of having cleared them with our nanomachine attacks and that last big fire. We haven't seen anything from them, so I'm going to assume we don't need to dedicate too much to worrying about them."

I nodded along. That was good. So our worry was now entirely about the underlake hive, which was basically sending more and more aliens our way.

"Do you have a plan already, or should we just dry the lake up and boil the fuckers?" I asked.

"That's plan B," Gomorrah said. "It's . . . somewhat extreme. I got some climate prediction software after what we did in New Montreal. If we burn off the entire lake's water supply, it'll . . . be pretty bad for the environment."

"God, I can't imagine," Sprout said. "Boiling the entire lake would just destroy any bit of its ecosystem left intact. There would be no saving it once the Antithesis are removed."

"Okay, so that's plan B, fine," I said. "What's plan A?

I noticed that a lot of people around us were starting to move differently, and the frequent retort of gunfire from around the wall picked up. It sounded like the aliens were testing us again.

"Plan A is to hold out until an expert arrives," Gomorrah said. "But that doesn't mean that we can't do *something* at the same time. I think we should create a firewall."

"Like on a computer?" I asked. "Did you pick the term because it has fire in it?"

"I was being a little more literal," Gomorrah said. "I have some explosives that can spray liquid fire around an area for an extended period of time. I want to create a wall between the Antithesis and the city."

"That's a stalling action," I said. The aliens on the other side would just have more time to group up and grow stronger.

"There's more," Sprout said. "I have some new seeds I want to spread. They'll need some time to grow, but once they do, they can turn the lost part of the city into a deathtrap for the Antithesis."

"Alright," I said. "Sounds easy enough. Gom, you need help with those bombs? I've got a few that might help with that wall of yours."

CHAPTER FIFTY-EIGHT

FINAL HOURS

For long-ranged travel, the aircraft is still the best option, but as time progresses and hovercraft become more common, we are seeing a harsh decrease in commercial flights, especially more localized ones.

A clever traveler can hop from city to city using different hovercar services for relatively cheap, and since the distance covered by a hovercar is significantly greater than that covered by a traditional car, we're starting to see the entire airline economy crumbling.

Which is why we want to push for more luxury-based airplane accommodations. Let's jack up the price and make airline travel something for the rich and influential and those who wish they were both.

—Beta Airlines internal memo, 2031

Gomorrah volunteered the Fury to deliver her explosive payload, and I was totally okay with the idea that we'd be dropping stuff onto the aliens from the relative safety of the air.

But that would only cover a little bit, and I didn't want Gomorrah to be alone up there.

"Alright," I said while we were all still in the planning . . . shed. "Gomorrah, you get the Fury up in the air. I'll see if the militia has any hovercars. I can probably give them something to drop bombs with, and we can load them up with enough munitions to cover everything. I know you can just go up and keep dropping things, but I'm worried that you'll just be one vehicle alone in the air."

Gomorrah shrugged. "It's a fair worry. I'll be closer to the water, and there might be larger Antithesis that can fly in the lake. They might come out if they see the Fury dropping bombs along the shore."

"Right, exactly," I said. "I wish we had more AA guns down here too."

"Franny will be here in twenty minutes with another load of turrets from your place," Gomorrah said.

"Really? That's not bad," I said.

"She brought some in last night as well. I got the militia to install them across the city. They're not exactly strong, you know?"

"Yeah, but they can take out the weaker aliens without too much of a fuss, and they don't need a person controlling them to work," I argued.

More turrets would be nice, in any case. We could get them up on all of the buildings on this side of downtown. I wasn't sure if their range was enough to really help during bombing runs or anything, but they'd certainly help if a flying car returned with some aliens on its ass. "I'll chat with Intel-chan, get things organized. Sprout, do you need to be there to spread your, uh, seeds?"

"That'd be ideal," he said. "But I think anyone could manage if you train them just a little."

"Cool. Do you want to go out with Arm-a-Geddon here? Both of you working together should be able to stay alive."

I noted that he still had that gun I'd given him a bit ago. Arm-a-Geddon had upgraded himself a bit. New arms, again, this time with what looked like several guns built into his forearms that I imagined could spring out of them.

Not my kind of thing, but whatever. I bet it made him a bit tankier, and we might need that.

"We'll arrange a few squads, then. Maybe mix the militia folk with some of the Kittens. They should be easier to get volunteers from to learn some, uh, advanced frontline gardening," I said.

Sprout nodded, and since he seemed pretty happy with that, I nodded myself. "Good. Gomorrah, can you help with the bombs? I'll get in touch with Intel-chan right now. Oh, and can you direct Franny once she arrives?"

"When did you want to put our plan into motion?" Gomorrah asked. "Because it sounds like you have a lot of prep-work to do."

I considered it for a moment, then looked at the time. "Call it . . . two p.m., on the dot. That gives us just a bit over an hour to get everything ready."

"I can work with that," Gomorrah said. Sprout looked a bit nervous, but he had an hour to get over those nerves.

In the meantime, I stepped out and headed toward the wall. Just because I had a lot of calls to make didn't mean that I couldn't help on the wall a little. I made two calls at the same time. One to Intel-chan, who'd get me in touch with all of the militia, and another to Jennifer. Neither call had time to ring once before they picked up.

"*Ohio*, Neko-sama."

"Hello, sexy."

There was a long pause, then Intel-chan spoke up. "Miss Stray Cat. Who is that?"

"That's Jennifer," I said and I pushed the two boxes that had popped up with the images of the people I was talking to toward the side. Intel-chan's little VTuber avatar squeezed in next to Jennifer's . . . also an avatar, probably. "She's Lucy's sexy robot secretary. Don't fall in love. Also, why did you call me sexy?" That last was directed to Jennifer herself.

"It's what Miss Lucy calls you in our internal notes," she said. "Also, I thought it was funny."

"Huh," I said. "Right, maybe don't? Anyway, I need volunteers, maybe Kittens, maybe not. People who know a bit about gardening and who aren't afraid of being eaten alive by homicidal aliens."

"Finding people with gardening-related skills will be difficult," she said.

"And not the other part?" I asked.

"Not really. Humans tend to have a strange relationship with fear until such a time as the fear-causing thing is already too close to be avoided. Where do you need these people? How many volunteers do you need?"

"We're going to send groups out past the wall to plant some stuff Sprout has cooked up. I don't want this to be a suicide mission, so we'll be sending them out in squads. Maybe one armored vehicle each, with enough armed folk to keep our gardeners safe? So yeah, however many squads like that you two can arrange, that's how many volunteers we'll need."

"I think we can supply some technicals," Intel-chan said. "We have a number of cars free right now."

"Good. Now, on the subject of cars. Does the militia have any sort of armored flying vehicles?"

Intel-chan's avatar bobbed its head. "Yup! We have three pursuit VTOLs, and five heavy lift vans for troop transportation. We also have a number of police cruisers on loan. They have turreted weapons, but they're not designed to kill organics."

"That might do. Bring them over here. We're going to turn them into bombers," I said.

Intel-chan clapped. "Oh, nice. You're going to get a ton of volunteers for that."

Yeah, that tracked. Giving a bunch of people access to heavy-ordnance and telling them to drop it onto the heads of the pesky aliens below was always going to be popular. "Just get the cars over here, I'll figure out a way to set them up to drop bombs. And remind our new bomber pilots that this shit's dangerous, we don't have good AA."

"Noted," Intel-chan said. "Still gonna get lots of volunteers. Expect the cars within the hour."

"Make it faster than that, we're starting the bombing runs at two p.m.."

"Oh, that's soon, I'll have everyone hurry up, then," they said.

"When do you need the gardeners?" Jennifer asked.

I shook my head. "Ideally they should be here already, but we can't have that. So just get them over as quickly as possible." There were some scaffolds set up on the inner side of the wall, with ladders slanted at an angle to act as OSHA-violating steps so that people could carry stuff to the top of the barricade.

A few heavier-looking machine guns were set up there already, rattling away as they sprayed at what I hoped was a horde of aliens. I ran up the ladder, tail swaying automatically to keep me balanced, then I climbed up another level to see over the top of the barricade.

There were heaps of alien bodies strewn across an otherwise empty street, with more aliens charging down from around the corner. There were lots of them, but it was far from one of those endless tides like I'd seen in New Montreal before. This was more of an endless trickle of lower-tiered models.

It was more than what they'd been seeing the day before, however, and that was concerning all on its own. We had three guns firing nearly nonstop up here, with pauses only happening when they needed to reload or change belts.

Eventually we'd run out of ammo. Maybe before the aliens ran out of bodies.

I wasn't liking the math here.

I flung a couple of grenades ahead. Just a few plain old resonators, to help melt the bodies that were piling up before they could turn into make-shift barricades. I made a note to leave some better 'nades behind too, in case bigger, meaner aliens started to show up. Even some in the early dou-ble-digit range could really mess things up.

Meh, we'd be fine. We just had to hold out for a little while longer. I was feeling pretty good about our odds.

CHAPTER FIFTY-NINE

ENJOYING THE VIEW

Why? Because this piece of shit runs off the same trash software some guy made in his mother's basement in the fucking eighties! That's why!

—About modern printers, 2057

It's going to have to be a custom job for each one.

I frowned, but it made sense.

I had three cars sitting before me and five armored vans. The cars were all sharp angles and boxy frames. They looked like they could move fast and punch through reinforced walls with ease. The kind of overly manly design language that got the little knobs of cops around the world all hard.

Having the Fury parked nearby kinda ripped the wind out of their sails, however. These things were at best armed with piddly little turreted auto-cannons designed to punch cars out of the air. They might have been police pursuit vehicles, but they weren't rated to do much against the Antithesis.

The five vans parked behind them were a bit better. I noticed three distinct models there, but they all followed more or less the same design language. Rounded fronts as a slight concession to aerodynamics and a big bulky box of a body with side-opened doors. Three of them had side-mounted turrets with the guns missing. A few techs were installing them in a hurry, though.

Yeah, those would do.

"Alright," I said. There was a gathering of pilots and volunteers from the militia nearby. "We're going to arm up the vans with something to drop bombs. You're going to need someone inside to reload the bomb-dropping thing, but it should be able to drop them on the right spot."

I was half talking to these guys and half to Myalis. I didn't want to have to trust some bozo with dropping bombs. You'd have to be a special kind of stupid to give someone with no training access to exotic explosives.

Clearing my throat, I gestured to the three pursuit vehicles. "We can add a cheap laser turret onto these. It'll make them a bit better in the air. That autocannon looks like it's enough to take out some of the earlier double-digit aliens without too much trouble."

Franny was arriving soon, and it wouldn't be too hard to divert three of those turrets over. Plus it would save me a few points.

I walked over to each van in turn and scanned their interiors with my augs to give Myalis a good idea of the amount of space we were dealing with. Then I ordered up the bomb-dropping mechanism for each. They were a hundred and twenty points each, which . . . I wasn't sure if that was a rip-off or not. Each was relatively large, able to fit into the door and block it completely, with a sort of deployable tube thing on the side to actually drop the bombs from.

Of course, I left the installation to the nearby techs. Just scanning the interiors for Myalis and ordering the shit was enough work for me.

"Will you be riding along with them?" Intel-chan asked. We had a voice channel up and running at all times now. The other nearby samurai were on it, but we'd split things up into individual channels so that we wouldn't be bothering each other with constant chatter. There was a "loud" channel where everyone would hear anything said, but that was more for emergencies.

"Nah," I said. "I'll go with Gomorrah. The Fury is a much nicer ride and we'll want to see what we can of the shoreline from the air. That'll be a lot easier with the Fury than in one of these cheap things."

"Fair enough. We've got as many volunteers as we need already, and a few more besides," Intel-chan said.

I nodded along. That much was pretty clear already. The area had picked up in activity, and there were a lot more people standing around or trying to look busy than before.

I was a little worried about the friction between the militia and the Kittens, but so far it wasn't all that bad. The Kittens seemed to lean more toward the . . . I guess "casual" side of things, especially whenever the militia were around. And on the opposite end of the spectrum, the militia were walking with an even stiffer rod up their asses whenever they passed the Kittens.

Typical monkey "my group's better than yours" behavior, basically. Kind of weird seeing it from a distance, usually I'd be there strutting with the rest of them.

Alright, the bombers were being set up . . . we still needed ammo for them to drop, which meant that I had to find Gomorrah.

Fortunately, she wasn't that hard to find. Less fortunately, she was standing next to a familiar hovercar, hands moving with uncertainty while Franny was bent over double to squeeze into the hovercar and remove folded-up laser turrets that looked like they were fresh off the presses.

I debated heading over or not for a moment before giving in and just walking to stand next to Gomorrah. "Enjoying the view?" I asked as we watched Franny unfold herself from the car. It looked like one of the turrets had gotten stuck at the bottom there.

Gomorrah straightened, then turned her featureless mask toward me. "I know that denying that I was looking would be pointless, but could you pretend that you didn't notice anyway?"

I grinned, then shrugged. "Sure. But you know, maybe she'd appreciate knowing that you were?" I stepped toward Franny and gave her a little wave. "Hey, how'd the trip over go?"

"Not bad," the redhead said. She brushed a few stray locks out of her face. "I might have to delay the next trip, though. The New Montreal police didn't want me flying out of their airspace and they barely bought my story about delivering supplies to here. Same when I crossed the border. And there's a lot of flying aliens in the air going around in flocks and hitting random vehicles. It's really not safe, except for in big circles around most cities."

"Shit," I said. "We should have given you something to get the law off your back."

"The Family actually stepped in," she said. "So it wasn't all that bad. And there's a few apps that'll tell you where the biggest sightings of fliers were. It was worth the credits to get them, I think."

Of course someone was monetizing that. "Well, glad you're here. If you want, Lucy's over at the mall. She can find you a place to stay. She'll definitely put you to work, though."

Franny shrugged. "I'm not averse to a little hard work. Next batch of turrets should be ready in about twelve hours though. We got the kittens working on loading up the machine. Rac sourced a bunch of supplies too."

There was a bit of warm pride in my chest at hearing that. My kittens were doing good work. Not that they were really *mine*, but whatever. I'd take credit for basically raising them as long as they were doing good.

The moment they fucked up, I'd pretend I had nothing to do with it, of course.

"Hey, can you set aside three turrets for the interceptors? We're going to be using them to keep the bombers safe," I said. "Ah, speaking of which. Gom, as much as I'd love to see your bumbling attempts at flirting, do you think you can put it off for a little bit? We need to discuss bombs."

Gomorrah's shoulders moved in a way that suggested she was sighing. Was it because she was sad that she wouldn't get to flirt, or was it something else? "Yeah, that's fine," she said. "Franny, you probably should go see Lucy. I think she could use the help. Cat here keeps giving her more work."

"Hey," I complained.

Wait, was that true? Was I overworking Lucy? Fuck, I wasn't even paying her, was I?

How much was a person like Lucy worth? Organizing an impromptu army, putting down dissidents, arranging to feed an entire city, and running a PR campaign at the same time . . .

Double fuck, I wasn't making enough money to afford her at all, was I?

"So, I was thinking of keeping it simple. Longer-lasting firebombs. Atyacus has a few chemicals that will burn for days at a time. They're not as powerful as some liquids I have, but the duration is important here."

"I think I can get Myalis to give me resonators that'll keep going for a long time and that'll be tough enough to endure the drop," I said. "I guess we're going to mostly aim for duration, then?"

"The problem is the spread, in that case. Even if our bombs overlap where they land, they'll only cover a relatively small area. It'll take thousands of them to create a complete barrier," Gomorrah said.

"Tricky," I said.

Mostly, I was still thinking of how to pay Lucy back. Would foot rubs count?

CHAPTER SIXTY

CALLSIGNS

We need a new minority to pin things on. It's becoming increasingly difficult to blame trans people or the gays. I can't think of any new group to marginalize though. We have a few options, but none of them fit all of our criteria:

1. We need them to be relatively poor.

2. We can't have that group be associated with us politically already.

3. They need a distinct culture.

4. They can't be a group that's well integrated with our own community.

5. The less media representation they have, the better. We'll take care of first impressions.

6. If they have historical reasons for being disliked, then that would be a bonus.

I'm thinking we can have the people in the south turn against the French? There's a small but strong French community around New Orleans that we could pin things on. But then the actual French are pretty strong, so it could blow back against us.

Ideas?

—Internal memo from Rep. G. Tean, 2031

I jumped into the Fury next to Gomorrah and then settled into place. Around us, the borrowed vans were starting to rise from the road, and the interceptors were already in the air, flying circles above.

There was surprisingly little talk as we got ready. I half turned in my seat and checked out the bomb-launcher in the back of the car. Gomorrah had just installed it, and it was basically just a bigger, more complex version of the bomb-dropping device we'd installed in the vans. There was an opening to place grenades into, so that's what I did.

"Right, we're going for longer-lasting things. And they need to survive the drop. Resonators are my go-to area-denial. Gomorrah's dropping fire. What else?"

Perhaps explosives that are proximity-detonated? They can fill any gaps in the line, and when an Antithesis tries to go around the fire left by Gomorrah's payload, they can detonate.

"As long as they don't go off when a person's nearby, that's not a bad idea," I said.

That's easy to arrange. Might I suggest some nyanpalm as well? It'd be a shame to have created a whole new kind of flammable weapon only to leave it unused.

I sighed, but she was probably right. "Yeah, that's not a terrible idea. Let's load this sucker up."

Points Reduced from 37,854, to 37,764

That stung a bit. Not so long ago I was in the fifty thousand point range. But that was before buying loads of food, more equipment, mounts, bomb-dropping devices, and literally thousands of bombs. Oh, and some spatulas.

If everything I purchased (spatulas aside) got used to murder aliens, then I'd be back to where I was before, and probably past that.

Gomorrah opened the driver's-side door and slipped in. "Is it loaded?" she asked.

"At one hundred percent," I said. "We've got bombs for days."

"Not really," she said more seriously. "We have enough to cover something like a four-hundred-meter stretch. Each bomber . . . van we have can cover another hundred or so. But the shoreline is several kilometers long."

"Right, we're going to have to bomb and return," I said. "Unless you want us to do all the work from here? We can refill in midair, the vans can't, can they?"

"They can," Gomorrah said. "It's a big purchase each time, but I can do it from here. I asked Atyacus about it. There's . . . rules about summoning items and where they appear. You can't buy an item and have it appear too far from where you are, but the vans should be able to fly into range."

That wasn't something I'd ever thought about. I'd have to annoy Myalis about it later. After all, buying a grenade and having it appear *inside* the nearest alien would save me having to throw the damned thing.

"Alright, I think Intel-chan's keeping a digital eye on our bomber's load-outs. We'll know when one of them hits empty."

Gomorrah nodded once. "Are we ready then?"

"Let's hit it," I agreed.

Gomorrah brought the Fury up with a sudden lurch and I hung onto the little strap above the door.

With a flick of a switch on my augs, I connected to the main communication channel being used by the bombers and interceptors. I supposed that that would be my job from now on. It wasn't like I could do much while Gomorrah was driving us around.

"Ah, this is God's Righteous Fury, we're airborne. The rest of you can start climbing. We're going to circle overhead, then head out to the shoreline for our first run. Intel-chan, you got the coordinates?"

Intel-chan's voice popped onto the channel. "Mapped out and sent to all pilots. Have fun! Pilots, all call signs, check in."

"This is Nutcracker one, climbing," one of the pilots said. I matched his location on my map, each van having an IFF. The vans had been numbered, but now their names were changing to match what the pilots were calling themselves.

"Rear Ender two, coming in hot."

"Cockpit Crusher three, rising."

"Gorilla four, ready to ooga some boogas."

"Oscar-Oscar-Foxtrot five, ready to bring the pain," the last pilot called out.

And I was surrounded by fucking morons. This was going to go fantastically. "Alright, children, form up behind the Fury, and keep the line clear unless there's an actual problem." I muted myself and shook my head. The pilots were all volunteers, sure, but they were all supposed to be professionals too.

"Are we good?" Gomorrah asked.

"We're peachy," I said. "We're starting the bombing run along the southern shore here, and heading northward. Nice and easy-like. Arm-a-Geddon and Sprout are going to head out now too. They might call out for fire support if they need it."

"We could help, sure," Gomorrah said. "How are you on points?"

"Not bad, but I've been spending them fast. Kinda hoping this'll refill me, you know?"

Gomorrah nodded along. "I understand. Still, points not spent are points wasted."

"I guess," I said. "I have a hard time justifying the spending. I dunno. How about you?"

"I'm saving up for something big," Gomorrah said. "Something that'll let me punch far above my weight class."

"Oh?" I asked. "What would that look like?"

"I'm thinking a warmech."

I blinked. That was . . . something. "How big are we talking here? Because warmech sounds bigger than, like, power armor. The kind of shit you'd expect to see from a top-tier samurai who isn't holding back at all."

"It's surprisingly worse than you'd expect, actually," Gomorrah said. "A big mobile weapons platform can only really be used in a few specific scenarios. It's like a tank. Sure, it's strong and can destroy things well, but most of the time we're clearing hives or clearing places room-by-room, or we need to navigate through a city. A tank can't really do that. A warmech has a few advantages, but not that many."

"Yeah," I said. It kinda made sense. "But it's also a fucking warmech."

"Exactly," Gomorrah said. "Perfect for fighting very large Antithesis. Things in the upper twenties and thirties. And it's decent for defending a location if the location's safety doesn't matter that much."

I liked the idea, but it sounded expensive. "Maybe I should get one."

"It would go counter to your usual MO," Gomorrah said. "The stealth part, at least."

"I'm sure Myalis could get me an invisible warmech."

I certainly could. Your Sun Watcher catalog actually has a few options.

Sun Watcher? I supposed that made sense. That same catalog had given me power armor before, so it having something larger wasn't too surprising.

Do you want to peruse the catalog? I'm sure we could find something you'd like!

"Are you just going to tempt me into buying something big?" I asked.

I'm pretty sure it will work too.

A secondary screen opened on my augs, and Myalis uploaded a rotating image onto it. It was a highly detailed scan of a quadrupedal machine. It reminded me a little bit of the cat bots I'd purchased before. Only this one had a small human figure next to it. The figure was just barely as tall as the warmech's legs.

This model is made of reinforced titanium and aluminium, making it surprisingly light. It has twin 105mm cannons, a railgun running through the center of the body, two 10mm Gatling guns mounted on its shoulders, a full sensor suite, and its tail and claws can deploy the same kind of blade as your Void Terminus. The pilot sits here, in the center of the unit within an armored and air-conditioned cockpit. The controls are entirely intuitive, and there's an onboard AI to help coordinate and balance the warmech.

I licked my lips. Fuck, it was kinda hot.

"Alright, focus," I said, shaking my head to clear the thoughts of warmechs from my mind. "We have a job to do right now. Warmechs can wait."

Gomorrah chuckled. "You're right. Let's get this operation underway and worry about the toys later."

I nodded in agreement, and with that, we started our bombing run. The vans fell in line behind us, and we all advanced toward the shoreline, prepared to unleash our arsenal on the unsuspecting Antithesis. We flew in a sort of arrow formation, the Fury at the front, with an interceptor on either side, then the vans behind in a trail with the third interceptor way at the back.

We swept around in a big curve that lined us up with the shoreline, then Gomorrah brought us all down lower toward the ground until we were only a hundred meters off. "Bombs away," she said.

There was a constant *clunk-clunk-clunk* as bombs dropped out beneath us. I watched through one of the car's rear cameras as we turned the otherwise peaceful shoreline, lined with waterside homes and old wooden piers, into a warzone.

"Beautiful," I said. "Nutcracker one, drop your load right after the end of ours, then pull up to circle. Rear Ender, you're next."

CHAPTER SIXTY-ONE

KITTYKOPTER

Deadvods are videos, usually uploaded to a site like YouTube or one of its competitors, which features a content creator doing . . . whatever it is that they normally do.

Game, beauty, movie reviews, commentary on events, creating memes, uploading minidocumentaries, etc. On a mechanical level, they're not so different from a normal channel.

Except that the creator is dead.

The videos are prerecorded. Often by an ill content creator, or one who is planning on taking their own life. They often make light of their own demise, using it as a macabre punchline which resonates well with an equally dead-inside generation of viewers.

With the advent of greater deepfakes, the number of such videos, even created against the explicit desires of their once-living creators, had increased tremendously.

—"On Deathtubers and Deadvods," *Mox* article, 2027

The run's start was . . . not exactly textbook.

Or maybe it would be textbook, if someone ever decided to write a book about perfectly mediocre combat maneuvers that kinda worked but only barely.

The Fury's run planted dozens of fiery explosions in a line across the shore, and the follow-up by the ragtag group of vans elongated that line by . . . less than we'd hoped.

Mostly that was because even with decent tech helping our pilots aim, it didn't ensure that every bomb went off exactly where they were wanted. The line ended up being much thicker and shorter than what we'd planned for, mostly so that the small gaps left between explosives were properly covered.

Sucked, but that was how it was going to work out.

We circled the air above the burning patch of coast for a bit while Gomorrah and I spent points reloading the bombers and we prepared to come in for a second run. The smoke was going to make organic verification a little hard, but that was fine. The stretch we'd bombed was about eighty meters long, which meant . . . we'd be here for a while.

"Do you think we should split the bombers up?" I asked. "Send each one farther ahead to create more, smaller blocks?"

"They need to be within range for reloading. And that would mean that they'll be all spread out if the Antithesis decide to show up," Gomorrah said.

I nodded along, not disappointed to have my idea shot down. I wasn't married to it.

"Alright, welp, let's keep at it."

I actually had very little to keep at. Gomorrah was the one doing the flying, and I realized that I was mostly just along for the ride at this point. Maybe I could have stayed back in Downtown to put out one or two more fires instead of sitting in the Fury to watch Gomorrah set some non-metaphorical fires alight.

I decided to be at least a little productive. "Myalis, do we have much of an idea of where the aliens are in all that water?"

Not an exact idea, no. The best I can give you are estimates based on satellite surveillance and observations from climate-change analysis devices in the region. It all points to a rather large hive, but my data could be fooled.

"What could do that?" I asked, genuinely curious.

While I am so close to perfection that mere humanity cannot begin to measure it, the human-made devices I have no choice in using are not so well-crafted. The same kind of sensors and analysis devices have been fooled by things such as geothermal venting and clandestine chemical dumping.

"Huh," I said. That made sense. But it led to another question. "Hey, is your obsession with cats something you have because they also think that they're perfect?"

No comment.

"Alright, get me a little drone or something. Something small that'll handle the water. If we're going to do nothing, we'll do nothing productively."

"I could turn on the radio, if you're bored," Gomorrah said.

"This thing has a radio?" I asked.

She gave me a masked-face *look* that I shrugged off with the ease of someone used to that "are you a moron" kind of expression.

New Purchase: KittyKopter Model One
Points Reduced from 37,644, to 37,634

A small box plopped onto my lap and I popped it open, revealing a small drone with a trio of off-center propellers. They were those weird asymmetrical ones, with a loop missing out of the middle. It was black, with currently pink RGB illuminating the inside of the prop rings, and the front had a little cat face sticker on it.

I rolled down the window with a press of a button, then flung the drone out the side while connecting to it with my augs.

It took a millionth of a second or so, and then I had a second set of "eyes" and a sonar system jacked into my hearing that painted a picture of the world around the drone.

I pointed it toward the water. The drone paused for a moment in midair, spun itself around to face the right way, then zipped forward, whisper-quiet so as to not interfere with its own sonar. Or was it just quiet because not being quiet would be stupid for a spy drone?

Maybe a bit of both?

The drone slowed considerably before hitting the water, but then it picked up the pace again.

"Got that heatmap?" I asked, and Myalis overlaid it with my vision. The drone angled itself to the side a little, and pushed toward the generated source of warmth.

I saw some seaweed move by, and some underwater shit. There was surprisingly little trash once the drone moved past the edges of the shore.

"Looks like a normal lake to me," I said.

This lake was once home to a large number of fish. A prohibition on large-scale industrial fishing from the 1970s has been kept up to this day, and with few nearby factories dumping anything into the lake, this was one of the cleanest lakes in the North American region. Easily in the top fifty. It should be inhabited.

I had the drone kick up the juice on its sonar and let my eyes go half-lidded as I listened. Gomorrah and the others were starting on their next bombing run already, but my attention was entirely on what I was seeing and hearing from the drone.

"No fishies," I said.

A disquieting fact, yes.

"Do you think the aliens got them all? Could they have? I can't imagine a model three with a little fishing line waiting for a fish to bite . . . okay, yes, I can imagine that . . . they'd have one of those floppy hats with the little hooks on."

"Cat," Gomorrah said.

"Yeah?"

"Stop imagining the enemy as cute."

"What, it's not like I wouldn't shoot them anyway."

The Antithesis do have aquatic-specializing models, as well as modifications to existing models that make them more viable for aquatic environments. In this case, however, a large number of model ones could clear out a lake of this size in a few days to hours, depending on the number of them.

Right, the bird-like ones were probably about as big as the average fish.

I sat up straighter as something flew toward the drone. It wasn't creating much turbulence as it moved, but it was probably at least somewhat noticeable.

I checked the controls, found the *Evasive Maneuvers* option, and then toggled that on a moment before a model one tried to clamp down on the drone.

Unfortunately for the bird, the drone was faster on the straightaway, and it shot away before it could do anything.

The bombing run ended, and we almost immediately started on the next one. I was barely paying attention to that anymore.

There was more than a single mean alien down here.

The drone's sonar fired, revealing a lakefloor hive that stretched on to the very edges of the sonar's range. Large roots were all over, with heavy sacs next to them filled with unborn aliens. Corrals, like pens for angry cows, held in thousands of smaller models while others moved along the surface of the hive.

I saw a number of them pushing dead meat into bulging organic bags filled with whatever crap the hive was using as digestive juices.

"Ah, fuck," I said.

Worse was the large line of aliens slowly walking its way to the shore.

I had the drone follow them, and quickly realized that it stretched almost all the way to the shore.

At the head of the line were several model twenty-twos. Huge mobile hives currently encircled by entire flocks of smaller aliens. They were forcing their way through the water on six massive legs each.

They were a concern all on their own. Any one of them planting themselves close to Downtown could wreck the entire place if left unchecked, spawning a ready-made hive in no time at all.

But the even bigger alien, the one whose model number I didn't even know . . . yeah, that one had me a lot more worried.

I sent the video I had to Gomorrah and felt her sitting straighter a moment later. "That's going to be a problem," she said.

"We're bombing the wrong damned place," I said. "And I don't think our bombs are big enough."

That warmech is still within your price range, Catherine.

CHAPTER SIXTY-TWO

QUICK THINKING

During the early 2010s, several companies ran this advertising campaign that encouraged people to name their children after a brand or corporation.

These children would, in theory, benefit from discounts and rebates while shopping at those locations.

Of course, that backfired spectacularly when most corporations forgot all about that by the time those children were old enough to purchase things themselves.

—Interview with Walmart "Walt" McDonalds, 2034

"I have a plan," I said.

"That was quick," Gomorrah said.

"The plan is that I'll jump out of this car and summon a giant warmech so that I can fight and hold off the aliens while you keep bombing the ground around me," I said.

Gomorrah paused for a long few seconds. "I see now why the plan was quick."

"Hey, it's got decent odds of success, I think. We need to slow down the advance of those bastards, and this'll let the vans continue to drop bombs along the shoreline." The vans were coming around for another bombing run already, continuing the line that we'd started. Gomorrah and I had left them to it and were racing to where the Antithesis were actually coming from, about a kilometer and a half farther down.

"Fine," Gomorrah said. "Don't die."

I grinned. "I won't," I promised. "Myalis, how far can that mech you were talking about drop from, and can you summon it with me inside?"

I see where you're going with that line of questioning, and while the attempt does sound spectacular, it also sounds foolhardy. The warmech I proposed earlier can drop from a height of seven meters without any issue. Above that it will suffer increasing amounts of damage from the fall. As for the summoning, yes, I could summon the vehicle around you in midair. Or you could politely ask Gomorrah to swing down and drop you off at ground level.

I groaned, but she was probably right.

It wasn't nearly as badass though, to be dropped off than to jump out of a moving car, summon a warmech around me, then land with that. "Gom, can you drop me off . . . about over there?" I pointed to a spot some fifty-ish meters from the shore. There were some wooden piers over the lakeside where the water ended at a set of cement walls. The piers stretched out over the water, and there were some restaurants nearby using them as sitting space.

A few smaller models were already pulling themselves over the edge of the pier. Doglike model threes, some tentacle-covered assholes too, and of course, a bunch of model ones were flying right out of the water and into the air for a short distance. A flock of these were hanging on to the rails, like seagulls on a wire, only worse in every way.

Gomorrah brought the Fury down low and quick, the hood popping open to release a flamethrower which did flamethrower things to the nearest aliens.

I waited for the fire to die down before stepping out. "Stay safe," I said.

"You're the one going out there," she said.

"Yeah, but I'll be fine," I said as I clicked the door shut. The Fury rose up past me in a wash of broiling air and I was left standing in the circle of burning pier over increasingly agitated waters. "Gonna wanna back up a bit," I said to myself.

Are you ready?

"How much is this going to cost?" I asked.

The more you put into it, the more you'll get out of it.

That was fair enough, I supposed. "What's my point total right now?" I asked.

Current Point Total: 37,634

I let out a long breath. "What was that big model? The really big fucker that I saw with the KittyKopter."

That was a model twenty-three. It is worth six hundred points if you manage to kill it. A rapid estimate suggests that the entire value of the Antithesis column moving in your direction is close to twenty-five thousand points.

I worked my jaw, then watched more model threes start to climb up onto the pier. No time to waste, then. "Myalis, sink twenty K into that warmech, and make it fucking fantastic."

Understood. Summoning a Mark IV Mechcatular Nyanzerfaust. Prepare for arrival.

"Wait, it's called the what?" I asked.

Then I was interrupted by a glimmer from above. By the time I started to look up, the thing was already crashing down onto the ground next to me. The burst of wind from its passing kicked up the flames all around me and its landing buckled and splintered the pier, sending wooden planks flying into the air.

New Purchase: Mark IV Mechcatular Nyanzerfaust
Points Reduced from 37,634, to 17,634

The robot was three meters tall and twice as long, all black and chrome and pent-up violence. It sat on four legs, hunched and mean, like a cat on the prowl. Its eyes lit up, pink and bright, then the light washed out across its entire frame, skimming along its sensor-whiskers, then along its mane and through its body. It flashed as it reached each individual paw and glowed faintly for a moment as it touched the thagomizer on the mecha's tail.

It was several tons of composite, alien armor, and corded artificial muscles, and it looked like it could fuck any Antithesis's day up.

The mech turned its head my way, locking eyes with me, then it bent down in a feline bow, the plates along its neck hissing apart to reveal a seat surrounded by control surfaces nestled deep within the mecha's body.

"Ah, fuck yeah," I said. "I don't know what I'm feeling, Myalis, but it's a good feeling."

It's a little disturbing, actually.

I planted a foot on one of the slid-back armored plates, then leapt up and into the cockpit. "Just don't tell Lucy."

That you were turned on by a multi-ton warmech?

"Actually . . . maybe Lucy would understand," I admitted.

The cockpit and the mech immediately linked up with my augs and my vision filled with a confusing mess of commands and controls. Fortunately, the one to close the cockpit was dead center, and I tapped it.

The armor slid back into place, and the inside closed up fully. I could feel it going airtight with a faint pop in my ears. Then a whisper-quiet hum filled the space around me and the air started to taste different.

The seat shifted suddenly, and I almost gasped before I realized that I was meant to be lying on my stomach, legs braced into a pair of holes and chest pressed up against a soft cushion. My hands naturally fell onto a pair of joysticks surrounded on the outside by dozens of buttons, and the world around me opened up as a projected screen came to life.

"Fuuuck," I muttered. This was some top-tier sci-fi B-movie shit. "Uh . . . how do I pilot this?"

It has an autopilot, though it is designed to be fully controlled by the person riding within it, otherwise you might as well exit the vehicle and just let it fight on its own without any added weight.

"Ouch," I said.

There are tutorials built into the mech to teach you how to fly it.

"How long do I have before that model twenty-three shows up?" I asked.

Approximately two minutes.

I nodded. "How long's the tutorial?"

Significantly longer than two minutes, Catherine. This is a full-on stealth capable warmech. Piloting it without assistance makes piloting a modern main battle tank look like riding a tricycle. The upside is that the wide control range means that a pilot can do some spectacular things with a vehicle like this one.

I ground my teeth. Sure, letting the autopilot take care of things would be fine . . . but I really wanted to do the piloting myself. It was too cool not to be something I wanted. And I could just imagine the ladyboner Lucy would get once she found out.

"Do you have one of those implantable knowledge things?" I asked.

For a few points, certainly.

I rolled my eyes. "Really, Myalis?"

Actually, the Mark IV Mechcatular Nyanzerfaust comes equipped with its own learning architecture. All you're missing are the neural uplinks to truly make use of it all.

"Fine," I said. "But nothing too intrusive. Call it two hundred or so points? I'm feeling cheap right about now."

New Purchase: Internal Neural Uplink System
Points Reduced from 17,634 to 17,434

What Myalis got me came in the form of a small, boxy syringe with the words "Press to forehead" written on one side.

I did just that, and immediately felt a wave of cold washing over my head, like a sudden brain freeze. Little tendrils raced across and out of the box, and I almost ripped it away only to realize it was stuck there. Then my head *vibrated* for just a moment and I was hit with a sudden sense of déjà vu.

System installed. There should be a new jack along the back of your ears. You'll find a connector on the ceiling, jack it in.

I felt at the side of my head and found what she was talking about, a tiny pinprick hole that hadn't been there before. "Wait, did that drill through my skull?"

Just a little bit. Don't worry, it's stronger than it was before.

I frowned as I tugged the jack out of the ceiling and shoved it into place. There was a noise, like connecting one of those old aug cables, then . . . then I felt myself.

My vision doubled. I was at once in the cockpit, and also seeing out of the eyes of the mech.

I moved my arm back into place, then raised a paw.

"Whoa," I said.

This . . . was fucky.

And unfortunately, as the pier exploded out around me, I was out of time to explore that fuckiness.

CHAPTER SIXTY-THREE

MECHCATULAR NYANZERFAUST ACTIVATE

Knowledge-download tech was seen as a massive step forward in the early 2030s. It allowed someone, anyone, to instantly become an expert in a specific field. Things like learning a new instrument or a new language in an instant is fantastic, and all it costs is a small fortune, but sometimes that price is worth it. A thousand hours spent learning Spanish, or thirty thousand USD? What's worth more to you? Tons of people signed on and got those early operations, and initially everything was fine.

Then the downsides started to show up.

What happens when your brain suddenly has a lot of new data with no concrete memories to go with it?

It starts to make things up to fill the gaps. People imagined, and believed, in entire false backstories that didn't mesh with reality just to match the knowledge they now had.

Then you had what we started to call PBS, or personality bleed syndrome, which is still barely understood, and yet can lead to all sorts of new and terrifying mental issues.

—Doctor Lopez, McRill neurosurgeon in a podcast interview, 2037

I jumped back, all four legs spreading wide even as they opened up and the jet engines mounted into them fired.

It wasn't enough thrust to lift me up, but it was enough, combined with a backward leap, to send me flying off the pier. I landed roughly on all fours, claws digging furrows into asphalt until the mech came to a full stop.

I paused then.

All of that had been *reflex*. Like twirling my arm to stop myself from falling after catching my foot in a carpet or something. It was all done without *thinking*. And that would be fine, usually, only it wasn't my body that I'd moved, but the warmech's.

I ran over every action I'd just taken. There had been several inputs on the two joysticks, and I'd pressed it on the foot pedals a few times too. Fuck, I hadn't even *known* that this cockpit had foot pedals a moment ago. "Myalis, this is some weird shit," I said.

It can take a moment for newly uploaded knowledge to begin to feel natural. If you dislike the feeling, then we can always focus more on training modules in the future. Several Vanguard have suggested a strong dislike of memory downloads in the past.

"Yeah, I can see why," I said. It didn't feel wrong, but it sure as shit didn't feel right either.

A tool then, neutral depending on how it was used.

For something like this, needing to learn something right then and there with no time to practice or do things right, that was acceptable, I supposed, but it still felt off.

If I had learned how to move this mecha myself, would I have moved the way I had just then? How much of me was there in my actions if they were actions downloaded from some file or something?

I didn't like it, basically.

Well, no, that wasn't entirely truthful. I didn't like the mind fuckery bit. But piloting a multi-ton warmech so well that I was practically dancing between explosions? That was fucking awesome.

My thumb flicked across a little wheel mounted on a joystick and with a three-button prompt, the shoulder of the warmech unfolded and a pair of multi-barreled Gatling guns locked into place. My vision split into three, two of the new screens allowing me to aim and lock the guns on the pier ahead.

When the smoke cleared, it revealed a large model eighteen ripping its way out of the wooden pier. Smaller models were using it to rush out of the water in droves.

I locked both guns on the massive monster, felt two triggers pop out of the joysticks under my index, and I pulled.

There was an impossibly loud pair of *brrrts* and the entire mech had to take a small step back to compensate for the recoil. I only fired for half a second, but my ammo counter had dropped by three hundred rounds.

The smoke cleared, and the big model eighteen was still clearly alive. A lot of the smaller aliens around it, however, were paste.

"What does this fire?" I asked.

10mm rounds. Very small and economical, but not nearly as impactful as larger rounds. You're firing a mixture of armor-piercing, hollow point, and ultra-heavy rounds, as well as phosphorus tracer rounds.

I stepped to the side and fired at the crowd of aliens again, sweeping the fire from left to right quickly. That was enough to saw one of the big alien's legs right off and it ripped apart any of the smaller ones hanging around it.

I could live with this.

The pier fell apart entirely as the model eighteen finally died. The posts on the edge broke apart, and a chunk of the walkway next to the pier was ripped back and dragged into the water with a heavy splash.

I started to pace along the shore, shoulder-mounted guns sliding back into place while I got used to the strangely flowy motions of the warmech. It wasn't like riding in a car. There was too much up-and-down motion for that as the mech walked, but it wasn't as jarring as I might have feared.

I scrolled through the weapon options I had while I was at it.

Two 105mm cannons on the sides with some slight amount of maneuverability. They were in the cat's ribs, more or less, so when they deployed I could aim them forward and down. The railgun basically fired out of the cat's open mouth, but its barrel ran along the entire length of the body with . . . with the gas release in the rear.

Fucking Myalis.

There were some warnings about heat management there too. The cockpit would warm up after every shot. I'd live with it.

The claws and teeth on this thing were similar to my sword in that they were basically double-sided portals with sharp edges. There was a similar setup in the tail.

And I discovered a set of deployable mortars in the cat's back, six chubby barrels that could unfold and launch basic grenades on parabolic arcs with a burst of compressed air.

Basically, I had about as many guns as a modern tank, but I could move faster and claw shit to death, which made me objectively cooler.

My ruminations on how awesome I was came to an end as the shore crumbled away even more and a large leg grabbed onto the edge and pulled.

A model twenty-two rose from the depth, water washing off of its massive frame. Its downward tilted face—a little too human looking, if dull— came into view as its four front legs clambered up onto the shore. More models were clinging to it, using the bigger monster as a living ramp to come onto the shore, though it was doing a good job of creating a more normal ramp already just thanks to its sheer bulk crumbling the waterside apart.

I shifted, brought my mech low, then opened its mouth.

If the Antithesis were going to line themselves up for me, then I wasn't going to complain. I had a whole lot of points to make up for.

The railgun charged in a split second, and I felt every hair in my body standing on end while I aimed the entire warmech's body at the biggest alien in the bunch.

Then I pulled the trigger, and before I could register what happened to the alien, I felt the temperature in the cockpit jump up a dozen degrees all at once.

It immediately started to cool down, but still. Damn.

The alien got pretty hot too.

I watched as it floundered, a hole large enough to crawl through punched right through its massive frame.

The model twenty-two stumbled, then its eyes turned toward me and it let out a long, low note, like someone imitating a foghorn with one nose plugged, only at actual foghorn levels.

The other Antithesis started to rush forward, and the sides of the model twenty-two opened up to vomit out dozens of smaller models all over the ground.

It trampled on a few of those as it continued to move.

"How in the fuck is that still alive?" I asked.

Decentralized nervous system, mostly. It's essentially a mobile hive, after all. Try your cannons. The first two rounds are high explosive. They should help to carve into the model twenty-two.

My cannons slid out of the warmech's sides and I barely had to aim before opening fire. Surprisingly, the kick from these was easier to handle than the kick from the Gatling guns. It was just a question of shifting the mech's weight down a little after every shot as opposed to fighting back against constant recoil.

I fired a round from each cannon, this time paying a lot more attention to the hit itself.

Both rounds punched into the mass of the model twenty-two, then almost immediately exploded, sending fire and plant guts and shrapnel flying.

The model twenty-two, now missing three of its six limbs and a good chunk of its body, crashed to the ground.

"Nice," I said as I checked my ammo. The cannons were magazine fed, with each internal magazine holding five rounds of high explosive armor-piercing gyro-stabilized discarding anti-personnel bullshit. "What even are these rounds?" I asked.

They're twenty-five points each. The primary sabot is surrounded by plastic-coated balls of cesium that disperse in a tight cone ahead of where you fire, ensuring that even if the main projectile misses, the target will still be peppered with supersonic projectiles that will immediately ignite.

I watched as the number of aliens ripping themselves out of the water kept growing, even if a number of them were on fire.

"I hope that'll be enough," I said.

CHAPTER SIXTY-FOUR

GETTING HOT

Why is it always giant mechs with those damned samurai?
Respectfully, sir, because they're cool.
—Exchange between staff sergeant and general,
the Pergignan incursion of 2032

I hopped to the side, then swiped a paw forward. With my claws fully extended, the Void Terminus blades simply moved through the space occupied by any of the aliens in their path, leaving nothing but chunks behind.

My attention wasn't just on those nearby, however. I had half an eye aiming my twin Gatling guns, which were both raining constant fire on any of the smaller models around. It only took a split second of concentrated fire to rip through an entire swarm of model ones, and barely any more than that to kill dozens of model threes.

Which was good, because the Antithesis here were really going all out with the numbers.

A small siren rang in the back of my head and I fired up the jump thrusters in the mech's feet while pushing back with my . . . *its* rear legs, sending me and the mech flying back half a dozen meters.

It was enough to avoid the exploding, tangled mess of an Antithesis artillery ball.

Where had that warning come from? A quick check of my systems showed that I'd received a ping from the warmech's lidar system that had detected an oncoming projectile and beamed the warning right into my brain.

I shook my head, and only realized a split second later that I'd made the mech shake its head too.

This was getting weird.

I wasn't exactly sharing most of my senses with the Mechcatular Nyanzerfaust, but a lot of its controls were linked to my augs, and I was controlling it with an ease and familiarity that was freaky. It was like getting dressed with the lights off while I knew exactly where I'd thrown my pants.

Or something like that. I was moving and acting and controlling this thing as if it was second nature, but I hadn't practiced for it. Some bits of me were confused as hell.

The rest of me really wanted to just kick back and have fun, because this was a fucking blast. I mecha-shifted my sides open and watched as a dozen model threes charged my way, each one of them salivating at the thought of taking a chomp out of me.

So I deployed my 105mm guns and fired both.

The explosion changed the minds of the aliens in a rather permanent fashion as it spread them over a couple of acres.

The guns reloaded automatically, ejecting a pair of casings that I could fit my arm into with a very satisfying *ker-chunk* while I sprayed another horizontal sweep with my Gatling guns through the smoke the explosion had knocked up.

"Having fun?" Gomorrah's voice asked in my ears.

"Tons," I said.

"Ready for a bombing run now. Going to do it right across your nose."

"Uh," I said. "One sec, I'm not sure how fireproof this thing is."

It's capable of enduring high heat, though your stealth systems do need to be within a certain temperature range to function correctly and some of your sensors will have to remain shielded. I'd also suggest keeping your cannons locked up for the moment, they are not rated for direct flame contact.

I tugged the guns back in. "Should be okay, more or less," I said.

"Don't worry. I loaded up on weaker bombs than before. These are just kerosene cluster bombs. No hotter than an oven."

"That's . . . awesome, thanks," I said.

"I do try to think of my friends," Gomorrah said.

I watched the Fury fly low over the shore, tiny black pinpricks dropping out from beneath it and spinning through the air before they burst apart and sent even smaller specks flying every which way. Those ignited in the air just before hitting the ground.

There were thousands of them.

I stepped back a couple of paces, making room as small bombs, no bigger than my fist, exploded over the ground and spread massive circles of liquid fire around.

The restaurants and other buildings along the shore weren't spared, and soon rooftops were blazing infernos and the entire close end of the pier was covered in a wash of low flames.

I wasn't too surprised to find that the mech had thermal vision as well, though now it was made almost entirely useless by all the fire all over.

I stood on the edge of the flames, watching the few aliens caught in them thrash and writhe as they died a no doubt awful death.

The worst thing was how ineffective it was. A few of the slightly-larger models on the far end just turned around and jumped into the lake, then came splashing out a moment later, smoking and scarred, but still alive.

"How long is this going to burn for?" I asked.

"About an hour," Gomorrah said. "Long enough for me to drop better explosives along the rest of the shore. The others are working as quickly as they can as well. We'll have a full cordon up within two, maybe three hours. I left this corner weak since you're there to cover it."

"Right, thanks," I said. "Keep safe up there."

"Will do." I saw the Fury wiggle from side to side before Gomorrah executed a half-loop turn and headed back the way she'd come, probably to go help the bombers.

Which left me here, with nothing but a small wall of flames between myself and a growing crowd of aliens that seemed reluctant to throw themselves into the fire.

I saw the smaller models clinging onto the shore and the remains of the pier be joined by bigger, meaner aliens, and I decided to start taunting the bastards. First, by aiming at their artillery models, especially when one of them flung another of those needle balls in my direction and I had to move out of the way or get crushed by a large mass of spikes.

I redeployed the 105mm guns and fired, letting the mech's auto-targeting software do most of the work after I highlighted the targets I wanted dead.

And they did a fantastic job of making them very dead.

That seemed to piss them off, at least judging by the way they all stared at me, some of them pacing the edge as if waiting. It struck me just how fucking alien these aliens were. They were too calm.

Then the water behind them bulged out in two places. To the right came a model twenty-two, a mobile hive like the one I'd just put down a few minutes ago. It clambered onto the shore with the ponderous movements of a lazy elephant and ten times the girth. Smaller flying models were already pouring off of it and taking to the air to swarm above. It pushed the entire line of aliens forward, sending dozens to their deaths as they fell into the flames.

To the left came that one model that I'd only caught a glimpse of underwater.

Now I could see it in the ultra-sharp contrast provided by my mech's sensor suite.

It was long and tall, with a head half the size of my mech and jaws that looked like it could chew concrete and two very, very long legs that were longer than all the rest of it.

The legs were really throwing me off, actually. The model twenty-three was a good two or three meters taller than my mech, but that was while it was crouched. This thing basically had chicken-style legs, with fat, armored thighs and a skinny pair of forearms that looked way too human for comfort, even if their size was all wrong.

Basically, it was a fucking T. rex if a T. rex could be made out of weeds.

The alien swiveled its head, and its too-many eyes locked onto me across the sweltering sheen of fire between us.

Then it ran.

"Is that thing fireproof?" I asked.

Yes.

"Fuck!"

I quickly aimed right at it and fired from both cannons, then watched in disbelief as one of the rounds ricocheted right off its thigh with nothing to show for it but a small explosion and some light searing. The other punched into its chest and did fuck-all.

You might want to move. This mech isn't rated to resist the biting force of a model twenty-three.

"Got it," I said. Didn't need to be told twice.

I turned, fired a parting shot with the one cannon still able to turn enough to shoot toward it, then I tucked the guns away and took off running.

We were in a residential area, with plenty of lakeside apartments and nicer homes with little lawns.

I'd have to see if I could get this thing to lose me in all of this mess so that I could punch a hole through its ugly head.

CHAPTER SIXTY-FIVE

T. REX VS GIANT MECHA CAT

SexyHawk: Ohhh! Go catmech!
TigerA: What's the t-rex looking one?
SDC: Cant be a trex, no feathers
Storyteller: stfu, you know what they meant. It's an m23
October: can we get an interior view?
Someone: Mess them up Stray Cat!

—Witch commentary on the live drone footage
of the Burlington Incursion, 2057

I ran, and the model twenty-three chased.

A few things became immediately obvious. While I had a lot more maneuverability and could turn and move in the air much faster than it could, the damned thing was *fast*.

The other thing that became obvious was my lack of rear-facing weaponry.

The Gatling guns mounted on the mech's shoulders could turn all the way around to fire backward, but that was about it, and while a constant stream of armor-piercing 10mm was doing something, it wasn't doing something fast enough.

I came around a corner, claws throwing up sparks as I scrambled for purchase on an old-school cobbled road.

The T. rex–looking motherfucker behind me just rammed through the building on the street corner, then opened its mouth wide to try and take a bite out of my ass while masonry crashed and skid across the road.

I kept moving, whipping my thagomizer-equipped tail into its face with its Void Terminus blades lit and extended. The crack of tail-meeting-face made the model twenty-three flinch aside, and it scored a long cut across its face.

Not nearly enough to kill the damned thing, but hopefully enough to hurt it.

I kept running, ducking into an alleyway between two smaller businesses. The model twenty-three paused at the entrance and glared at my back.

It couldn't follow through the narrow gap, not without ripping through the entire thing and risking getting itself stuck.

So it went up instead, powerful legs bunching beneath it before it leapt, ripping apart the road under it before crashing onto the roof of the building to my right.

The building instantly collapsed under several tons of rampaging alien mass. I swore as I ducked down lower and pushed myself to move faster and slip out of the far end before I was the one to get stuck in the crashing building.

"You okay?" Gomorrah asked.

"Ask me once I've killed this fucker," I snapped.

I needed to hit it with *something* better.

I dug one claw into the ground and used that as a pivot to turn around while the model twenty-three ripped its way out of the ruined building. I didn't quite have time to fire my railgun, but that didn't stop me from unfolding my 105mm cannons and firing both.

At the same time, the mortars on the cat's back popped open and fired, all six of them tossing grenades forward with a nearly silent *thump* that I felt more than heard. "What were those?" I asked.

Resonators. I equipped you with those since you seem to enjoy them. Forgive me, they're not quite as useful in this situation.

The grenades clanked around the alien, all six screeching but probably doing very little to the bastard. The 105mms reloaded and I fired another volley at it. The armor-piercing sabots rammed into its armored chest and detonated, sending some plant meat flying.

But not enough.

As the smoke cleared I discovered the alien was too damned close, jaw almost unhinged to reveal teeth nearly as long as I was tall.

I jumped forward and to the side, narrowly avoiding getting bitten as I slid past the alien while pulling my guns back in.

It wasn't quite fast enough.

My world suddenly spun and I was thrown around inside the cockpit, even with the harnesses in there keeping me as snug as they could.

The mech had been spun around, so I immediately grabbed onto the controls and spun it back to its feet, found a cleared stretch of road, and ran while my attention wandered over three things. What the hell had just happened, where the hell the alien was, and what the hell had broken.

The first was easy to check. A quick recording from five seconds prior showed the model twenty-three basically horse kicking me as I went by.

The damned thing had stumbled forward after the kick, but it had regained its footing and was coming around, salivating for a taste of some good Cat.

The damage was . . . not great, but not awful. One of my Gatling guns was ripped off, and stray shells were clinking out of their chain and onto the ground as I moved. The 105mm on that side hadn't finished sliding back into place when I got struck, and now some of its parts were reading orange on the damage readout. Otherwise, everything seemed more or less fine. A few yellow-greens, but nothing that would interfere too much.

"Reload the mortars," I said.

High explosives?

"No, something sticky," I said. "I want to glue the fucker down."

Interesting. Loaded.

"This thing needs rear-facing guns," I said.

Noted. I wasn't expecting so much running, but I'll add a note for any future modifications.

I had a good idea of where the model twenty-three was in relation to me, so as I ran I took a sharp right, then spun around an abandoned minivan and immediately kicked on my stealth features. The skin of my mech warped a little bit, as if I was seeing it through a heat haze, then it faded away, and I was entirely invisible.

The model twenty-three came rushing around the corner and kept going, but I saw its many eyes scanning around, trying to spot me.

So I fired my mortars again and grinned like the cat who'd caught the canary as they exploded all around the alien, covering it in expanding mounds of sticky foam.

That won't stop it forever.

"Reload with HE," I said. "And tell me where that asshole's brain is."

Upper chest, about half a meter below the nape of its neck. Highlighting now. Mortars are loaded.

My mech's chest opened and I pulled the trigger.

Immediately, the cockpit warmed up as I fired the railgun.

The alien's chest gained a hole I could crawl through even as six high explosive grenades landed in the goop around it and detonated.

I waited for just a moment, then shrugged and fired the railgun again, then unfolded the 105mm guns and fired the remaining rounds I had left before needing to reload about where the model twenty-three was.

Then I waited, and as the dust settled it revealed a very fucked up alien, its upper body shredded apart, one arm missing, and head flopped to the side.

It's technically still alive.

"Wow," I said. "Well, let's make Gomorrah proud then. I've got to have some sort of burning grenade that'll melt that thing."

I watched for a few merry moments as the model twenty-three cooked. I was feeling pretty good about myself, all things told.

"If you're done, can you do something about the rest of the aliens?" Gomorrah asked. "They're making it past the firewall, and I'm busy over here."

"Ah, right, got it. Consider me on the way," I said. I let go of the mech's controls for a moment and rubbed at the back of my neck and shifted my legs a bit to stretch them. That had been kinda awesome, but also stressful as hell.

Who knew giant-mecha-on-monster combat could be so nerve-wracking.

My break over, I checked my GPS, realized that I'd gotten turned around at some point, then realigned myself with the shore and took off running while ordering up a reload of everything. More mortars, more shells for my guns.

I'd live with just one Gatling gun for now. It was something I could fix later. And maybe I'd use replacing it as an excuse to upgrade my new toy, because I couldn't see myself *not* using this in the future.

Would Lucy fit in the cockpit or would it be too tight? Or would she have to like . . . ride on top.

I could very vaguely recall her once saying that she wanted to ride a horse one day, back when she was much younger and really into ancient horse movies for whatever reason. I wondered if this was a suitable replacement for a horse.

Giant robot cats were so much cooler than horses. (Although, now that I was thinking about it, some of that obsession might have been inspired by riding pants.)

"Cat, are you getting there, or not?" Gomorrah asked.

"Yeah, yeah," I sent back before pushing the mech to move a little faster.

Once I got closer to the pier, I could see why Gomorrah was getting nervous.

There were a lot of aliens here. Hundreds, maybe thousands of them. Most in the single-digits, but a few bigger ones, though none as large as the model twenty-three I'd just killed. There was a mobile hive left, however, slowly trudging through the burnt ground without a care in the world.

I'd have to change that. Remind these aliens that there very much was a reason to worry.

CHAPTER SIXTY-SIX

SPINNING A YARN

League of Samurai Legends is a Massive Online Battle Arena that is quite unique, or was when it first released. The game plays as a 3v1, with three players on the "samurai" team working together against an "Antithesis" player who controls the opposing faction.

The samurai players control various historical and current samurai, as well as a few original characters, buying gear as they rack up points for completing objectives and killing Antithesis NPCs.

The Antithesis player interacts with the game in an entirely different way, controlling it as a micro-management-heavy RTS wherein they create and react to the choices of the samurai players.

Games can be extremely tight, and it affords and encourages a wide range of tactics and playstyles.

—*LoSL* wiki page, 2034

I lurched forward, claws swiping toward a model five that I grabbed with almost contemptuous ease. Then, while shifting back and to the side to avoid a rush from some smaller aliens, I raised my mech up onto its hind-legs for just a moment and *spiked* the tanky model five into its comrades.

I didn't stick around, however, and bounded ahead with several leaps while my remaining Gatling gun fired off small bursts into the more densely packed crowds of aliens.

The nice thing about being in a several-ton warmech was that the little aliens were basically a non-threat, and most of the Antithesis here were little ones.

Advanced stealth bullshit meant the Antithesis only knew where I was when I stopped to wreck their shit. The rest of the time, they were just running around, clueless.

The Antithesis were circling around their mobile hive, a few hundred of them bumping into each other as they created a cordon of plant meat around the biggest alien, keeping it safe.

Well, not really that safe.

A flick of my thumb folded the mech's back plates just enough for the mortars to poke out and fire. A subsystem of a subsystem tracked their trajectory as they flew in a nice arc and landed spread out amongst the aliens.

Then they detonated, and alien meat was sent flying all over.

I continued to move, back clasping shut even as I avoided a swarm of model ones swooping over the spot where I'd been with suicidal speed.

On a whim, I turned around and pinged one of the black birds in the middle of the flock. The mech's auto-targeting started to draw lines to it, telling me exactly where I needed to aim and how much leeway I had in positioning myself. I unfolded the 105mm cannon on my right side and adjusted the mech's stance so that the gun could align itself on the fly.

I fired the moment the auto-targeting went green, and my mech's hind-claws dug into the road as it absorbed the recoil.

The shell detonated in the middle of the model ones, fire and shrapnel and a powerful concussive blast turning the entire flock into cooked meat.

That had given away my position, but at this point, I wasn't caring as much.

There were three artillery models near the shoreline, hanging back until they had an idea of where I was. An alarm rang in my head as they fired, so I moved, running around in a large curve. Halfway there, I pounced up and landed onto a model four, squishing it beneath my weight before I started to jump ahead in a zigzag pattern. My thagomizer-tail flicked from side to side, splattering aliens with every swipe.

Then I was among the artillery models and ripping them apart.

There was something insanely visceral about chomping down on an alien the length of a school bus and then shaking my head around while bits of it flew off in every direction.

Yeah, I was having too much fun in melee range, but I was also in a giant warmech, which made it possible to be this close without worrying too much.

Once the last of the aliens was spread out across a couple of acres, I found myself panting in my cockpit with exhilaration and looking for my next target.

The mobile hive. It was still being protected.

But it wasn't looking my way, and a hundred-odd little shits wasn't going to stop me.

I laughed within the confines of my cockpit as I sprinted across the distance between us, then leapt across the last sixty or so meters, guns unfolding on my side to fire while I was in midair even as the thrusters built into the mech's legs fired off, giving me a bit more forward momentum and cooking the aliens below me.

Then I crashed into the alien, claws digging into armored scales able to deflect tank shells as if they were butter.

I rolled into a ball, the longer claws of my hindlegs scratching wildly into the alien's side even as I bit onto its back to keep myself in place.

Aliens were charging in from all over, coming around the model twenty-two and leaping up onto me as the bigger model struggled to stay standing, even with six trunk-like legs.

I was getting rid of the smaller ones, though, swiping them away with whip-cracking strikes from my tail and with constant fire from my Gatling guns.

Still, they were starting to be an annoyance. I had at least a dozen model threes chewing ineffectually at my armor, but there was a tiny chance they'd ding my paint.

"Load up the mortars. Two concussive, four resonators," I said.

Done.

I opened the mech's back and instantly fired the mortars, but I adjusted them to fire with barely enough force to just drop onto the ground next to me.

The concussion grenades went off a split second after I closed my back up.

The explosions splashed the model threes and their bigger buddies, clearing out the entire side of the model twenty-two.

I shoved off, landed on my forepaws, then ran a bit, tail slicing into the alien's skin as I shot past it.

Then I turned hard, jaw opening up even as I locked onto the ugly alien's face and got ready to be warmed up.

The railgun fired, then reloaded and fired again.

For good measure, I unloaded the last couple of rounds left in my 105mm cannons.

The model twenty-two stumbled to the side, then crashed to the ground with enough mass left to it to shake the entire street.

The last of the aliens left around here charged my way, but a quick swipe of a paw splattered them, and a roar from my Gatling gun took care of those that weren't close enough for that.

I turned, attention to my sensors as I looked for more . . . only there weren't any. "Huh," I said.

Well done. The area's cleared.

The area was more than cleared. It was fucked. Every building in the area was either on fire or would have looked better if it was. Dozens of very loud cannons going off and stray 10mm rounds from my Gatling guns had shredded homes and lakeside businesses.

That wasn't accounting for the street itself.

Claw marks deep enough to crouch in marked the road, painting a wild picture of everywhere I'd run. Bodies, most of them in several pieces, were splattered all over the place, and the road was painted in soot and chlorophyll.

The biggest corpse was still smoking, its insides burning.

As I watched, a small egg-like thing flopped out of the side of the model twenty-two and squirmed for a moment. Then a tiny model three broke free from the shell it was born in and shook itself.

I walked over and crushed it into the road. "Well, I guess, uh . . . yeah, that was something."

You might want to take a moment to cool down. Your heart is still racing at nearly dangerous levels and your body temperature is higher than optimal.

The AC kicked on properly, and I let out a sigh. She was probably right. I blinked a few times, my organic eye burning and somewhat exhausted. "Gomorrah, things are cleared up here," I said.

"Got it. Bombing run's finishing up along the shore. I'll be passing back over where you are and dropping something a little more permanent in . . . about five minutes."

"Alright," I said as I sat the mech down. I was tempted to lick the blood off my paws, then I realized that it didn't matter, and I didn't have a tongue and . . . why the fuck would I do that? "I'll uh, stay here for a bit then."

"That was impressive, Stray Neko-Sama!" Intel-chan said. "I saw from the bomber's feed. Well, I saw some of it. You were invisible for most of that, but it was still awesome to see. Too bad the aliens don't have morale, because if they did, we'd just send them the vid and they'd surrender."

"Thanks, I think," I said.

"Do you mind if I share it? It'll be good for our morale, at least. And you're less likely to be shot on the way back!"

I snorted. "Yeah, sure, if it'll help a little."

"Nice! In any case, I put in a special order for you, and also, the reinforcements are arriving early. ETA one hour."

Reinforcements . . . holy shit, about time. I could feel a bit of stress leaking from my back, but I tried to keep my hopes in check. "What's the order?" I asked, curious.

"A big, *big* ball of yarn," Intel-chan said.

CHAPTER SIXTY-SEVEN

LATE

The best thing to happen to sports was the dissolving of most major sporting leagues and associations. It occurred rather suddenly in the late 2020s and into the early 2030s, but interest in sports had been waning for some time before that.

What replaced them were more extreme and audience-friendly forms of entertainment. No bars nor barriers—sports where every player is a perfect machine, pushing what humanity can do the same way racing cars were tuned to near perfection in their own sport.

—*Sports in the 21st Century: A Biography of an Art*, 2041

I returned to Downtown at my own pace. Which meant pretty damned quickly, all told.

Mostly that was because my new warmech, even with a few dents in it, could top out at seventy kilometers an hour on a straightaway, and it wasn't like I had to deal with any traffic on the dead streets.

I had half my attention split on my damage readouts and on the internal repairs of the mech. It had a pretty in-depth self-repair system. Nothing too fancy. It wasn't like it had nanomachines or anything over the top like that. But every system did have multiple levels of redundancy, and the mech was slowly testing out the systems that had been shut down, seeing what they could take now that the fighting was over.

"How much is it gonna cost to get this thing back up to functional?" I asked.

Not nearly as much as the initial price. Though, there are multiple ways to repair the Mechcatular Nyanzerfaust. The simplest and least cost-effective would be to buy all the missing parts as new, with a small surcharge to have them appear on the vehicle itself. The much more affordable option would be to simply return to your New Montreal fabricator and build the damaged parts there. Seeing as how you don't have the complex education needed to repair the system yourself, or replace its parts, I'd suggest buying a repair drone for a few hundred points and allow it to effect the repairs itself.

"Sounds slow," I said.

I believe that you will be afforded that time soon enough.

Frowning, I poked at my friendly AI. "What's that mean?"

Even though you are not officially a member of the Family, they have been treating you as one to some degree. According to their internal protocols, after the last 48 hours—which they would classify as mid-high on their stress charts, you would be afforded five days of obligatory rest.

"Obligatory rest?" I asked. "That sounds like a terrible deal. I don't wanna obligatory anything. Besides, I'm still good to go."

The rest period is to give the Vanguard time to destress and heal from any injuries. Prolonged periods of high stress can lead to mental fatigue, cumulative stress injuries, and a whole host of other issues. But you are correct. You are still capable of continuing.

I . . . wasn't expecting Myalis to agree to the last part. "Thanks, I guess?"

You are, and this is said with all due fondness, very much abnormal, Catherine. Your brain is wired wrong in the most entertaining way. I almost want to see you trying to take five days off, just to see the panic of inaction settle in, but that would be cruel and unusual and surprisingly unhealthy.

Sitting on my ass for five days would drive me a little mad. Lucy too, because as much as I didn't want to, I'd totally drag her into the madness too. "Yeah, I can kinda see that. So we tell the Family to piss off?"

I would actually suggest taking them up on their offer. The lake-and-oceans specialized Vanguard is arriving shortly, and the current reinforcements include a number of low-tier Vanguard, similar to those you found in Burlington on arriving. In any case, you accomplished what you set out to accomplish. The city is, in a way, saved. Passing on the torch wouldn't be harmful at this point, and it would allow you to shift your focus closer to home.

I thought about it as I continued to run toward the city.

Maybe she wasn't so wrong about it. What did I still have to do here? Hell, why had I come here in the first place?

Some of it was wanting to help, but I wouldn't have wanted that at all if Gomorrah hadn't dragged me into it. Now that I was here, I felt responsible for this city, but it wasn't *mine*. It wasn't home.

Home was back in New Montreal, where I was sure I'd find plenty of problems waiting for me.

Still, I'd . . . done good, hadn't I? Whipped the locals up, got Lucy to help, fucked up in a few new and creative ways, but still managed to keep things from imploding on themselves. Killed a whole lot of aliens.

Yeah, I'd done alright.

Maybe I would head back home for a day or two. Chill out in my little pool, then come back once the place was on fire because some moron bungled the whole thing up.

There was another consideration. Lucy. Heck, Gomorrah too, and to a degree Franny as well.

As long as I didn't stop myself, none of them would be able to stop either. I got the sense that Gomorrah especially would try to match me beat for beat. Lucy was obstinate enough that if she needed a break, she'd get one no matter what, but she'd still push herself to keep up for a while, and she was still healing, no matter what Myalis said about their miraculous medication.

Yeah, I was gonna take a nice, quiet couple of days off.

I made up my mind at about the same time as I reached the city walls.

I saw eyes widen and picked up a few panicked calls as I jumped to the top of the wall, crumpling a small section of it, then leapt down on the other side.

There was a jet parked nearby, and I paused a bit as I took it in. It wasn't a little fighter thing, but a big chunky cargo plane with its wings turned back. One of those fancy vertical takeoff planes? It looked like they were unloading shit from the plane.

I didn't recognize the uniform of the new soldiers.

"What's all this?" I asked.

The reinforcements you requested.

Oh, yeah, that made some sense. I walked my mech over, keeping it low and slow so that I had time to take in the scene.

There were a good hundred or so people in navy-blue uniforms with armored cuirasses, arms, and kneepads moving around. They were better equipped than the local militia and it showed. I wasn't sure if it was samurai tech though. Probably not.

Then I noticed a small group looking my way, four figures dressed in wildly different styles. I recognized one of them though, a younger man in what looked like jeans and a faintly glowing chest piece covered by a long leather coat. He had a long wooden rifle slung over his back and a tipped back cowboy hat that looked like something had chewed on it.

Crackshot Cowboy, from New Montreal.

Which made the others around him samurai as well. I glanced over the other three. Two girls, another guy. One of the girls was tiny. Not young, just really small, with an outsized backpack and what looked like flame-throwers? The white costume and glowing neon snowflakes on her outfit suggested the opposite.

The other woman was dressed like an old-school racecar driver. I didn't see any weapons on them, but her helmet was clearly some samurai-grade shit, and the suit looked too good to be commercial.

The last was a tall guy in a leotard with mechanical bunny ears stuck to his head and disgustingly hairy legs, and I really didn't feel like inspecting him too closely.

I wasn't an expert at shit all, but something told me this bunch was entirely made up of new samurai. "They didn't send the cream, did they?"

I suspect that Burlington's going to be used as a safer location for new Family-related Vanguard to train.

Well, that made some sense.

I crouched my warmech down, then opened the cockpit. Something scraped, but the top of the mech opened up all the same and I yoinked my connection out from the side of my head with a swipe, then resisted the urge to vomit all over the cockpit.

There's a shut-down process for a reason, Catherine.

I went from being the machine, or at least having it in my brain, to not in a split second, and it felt . . . weird, like disconnecting my prosthetic arm, but all over and all at once.

But I had noobs to show up, so I fought past it, then stood up atop my mech.

I hadn't realized from within just how battered it looked. There were dents all over, and several hundred liters of plant blood painted on its exterior. I checked on the missing Gatling gun and held back a wince. That was going to cost something to replace.

But for now, I had to get started on making a good first impression.

"You're fucking late," I said.

CHAPTER SIXTY-EIGHT

PAPERWORKER

The Family is many things, but most of all, it's a place for the buck to stop.
—Agent Argent, 2032

I jumped off my warmech and landed in a crouch, boots muffling any of the noise I should have made dropping to the ground like that. My coat flapped a bit, so I straightened it as I stood up. "Crackshot, nice to see you again," I said.

"Miss Stray Cat," he said with a nod. "Pleased to see you too. Didn't know you'd be here when they sent me over, but I'm happy to see you again."

"You know her?" the girl with the ice-themed gear asked. I think she pitched her voice low enough not to carry, but that didn't really matter to me.

"Crackshot and I have a bit of history," I said. "Was it me or Gomorrah who gave you the name?" I asked.

"Ah, that was you," he said with a grin. "Pleased with it so far too. So thanks for that. And yeah, Miss Stray Cat helped me a heap when I was just starting off. Still haven't spent all the points I made during that big wave."

I nodded along and buried my envy. I'd made some points back today, but I was probably going to leave Burrlington with about the same amount I'd gone in with.

Then again, that might change. Some of the gear I'd bought was going to generate a small trickle of points as long as the city kept up its defenses. In any case, that was a worry for later. "So, who're your friends?" I asked.

"Oh, right," Crackshot said. "This is Shiverinn," he gestured to the small woman standing next to him. She blinked, raised a hand, then waved, all with quick, jerky motions that came off as extremely nervous, like she was some sort of human chihuahua. "This is Rod." He gestured to the chick in the racing outfit who nodded once. "And that's Hairy."

Hairy smiled at me, and I decided to studiously ignore him.

"Well, welcome to Burlington," I said. "Things have been . . . all over the place, honestly, but overall, not that bad. Is one of you the underwater specialist?" I asked.

I got four head shakes there. "Family mentioned that someone called Drowning Man was heading over from the other end of the Great Lakes. Supposed to be here tonight or tomorrow morning," Crackshot said.

"That'll do it. They'll have their work cut out for them. There's a fuck-huge hive in the lake. What do you guys know about the situation here? And are you four . . . taking over from here, or am I just getting my hopes up for some time off?"

Crackshot rubbed at the back of his neck. "Well, we're supposed to be under Drowning Man's command. I think he's coming over with his own team to take over from there. Don't know how the handoff's supposed to work though. The battalion here's all Family-related folk."

I could feel a fresh headache coming on already, and part of me could already picture what was going to happen.

The militia here got along . . . somewhat well with me. They genuinely seemed to like the local samurai as well, since they were locals and they'd worked together. They also got along well with the Kittens.

The Kittens here were all gung-ho about helping, but they were also big on community stuff, and since the Militia was homegrown, they got along well despite a few grudges. The Kittens were very obviously built to support the Militia, and that made them get along.

Now we were bringing in outsiders who seemed to know what they were doing, and who I would bet were going to rub the fact in.

Thank fuck it wouldn't be my problem to sort it all out.

"Well, that sounds awesome. Nice to meet you all. Hope you enjoy your stay. If you want to get ahead and make a few quick points, just hop on over the wall. There's some aliens out there if you're willing to search around for them."

"I don't know if we're that equipped," Crackshot said. His eyes wandered over to my warmech.

"Oh, you don't need anything like that," I said. "That's because I was out near the shore. Just . . . don't go near the shore. Not that you can, it's all on fire now."

"On fire?" Shiverinn asked.

"Gomorrah was around. Anyway! You'll want to figure out whoever's in charge of the Kittens. They're the nice folk in the cute outfits with the ears. Try getting Intel-chan's attention too. He, or she, or whatever they are, has a pretty good idea of where the next fire that needs putting out is."

"You're not sticking around?" Crackshot asked.

I shrugged. "I might. I might not. The fun part of not being part of any organization or anything is that I get to do what I want. And maybe what

I want is to sleep in my own bed." I patted him on the shoulder. "But don't worry. I'll listen to the news. If you're in deep, *deep* shit, then give me a call, yeah?"

"Right, yeah, of course," he said.

I nodded to him, then headed back to my mech. "Good luck!" I said as I grabbed onto the side, then pulled myself up. Soon enough I was lying back down in my cockpit and gingerly jacking myself back into the mech's control system. "Hope they manage."

I suspect they will. And the added challenge of not having someone as aware of the issues as you are will allow them to grow even more.

"That's a nice way of putting it. Kind of a shitty justification, but nice-sounding," I said as I turned the warmech around and started heading deeper into downtown.

It's the same justification that other Vanguard used for not assisting you, and so far it has proven worthwhile, hasn't it? You have faced great challenges and have grown from them.

I supposed I couldn't shit on the idea that hard, but it still felt a bit raw.

I arrived at the mall in short order. My mech wasn't quite as fast as a car could go, but I had the fantastic ability to ignore what little traffic there was. Cars tended to move aside when they saw a giant mechanical warmech running in their general direction. I didn't waste the time heading over, either. I placed a few quick calls to Intel-chan, informing them that there were new people to coordinate with. Then I checked up on Sprout and Arm-a-Geddon, just to make sure they were still alive.

At some point, Manic had joined them out in the field, so that was good to know. It probably meant that her little excursion had been a success then.

Good news all around.

I brought the mech to a stop in front of the mall and climbed out of it, this time being a whole lot more careful while unplugging myself from the mech's control system. Surprisingly, doing things the "right" way didn't lead to sudden massive headaches, which was nice to know.

By the time I dismounted, Lucy had come down and was waiting for me by the entrance. "Cat!" she cheered.

Instantly, all of the sour thoughts I'd been having were wiped away, and I found myself smiling like a moron. "Hey," I said as I jumped off the side of the mech. "Look, I got a warmech!" I said while unclasping my helmet and removing it.

Lucy laughed as she pulled me into a hug. "You did. And it's already messy and covered in dents. If I ever buy a car, you're not allowed to drive it."

I scoffed. "And here I was going to let you ride my giant cat mech," I said.

"If I want to ride a Cat, then I have plenty of options," she purred, and my smile turned from moronic to goofy for a moment. "How did things go?"

"Not bad," I said. "Bunch of Family troops just arrived. Our reinforcements."

"Aren't they early?" she asked.

"Maybe, but I won't let them know it," I said before stealing a kiss. "Hey, I was thinking, maybe we could head home?"

"Right now?" she asked.

I nodded. "Sure, why not?"

Lucy laughed. "Why not? Cat . . ." It was her turn to steal a quick kiss. "You can't just drop a heap of responsibility on a girl's lap, then ask her to run off into the sunset with you right after. At least give me a few hours to make sure the Kittens here will be fine?"

"Ah, yeah, I guess that makes sense."

She grinned. "You're the best. But you'd be even better if you lent me Myalis to help with all of this paperwork."

I'm afraid you can't "lend" me to anyone. On the other hand, if you help her yourself, I can assist you in assisting her.

Which meant doing some of the paperwork myself.

The shit I did for Lucy. Unbelievable.

CHAPTER SIXTY-NINE

NICE

I'm proud to announce my re-election in the last emergency mayoral elections. New Montreal is facing a number of hardships, and I promise I'll be there to address them as best I can. You have nothing to worry about while Dupont is here!
—Mayor Dupont's post-election speech, New Montreal, 2057

"Is this the last one? Please tell me this is the last one," I said as I swiped to the side and looked at a new form. It was a small wall of text, without even little drawings to make sense of the corporatese and legal gobbledygook that filled the form from top to bottom.

"Cat, you're barely doing any of the work yourself, don't complain so much," Lucy said.

Lucy, Franny, and I were in Lucy's office space, working through the tedious process of making sure nothing imploded the moment Lucy and I weren't here watching over things.

Jennifer the sex bot was coming in and out periodically, carrying some actual paper documentation for Lucy to look over. She was also answering calls and filling out a constant stream of emails with auto-generated replies.

The transition was going to be . . . tricky.

Basically, Lucy was transferring power to a governing body composed of some dozen members that she thought wouldn't fuck everything up immediately. The Kittens were still, nominally, under Lucy's control, but if she wasn't going to be right there sitting on top of it, then someone had to make the minute-to-minute choices.

I wasn't sure if electing Jennifer as the leader was a fantastic idea or not, but Lucy seemed tickled by the idea, and I hadn't come this far by telling her no.

In any case, the more forms I skimmed through, the more I was impressed by all the shit Lucy pulled. She had taken a bunch of volunteers, gave them a purpose, encouraged them to work together for their own interests, then somehow turned them into a passable fighting force with a generous hierarchy, decent pay, and enough momentum that I suspected that the Burlington branch of the Kittens wouldn't be the only one.

"Did I ever tell you that you're scary?" I murmured to Lucy.

She grinned, big and proud. "No, you haven't. But I'll take it."

"I'm not sure about scary, but this is pretty impressive," Franny said. She tossed a small tablet computer onto one of the desks. "When'd you find time to set all of this up while also doing . . . well, everything else?"

"Oh, I cheated," Lucy said with a nod. "The trick isn't just being good enough that you can do everything yourself. It's finding people to do parts of it for you, then sweeping in and correcting them afterward. There's an entire out-of-work city's worth of people to pick from, so I just had Myalis help me find people that were actually competent, then I asked them nicely to do the stuff they're good at."

"So, the same as asking the kittens back home to do different chores based on how old they are and how many limbs they have," I said with a nod.

Franny looked between us, then shook her head. "We didn't have the same sort of upbringing at all," she said.

"Aren't you an orphan too?" Lucy asked.

"No, actually. Still have parents. They're corpo, some middle-upper sorts. They tossed me to the nunnery because you can get a kid raised there for relatively cheap, and there's a lot of other ex-nun-raised girls who have gone on to do really well in business."

"I don't see the relation between being a good nun and being good at business," I said.

Franny grinned. "The way the old nuns put it, it's all about self-discipline and that kind of nonsense. I think it's mostly that you learn how to be underhanded while looking earnest, but what do I know? I'm not exactly a shining example of what they want. Delilah, on the other hand, is *exactly* the kind of girl they try to produce."

"She *is* a little uptight," I said with a good-natured grin.

Franny chuckled. "Yeah. Exactly. Now imagine her in one of those corpo outfits instead of looking like a nun, and you've got a complete picture."

"I'm sure we'd all love to spend time thinking of Gomorrah in a pencil skirt," Lucy said. "But we can do that later! We're almost done here."

I laughed, signed off on the final form without really reading it too well, then sat down on Lucy's desk. "What's next?"

Lucy looked around her office, then blinked a few times, eyes twitching in that telltale way that meant she was looking at screens I couldn't see. "I think . . . that we're pretty much done here," Lucy said.

I felt myself tense up for a moment before it all kind of just . . . washed away. I wasn't expecting it, but I supposed that for the last couple of days I'd been running on lots of stress. Now things were, more or less, over.

"Are we going to pick up Gomorrah?" I asked. "I imagine she'll want to head home too?"

Franny perked up. "I sent her a message. She's on her way back. But, ah. There's only room for two in the Fury."

"Well, I'm not going to get in between you and your girlfriend," I said.

Franny's cheeks warmed up so much they almost matched her orange hair. "It's . . . we're not . . . urgh. You're too much like Lucy," she said.

I shared a grin with Lucy. "So, she has a way home. What about us?"

"I don't imagine taking a taxi is possible, is it?" Lucy asked.

I laughed. "I don't think so. Besides, I don't want to leave my giant warmech behind."

For a couple of hundred points, you could buy the Mechanized Warfare Platform Flight Systems catalog. Then bringing the Mechcatular Nyanzerfaust back to your home wouldn't be as much of a challenge.

I glanced to the side, to make sure no one thought I was talking to them, directly. "And how exactly would that work out?"

I suppose it depends on what sort of flight system you purchase. I'd suggest foldable wings that can lock onto the side of the Mechcatular Nyanzerfaust with an engine pack for lift. With some slight VTOL abilities, landing the mech back at your home should be relatively easy.

"Yeah, yeah, we could do something like that. But then . . . Hey, Lucy, would you rather be stuck with me inside of a very tight cockpit, or would you rather ride on top of a giant warmech?"

Lucy stared at me for a moment, then her brows drew together as she actually thought about it. "How safe is riding the mech? And how much are we wearing inside that cockpit?"

"Well, I'd make sure you have a strap or something. Maybe a saddle? I don't think there is much we can do to *actually* make it comfortable, honestly. It's pretty wide at the shoulders, so it wouldn't be like riding a horse or something. As for the cockpit." I grinned. "I can wear as little as you want."

"Right," Franny said as she dropped some stuff off. "I'm heading out. Maybe we can have lunch or something one of these days. Lucy, thanks for the . . . advice earlier." She cleared her throat, and I couldn't help but notice the blush still clinging to her cheeks. "Have a safe ride back, you two. But like . . . take a car. Like normal people."

"We'll think about it," I said. "Stay safe, Franny. And say hi to Gom for me."

"Don't forget what I told you, about the tongue," Lucy added.

I turned toward Lucy while Franny made a quick exit. "What did you tell her?" I asked.

"I just gave her some friendly advice," Lucy said. "Delilah and Franny are cute together, but they're both really useless."

I shrugged. "We weren't always so good about stuff ourselves."

"Yeah, exactly," Lucy said. She wandered over, and very casually wrapped her arms around my waist and let her head fall onto my shoulder.

I hugged her back, artificial arm around the small of her back, my other hand slipping into the soft fluff of her hair to scratch at the back of her head. We didn't talk for a couple of minutes, just hung onto each other. I didn't know if Lucy was destressing, but it didn't feel like it. This was more . . . hugging for the sake of hugging.

"You did well," Lucy said.

I tensed up for a moment, and Lucy hugged me harder in response, so I just melted into it more. "Thanks," I said. "I think I could have done better."

"Next time," she murmured. "There's always going to be another fire. You know how it is, Cat."

"Same as it ever was," I complained. Then I pressed a kiss into Lucy's forehead, and I felt like even if all I ever did was run around and try to stamp out problems, maybe that wasn't so bad if I had something to return to.

Lucy sat in the kiddie pool, an energy drink in one hand, the other splayed out over the edge of the pool. She was contorted in a position that was as comfortable as it was bad for her spine.

She had bought a TV, even if it was a stupid luxury to buy when anyone with sense could just look at virtual screens projected from their augs. Still, she liked having the big flatscreen pressed up against the wall.

It was turned to a Burlington news channel. It was a small local channel that had been taken over by a few reporters who wanted to . . . well, report stuff. It was very jank at the moment, with most of their footage being shaky-cam and interviews with randos, and what news they said that Lucy could fact-check came back as mostly wrong. Which was par for the course as far as news went.

Still, it was nice to see that the city wasn't a burning husk now that she was back home.

The lake *was* on fire, but only a little, and for once it wasn't Gomorrah's fault. Probably that underwater samurai whose name she'd forgotten.

Lucy took a sip of her drink, then suppressed a shiver as the sugar hit her.

She needed to get a better kiddie pool, maybe something with a heating element in it?

But then, she might as well get a Jacuzzi.

And if she got one of those, there was a very real chance she'd never leave it again. So maybe it was for the best that she didn't. The last couple of days had been stressful.

Actually, the last couple of weeks had been pretty bad, as far as stress went.

Lucy tilted her head back and took in the massive bedroom that was now hers, with its Protector-made architecture, sheltered within a larger penthouse floor that was practically a modern mansion near the center of one of the largest cities in the world. The kind of place that cost more than most people could ever imagine having.

So yeah, while the stress had been a bit bad, on the whole of it, things were going pretty well. It was a lot of work to keep it all up, but she was glad to do it. It was *helping* and while she never believed herself to be anything but a practical sort of altruist, she'd help others if it meant coming out on top herself.

She had a couple dozen emails waiting for her. They were offers, polite and otherwise, asking for her to join their group in one form or another.

Either she'd *really* impressed a bunch of big wigs, or they were trying to get her to look at them favorably since she had connections to Cat.

The idiots. As if she'd ever leave such a cushy position to work for a corpo.

The door to the room opened, and Lucy casually draped an arm across her chest until she saw that it was Cat who'd stepped in.

Her girlfriend was frowning as she looked around, then she spotted Lucy and froze in the act of closing the door. Her eyes flitted from Lucy's face to Lucy's chest and stayed there. "You're in my pool," Cat said.

"Mm-hmm," Lucy agreed.

"You're not wearing anything," Cat said next. Another statement of fact.

"I haven't had time to buy a nice swimsuit," Lucy said. She gently lowered her arm, and Cat stared, as if her breasts were the red dot and Cat was very much the animal she was named after. "I was thinking of getting a Jacuzzi, do you think we could get away with that?"

"In the bedroom?" Cat asked, finally snapping her attention up.

"Why not?" Lucy asked.

Cat blinked. "Fuck it, sure," she said.

Lucy grinned. Yeah, life was a bit stressful, but it was worth living these days.

ABOUT THE AUTHOR

RavensDagger is a Canadian writer who wants to make people smile. The best way to do that, he has found, is by pecking away at the keyboard and hoping for the best.